Also by Lynn Kiele Bonasia

Some Assembly Required

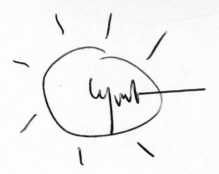

SUMMER
SHIFT

Lynn Kiele Bonasia

A TOUCHSTONE BOOK
Published by Simon & Schuster
New York   London   Toronto   Sydney

Touchstone
A Division of Simon & Schuster, Inc.
1230 Avenue of the Americas
New York, NY 10020

Copyright © 2010 by Lynn Kiele Bonasia

First Touchstone trade paperback edition June 2010

TOUCHSTONE and colophon are registered trademarks of Simon & Schuster, Inc.

For information about special discounts for bulk purchases, please contact Simon & Schuster Special Sales at 1-866-506-1949 or business@simonandschuster.com.

The Simon & Schuster Speakers Bureau can bring authors to your live event. For more information or to book an event, contact the Simon & Schuster Speakers Bureau at 1-866-248-3049 or visit our website at www.simonspeakers.com.

Designed by Renata Di Biase

Manufactured in the United States of America

10   9   8   7   6   5   4   3   2   1

Library of Congress Cataloging-in-Publication Data
Bonasia, Lynn Kiele.
    Summer shift / by Lynn Kiele Bonasia.
        p.   cm.
        1. Cape Cod (Mass.)—Fiction. I. Title.
PS3602.O6563S86 2010
813'.6—dc22
                                                    2010011940

ISBN 978-1-4391-2897-8
ISBN 978-1-4391-4952-2 (ebook)

For my dear Auntie

It seemed to me . . . that we could step into uncharted territory and relax with the groundlessness of our situation. . . . My teacher . . . described this as "leaning into the sharp points."

PEMA CHODRON, *WHEN THINGS FALL APART*

May

1992

The late afternoon sun yawned off the newly shellacked bar. Mary and Robbie stood inside the door to the dining room, which still smelled of gray deck paint and the plastic window tarps that had been delivered earlier that unseasonably warm spring day.

"What's wrong?" Robbie asked. He knew her so well.

"It's that lobster," Mary said. She wiped the sweat off her brow with the back of her hand and pointed to the rafters. "It's overkill."

Robbie folded his arms in front of him. His light blue work shirt was unbuttoned to the waist, his tan chest speckled with paint. With less than a week to go before Memorial Day weekend, they'd been working around the clock to set things up. "This is a clam bar. I think the town fines you if you don't have the requisite lobster buoys, fish nets, and plastic critters."

Mary peeled the sweaty T-shirt fabric from her skin. She moved to take a step down the center aisle, but Robbie grabbed her hand and pulled her to him. "You fixin' to break the law, missy?" he said.

Mary fell into his arms. She was exhausted, but in a good way, with a healthy ache in her young muscles. They kissed. Mary smelled alcohol on Robbie's breath and wondered when he'd managed a drink. They'd been together all day.

"I can't believe it's really ours," Robbie said.

"I can't either." *Thanks, Mom and Dad,* Mary thought. She knew Robbie liked to downplay their contribution, which was why she didn't readily share these thoughts with her husband, how she secretly carried her parents with her into this venture, consulting them at every turn—how her mother, who'd had a good eye for design, might have laid out the interior, or what kind of bargain her father might have struck with the shellfishermen out on the cove. Things may not have gone down between Robbie and her father the way Mary would have liked, but the restaurant wouldn't have happened without the money they'd left her. She was hell-bent on making it succeed, as much for her parents as for herself.

From as far back as Mary could remember, running a restaurant was what she always knew she was meant to do. Her great-grandfather, referred to only ever as "the Captain," had operated a legendary clam shack off the Mid-Cape Highway in Eastham that was long gone by the time Mary was born. But she'd grown up with a sepia photograph of him framed in the upstairs hall, him standing in the doorway of his establishment holding an enormous live lobster. Something about that bit of family lore had captured her imagination, this and a love for the food she'd enjoyed as a Cape Codder from her earliest days.

Mary nestled her chin into Robbie's neck, looking over his shoulder at the new carved wood Clambake sign at the end of the driveway. "I just know this place is going to make it. I can feel it," she said.

"You can feel it, huh?" Robbie let her go and walked down the aisle. He bent over to collect a speck of paper from the floor. Seventy-Eight dove out from beneath one of the tables and lunged at his fingers.

"I mean it," Mary said. "I know I'll be good at this."

"Let's hope so." He scratched the tiger kitten behind its ears as it wove in and around his ankles.

"Unless this lobster jinxes us," she added, glancing upward.

The door opened and a breeze rushed in, carrying with it a few blades of fresh-cut grass and Mary's great-aunt, Lovey. She was wearing her drip-dry navy polyester slacks and a beige short-sleeve sweater with a gold circle pin centered below her collarbone.

Seventy-Eight made a dash for freedom before the door swung shut.

The older woman slid her tan pocketbook up on her forearm and clapped her hands. She brought them to her chin. "My goodness, will you look at the place," she said. Her blue eyes sparkled.

"Auntie!" Mary said. Since she was a child, Mary had always lived to make her aunt proud. "The tarps came today. And the tables. Of course no chairs yet, but they're coming Wednesday. What do you think?" Mary held her breath.

Lovey took her time looking around, eating up every square inch. "It looks like a real restaurant. Why, I'd love nothing more than to sit here on a brisk summer evening with a cup of hot chowder—"

"You will, every night if you like," Robbie said. He came up and gave Lovey a peck on the cheek. "I'm glad you're here. You can help Mary and me settle a dispute."

"Can I get you a glass of wine?" Mary asked. She started for the bar. It wasn't stocked yet, but there were a few bottles in the cooler that Mary had brought from the house.

"That would be nice." Lovey set her handbag down on the nearest table. She turned to Robbie. "What is it I can help you with, dear?"

"It's about the lobster," Robbie said.

She wagged her finger at him. "I saw something on Julia Child the other day. Do you have any idea how they make baked stuffed lobster?" Her face reddened. "They take and slice the lobster right down the tail"—with the heel of her right hand, she sawed at her left palm—"while it's still alive!" Her eyes widened. "Then they spoon the dressing right in the gash and then into the oven he goes! Ach!" Lovey pressed her hands to her mouth, then shook them out. "Who could do such a thing?"

Mary smiled. Her aunt had always been an empathetic soul, particularly when it came to "God's creatures," as she called them. Though empathy was one thing and the woman's love of a good lobster roll was quite another. "We're only going to steam them, Auntie. They die instantly."

Lovey's shoulders relaxed.

"The doors to the steamer are so thick you can't hear them scream," Robbie added.

From behind the bar, Mary gave him the evil eye, trying not to smile. She found the wine. There were two bottles, though she could have sworn she'd brought over three. Then again, she'd been making so many trips back and forth, she couldn't keep track of where anything was at this point.

"Anyway, we weren't talking about real lobsters, Lovey, though baked stuffed does sound yummy." Robbie grinned. Mary admired her handsome husband, even more so with that mischievous flicker in his eye. "In any case, we meant *that* lobster," Robbie said. He pointed to the rafters, to the larger-than-life red crustacean caught in the net.

Lovey ignored his teasing and looked up. "What's the trouble? I think it looks fine."

Robbie grinned, victorious. *Not so fast,* Mary thought. She knew her aunt better than anyone.

Lovey walked down the aisle until she stood directly beneath the plastic creature. She cocked her head. "Though I see why some might take issue with it." She tapped her cheek with her forefinger.

"Why's that?" Mary asked.

"Well, we don't cast nets for lobster, do we?" Lovey turned to Mary. "Your father kept dozens of pots out back. Don't you remember—?" Lovey stopped mid sentence and looked at Mary. Her face grew long, as though she'd immediately regretted bringing up Mary's father, who'd died just two years earlier.

"It's okay," Mary said. She smiled. It was good to talk about her parents. How else would they be remembered? "Of course. I used to love helping him set the traps."

With that, her aunt seemed to relax. "I'm just saying, if someone's a stickler, you might catch an earful." Lovey Rollwagon being the Queen of Sticklers.

"You're being too literal—," Robbie started.

"And I supposed the most egregious error of all is that the lobster is *red,*" Lovey said. She folded her arms and shifted her weight from one foot to the other.

"So?" Robbie said.

"*So,* they don't turn red till you cook them!" Lovey said.

Robbie frowned. "Oh, yeah." For once he seemed at a loss.

"Unless the oceans are getting *that* hot," Lovey continued. "Did you know about that, dear?" She turned to Mary. "That the oceans are warming up? They think the whole planet is getting hotter thanks to pollution. I read something about it in the *National Geographic.* 'Global warming,' it's called."

"That sounds awful," Mary said. Her aunt was always informing them of the latest impending catastrophes and natural disasters, though this one Mary had already done her share of fretting over. The idea of the sea level rising as a result of melting polar ice caps didn't bode well for the Cape. One day this place would be waterfront. "But you're absolutely right about the lobster. It makes no sense." Mary scanned the counter for a corkscrew. "And never mind that, it's *tacky.*"

"I can't imagine anyone eating a lobster *that* size, can you? My goodness. Imagine the leftovers. Lobster salad up the *wazoo.*" Lovey let loose with her staccato laugh.

"I don't think they even sell fake uncooked lobsters," Robbie said. "They're all red."

"Because they're made in China," Mary said. She found a wine opener in the sink and screwed the metal spiral into the cork. "Do they even *have* lobsters in China?"

Lovey turned to her great-nephew-in-law. She patted down the hem of her sweater. "Well, dear, as a decoration, I'm sure it's fine," she said. "But you *did* ask."

"That he did," Mary said. A little leverage and the cork gave way.

"If it's any consolation, I imagine the folks who come here from places like New York don't know red lobster from green," Lovey said. "Just like they don't know red chowder from white."

Robbie laughed. "Now you're just being a snob," he said. "Far as I can tell, the people who get most upset about red chowder are the ones who once came from places that serve it. I've lived here all my life and I have nothing against red chowder."

Lovey wrinkled her nose and turned to Mary, who was coming around the bar with a glass of wine. "You're not planning to serve that *Manhattan* variety, are you?" she asked, as she took the drink with both hands. If there was one thing Lovely regretted, it was having been born in the Bronx.

"Never," Mary replied. Challenging the unwritten plastic-lobster rule was one thing. Serving Manhattan clam chowder was simply against the clam bar code, a matter of ethics, heritage. Loyalty, even.

June

2009

There was a chill in the air that Mary could feel through the windowpanes. She took a sip of wine. It left a hint of pepper on her tongue.

Mary had a perch where she sat in the restaurant kitchen, a small stool in a corner nook near the take-out window where she could see the entrance and out onto the floor. This gave her the opportunity to observe what was going on in the kitchen while keeping an eye on the dining room, all without being seen by patrons. Here she had spent most of the last seventeen years.

It was close to five o'clock. Nate, a line cook, and one of the bartenders were tying up trash bags from lunch that would be loaded onto the pickup and deposited in the Dumpster out back.

Mary watched as a Styrofoam chowder cup drifted to the ground. The breeze caught it and sent it skipping across the parking lot gravel. At the Clambake, most of the food left the kitchen in paper-lined baskets and red-and-white cardboard cartons that could be tossed at the end of the meal. It occurred to Mary that a restaurant owner could probably learn a lot about her business from its trash, what people didn't like or what one could get away with serving less of. It was something Mary hadn't considered until now. It was this willingness to consider things others overlooked, she knew, coupled with an unflinching ability to do whatever it took, that made her one of the most successful restaurant owners on the Cape.

Nate flipped the blond hair from his eyes. His back broadened as he lifted the bag from the plastic bin. She imagined the strong hamstrings tensing beneath his jeans. This morning his sunburned thigh had peeked out from under the white sheet like a slab of raw tuna, all muscle and reddish brown. She had watched as his breath came soft and sleep erased more years from his face so that he looked like a child. This had irritated her.

Wayne erupted. "Does she want me to come out there and butter her corn for her too?" he said.

Mary looked up from the dinner-specials board she was hand-lettering. Wayne's face was dark and his black hair was jutting out in all directions. "Where the hell is Vanessa?" he added. There were three baskets of fish and chips sitting on the counter, five big orders had come in at once, and now a waitress had requested a lazy man's lobster, which meant it had to be taken out of its shell. It wasn't an outrageous request. They did it all the time for customers. With Wayne, it was always just a matter of timing. Sometimes he could be downright accommodating. Other times, he would reduce the girls to tears. Then Mary had to step in. A crying waitress was no good to anyone out on the floor.

"I'm sorry, I thought—," the waitress said. She was new this season. Mary didn't have all their names down yet. The girl had two earrings in one ear and a birthmark on her neck that looked like a whale. When she'd come for the interview, Mary'd first thought it was a tattoo, which would have been reason to turn her away. The girls who worked at the Clambake had a wholesome image to uphold. They had to have an aura of innocence about them, whether or not it was genuine. As for the whale birthmark, Mary had thought the customers would get a kick out of it. *Sweat the details.* It was her motto—one of them anyway.

Nate had already washed his hands and was back in the line.

"You *thought.* Hey, everyone, here's a first. Anicca *thought,*" Wayne said. One of the steam cooks laughed.

"Give her a break, dickweed," Nate said to Wayne.

Blood rushed to the girl's cheeks. She looked at Mary. "But you said it was okay—"

Mary shrugged. A betrayal. She felt some remorse but knew to stay out of it. Part of the job for these girls was to learn how to manage the kitchen crew, her excitable head cook in particular.

"See *this?*" Wayne lifted a gallon container of fresh-shucked steamers and let it crash down onto the metal countertop. The waitress and the counter girls jumped. "This is the sixth gallon of clams we've opened today. That would indicate that we're a little busy. So if you want to come back here with us and take Mr. Lobster out of his shell for the nice lady, that's just splendid. But we don't have the fucking time—"

"Get over yourself," Nate muttered under his breath.

Mary knew it was time to intervene. "Maureen, you do it," she said.

Maureen's short brown hair was clipped behind her protruding ears, a hairstyle that emphasized her receding chin. "But, Mary, I'm trying to get these orders—" She looked at Mary and must have realized there was no point in arguing. "Okay, okay."

"Thanks, Maureen, I owe you one," Anicca said. Mary could see she was on the verge of tears.

"*Thanks, Maureen, I owe you one,*" Maureen mimicked. Maureen Donovan hated the waitresses, not because they caused her more work, but because they were pretty and she wasn't. Try as Mary might to convince herself otherwise, good-looking people who came in to apply for jobs at the Clambake usually ended up out on the floor. The rest ended up in the kitchen, chained to greasy fryers and hot lobster steamers, elbow-deep in mayo and macaroni salad. Their fates were sealed. Long after their dining room friends had tipped out and made their way across town to one of the local pubs, they were still swabbing floors and scrubbing counters, smelling so rank and foody that no shower could exorcise the grease from their hair. No amount of supercharged laundry detergent could eliminate the stains and seafood from their clothes. Worst of all, their earnings over the summer were pitifully less than those of their server counterparts, all because they lacked clear complexions, straight noses, and dashing smiles. In the end, Mary had to confess, a Sea Breeze just tasted better served up by a handsome young man. A foot-long hot dog, just better with a little sun-kissed cleavage on the side. She didn't write the rules. It was the same at restaurants all over town.

Mary's house rose from the sand like a top-heavy cake, rounded with four layers and crowned with a copper whale that swam above the tree line, visible for miles in all directions, except when the fog was thick and palpable, as it had been earlier that morning.

Mary had roused Nate at the crack of dawn and sent him home to clean up for work. It was his turn to open the restaurant. On these mornings, she had an extra hour before she had to come in. Over the steam from her coffee, she was staring out the window into the coal eyes of a red coyote that had just relieved itself in the middle of her crushed shell driveway. The two were locked in a standoff.

Nate's Clambake sweatshirt sat in a ball on the kitchen island. He'd forgotten it, and now, thanks to the distraction, she'd broken her stare and the animal had disappeared into a darkening in the thicket of wild roses.

She'd bought the house on a whim fewer than eight months ago, sure that the change of scenery would do her good. It had been intended for the young mistress of a wealthy hedge fund manager, who had hired lawyers to push through his ambitious plans, finding loopholes in building regulations so that he could build on the small lot. When his wife found out about the affair, she divorced him and was awarded the house. According to the real estate agent, two months after the paperwork went through, the house quietly was put on the market. Mary figured the wife had never been interested in living here. It was the idea of the girlfriend getting it that had been too much to bear.

When the listing came on the market, something about the house, the over-the-topness of it, had intrigued Mary. And she could afford it. The restaurant business had been good to her, the last few years in particular. Still, she hadn't been actively looking to move from her place down the street from the Clambake, the old captain's house she and Robbie had bought and fixed up more than sixteen years earlier, but somehow she felt it was time. Even so, letting go of the old place had been harder than she would have imagined, even after all these years. She often wondered if it had been the right move. Why *this* house? Why now?

Until this house, she'd invested only in land and rental properties here and there, usually fixing them up and flipping them at just the right time. She had a knack for it and a secret passion for real estate in general, which had less to do with making lucrative investments than it did with her liking to imagine herself existing in different spaces, the idea of expanding into them, making them her own, something she'd done as long as she could remember. On Fridays, when the local paper came out, she always turned to the real estate listings in the back. Sometimes it was a dilapidated fixer-upper that caught her eye, a tiny cottage she might scrub clean, then decorate with gingham curtains, perhaps even stencil the floors. She'd plant a little perennial garden out back that she could go out to each morning and pick a few fresh blooms for the small cranberry glass vase on the sill. Or it might be a historic home that would capture her imagination, a house that came with its own ghost. Or one of those new zero-maintenance condominiums where she'd never have to lift a finger. Or it might be a different kind of space entirely, a mansion overlooking the inlet with sweeping views of the ocean beyond, where she might lounge on a chaise on the deck and listen to classical music piped through built-in speakers. A place so big and rambling that she'd need a second cat, perhaps the fat, fluffy kind that ate out of crystal goblets, a companion for dear old Seventy-Eight, whom she and Robbie had named for the blizzard that pummeled the Cape with hurricane-force winds and a tidal surge great enough to cause the first big break in the Outer Beach.

It was as if by looking at all kinds of houses, Mary could allow herself to slip into different lives, and imagine how hers might play out within different sets of walls, as if her key to happiness was only a matter of finding the right ones.

This new house, with its sweeping views of the salt marsh and the bay beyond, cut a dramatic silhouette into the landscape. It was an albatross among the fifty-year-old summer shacks peppered throughout the dunes. Mary was only just coming to understand how upset some of the locals had been over its construction. "One Skaket Drive" might as well have been an obscenity to the propane salesman at the hardware store and the old dame who sold Mary her rugs from the antique shop on Main Street. Of course, prior to buying the house, Mary had been oblivious to such drama, insulating herself as she typically did from everyone but the people who put the food on her tables in the summer. A loner like her father, she had better things to do than get wrapped up in town gossip. It was a fine house. A little showy for her taste, but through years of kitchen grease and tenacity, she'd earned the right to call it home. It wasn't until she actually moved in that she saw the small homes behind her whose views had been obliterated by walls of shingles. It made her uncomfortable, like being in a movie theater in front of a group of small children you know can't see the screen because your head is in the way, so you shrink down in your seat a little. But with this house, there was no shrinking.

Mary tightened her bathrobe. She'd left the windows open last night and the air inside the house was thick and cold. She heated up her coffee in the microwave, then retreated to the master bath, where she turned on the shower, eager for the hot stream to pulse away the chill in her bones. She slipped out of her robe and kicked it into a ball on the floor, trying to avoid looking in the mirror, reluctant to confront the middle-aged woman with puffy eyes, matted hair, and dry skin. A woman trying to hang on to something that was dangling by a thread.

Mary brushed the blond bangs from her eyes. She looked down at her thin limbs, which could have used some color. She smiled and thought of her mother, who she seemed to be resembling more each day. Though there were worse middle-aged women to have to resemble than Claire Hopkins, who died when Mary was still in high school. Mary's mother had been attractive, her high cheekbones framing a face that never saw many wrinkles. Mary's neck was long, like Claire's. Where Mary only really resembled her father was in his coloring—his more sallow complexion and sandy-blond hair—whereas Claire had been fair and freckled, with a coal-dark mane. And while both parents had blue eyes, Mary's were deeper, like her father's, "the color of Pleasant Bay on a sunny morning," her mother used to say.

Like so many women of the era, Claire Hopkins had been a sun-worshiper. Mary remembered the eerie glow of the sunlamp coming from under the bedroom door, a signal to stay out, like the ON AIR light outside a radio recording booth. As soon as the weather was warm enough, Claire would break out the folding chair and the sun reflector, which had consisted of an Elton John *Captain Fantastic* album covered in tinfoil. To her, a tan was like keys or a pocketbook, something she couldn't leave the house without. But try as she might, Claire never got as dark as her best friend, Suze, who always achieved that coveted grocery bag brown. Even Mary's young skin tanned more deeply and evenly than her mother's. Some people get away with sunning themselves their entire lives. Others have black flowers suddenly appear on the soles of their feet, ironically a place on Claire's body that probably saw the least sun of all.

We interrupt this idyllic childhood to bring you unfathomable pain.

Her mother's death hardened Mary, like those pellets of sand on the beach that crumble as soon as you try to pick them up. It left her fragile, easily broken. As an only child, she'd been close to her mother, even if they had their differences. Claire had been a stay-at-home mom until Mary reached middle school; then she went to work at Hair of the Cod, a popular salon. She was always bringing back stories of the characters in town, the latest steamy affair, a local drug bust, and once even a story about a woman from a neighboring town who pretended she had a daughter, a child who'd never existed, and carried on the charade for twenty some-odd years, even though everyone knew the truth. While Mary found the stories interesting in a train-wreck-fascination sort of way, they depressed her too. She was turned off by idle gossip and cattiness, and vowed she would never partake. She would be more like her father, who, no matter how juicy the story, never seemed to want to know more. People's business was their own. He had been a fiercely private person, which sometimes made him seem distant and unapproachable, often admonishing Claire for sticking her nose where it didn't belong.

"I'm a hairdresser, for God's sake," Mary's mother would say, fluffing up her own frosted shag, twisting the wisps of hair at the cheekbones and flattening them with her palms. "People tell me things. It's like being a bartender. Or a priest."

At that, Tom Hopkins would roll his eyes.

"Never mind. It helps them or they wouldn't tell me." Claire never let Tom's ways get to her. Somewhere, on some subterranean level, there was a deep understanding between the two of them, a powerful bond. Theirs was a true love story. Mary often marveled at what her parents had, took comfort in it, and hoped for the same for herself one day.

Not that it ever materialized. Now Mary could see that her father's sudden death from a heart attack had plenty to do with how fast she and Robbie had gotten married. There had been no love lost between Tom Hopkins and Robbie, who had never managed to earn her father's respect. Mary's father just couldn't understand what she saw in Robbie, and Mary, when she wasn't being defensive, hadn't been sure what it was either, aside from his carefree attitude, so unlike her own, and his physical beauty. After her father died at fifty-seven, Mary, then just twenty-five, was free to marry whomever she liked. But if she was being honest, most of her rush to the altar had to do with her not wanting to be alone.

Mary sighed. She stepped over her robe and into the shower. She looked down at her breasts, still full and firm. Never having kids had spared them. Her nipples were dark and wide, like sand dollars. A former lover had pointed that out to her once, though she couldn't remember which one. Over the years, she'd collected comments about her body like seashells. She remembered a time when she thought of sex as a hot spring that seeped from a vent at the bottom of the ocean, or like the sea itself, with its dark salt rhythms and undulations. After all these years, at least her flesh hadn't let her down. She was still an attractive woman, in some ways more attractive than she'd been as a girl, as she'd grown into her height and proportions. After Robbie, there had been others to appreciate her attributes, though it had surely been a while since.

The kitchen at the Clambake was a large rectangular room broken into serviceable stations. In the back near the door and the time clock stood the lone dishwasher, who tugged with Quasimodo-like gloom on the lever that lowered the stainless steel hood over racks of dirty pots, pans, and utensils. Next, and just slightly higher on the food chain, were the steam cooks, who sent clouds of vapor billowing through the room each time they opened the heavy metal doors. It was the steam cooks who did the prep work, which meant they had to come in hours early (while the waitresses were still on the beach) to chop the celery and onions for the tuna salad, rinse and soak the steamers in tap water to coax the sand out of them, boil the quahogs for chowder, scrub and de-beard the mussels, shuck the corn, shred the cabbage for slaw, slice the lemons, and mix the dressing.

Running down the right side of the room were the broiler oven, grill, and fryers, all of which fell under Wayne's dominion. To the left was the station where orders were prepped, a long steel table lined with individual iced bins of sliced lemons, kale, and cherry tomatoes; plastic cups of tartar sauce, cocktail sauce, and mayonnaise; and foil-wrapped pats of butter. Beneath the table, the large cork-lined oval trays were stacked vertically. Behind the station were three large refrigerators stocked with plastic bowls of pre-made tuna and crab salad, coleslaw, and baked beans; ears of shucked corn; and backup vats of chowder and condiments. When an order was up from the cooks, the girls who worked the line snapped into action, assembling the dishes, setting them on trays, and adding the finishing touches—a lemon wedge placed on the side of a broiled-dinner plate, a plastic cup of tartar sauce tucked in with the fried scallops, or a glob of mayo wiped from the rim of a tray before it headed out onto the floor. Then they'd call the waitress's name over the loud-speaker to let her know her order was up. There were several qualities Mary looked for in the girls who ran this station. They had to be smart, reliable, and unflappable. No criers or diva personalities, or girls who weren't tough enough to take the incessant stream of obscenities that spewed from Wayne's mouth and were often directed at them. They had to be able to say "Vanessa" and "Jennifer" over the loudspeaker like phone-sex operators while lopping off the heads of fish or rinsing eggs out of lobsters sent back to the kitchen by squeamish patrons. It was in these girls, of all the people who worked in the kitchen, that Mary often saw herself most. She had a soft spot for them. They worked harder than anyone.

To the left of the prep station was the take-out window, staffed by the order line girls as well. To the right, separated by heat lamps and a steel shelf for the food-laden trays, was the area where the waitresses deposited orders and picked up food and got their utensils, Styrofoam cups of chowder, oyster crackers, plastic spoons, creams, and sugars. There were two clearly marked doors through which the waitresses were instructed to enter and exit the kitchen. The concept was that they were to go in the "in" door and out the "out" door to avoid collision and injury: the mastering of which usually involved a few days' practice for some and a knot on the head for others.

At two in the afternoon, the small of Mary's back was being mashed into an open carton of plastic drink straws. She thought about the imprint of one hundred tiny zeros at the base of her spine. She'd have to throw away the entire box.

"Nate! What is it?" she asked. Mary had come up to the store-room to check the stock of citronella candles. The next thing she knew, Nate had followed her in and closed the door behind them.

His heel caught the doorstop and he stumbled toward her, catching himself just in time.

"I'm sorry about what happened last night," Nate said. His breath smelled like the lemon peels he chewed to mask the odor of the cooking grease he hovered over—and, on this day, probably to mask the liquor still on his breath from last night.

She blushed. "Nothing *happened*." Every now and then a kid came along who made Mary wish she were twenty-two and not forty-four. Last summer, Nate had been her crush. When Mary found out he was coming back, she wondered whether she'd still feel the same way. To her relief, it had mostly worn off. However, seeing him on her couch like that this morning hadn't helped the cause. And being trapped in close quarters with him now wasn't helping either.

He took a gulp of air. "I mean for showing up at your house like that."

"I'm just glad you made it there in one piece." The air in the room was thickening. Mary felt a familiar anger flare up in her chest. "What were you *thinking* getting behind the wheel like that?" she said. She scowled at him. "You know how many people get themselves killed—"

Nate stepped back and his heel accidentally kicked a box of empty salt and pepper shakers. They clinked together so hard she wondered if some might have broken. "I got in a fight with my girlfriend," he said. "By the end of the night, I was too lit to go home. My folks would have killed me." Nate exhaled. "They'd've taken away the car."

Had she heard him right? "I didn't know you had a girlfriend." Had he had one last summer too? He never talked about girls, so she'd just assumed he didn't.

"I probably don't anymore. She was pretty pissed off at me."

"How come?"

"You don't want me to bore you with—"

"Who knows? Maybe I can help." Though it was truly more curiosity than altruism.

He cast his eyes down toward the floor. "She has this crazy jealous streak." His voice was hoarse.

"She thinks you're cheating?"

"She doesn't like me working here. She thinks the waitresses are too pretty."

Mary felt a wave of embarrassment. It was true. "Because she thinks you'll be tempted." Mary felt some sweat drip down the small of her back. "We should probably open the door," she said.

"Not that I ever would." He stuffed the box he'd tripped on back under the shelf. Then he looked up at Mary. "Can I ask you something?" He leaned in closer. "I don't come across as some kind of awful flirt, do I?"

Nate's face was wide open, his expression unbearably earnest. *Quite the contrary,* she thought. That was part of his charm.

"Not at all," Mary said. "Nate, you're a great guy. But you don't need to take everything so seriously. You're twenty-two, for God's sake. Lighten up and have a little fun. That's my advice." Then she added, "Though that doesn't mean getting trashed out of your mind and getting behind the wheel. If I ever catch you doing that again, I'll fire you. I mean it."

Nate's eyes widened. Mary knew how much he needed this job. That's why she'd said it. "It won't happen again," he said. "Honest."

Mary had no choice but to believe him. "And showing up at your boss's house in the middle of the night isn't all that considerate either." She wanted him to think she was just feeling put out. But what she really meant was that for a woman who'd gone without for as long as she had, having an inebriated, handsome young guy in her house was outright torture.

She leaned in and gave him a motherly pinch on the cheek, allowing her hand to rest on his face perhaps a little longer than was necessary. Then she opened the door and moved for the stairs.

As she left Nate in the storage closet, it occurred to her that she'd sounded a bit like she'd been reading from someone else's script, the part where the prim, excruciatingly repressed and long-suffering middle-aged woman (played by Emma Thompson) once again forgoes the opportunity to seduce the excitable young buck (played by a young Brad Pitt). Why did it always have to play out that way? Last year's harmless crush had taken on a tragic air. As Mary brushed the dust and cardboard bits from her T-shirt, she realized she felt old.

Two

*C*rash. A tray was down in the dining room. An old woman dropped her chowder spoon. A mother instinctively put her hand on her four-year-old's chest, first to see if he was okay, then to make sure he wasn't the culprit. A man looked down to find beer splattered on the cuffs of his pants and a tidal wave of pilsner rushing toward his feet. The oyster knife slipped in the bartender's hand and blood trickled out over the vat of crushed ice, turning it sno-cone red.

Seven o'clock and Mary was now down a bartender, and perhaps even a steam cook if one of them had to take the injured kid to the hospital for stitches. The dishwasher would have to get out on the floor to clean up the smashed mugs and beer bottles before someone stepped on a piece of glass and decided to sue. With the dishwasher away from his job, they'd soon be low on clean glasses for the bar.

"You order fried clams, you get fried clams," Wayne said to a waitress. Mary couldn't recall this one's name either. Some kind of herb. Rosemary? On a tension scale of one to ten, Wayne was now at about a seven, and waving a basket of fried food in the air.

"But my customer doesn't *want* clams with the bellies. He wants *littlenecks*. I *told* you that when I dropped the order," the waitress said.

"You eat littlenecks on the half shell." Wayne stuck his gloved hand deep into an open container of clams and pulled up a dripping handful, their long protuberances and swollen bellies bulging through his knuckles. He was really trying to repulse the girl. *Must be love,* Mary thought. "*These* are sea clams," he went on. "*These* are what we fry here on Cape Cod. That's it for Clams-fucking-101." He tossed the bivalves back into the container, wiped his hand on his grease-stained apron, and turned his back to the girl.

"Hey!" the waitress said.

The sound of her voice cut through the kitchen so that the steam cook, with a live lobster hinging in each hand, stopped and looked up. The order line girl with her lips to the microphone drew back and slid her finger off the speaker button. "I don't need this," the waitress continued. "I've got two new tables and a tray of food that's sitting here getting cold." Nobody but Mary or Nate ever dished it back to Wayne. "Look, Wayne," the waitress said. She was a beauty, even with the sweaty hair plastered to her head. Her tone changed and got creamy. "Can't you help me out just this once and fry up some littlenecks?" She smiled. Mary had found her new head waitress for the season. If she could just remember her name. She'd have to check the schedule. Maureen had done it these last two weeks.

Wayne still had his back to her. He grunted. "Get the bartender to shuck 'em," he said.

The waitress smiled. She bounded for the door.

"Hang on a minute," Mary said. "Tell your customer we'll be happy to fry up some littlenecks but he's going to have to pay three dollars more," she said. "For the labor," she added. People often thought Mary was cheap, but she didn't get to where she was by giving things away.

"Are you kidding?" the girl said, annoyed. Mary's face must have told her this was no joke. "Okay, okay."

As soon as Wayne heard the screen door slam, he said, "What's wrong with these people? You don't fry goddamn littlenecks."

Mary had been to enough parts of the world to know that wasn't true. She didn't say anything. Wayne had been humbled. Imagine that.

"Maureen, call Hope in here," Mary said. "I want to know who dropped the tray."

Moments later, Wayne's waitress burst back into the kitchen, hands on her hips. "Thanks a lot. The guy didn't want to pay extra. He told me what I could do with my littlenecks. Wanna know where he told me to put them, Wayne?" she said. "Just make me a hamburger."

Mary waited for Wayne's comeback. And she waited. None came. *He must really have it bad for this one,* she thought. That was his problem. He set his sights too high.

Few were ever admitted into Mary's inner sanctum, a tiny room down the hall from the storeroom and atop a set of steep, creaky stairs. It was here Mary liked to wallow in paperwork, in the company of her cat, when she wasn't needed downstairs. This half of the restaurant had once been part of a house, and the ceilings were pitched at steep angles. The room was only big enough for a desk and two chairs, a small bookcase, and a file cabinet holding a dusty TV that hadn't been switched on since the O. J. Simpson trial. If Mary's restaurant was a picture of cleanliness and organization, her office was the opposite, with magazines piled high and papers strewn everywhere, cobwebs in the rafters, and an overflowing wastebasket. This was the only space in Mary's life where she allowed clutter, and one of the few places where she truly felt comfortable, being something of a pack rat by nature—a trait she'd inherited from her aunt Lovey, who'd contributed the heavy pink-and-maroon afghan that was slung over Mary's chair, and, on her desk, the silk rose encased in a crystal ball that Mary had admired as a child.

Mary's office was a sanctuary replete with such personal treasures—a smooth stone with a vein of quartz running through it given her by Robbie on their honeymoon that she'd been meaning to skim on the waves for fourteen years; a lobster claw, the size of a grapefruit, mounted on a wood plaque; a five-euro prayer candle from one winter's trip to Notre-Dame. Her only indulgence: a vase that was always billowing with fresh blooms from the farmers' market across the street. Tonight it held irises.

"Hey," Nate said. Somehow he'd managed to sneak up on her in her office without making a sound. Mary swiveled around in her desk chair. "Just sent the last order out," he said. Things must have died down fast. It wasn't even nine.

Mary turned back around and pretended to be reading an issue of *SeaFood Business* magazine, opened to an article on salmon franks and panko-coated crab nuggets. She adjusted her reading glasses. "So did you have a chance to work things out with your girlfriend?"

"Not exactly," he said.

Mary turned and slid her glasses down her nose. "What happened?"

"Really want to know?" Nate flipped the hair out of his eyes.

"Sure."

He looked down at the floor. "She found out where I slept last night and now she thinks I'm having an affair with you."

Mary's face grew hot. "That's crazy!" Had the story already made it all over town?

"I'm sorry. I never should have come to your house in the first place," Nate said.

Mary closed the magazine. "Why *did* you? You must have other places where you could have crashed."

"I don't know," Nate said. "Maybe she's right. Maybe I do have a thing for you."

"*What?*" Mary whipped around, worried that someone else might have overheard. But there was just ancient Seventy-Eight, whom Mary had moved to her office after the first time she'd seen that coyote loitering around the new house. Now on his cushion on the window seat, the cat was so still that Mary was compelled to go over and check to see he was still breathing. But there, his belly moved. Her eyes settled back on Nate.

He was grinning. "I'm *kidding.* I just knew where you kept the spare key from when I delivered those cases of wine to your house last summer," he said. "Seemed like a no-brainer. I planned to get up and leave before you even knew I was there. Then again, I wasn't exactly operating with a full deck."

Mary felt her neck spasm, which happened when she was nervous. She gave it a squeeze.

"Let me," Nate said. He pressed his thumbs on either side of her spine and started gently rotating them.

Mary felt her shoulders release. She closed her eyes. Her body felt like a pat of butter on an ear of corn as it slowly drips down to a puddle on the plate. She dropped her head back, opened her eyes, and saw the hopeful look on Nate's face.

Mary bolted upright in her chair. "Wow, thanks. That was great." She took off her glasses and set them on the desk. "So, about the kitchen."

"I was an Exercise Science major, for one semester anyway," Nate said. "Feels better now, right?" he added. There was what the hopefulness had been about.

"Much better, thanks." Though now every muscle in her body had constricted. Mary smoothed the shoulders of her sweater. "No one else will be coming in at this hour. Let's close." He'd started to leave when Mary asked, "By the way, how was Anicca the rest of the night?" Hope had told Mary that Anicca, the girl with the birthmark, had been the one who dropped the tray. "Did she get her act together down there?"

"I don't know. I guess."

It was close to eleven o'clock. All the servers had cleared out, including Anicca, with whom Mary had planned to have a talk. She'd vanished before Mary ever had the chance.

Wayne was chewing something. Mary saw a flash of green between his teeth. "What are you eating?" she asked.

"Nothing," Wayne said.

"He just tore off a bunch of parsley and stuffed it in his mouth," Nate said. He was scouring the sink with steel wool. "Like a cow or something."

"Good for the breath," Wayne said. "You should try some."

"No, thanks," Nate said.

"No, *really*. Do us a favor."

"Piss off."

Mary ignored them. She was used to the banter, this being Wayne's third season at the restaurant. He had an amazing talent for being able to provoke just about anyone, even good-natured Nate.

Mary was nearly finished going over the liquor order. She'd review it once more with a fresh eye in the morning. She shuffled the papers together, tapped them on the window ledge, and set them down. She studied Wayne as he restocked the broiler plates on the shelf below the stainless steel counter. The parsley was something new. What effect did it have on him? What shapes did it make him feel? Of course, he'd kill her if she came right out and asked in front of Nate. But over the years, Mary had compiled quite a list of Wayne's sensations. For example, she knew that grape bubble gum somehow manifested as three-dimensional honeycombs, and that mint chocolate chip ice cream made his cheeks burn as if he'd been slapped, whereas menthol cigarettes conjured up row upon row of smooth glass columns that, according to him, seemed to go on forever.

The last of the order line girls was breaking down condiments, wrapping sliced lemons and kale garnishes in plastic for tomorrow's lunch.

Nate dumped an empty pot on the metal grate of one of the burners. He opened the cellar door and clomped down the stairs.

"So you guys are sleeping together?" Wayne spit the chewed-up green wad into the trash barrel and wiped his mouth with his sleeve.

"What? Are you out of your mind?" Mary said. "What have you heard?"

"There was something to hear?" he said. One of his brows inched up.

He'd just been busting on her over last year's crush. He hadn't heard anything. Mary relaxed. She poured herself a last finger of wine. She took a sip, pooled it on her tongue, then swallowed. "Give me a break. He's twenty-two."

"I'm twenty-six," Wayne said.

"So?"

Wayne yanked the dirty hand towel out of his waistband and tossed it on the laundry pile on the floor. "So, I'm no kid. Why can't we have a go at it?"

Wayne wasn't good-looking in a classic sense, but there was something about him, with his lean Asian build and strong forearms, his dagger-shaped eyebrows, and a roughness around the edges that always made him look as if he just rolled out of bed. Or course, head cooks were as off-limits as the rest of them. But sometimes Mary found herself wondering what it would be like to be with him, and to what shape she might be assigned, whether her lips might be perceived as a cone or a grid or even a nice sexy triangle.

Nate was downstairs. The order line girl had her head in the fridge. Mary took advantage of the opportunity. "Wayne," she whispered. "The *parsley.*" She nodded in the direction of the trash barrel. "What—?"

"Ugh." Wayne rolled his eyes and turned away from her.

"Come on," she said, a little louder.

He must have known Mary wasn't going to be satisfied until she had her answer. He leaned over to make sure the order line girl wasn't looking.

He turned toward Mary. "Springy," he said behind his hand. He brought his thumb and fingers together and released, repeating the gesture a couple of times.

Springy. Mary mimicked his fingers. "Really?"

He nodded. "With bumps," he added.

Bumps! "And that's *good?*"

Wayne shrugged, squirted some cleaner, and started wiping the knobs on the stove.

Wayne was the only Asian kid Mary had ever met with an honest-to-goodness New England accent. He'd grown up on the Cape, brought to the United States from Beijing as an infant as part of his father's American dream to open a chain of Chinese restaurants. Wayne's father had five dining rooms, one in Falmouth, one in Mashpee, two in Hyannis, and one here in town, but for reasons initially undisclosed to Mary, Raymond Chen's son wound up on her own doorstep three summers ago and had been her head cook ever since. Of course, at

first she was curious about why he didn't work for the family business. She thought Wayne and his father might have had some falling
out. The real reason was too bizarre for even her to have dreamed
up. The first time she'd caught on that something was different
about Wayne was just a few weeks after he started.

During a quiet afternoon early that first season, he and Mary had
been testing out some new dishes. One of them was a lightly sea-
soned haddock. He had taken a metal plate out of the broiler and set
it on an oven mitt in front of Mary.

"Smells great," she said. She'd been impressed with her new hire
from the start.

With the corner of a spatula, he flaked off some fish and tasted
it. Then he dropped the utensil on the counter and pushed the plate
away. "Damn," he said. He went to the spice drawer.

"What's the matter?" she said.

"Not enough points." As soon as he said it, a look of panic came
over his face.

"What?"

"Never mind," he said. He turned away from her.

"You said *points*. What do you mean, *points*?" Running a glori-
fied clam bar often made Mary feel like she was out of the culinary
loop, which was why she watched cooking shows and kept up her
subscriptions to the trade journals. *Points.* Was this some new flavor-
rating system?

"Forget it," Wayne said. He took another raw fillet of haddock
from the fridge and set it on the counter.

Mary wasn't about to let it go. She was in secret awe of people
who had such an intuitive way with food, such cultivated taste buds.
She envied him. "You mean you want the flavor to be more *sharp*?
But who wants sharp-tasting fish?" Mary thought of bluefish and
how there was always so much left over on nights when it was the
special, and how she kept telling Ernie Smith, her fish guy, that if she
found those big yellow eyes staring up at her in the walk-in one more
time, she'd be finding herself another fish guy.

Wayne rinsed the fillet and patted it down with paper towels. "That's a metaphor. I didn't mean *sharp*. Just needs more flavor." He set the fish on a clean broiler plate and squeezed lemon over it.

"But you said *points*. What did you mean?" He didn't answer. "I'm not dropping this till you tell me." She folded her arms.

Wayne shook his head. "You'll think I'm a nutcase."

"I already think that," Mary said. She smiled.

He wiped his hands on his apron, then looked up at her. "I have this thing that when I taste something, I see shapes."

"Shapes," Mary repeated.

"Actually more like *feel* them." He raised his right arm into the air in front of him. "When I taste something intense, the feeling sweeps down my arms into my fingertips. I feel its shape, its weight, its texture, whether it's hot or cold."

Was he kidding? Mary eyed him. There was a lime on the counter. It was round. Limes are round. What more did anyone need to know? "That's crazy," she said.

"I *told* you." He shrugged and drizzled some melted butter on the fish. "When I was a kid, I thought it happened to everyone. Embarrassed the hell out myself in the school cafeteria a few times before I figured out I was *special*."

"You've had this all your life?"

"Yeah." He went to the fridge and got some fresh herbs in a plastic baggie.

"So what was wrong with *this* fish?" Mary said. She pointed to the abandoned fillet.

"I wanted it to have more *points* but it came out round, almost *spherical*," he said. He screwed up his mouth like he'd tasted some terrible.

"Remarkable," Mary said. She took a piece of the fish onto her fork and tasted. It was actually pretty good, a little bland but not bad. Was it possible that this shape thing was what made Wayne such a good cook? "Is there a name for this . . . affliction?"

"Synesthesia. And it's not really an affliction. I mean, most of the time, it's a good feeling. If you told me you could snap your fingers and take it away, I wouldn't want you to." Wayne scraped the "spherical" fish off the plate and into the trash. "Of course, my father would have it gone in a heartbeat."

"How come?"

Wayne deposited the dirty plate in the sink, letting go a little too soon. "Haven't you ever wondered why I'm working for you instead of him?"

"I just figured you're a hothead—"

"It's because Chinese food is the only kind of food in the world that causes me to feel like my hand is being pressed down onto a bed of razor-sharp nails. Sometimes I feel it all over my body. It's horrible." He looked up at Mary and she thought she saw him shiver. "There's just too much going on. I can't take it."

"So you couldn't work in his kitchen. You couldn't taste what you were cooking." She studied Wayne's hands as he stripped the leaves from a sprig of thyme. "Besides your parents and me, who else knows?"

"Hardly anyone. And I'd like to keep it that way, if it's all the same to you," Wayne said.

"Sure." Mary figured it could only be a distraction if others knew. But she had to admit, it tickled her. She'd already begun to think Wayne was one in a million, and this confirmed it. In the meantime, she'd just chalk it up to the idiosyncrasies of a genius, and one in her employ. Her very own culinary savant.

In the days that followed, Mary's own curiosity, coupled with the secret fear that her leg was being pulled, led her to the Internet, where she learned of cases of synesthesia that had been documented as far back as the 1700s. At least one person in two thousand, perhaps more, had some form of this hypersensitivity; among them had been artist Wassily Kandinsky, poet Arthur Rimbaud, and even author Vladimir Nabokov, who wrote about the experience in his memoir *Speak, Memory*. She also learned that Wayne's particular form of it was extremely rare, occurring in perhaps fewer than ten in a million.

Mary read about a celebrated pianist who *heard* colors, each note having its own distinct hue, and about individuals who attributed colors to letters of the alphabet, numbers, environmental sounds, even whole words, though no two synesthetes assigned the *same* colors, shapes, or sounds to the same stimuli. Every now and then, Wayne would let some comment slip. He might run his hand through the air in an odd gesture that the kitchen crew never picked up on—or if they did, knew better than to challenge their acid-tongued boss when the line was chugging along full steam. But Mary knew what it meant. He was tasting a cone or a cylinder or a bunch of bumps. Mary grew jealous of Wayne's extrasensory perception, the way a blind person might envy the sighted. Sometimes she'd close her eyes while gnawing on a bread stick or a lemon peel, opening herself to the possibilities of color, numbers, or shapes.

After that first season, Mary learned to accept Wayne's special ability. While his condition continued to intrigue her, eventually the novelty wore off and most of the time it didn't matter what shapes Wayne saw as long as the customers kept coming back for more.

Around eleven twenty, the order line girl had finally left in a Jeep with a bearded guy Mary prayed was her father. Nate had been down in the basement checking the afternoon's fish delivery. When he came back up, he went over to Mary's perch by the window. He lifted a paper cup filled with ice, put it to his lips, and flung his head back. Mary watched his Adam's apple dance as the water dripped down his throat. Young men had such pronounced Adam's apples. Then they got to be her age, their necks thickened, swelled and you couldn't see them anymore.

"There's a hunk of swordfish down there," Nate said. He set down the cup and took off his apron.

Mary realized she'd been staring at him. What was wrong with her? She dropped her head and slid her hands under her thighs. "Swordfish. That's great," she said. Fresh swordfish caught off the coast of Nantucket was a real treat, and infinitely better than the stuff she could get frozen. "What do you think, Wayne?" Mary said. "Maybe serve it up with a light dill mayonnaise, some tomatoes on the side—"

"Anchovy paste. Roasted peppers. Red wine vinegar," Wayne said. "The *wavy* kind," he added behind his hand. His eyes sparkled as if he were a mathematician working equations. He wiped his greasy hands on his already grimy apron, leaving two brown tracks.

Mary had to admit his suggestion sounded more appealing, waves and all. "Try it," she said.

Mary walked over to the time clock at the back of the kitchen. She ran her finger up the yellow cards until she came to the one with "Anicca Sutherland" at the top. Mary pulled out the card. Just as she suspected, the girl had forgotten to punch out. At that instant, Mary knew the soft-spoken slender blonde with the whale birthmark on her neck wasn't long for the Clambake. She just didn't have it. Every year brought one or two who didn't make it. Mary could pick them out right from the start. Her instincts on this were always dead on.

Three

The next morning, Mary stood at the sink with her toothbrush in her mouth. From her bathroom window, she could see the old man who lived behind her. He was breaking up his shredded wheat with a spoon. She hadn't realized until she moved in how close her house was to his, how on top of it, and how he once must've awakened to the sunlight stretching over the flats each morning, while now he had a stunning view of her outdoor shower and bulkhead. *Bad house karma,* she thought. And rather bad of her to be spying on the poor, unsuspecting man in his blue pajamas as he poured milk into his shallow bowl, then tossed in a couple of teaspoons of sugar. And now, as he bored holes into the brick of cereal, twisting his spoon gently so as not to upset the milk, captivating her with his slow, deliberate movements.

The phone rang. Mary spit out her toothpaste. *Someone calling in sick,* she thought. *They know better than to call me this early.* She grabbed a towel and wiped her face. The phone kept ringing. Every season it was a new group of employees with new reasons why they couldn't come in to work. Only they were usually the same old reason: that they were hungover from having partied all night, which of course they never admitted. Instead, they came up with the same tired fairy tales: car trouble, poison ivy, a case of the flu. Mary remembered a girl who claimed to have accidentally eaten a piece of shrimp from a coworker's dinner plate, thinking it was an onion ring, and then gone into anaphylactic shock. Come to think of it, that one might have been legitimate. But there was another girl who came down with a mysterious case of shingles every time her boyfriend came to visit. And a bartender who faked a limp for a week so he could go to a Dropkick Murphys concert, Mary knew, because another waitress that summer had confessed she'd seen the kid in the mosh pit.

Mary let the machine pick up. She looked in the mirror. Pouches of fluid had collected beneath her eyes. She tapped one lightly with her finger and the ripple traveled toward her nose.

"Mary, it's me." The voice was Nate's. He sounded different, smaller. After yesterday, she obviously needed to reestablish some boundaries. She was his boss, not is confidante, and this was her home, not his crash pad.

"Something happened last night. One of the waitresses— Just call me back, okay?" He hung up.

Ah, so that was it. Perhaps he'd taken her advice after all and had a little fun. And now he was feeling remorseful? Or worried about the girlfriend finding out? Mary smiled. She reached for the deodorant and sighed. She slipped a white tank top over her head. There were really very few markers for the passage of time at the Clambake. Not the drama, not the excuses for not coming to work, not even the names of the servers ever seemed to change. Each year there was always at least one Ashley, Megan, or Heather. Always more than one Jennifer. And at least one or two wild cards: last year, a girl named Grayson. This year, an Anicca.

If only to keep sane, Mary saw to it that some small changes were implemented each season: a new cleaning procedure, a new entrée, or something she'd buy to spruce up the restaurant, like yellow umbrellas for the patio. One year she'd wrapped white Christmas lights up the old wood beams. Another, she'd put geraniums on the tables. Two summers ago, she'd found rubber caps that turned empty beer bottles into salt and pepper shakers, thinking she could save a few dollars. Instead, people liked the shakers so much they kept swiping the caps, which resulted in more than a few plates of food being doused in salt and pepper by unsuspecting customers.

Mary turned her head upside down and shook the wet hair away from her scalp.

Toward the end of last summer, a woman who had been one of

her very first girls came in for dinner with her husband and three kids who were eight, eleven, and fifteen. It made Mary feel so old. Not only that, but like nothing had changed for her since she opened the place. It made her feel as if some of the most important parts of life had passed her by while she was caught in a loop of living season to season, the same thing year after year, a modern-day Cape Cod Sisyphus rolling her clams up the dune only to have them roll back down again and again.

Why put it off any longer? She grabbed the phone at the side of the bed and dialed Nate's cell phone. "You called?"

"Mary." There was a pause, then: "Something awful . . . I don't even know how to—"

Mary laughed. It never ceased to amaze her how dramatic kids could be. How self-important. It took some living to realize people didn't live and die on your every breath. "Whatever it is, Nate, I'm sure you'll survive—"

"It's Anicca. The waitress. She's dead."

Mary heard the words but they didn't register.

"There was a cop at the restaurant when I showed up," Nate continued. "She went out after work. I guess she'd been drinking, though that's not the official report yet. But he smelled liquor. He thinks she was going too fast on her way home and lost control of her car. He said she hit a tree, right on 28. She was already dead when the ambulance got there."

"Jesus," Mary said. She felt a cold pinch in her chest. She looked down at her hands, which had begun to shake. A feeling of déjà vu welled up from her gut and spread to her chest. Before she could grasp it with her mind, it vanished.

"I know what you're thinking. That this was because of all that stuff that happened at work. But having a bad day isn't enough reason for her to get shitfaced. I mean . . ." His voice trailed off. Hadn't he done precisely the same thing the night before?

It might easily have been enough reason. She could see the girl now, the look on her face when Mary had acted like she'd never said it was okay to request a lazy man's lobster. She'd thrown the kid under the bus. And the poor thing never recovered. She'd gone on to drop a tray, which must have been humiliating. She was in such a hurry to get out of there, she didn't even punch out. And rather than be sympathetic, Mary had written her off, ready to toss her out like an empty chowder cup.

"Mary, are you there? How do you want me to handle it with the employees? Do you want to send them home? Should we close for the day? Do you want me to call anyone?"

Mary sat down on the edge of the bed. The belt of her bathrobe had come untied and the robe had opened, her nakedness spilling out. She looked down at herself and felt disconnected from her body. Whose legs were these? Whose belly?

So familiar. She'd been here before. Right here. "I gotta go."

"Wait. What do you want me to do?" Nate asked.

"Whatever you think is best."

"Mary, this is *your* restaurant," Nate said. "Besides, the cop told me he wants to talk to you. Just to find out what happened."

Mary felt a cold shiver fanning out to goose bumps.

"Do you want me to come over there?" he asked. She heard the concern in his voice.

"No." She started to hang up the phone.

Before she got the receiver down, she heard: "Mary."

She raised the phone back up to her cheek. She didn't say anything.

"This didn't happen because of anything *we* did or didn't do." His voice reached through the phone and held her. "*God* gets credit for this one. Okay?"

Mary hung up. She'd never been much of a believer in God. The fact that something like this could be happening again didn't make her much of a believer now.

Mary sat on her bed and looked out at the bay. The tide was out for a couple of miles, so that as far as the eye could see there was just sand that disappeared into the haze. Every so often she'd heard about joggers on the flats who got lost in the fog at low tide, disoriented, unable to see land and not knowing which way the water was coming in, and then it would come in so fast and they found themselves too far from shore to swim back. They didn't even know where "back" was. Mary felt like that now. Someone had died and there was no going back. And the worst part was, she hadn't even been able to remember the girl's name until a day ago. She didn't know where she went to college or what she majored in. She hadn't met her folks. She didn't know where Anicca had grown up or if she had a boyfriend or what kind of music she liked. She knew as much about Anicca as she did about the rest of them. To her they were just ponytails and fresh faces who kept her in business. They were just kids who owed her for the opportunity to work for her. Girls in skimpy uniforms. What if Anicca had problems? What if she'd been struggling with addiction or trouble at home? What if she was just thin-skinned? *Tough,* Mary would have said. *If you can't take the heat . . .*

She closed up her bathrobe and knotted the belt tight. She knew all too well the steps to this dance.

Mary went into the bathroom. She splashed some cold water on her face, then looked down into the old man's window. He'd finished breakfast. His bowl was gone. There was just a band of light that cut across an empty chair. And there was something else on the table, just outside the light. A newspaper. Had the story already gone out to the press? Was it on the news? It wasn't too late to learn something of who the girl had been.

Mary went out to the living room and opened up the armoire that housed the fancy entertainment system she never used. She turned on the radio. An old song about drinking alone came on. She tried to tune in another station, but without cable this was the only one that came in. After the song, a few bad local commercials and then this:

"Last night, a fatal car crash on Route 28 took the life of twenty-six-year-old Anicca Sutherland. The young mother died when her car hit a tree just south of the intersection of Route 28 and Jessop's Lane. There were no

passengers. Authorities are investigating whether alcohol may have been a factor."

Young mother? Had she heard that right? Anicca had a child? Children? How could Mary not know a thing like that? Did the job application even ask such a question? *How many kids do you have?* Had she known, would she ever have hired Anicca in the first place? Or would she have seen a child as a potential reason for missed shifts and distractions, and found some other, more legally acceptable, reason for having turned the girl away. Lack of experience, perhaps. Maybe the child had been the cause of Anicca's distraction at the restaurant yesterday. This didn't make Mary feel any better.

The accident scene was about a mile and a half from Mary's house. As she pulled out of her driveway, the story came on the radio again and Mary clung to the words, hoping that they might have changed, that the newspeople had made some mistake, if not about Anicca's death, at least about her being a mother. But the words were identical to the ones she'd heard earlier. *"Last night, a fatal car crash on Route 28 took the life of twenty-six-year-old Anicca Sutherland. The young mother died—"*

Route 28 was a narrow two-lane road with lots of twists and turns and changes in elevation. The Orleans side was more densely wooded with pine and locust trees, and peppered with modest shingled houses. Toward Chatham, the road opened up to sweeping views of Pleasant Bay and historically significant homes with lush lawns that rolled down to meet the water's edge. Mary knew the road well. The intersection of Route 28 and Jessop's Lane came at the wooded end, at the bottom of a steep hill with a turn at the base. Coming from the Chatham side, it was easy to imagine how someone might miss the turn if she was going too fast. Mary passed the intersection, then made a U-turn in a driveway. As she approached the intersection from the other direction, she slowed. There were no cars behind her. She searched the side of the road for signs of the accident, some remnant of twisted metal that had been missed by the clean-up crew. What she saw at the turn was a large maple, at least three feet wide, that had been skinned of its bark—a raw wound that stood out from everything else in the landscape. Mary suspected the tree would survive. Trees had the capacity to mend themselves, bark rolling over their wounds the way tidewaters come in from all sides to fill a depression in the sand. One day, years from now, there'd be just a scar, some imperfection in the surface that would hold the memory of what had happened. Mary knew of such trees; one lay less than a quarter mile down that same road.

Broken glass sparkled at the edge of the pavement. Others had already been to the site. Beneath the tree were the beginnings of a makeshift shrine, with a few stuffed animals and bouquets of handpicked flowers. Someone had tacked a Clambake uniform shirt to the base of the tree. The poor girl had probably died in her uniform.

Mary knew she should go in to the restaurant, but she wasn't ready to face any of it yet. There was only one place she could escape to, at least for a little while, a place where time stood still. She would visit Lovey, who received no daily paper and watched no news, just the Weather Channel, and only then to keep track of the date, which always appeared at the top of the screen. Travel advisories, heat waves, and cold snaps were otherwise of little consequence to an old woman who dwelled in a government-subsidized, rent-controlled unit, heat and utilities included.

"Mary," Lovey said as she opened the door. "What a surprise." Mary kissed her and felt a prick from a hair growing out of the mole on her great-aunt's chin. "You should have phoned ahead. I would have put in my tooth. I'll be a minute." Lovey turned and headed for the bathroom, where Mary knew she kept her denture in a small plastic cup on a bed of folded paper towel.

"I brought you some macaroni salad," Mary said. After visiting the scene, she'd gone back to the house for something she could bring to her aunt. "I'll put it in the kitchen."

"Thank you, dear. Make yourself comfortable," Lovey said over the bathroom fan.

The smell of last night's Meals On Wheels lasagna hung heavy in the windowless kitchenette. All the pots and pans were on the countertops, leading Mary to believe she'd caught her aunt in the middle of cleaning out her cupboards. Mary opened the fridge and set the salad on a shelf next to a six-pack of nutritional milkshakes.

The apartment was small but adequate for one person—one bedroom, one bath, living room, dining area, and a tiny but functional kitchen. As Mary passed through the dining room, she stopped to look at the old montage of photos on the wall, mostly snapshots of Mary in her youth. A faded picture of her at four years old on the blue sofa in her parents' home. Another of her in her high school cap and gown, holding up her diploma. An image of her father standing before the frozen kettle pond behind their house the year after her mother died.

The Hopkinses hadn't been wealthy by any stretch, at least not in anything but *Mayflower* heritage, but they were comfortable enough, with a nice home and a big yard that backed up to water. Tom Hopkins and his generation had had the greatest opportunity to capitalize on the real estate boom on the Cape. Mary's parents' house had cost a mere fraction of what it eventually sold for. While her father never went to college, he was a smart, intuitive businessman who started out as a sheetrocker and ended up running his own construction company—a good business to be in during the 1970s and '80s. Tom had a decent nest egg saved for his retirement, one that illness prevented him and his wife from ever enjoying. As Mary looked at her father in this photograph now, there was something in his expression, a tightness about the eyes, that made her think he might have had an inkling of how his own life would play out now that the love of his life was gone.

And then there was the photo she'd come in close to see, one of herself and Robbie—the last one ever taken of the two together—that was already beginning to curl away from the glass, leaving some of its surface behind. It was a shot of the two of them at his company Christmas party down at the pier the year she turned twenty-six. They were standing behind a table of poinsettias. Just moments before the picture was snapped, Robbie had given notice to his boss that he was leaving his job to go to work full-time at the restaurant. Mary leaned in to get a closer look at the man she'd married. After fourteen years, there were things now that she could no longer remember, like the smell of his neck, the brand of underwear he wore, or the name of his sister's dog. And there were things she couldn't forget: his dashing smile, the clumsy way he kissed (how she felt his teeth through his lips), how he took his coffee (black, with two sugars), and how his face changed when he'd had too much to drink, the color draining from his flesh, a sheen of perspiration on his forehead and cheeks, and the slightest curl at corners of his lips, a Mona Lisa smile. Mary used to muse over the possibility that she'd solved the age-old mystery, that perhaps Leonardo da Vinci's muse had simply been inebriated.

There was that familiar furrow between Robbie's eyebrows, in this case reflecting his struggle to keep his dilated pupils directed toward the camera. And she recalled how, after the flash, he'd looked confused, as if the camera lens had taken something from him, so that she had grabbed his hand and held it tight. Looking back, she realized she already knew then that, no matter how hard she tried, she wouldn't be able to hold on to him.

Lovey came out of the bathroom smiling. She winked and pulled down her lower lip, pointing to the tooth, which was much whiter than the surrounding ones. She'd changed into her favorite house-coat, the one with owl pockets.

"Come, sit in the chair," she said.

"*You* sit in the chair. I'll sit on the couch." Lovey always offered the chair, but Mary never accepted. The green tweed recliner was where her aunt had spent most of the last quarter century. It was *her* chair. Besides, what was the height of comfort for Lovey was like putting on someone else's old shoes that rose and sunk in all the wrong places.

"What brings you by?"

"I was just driving," Mary said. She didn't look at her aunt. She took up the remote from the end table and clicked on the TV.

"With macaroni salad?" Aunt Lovey asked. She smiled.

Mary shrugged. "I haven't seen you in a while. I thought I'd swing by on my way to work."

The Weather Channel was airing a show on twisters, like the ones Mary now felt in her stomach and brain. F5s.

"Can I fix you a nice egg?" Aunt Lovely asked. As long as Mary could remember, eggs had been nice.

"No thanks. I ate," Mary lied. She pretended to be watching the TV. This was what the two of them did sometimes, rather than talk. Lovey had become less and less talkative in recent months, less interested in the daily goings-on at the restaurant or in Mary's life. Today, that was fine with Mary. It was enough for her to just be near the one person left in the world who loved her unconditionally. Maybe it was this morning's news, but Mary was now thinking of her mother, and how Mary and her father weren't the only ones devastated when she died.

Lovey had once told Mary how she regretted the times she'd complimented her niece, stroking her arms and saying, "How bronze. You look like a movie star," which was what she knew Claire had wanted to hear. Lovey said she felt in some ways responsible for Claire's death. Cancer had run in the family. She should have known better. She should have warned Claire. Lovey's sister had died of a brain tumor. Mary's grandfather lost his battle with stomach cancer when Mary was a child. If there was one thing Mary knew and accepted, it was that cancer would probably get her and Lovey in the end too. For years, she had secretly dreaded the day Lovey would be stricken with the disease. The old woman had already had one brush with a tumor.

Her aunt coughed. Mary could hear the dryness in it.

"You should have that checked out," Mary said. She looked at Lovey, who seemed to have aged some in the two weeks since

Mary's last visit. It was as if her hair had thinned and her jowls had grown more slack, though her cheeks were still pink and full at their apples. "I should get you a humidifier."

"What month is it again?" her aunt asked.

"June."

"That's what I thought. People don't run humidifiers in June."

"Well, then, let's open a window," Mary said. She walked over to the dining area and lifted the sash. "It's so dry in here. It's not good for your throat." When Lovey was in her fifties, she'd had a benign tumor that snaked around her carotid artery. She liked to tell the story of how, during the surgery to remove it, the doctor accidentally nicked the artery and her blood spurted up onto the ceiling. "And these weren't the ceilings they have in hospitals nowadays. These were the old ceilings that had to be fifteen or twenty feet high," she would say. In the end, they'd gotten the tumor, and the only real physical trade-off was that she'd lost her singing voice (though she still crooned along in a croaky voice when the spirit moved her) and occasionally her throat got scratchy.

The monetary fallout was different story. Lovey had always planned to retire in the country, perhaps in the Catskills, where her family had vacationed. She had never married, but a lifetime of working as a secretary in the accounting department of a big firm in Manhattan had left her with a sizable pension, which she'd had the option to either take in a lump sum when she turned fifty-five or continue to draw from each month as long as she lived. Learning of the tumor at the age of fifty-four affected her decision. Her doctors didn't know if they could operate. Even though the tumor was benign, it was aggressive. The prognosis wasn't good. Lovey decided she might as well take the money and enjoy it while she could. That turned out to be a mistake. A year later, the tumor had been successfully removed and Lovey was as healthy as could be. But now the money would probably run out before she did. After Claire had met and fallen in love with Thomas Hopkins one summer on a road trip with girlfriends, she'd thought it best for Lovey to follow her from

New York to the Cape. Lovey, who would agree only if she could maintain her independence, had the good fortune to secure a unit in this complex where rent was paid on a sliding scale based on income. So even with just her Social Security checks, Lovey would always have a roof over her head.

Years later, when Mary was in a position to help her financially, Lovey flatly refused. When Mary offered to set her up somewhere else, her own cottage, or at least a larger apartment with a better view and new appliances, Lovey would have none of it. "I'm perfectly happy here," she said, which Mary could understand, seeing as the woman had lived most of her days in a cramped tenement in the Bronx with her mother, sister, brother-in-law, and niece. To finally have a place to herself, however small, must have been heaven. And the unit still looked as brand-new as the day Lovey moved in, testament to her housekeeping.

Lovey had prided herself on being self-sufficient her entire life, and that she had to end up on the receiving end of government assistance was enough. She wasn't about to accept money from Mary. "Besides," she said, "they have all my bank records. Anything you give me I'll have to report, and then my rent will go up." Mary wondered how true that was, and suspected her aunt was just being stubborn.

Aunt Lovey's arms dripped over the wooden rests. Mary noticed how the old woman's skin had grown translucent, like a paper towel that has fallen into the sink. Her forearms were dappled with age spots, with fresh bruises near the bracelet the doctors made her wear all the time, with its chunky, tarnished chain and silver oval stamped with the word "pacemaker" in block letters, everything about it so vulgar and clumsy, a label forced on the woman as though she were a can of wax beans. It made Mary angry, the way old people were treated sometimes.

Mary reached over and touched her aunt's arm near the bruises. "Do they hurt?" she asked.

"Not at all," Aunt Lovey said. "Happens when I sleep."

Mary gave her aunt's arm a gentle squeeze. They stayed like that, watching the television for another ten minutes or so, long enough to see one barn and two trailer homes—awnings, curtains, and all—shredded by 210-miles-per-hour winds and sucked up toward the heavens. Mary grew restless. She knew she couldn't hide there forever.

"I suppose I should get to the restaurant," Mary said. "Besides, it looks like I caught you in the middle of cleaning."

"What was that, dear?"

"In the kitchen. All the pots and pans are out," Mary said.

Lovey's expression changed. The corners of her mouth turned downward and deep creases appeared on her forehead.

"What is it, Auntie?" Mary asked.

"I suppose it's time you knew. Someone's been breaking in here. They've been using my things. I didn't want to alarm you at first, but—"

"What?" Mary jumped up off the sofa and went to the kitchen.

By the time Lovey caught up with her, Mary had her glasses out of her purse and was examining a fry pan. It was a little scratched up, but then again, it was probably at least a decade old. "What makes you think someone's been here?" Mary asked.

Lovey took up a saucepan and chipped a bit of dried egg off the handle with her fingernail. Her face grew red. "Look at this filth. Is this the way I live?" Mary probably had worse-looking pans in her own cupboards, but her aunt had always been fastidious.

"When do you think someone could come in here? You never go out anymore, right?"

"Middle of the night. Or when I'm in the bathroom." Lovey shrugged and went back out to the living room and settled into her chair.

"Wouldn't you hear them?" Mary asked. "I mean, you'd hear someone banging pots around in your kitchen at night, wouldn't you?" Mary looked at her aunt and saw a mix of impatience and fury in her eyes.

"Who can hear a thing when that bathroom fan is going?" Lovey said.

"Auntie, why would someone want to use your kitchen? I mean, who would do that? All the people here have kitchens of their own."

"Are you saying you don't believe me?"

There had to be something going on. It wasn't like Lovey to make things up. "No, I— Of course not. I'll makes some calls and see what I can find out."

"Call that *Darlene*," Lovey said. She pointed a crooked finger toward the emergency office number taped to the fridge. "Maybe she'll listen to *you*." Almost immediately, she calmed down. The tension drained from her face.

Mary gathered her things. The old woman was now fixed on a new funnel cloud tearing through a church on the television screen. As Mary leaned in and kissed Lovey good-bye, she noticed the skin on her aunt's face was so thin that Mary drew up a little of the flesh from Lovey's cheek between her lips.

Four

A t 11 a.m., when Mary finally arrived at the Clambake, seven or eight of her crew were standing around outside. Some were dressed for work, others in regular clothes. They looked surprised to see her when she pulled into her space at the front of the restaurant. She got out of the car and felt their stares. They didn't say anything. They just parted like reeds in the wind to let her by.

Wayne was sitting out on the low stone wall in front of the take-out window. He was by himself, smoking. "Hey," he said. He shook his head. "Tough news."

"Yeah," she said. He must have been feeling some guilt over what had happened too.

On the door was a sign. She recognized Nate's handwriting: *Restaurant closed today due to the sudden passing of a coworker. Will reopen tomorrow.* He'd posted a Closed sign at the front of the driveway as well. It was a good decision.

She pushed through the screen door. The kitchen was empty. Nate was sitting on Mary's stool by the window, talking on her phone. His voice was filled with concern.

"I'll try to come by later. *No one* knew she had a kid. . . . Eighteen months . . . With the grandmother . . . I guess they're trying to figure out how much family she had and who's going to—" Nate looked up and saw Mary standing there. "Hey, listen, I gotta go." He hung up.

"Who was that?" Mary asked. She dropped her handbag down on the steel counter. The sound of it made her think of metal wrapping around a tree.

"Nelson," he said. Nelson was one of the line cooks. Nate got up from the stool. He took a step toward her and held out his arms. "Are you okay? I didn't think you were coming in."

She relaxed into his embrace and buried her head in his neck. She started to cry. When was the last time she'd cried?

"Hey, it's okay," Nate said. He rubbed her back.

She was mad at herself for falling apart. She drew away and took a deep breath. "I didn't know she had a kid," Mary said.

"None of us did."

"I heard you say eighteen months. Boy or girl?"

"Girl."

"Jesus." Somehow a girl made it worse. Mary wiped her face with the back of her hand. She looked out the window and saw the kids outside looking in. "They should go home," she said.

"I told them it was okay to congregate as long as they stayed outside. They're upset. They need each other," Nate said. He looked out the window. "Some didn't even know until they got here. They just showed up for work."

"Let them do it somewhere else. I don't need them judging me," Mary said. She rummaged through her purse for a tissue.

"*Judging* you?" Nate looked confused. He ran his hand through his hair.

It was too much for her to try to explain. Mary blew her nose. She crumpled the tissue and put it in her pocket. Her hands felt shaky. "Get rid of them, Nate," she said. "Please."

Nate didn't ask questions. He just went outside. Mary walked to the back of the kitchen so she wouldn't have to watch. Five minutes later he came back in. She heard cars starting up, then heard them pulling out into the street. She took a long, deep breath.

"The cop was on his way to your house. I guess he'll come back when he sees you're not there," Nate said. He pulled the waitress schedule in its plastic sleeve off the bulletin board near the time clock and handed it to her. "Better fix this before tomorrow," he said. "I'll make some calls if you want me to."

Mary took the schedule. She examined the column with that day's date. It would have been Anicca's day off. She'd probably planned to spend it with her daughter. Then she was back on the rest of the week. Mary leaned against the dishwasher. She felt some wet from the machine bleed through her shirt. "Was she married?" she asked. Mary would have noticed a ring.

"Don't think so. They're not pressing the grandmother for too many answers right now." Nate shook his head. "It's not supposed to happen."

"What?"

"Grandmothers outliving grandkids," he said.

Mary looked down. Her hands were clenched. "Where had she been drinking? She didn't get it here, did she?"

"They say she was at the Gunwale," Nate said. The Gunwale was in Chatham, which would explain the direction Anicca had been heading.

"Why did they keep serving her? Why didn't someone take her keys? Who was she with?"

"I guess it was packed last night. You know how it gets in the summer. She was with some people she knew from the convenience store she worked at last summer after the baby was born. I was talking to the kids outside this morning and they said she hadn't really gotten to know anyone here yet. She kept to herself."

He was talking about the kids outside. He was one of those kids. And yet he was handling this with more maturity than the owner, who was twice his age.

"Where was she from?"

"Somewhere outside Boston. Waltham, I think. But she'd been living down here with her grandmother since the baby was born," he said.

"Where does the grandmother live?" Mary asked.

"On Bridge Street." That was a cut-through street in the middle of town, zoned mainly for business but there were a few modest residences, small Capes mostly. Not one of the trophy neighborhoods, that was for sure.

"Who is she?" Mary asked.

"Meg Ryder. Don't know her. My folks might."

"The name sounds familiar."

They heard another vehicle pulling into the parking lot. A customer?

"Make whoever it is go away, Nate," Mary said.

He let go of her hand and went to the door.

"It's the police officer. Same one who was here earlier," Nate said. "Boyd." Nate wasn't one of the rich summer kids. He'd grown up here. He knew people.

Mary walked over to the window. She saw the cop get out of the cruiser and look at Wayne, who hadn't left with the others. Wayne nodded and lit another cigarette. She recognized the officer as the same one who'd directed traffic along the street leading to her house during the week it took town workers to trim the trees growing near the power lines. She'd seen him around other places too. It was a small town, smaller in the winter.

As the cop headed toward the door, Mary started to feel a squeeze in her gut. Had she done something wrong? Could they shut her down?

Nate went to greet the cop. "She's here," Nate said. "Didn't think she was coming in. Sorry for the runaround." He stepped back to make room for the officer, who stepped past the threshold, having to duck so his head wouldn't brush the top of the door frame. He was taller in person than on the street with the tree cutters, Mary thought.

"No problem," he said. Whiskers salted his face. He obviously hadn't had the time for his morning shave. He had on a short-sleeve button-down uniform shirt with a silver badge just above the pocket. Clipped to his belt were a handcuff pouch, a radio, and a pistol in a black holster. Mary could count on one hand the times that she'd ever been that close to a firearm.

"Mary, this is Officer Boyd."

"Ms. Hopkins?" He was sucking on something, a cough drop or a sour ball.

She nodded.

"You own this place?" he said. The candy lump came to rest between his cheek and gums.

"Seventeen years."

"And Anicca Sutherland worked for you as a server?"

"Just a couple of weeks, yes."

"Want me to pull some chairs from the dining room?" Nate asked.

"I'll stand. But feel free to have a seat if you wish," he said to Mary. "Can you give us a minute?" he said to Nate.

Nate nodded. He went outside and joined Wayne on the rock wall. Mary saw him bum a cigarette. She didn't even know he smoked. She slid onto her stool, trying to avoid looking at the cop's weapon while being unable to focus on anything else. This was how men must feel when confronted with cleavage.

"I'm sure by now you've heard the news," he said.

"It's horrible. We're all very upset," Mary said. "Anicca was a wonderful—" *Don't lay it on too thick,* she thought. "She seemed like a good kid."

"How well did you know her?" Boyd asked.

"Not very. I didn't even know she had a baby."

"How does something like that get past an employer?"

Mary lowered her head. "I guess I was a little out of touch."

"One of your workers was telling me that Ms. Sutherland had kind of a rough night here last night? And that there'd been some kind of conflict in the kitchen? Did you happen to catch any of that?"

"Did you talk to Wayne?" Mary said. "He was the kid on the wall outside when you came in."

"I got his version of things," Boyd said. "But the more people I talk to, the easier it is to piece things together."

She wondered what Wayne had said. "It wasn't really a conflict," she said. "More of a misunderstanding, really." She tried to nonchalantly wave her hand and wondered if he saw it was shaking.

"Why don't you tell me what happened," he said. "Assuming you were there."

Mary nodded and took a deep breath. "Anicca came into the kitchen with a request for a lobster to be taken out of its shell."

"That's not that uncommon, is it?"

"No, not at all," Mary said. "It's just that the kitchen was swamped and Wayne—" She looked to the window. "He's the head cook. I guess he gave her a little grief about it."

"He said as much."

Mary nodded. "Wayne's a good kid. But he's also a bit of a hot-head. He yells at everyone. Some kids take it better than others." Mary thought of the other waitress who'd wanted the fried little-necks, and how she'd given it right back to him.

"So he told her he didn't have time, in so many words?"

"Basically."

"And then what happened?"

"She looked at me," Mary said. The girl's face flashed before Mary's eyes. She'd stood almost in the exact spot where the cop was standing now, just a few hours ago. How could she be dead? It didn't seem possible. "See, in training I'd said it was okay to bring those requests into the kitchen and . . ." Mary's voice trailed off.

"And?"

"And when she looked at me to back her up, I didn't say anything. I should have. I just told one of the order line girls to do it. But right away I felt bad, like I'd betrayed her a little." Mary stared at a chip in the floor tile, afraid to look up. The cop was writing something down. Mary heard the pen scratching against the paper, until the refrigerator motor kicked on. Mary jumped.

"That's it?" he finally said. Wasn't *that* enough?

"And then later she dropped a tray," Mary said.

"Did she get reprimanded?"

She looked up. "Of course not. This is a busy restaurant. Stuff like that happens all the time."

Officer Boyd nodded. He riffled through his note pad and asked the next question without looking at her. "Did she seem to you like she might be incapacitated?"

"What?"

His eyes met hers. "Drunk or high? Do you think she was on something?"

"No, I don't think so," Mary said. He wrote something down. "I just think she wasn't cut out for waitressing. Some kids have it and some don't. By the end of last night's shift, I'd pretty much written her off."

Boyd raised one of his thick eyebrows that disintegrated past the arch like wisps of smoke. "I beg your pardon?"

"I didn't mean . . . I wasn't going to fire her or anything." Not that week, anyway. "I just could tell she wouldn't be here long."

"You got that right," he said. Mary knew he wasn't talking about the restaurant. She noticed the pouches under his eyes.

Mary shifted on her stool. "The baby. Will she go with Anicca's parents?"

"We're looking into all that." Boyd folded his pad shut and tucked it in his breast pocket. Mary noticed he had on a heavy gold ring commemorating New York City cops lost on 9/11. "One last thing. Did she seem upset when she left?" he asked.

"I was upstairs in my office when she left. I didn't see. She went out the back door. And she forgot to punch out."

"And then she got in her car and left?"

"I'm guessing."

"Thanks, Ms. Hopkins," Boyd said. "I'll let you know if we have any more questions." He started for the door.

Mary stood. "Where's the baby now?" she asked.

"With the grandmother."

Imagine what that woman is going through, Mary thought.

"If anything comes up, I'll be in touch," he said.

As Officer Boyd left the kitchen, Nate jumped off the low rock wall and crushed the cigarette under his foot, as if he'd been caught doing something illegal. "So long," Nate said. He, Mary, and Wayne all watched as the cop got into his cruiser and pulled out of the parking lot.

. . .

That afternoon, it was just she and Nate. He made calls and let people know about schedule changes. Mary started on some of the prep work for the next day. Some of the food they'd prepared for the day's lunch and dinner had to be thrown out.

As they worked side by side in the kitchen, they barely spoke. Mary waited for Nate to bring up the fact that what had happened to Anicca could just as easily have happened to him the night before. Sometimes one mistake was all it took. Other times, she knew firsthand, it took more.

As the sun hit the bark of the oaks lining the street, turning them gold, Nate said good night, got into his Jeep, and left.

The next morning, Mary waited in the kitchen while Nate assembled the staff out in the dining room. A mandatory meeting had been called for Sunday, and it was clear by the looks on some of their faces, Wayne's in particular, that 8 a.m. was a lot to ask, even given the circumstances. Mary sat on her stool and went over the notes she'd made. The meeting had been Nate's idea, something he'd come up with the previous afternoon. He thought it would be good to give everyone the chance to ask questions and share their grief. And a good way for Mary to make up for the insensitive way she'd kicked them all off the premises the day before.

Now she was scared to death. One-on-one she was fine, but speaking in front of large groups in a formal way sent swarms of bees up her spine.

Nate pressed his face to the screen, trying to make her laugh. "Think they're all here," he said.

Mary had never been much of a day drinker, but now she wished she'd taken a hit off that dusty tequila bottle on the bar in her living room before she'd left the house. She pressed her hands down along the sides of her linen blazer to flatten out the wrinkles, then slid off her stool.

"I'm coming," she said. "I'll just be a minute." She stuffed her notes into her jacket pocket.

"Come on, Mary. Half of them rolled out of bed on their day off to get here. Don't keep them waiting," he said.

"I forgot something," she lied. She ran up the stairs to her office, to the left-hand side desk drawer, and pulled it open. In it were a few promotional nips of sweet, nasty mixed drinks the liquor distributor had tried to talk her into selling—some kind of mudslide that looked the color of the sandy puddles out in the parking lot, and another concoction, cough syrup pink. She unscrewed the mini cap and downed the mini mudslide, then chased it with the reddish stuff that tasted like bubble gum. The combination made her gag. But then she felt the warm scratch of booze down her throat to her belly and right away she felt better. She licked the sweet stuff off her lips, smoothed her hair, and started downstairs.

By the time she entered the dining room, the buzz from her candy booze was already gone.

"Hi, everyone," she said. Her voice didn't sound like hers in her ears. "Thanks for coming in so early."

Some groaned. Others just offered up blank stares. It was strange to see them all sitting at the tables in the dining room. It felt like some kind of dream where suddenly she was expected to wait on them. Over the course of seventeen years, Mary had had her share of those dreams.

The room was divided by the center aisle, kitchen crew on the left, waitstaff and bartenders on the right, not by her design but by theirs. Those on the left sprawled out with their feet over the chairs, Wayne being the worst offender, taking up an extra chair for each foot. They looked slovenly, even in the way that their clothes were baggy and mismatched. The kids on the right sat more upright, as if the work had given them some kind of reverence for the dining room. The girl who'd given Wayne a hard time the other day was using her thumbnail to chip wax off the table. Her eyes were red. In fact, Mary could see the waitstaff looked more despondent, whereas the kitchen crew seemed their usual cynical selves, taking on postures that silently challenged Mary.

Mary took in a breath. "Of course, we're all here because we cared about Anicca, a young girl who died way before her time in an accident made even more horrible by the fact that she had a baby girl that none of us knew about." She sounded like a preacher. Mary looked up. She locked eyes with one of the Jennifers, the nicer one. The girl was wearing a Boston College sweatshirt. Her hair was pulled back in a loose ponytail, and her face looked scrubbed and sun-kissed. *Ah, youth,* Mary thought. Out of habit, she searched for Nate, and found him in the front with Maureen and the kitchen guys. She lost her train of thought and had to pull the notes out of her pocket. She heard people moving around in their seats. "Sorry, this has been hard for all of us," she said. "I'm really sorry for what happened to Anicca. As I'm sure all of you know, she had a rough time at work the night she died." Mary looked up at Wayne, whose head was down, face frozen. She continued, "Whether or not this is why she went to the Gunwale and proceeded to drink, then get behind the wheel, I'll never know. All I can do is tell you how sorry I am. And I want to do something to help Anicca's family, her kid especially. So we're starting up a college fund."

Mary was expecting maybe some of them would clap or say something positive, but no one did. "This summer, a portion of the proceeds from every meal we sell will go into a trust we're setting up. The newspapers will let everyone know about it, and patrons and locals will have the opportunity to donate as well. And maybe later in the summer, we can have some kind of benefit." Mary looked up. Their faces were unchanged. Her voice shook. "Another thing I plan to do is take the time to get to know all of you. I didn't do that with Anicca and I'll always live with my regret. I want to know who you are, what you care about, *everything.*"

Mary looked up, hopeful. Their tear-streaked faces now bore puzzled expressions. Some even looked slightly terrified.

"Okay," Nate said. He got up on his feet. He pointed to a stack of blue papers on a table. "So take one of these flyers with the details on the fund-raising plan on your way out so you can explain it all to customers if they ask. And check out the new waitress schedule in the kitchen. Some of you may have picked up a shift."

"Who died and made you boss?" Wayne, arms folded on his chest, said to Nate. As soon as he realized his gaffe, he kicked one of the chairs in front of him. It screeched across the floor. Wayne hung his head. Nate sat back down. No one else moved. They all pitied Wayne at that moment. Mary could feel it.

"I don't think you should blame yourselves," someone said, a small voice in the back. Mary looked up. The other Jennifer in the Smith College sweatshirt was standing. She took a step forward. "I heard from a friend of Anicca's from the convenience store that Anicca's boyfriend had told her he was going away that morning."

"The father of the kid?" Nate asked.

The girl ran her hand through her short blond hair. "I think she was hoping he'd marry her."

Courtney, one of the kitchen girls, started to cry.

"That sucks," Todd the bartender said.

Wayne let out a long breath. He took his other foot off the chair. Mary suspected he felt better knowing his words with Anicca that night probably had no bearing on her death.

Mary felt her neck grow hot. It hadn't been her fault either. At least this time, it hadn't. She coughed to clear her throat. "Okay, take a few minutes. Then those of you who aren't working the noon shift go on home. The rest of you, let's get going."

Moments later, back in the kitchen, Mary felt her anger folding on itself like laundry being stacked in a basket, piling up thicker and becoming more organized. She took comfort in her fury, as if it were a favorite towel, soft and worn, especially now that the anger could be directed at someone besides herself.

"How could the father of the kid just take off?" Mary said. She stood in front of the cash register, removing ones, fives, tens, and twenties from the blue vinyl pouch, tearing the brown bands and slipping the bills into their slots. She opened the drawer beneath the register to tuck away the empty pouch and found an unopened pack of cigarettes. It had to have been left behind by a customer. Aside from Wayne, hardly any of the kids smoked anymore. Mary could remember the early days when they all had cigarettes going right there in the kitchen. She tapped the box against her thigh. It left the imprint of a rectangle in her jeans.

"He was just a kid himself," Nate said.

Mary looked up at him. "Don't tell me you'd ever—"

"Mary"—Hope came into the kitchen—"there's a guy who wants to talk to you—"

"We're not open yet," Mary said.

"He said he just wants to say hi."

Mary scowled at the hostess. "And you told him I was taking my dog to the vet." A dog she didn't own. "Or that I was out hauling up lobster traps. *Something*, right?" These kids knew the drill. Mary didn't talk to customers unless it was absolutely necessary.

"He said he saw you in the kitchen," Hope whispered. She had lips like a Kewpie doll. And dimples.

Mary stepped back from the window. Most restaurant owners loved to schmooze with customers. Mary saw patrons who wanted to chitchat as vying for special treatment. She made the food, the customers paid for it. They were even. She didn't owe them anything further. In truth, it probably had as much to do with her being introverted and out of practice.

"Tell him I had to take an important phone call," Mary said. "Tell him when he comes back for dinner I'll be sure to come out and say hello." *Tell him not to hold his breath.* Nate looked at her with disapproval.

Mary tugged at the little string on the pack of cigarettes and peeled away the cellophane. She tried to drop the wrapper onto the counter but it stuck to her hand.

"Don't even think about saying anything," Mary said. She meant both about the man outside *and* the cigarettes.

"I didn't *say* anything," Nate said. "I would just think you'd be feeling better after what we learned out there," he said. "Now we know Anicca's drinking was probably over what had happened that morning with the father of her kid, not what happened here."

It was true. She should have felt better. But a girl was still dead. And then there was how it happened and all that had been churned up as a result.

Wayne came in and fired up the grill. Maureen and another order line girl pulled the morning checklist from its slot beside the cash register and began their chores, one wiping down the trays so they wouldn't slip out of the waitresses' hands, the other pulling the condiment bins from the fridge.

"Okay, I'll see you later," Nate said.

"Where are you going?" Mary asked.

"I don't come on till four," he said.

"Oh, right," Mary said. She was a little crestfallen. She didn't want Nate to go.

As he was leaving, Hope stuck her head in through the "out" door.

"Watch it," he said to her. "Wrong door."

The hostess backed away and let him out. Then she walked around to the "in" door. "You can come out. He's gone," Hope said to Mary. "He was nice. He said he knew you."

"Who?"

"The guy outside. He said he knew you from a long time ago," Hope said. Mary looked out the window. There was no one there.

The waitress named Vanessa rushed in the door. She lit the burner under the soup warmer. "Did you get a load of that guy? He looked like a pirate."

"What guy?" Mary set the cigarettes down and craned her neck to see, but whoever it was had apparently gone.

"The guy who came to see you," the hostess said. "Don't worry, I got rid of him. Come to think of it, he did look a little like a pirate, not like Johnny Depp or anything. He was a ton older. More like a cross between a pirate and one of those guys on the fish sticks box."

"He was wearing yellow pants," Vanessa said. She opened a carton of chowder-cracker packets and poured them into a basket. "I think they were made of rubber."

"Must be disco night at the Beachcomber," Wayne said.

"And he had an earring," Hope said.

"Lots of guys have earrings," Maureen said. She was slicing lemons. "Get a life."

Mary felt a prickling sensation spread down the back of her neck. It spread to her arms and out to her wrists. "Did he tell you his name? Did he say what he wanted?"

"His name, right. *Dan* something."

Mary felt her face flush.

"He said he was sorry about Anicca, only he didn't know her name. He just called her 'the girl.'" The hostess dug into the pocket of her skirt. "And he gave me this." Hope held out a hundred-dollar bill. "He said it was for the family."

"For God's sake, why didn't you get me?" Mary snatched up the bill.

There was some writing on it. Mary pulled the reading glasses out of her purse and slid them on. There was the letter *M* and a stick drawing of a sunshine on Franklin's forehead. *Mary Sunshine.* And there was a phone number beginning with the local area code in the space to the right.

"I'll be damned," Mary said. She clenched the bill in her fist and looked out the window. Then she folded it and slipped it into her pocket.

"Those are waders, by the way," Maureen said. "Not disco pants, you freaking wash-ashores."

"Can I go now?" the hostess asked.

Mary grabbed her shoulder. "If he comes back, get me. You understand?"

The girl cocked her head, then froze. "But I thought you said—"

"Who is he?" Wayne asked.

"Just a friend," Mary said. Mary saw Hope wink at Maureen as if to say, *Must've been* some *friend.* Mary took a deep breath and looked out the window at the kids setting up the dining room, folding plastic lobster bibs, replacing candles, and wiping bar trays. She thought of Anicca. She slid one of the smooth white cigarettes out of the pack and ran it along the soft flesh between her fingers. She put it to her lips. The idea of slowly killing herself seemed more appealing than any kind of sudden death.

Mary woke at her desk with a crick in her neck and the mud taste of tobacco in her mouth. How many had she smoked? The room was dark. Her throat was raw. There were still sounds coming from downstairs, kitchen sounds that comforted her, reminding her of her own kitchen when she was growing up, and of her mother and her grandmother, Lovey's sister, working side by side preparing the family meals. Fleeting visions of her youth were quickly replaced with the harsh reality that there was one little girl in this town who would never have memories like that. *Her* mother was dead. And then Mary remembered the visitor. She felt for the hundred-dollar bill in her pocket, just to see whether she'd dreamed the whole thing. She reached in and pulled it out. Had Dan Bassett really come by the restaurant? She flattened the bill with her palm. What else could the *M* and the sunshine drawing mean? And there was the phone number. What if she called right now? But she couldn't call now. It was the middle of the night. And even if it weren't so late, why would she want to bother with him now, after all these years? As far as she was concerned, he was as dead to her as Robbie.

The noises downstairs subsided. Mary lifted her head. From the window she saw the gravel by the take-out window fall into darkness. Someone had switched off the light. She heard footsteps outside.

Sometime before Nate came on, she'd told Wayne she was going upstairs. Now on her desk was the nearly empty pack of cigarettes, along with a candy tin that had served as a makeshift ashtray. It was brimming with butts. It was a miracle she hadn't burned the place down during her nicotine bender. There on the legal pad by the ashtray were the shapes she'd rendered in an attempt to capture the birthmark on Anicca's neck. Had it been a humpback whale, with long fins, or more of a sperm whale? She recalled it had a distinct tail. And a darkening at what would have been the blowhole. Such an unusual thing to have on one's neck. Not that it mattered anymore. She wondered if the baby had a similar mark. Lovey used to call birthmarks on babies "angel kisses."

Mary pushed back from the desk and rose to her feet. Maybe there was a little coffee left in the pot downstairs that she could re-heat. She moved slowly, mindful of the fragile state of her head, on the brink of aching, mindful of the crickets outside and the scent of pine floor cleaner, and the silence. She opened the door at the foot of the stairs. The cooler kitchen air washed over her face. Every-thing here was so peaceful and calm. A citronella candle still burned on the counter, its light dancing along the scratches in the freshly polished stainless steel.

Talk about burning the place down, she thought. Wayne would catch hell for this one. Final check was his responsibility, and here a candle had been left burning. That's when she saw the basement door had been left open. Strike two. It was supposed to be bolted closed from the kitchen.

Mary moved toward the doorway. One of the lights was on down there as well. Then she heard something, the sound of shoes scuffing along the floor. Did Ernie the fish guy make deliveries in the middle of the night these days? She was rarely here this late.

Then she heard a little moan. A vibration at the back of the throat. Had it escaped her? Mary moved closer to the top of the stairs. She listened.

"For the hundredth time, *nothing* happened." It was Nate.

"Whatever," a girl's voice said. Mary knew the voice.

"I know you believe me. You're just busting my balls," Nate said. "Come here." There was a long silence. "I missed you."

Mary heard the screech of something heavy on the floor, a chair maybe. "If you slept with her, I'll never speak to you again," the girl said. Not a waitress. "Besides, do you realize how *old* she is?"

"I didn't sleep with her. I was just trying to make you jealous," Nate said. Another interval of silence. "Hey, come back."

"I'm not a moron, Nate," she said.

"I'm sorry," he said. "I was just too drunk to drive home, okay?"

"Okay." Another pause.

"I wouldn't have blamed her if she fired me. I'm not sure why she didn't. Then I'd have been screwed. My parents don't live in the Heights like most of these assholes. I need this job."

"Stop talking," the girl said.

Mary strained to pick up everything she could, the clicks and sucking of two mouths joined. She imagined the loosening clothes. Her senses were heightened, her hearing was on high alert. A shiver ran through her. One step lower and she might have even been able to see. But she didn't have the courage. She didn't want to know any more about the kind of love that had passed her by.

"Mmmm," Nate said. Then, after a moment, "I love your throat."

The girl laughed. "Is that all?"

"I'm not kidding," he said. He moaned. Mary could almost feel the warm touch of his lips on her own neck. *Do you realize how old she is?* She remembered what it had been like to kiss her Aunt Lovey's cheek, the milky looseness of her flesh.

Mary finally realized who the girl was, and figured out that the person Nate had been talking to on the phone when she arrived at the restaurant the morning after the accident hadn't been Nelson.

Five

The mist had settled in. As she walked to her car, Mary felt the warm droplets on her face. She started the engine. If they heard the car pull out of the drive, they'd know they'd been caught. Did it matter?

Mary drove home slowly, focusing on the road just ahead and the water collecting on the windshield—how the wipers pushed and pooled it into a stream that trickled down the sides of the glass. Once she made it home to her own driveway, she was in no hurry to go inside. Her new knowledge would have a way of coloring things, changing their texture. She wasn't ready to see how Nate's sweatshirt still on the kitchen island would now appear in the shadows like an abandoned pet, something lumpy and sad, or how, thanks to Dan's return, her bed might now pick up more grays and blues in the light cast off from the bay, turning hard and cold.

In the beam from the spotlight on the side of the house, tiny beads of water darted off in unison with the sudden bursts of wind like schools of fish scattering and regrouping, as if pursued by something ominous. When Mary was a kid, she used to think she could see people's spirits swirling in the mist, pirates like Sam Bellamy, whose ship, the *Whydah,* ran aground in the shoals off Wellfleet in 1717. When she was around thirteen, she'd pulled a book called *The Narrow Land* off her mother's shelf and learned that Bellamy had had a lover on the Cape, a farm girl from Eastham whose name was Maria "Goody" Hallet. The story went that Bellamy got Goody pregnant, then left for the Caribbean. Mary thought of Anicca.

Goody gave birth to the child, only to have it die that same night. After that, they say, something in her snapped. For the rest of her life, she could be seen walking the dunes in the middle of the night, in the rain or snow and always alone, waiting for Bellamy to return. Of course, he never did. After Mary read that, it was Goody Hallet that she saw in the mists and whose voice she heard from time to time, calling her own name in the long steady tones of the channel buoys out in the bay. For centuries the Cape had been a place for broken hearts and ill-fated romances. For Mary, there had been Robbie. Then Dan. The residue of love was something that hung in the air, heavy and sad.

With a sudden urge to be by the water's edge, she reached down to take off her sandals. She got out of the car and made her way down the narrow path that led from the house to the beach. When she got there, the horizon was defined by a deeper shade of black. Covered by a thin veil, the moon threw off enough light for Mary to see something blue near her foot, perhaps a dried jellyfish that had gotten tangled in a clump of eelgrass churned up in a recent storm. Somewhere out there, a baby winter flounder had lost its home. Mary bent down to examine the blue object, a shard of glass, Noxema blue, not officially sea glass yet, too clean and sharp at the edges. She picked it up and tossed it out into the water, where it, like everything else in time's cauldron, would be sufficiently pulverized.

The water had nearly reached high tide, and gentle waves lapped the shore. She stepped in to her ankles, not caring that the bottom of her pants got wet. The water was warm, as it always was when the tide came in over the sun-baked flats. She waded in further, to her knees. It felt clean and refreshing.

Mary thought about what it would be like to drown. It was the kind of death she'd never been able to fully comprehend. Others were so much easier. Heart attacks. Gunshot wounds. Car wrecks. Yet she'd grown up hearing about people, tourists mostly, who slipped beneath the waves or got caught up in a riptide, fighting the current rather than just letting it carry them further down the shore. *Why didn't they just float?* she would wonder. There was a fearlessness born out of familiarity that Mary drew from the water's edge. And a naïveté as well, as she realized when a schoolmate was lost in a storm with his father after their boat capsized. But as a young child, she imagined that she herself couldn't possibly drown, and even that she could breathe underwater. Relaxing her whole body, she could go what seemed like minutes without air. Rather than clench the breath in her lungs, she held it softly so that she could barely tell where the air stopped and the water began. Now she imagined what it might be like to just let the water in through her mouth and nose, how the salt water might fill every orifice, bloating her like a water balloon, smoothing out the wrinkles, plumping her flesh, and restoring her pale ivory skin for one last time. It might be a fitting end, surrendering herself to the sea to honor all the creatures that had died to make her a rich woman, all the unsuspecting fish, mollusks, and crustaceans that had been plucked from their homes, only to end up on a blue plate, in a basket, or on a bed of kale.

Mary waded in to her waist. She felt something brush her hand, looked down, and saw the faint form of a tiny silver fish. *How brave,* she thought. *Or stupid.* For all it knew, she might be a bigger fish or a six-year-old with a net. Or a seafood restaurant owner. She let the fish kiss her for a moment more, then turned and headed back toward the house, feeling the weight of the wet, sandy pants dragging at her heels.

There came a knock on the front door. Mary opened her eyes. Light poured through her window, bleaching her dream. She'd been on a bed in the sand, out on the beach, where a soft breeze created wavelike ripples that moved through the sheets. She was dressed from head to toe in white shells. On her fingers, tiny white limpets. Sea clams and cockles running down her hips, down the length of her legs. She still could almost feel them on her skin. But how did they get there? Who had taken the time and care to place each one? In the shadows, there'd been a figure. *Robbie?*

Mary heard another rap on the door. Before she was entirely awake, the door clicked open.

"Hey, it's me. Nate."

She focused her eyes on the alarm clock digits. It was seven thirty.

"What are you doing here?" she called.

"I just came to get my sweatshirt." Nate started up the stairs. "Did you know there are pants on the steps?" he said. She stretched her feet across the mattress and felt the grit of sand. She'd never bothered to wipe off her feet before climbing into bed.

"It's in the kitchen. You don't need to come up—"

Nate entered the room. He was wearing his uniform shirt and jeans. Mary wondered if he'd ever gone home. He seemed nervous. "How did you get your car home?" Nate asked. "I thought you took a cab yesterday."

"I drove it," she said.

He turned toward the window. "When?"

"A little after midnight."

His head dropped a little. "You were upstairs."

"And then I came down to the kitchen and saw the candle, and then heard you," she said. "And *Maureen*." Maureen Donovan. Mary's best order line girl, that gangly, almost homely girl with the sharp tongue and the mind to match, who worked harder than anyone.

He turned to face her, folded his arms, and then jerked them awkwardly to his sides. "I was afraid of that. Look, I'm really sorry. I didn't want to tell you about us."

Mary drew the covers to her chin. She looked at Nate. His cheeks were red and his young, doughy mouth gaped, making him look like a kid who'd lost his mother in the department store. Between his brows was the beginning of a crease that would probably develop into a deep furrow over the years as he experienced the stuff of life. Mary wanted to press her thumbs between his brows and smooth it away. This was kid stuff, she thought. This was nothing. Save the frowning for the real pain. *You'll have your share,* she imagined. "How long have you been seeing each other?" she asked him.

Nate's shoulders slumped. He sat on the edge of the bed, bracing himself. "On and off since third grade."

Mary had forgotten Maureen was a local too. "I see."

Mary felt an inexplicable calm, as if the deep sensations of relaxation and adoration from her dream had carried over into real life. "I wouldn't have thought she was your type."

He looked at her. "Maureen may not be as pretty as some girls, but we've been together so long I don't even see what's on the outside."

Mary was proud of him for defending his girlfriend. How many young, good-looking kids like Nate focused more on insides than outsides? "You love her, don't you?" she said.

He lowered his head. "Sorta."

Mary sat up in bed. "I'll tell you what. I think it's great."

"You do?"

"Absolutely." She feigned an enthusiastic smile. Though perhaps some part of it was real. "Now go. And take your sweatshirt. Like I said, it's on the island downstairs. I'll see you later." She pulled the covers over her head. She felt the weight of him lift from the bed.

"One other thing, Mary," he said. She could tell from his voice that he was already across the room.

"What?" she said from beneath the covers.

"I found out the funeral is this morning. Some of the kids are going. I shuffled the schedule around a little yesterday afternoon. Hope you don't mind. I just wanted you to know."

The baby would be there. Did she look like her mother?

"I'm not going," he continued. "It's private. The only ones invited were part of a group who visited the grandmother after our meeting yesterday."

Mary sunk back down into the covers. "Okay, then. I'll see you *later*," she said, this time with enough edge that he got the hint. She listened until the front door latched shut. She'd have to remember to change the hiding place for that spare key.

Mary thought it would be best if she paid a personal visit to the manager of the senior housing complex, even though the woman was one of the few people in the world who actually intimidated her. To get to Darlene's office, Mary had to pass through the common area where residents often congregated to play cards, watch TV, or swap books and videos from the large collection on the wall. The room had a dusty smell to it. On a tweed lounger near the window there was a man who'd dozed off, his head slumped at an angle that was sure to cause him stiffness when he woke. Drew Carey was on TV, challenging a young Mexican woman in pink stretch pants to guess the price of a tube of Denture Grip.

Mary almost hoped the manager wouldn't be in her office but as she approached, she heard Darlene on the phone. "That's right, Mr. Eldridge. . . ." Mary stood in the doorway but Darlene didn't look up; she was tapping her pen on the desk as she spoke. "It says in your lease, *no pets.* . . . Of course a snake is a pet. . . . *You* tell *me* how it got into Mrs. Carlson's toilet. . . . I don't have time for this now, Mr. Eldridge. I want that snake out of here by the end of the day. . . . I'm sorry, those are the rules." She looked up at Mary but didn't acknowledge her. "Five o'clock. I'll come by then. *Good-bye,* Mr. Eldridge."

Mary guessed she'd practically hung up on the man by the way the volume of her voice rose at the end. Darlene let the pen tumble out of her fingers onto the desk.

"Nearly killed the poor woman," she said to Mary.

"Who?"

"Mrs. Carson. You know old people can't get up off of toilets as fast as the rest of us. Let's just leave it at that," Darlene said. "Now, what can I do for you?" Mary had been in to see Darlene numerous times on her aunt's behalf in the thirty-some-odd years Lovey had lived there, for eighteen of which Darlene had been in charge. Yet the woman never seemed to recognize her.

"I'm Mary Hopkins, Lovey Rollwagon's niece."

"Oh, right." Darlene said. Her short, wiry hair had gone gray since those early days. Mary would guess she was now in her mid-fifties. One of her trademarks was that she always wore yoked sweaters. Today she had on a lightweight tan cotton pullover with a yellow pattern around the neck. It washed her out. "I've been meaning to call you."

"About the break-ins? She told me someone's been coming into her apartment. I was over there yesterday and she showed me the pots and pans—"

"May I ask you a question, Ms. Hopkins?" Darlene picked up her pen, stuck it behind her ear, and didn't wait for Mary's answer. "Have you ever heard of a *cooking* bandit?" She opened the top drawer of her desk and took out a box of mints.

"No."

"Have you ever heard of people breaking into other peoples' apartments in the middle of the night to use their pots and pans?" She held the box out to Mary.

Mary shook her head. "Well, no. But I thought you said—"

"Are you aware that your aunt had cataract surgery a few months ago, and that her eyesight now is probably better than it was—"

"Of course, I took her—"

"And that just maybe she's seeing things on her pots and pans that she hadn't noticed before?"

It was something Mary hadn't considered.

Darlene took two mints and popped them into her mouth, then chased them with water as if they were aspirin. "Are you also aware that one in five people over eighty experiences some form of dementia? It might not be something you've thought of, but, trust me, after nearly twenty years on this job I can vouch for those numbers."

Mary felt the heat in her face seep down her neck. "My aunt doesn't have *dementia*," she said.

Darlene tossed the mints in the drawer and slammed it shut. "I suggest maybe you let a medical professional be the one to decide. And soon. In the meantime, I'd appreciate it if you could try to persuade her to stop calling me three times a day to tell me about the scratches on her skillets. As you can see, I've got a few things on my own plate." She pointed like Carol Merrill to the piles of paperwork on her desk. Mary heard the theme song of *The Price Is Right* playing on the TV in the other room.

"I'll talk to her," Mary said. Her chin dropped to her chest. Could things possibly get any worse?

"And if it turns out she does have dementia, you'll have to find her someplace else to live. It's all in the lease." Darlene shuffled some papers on her desk and didn't look at Mary. "It's to protect the other tenants. People with Alzheimer's can't live by themselves."

"Alzheimer's! Who said anything about—?" Mary stopped when she saw Darlene reach for the phone.

"Just take her to the doctor," Darlene said.

It was a simmering-hot day, the kind where molecules grow wavy above the asphalt. Mary was so upset over what Darlene had said about her aunt that she almost drove right past the funeral home. She'd expected the parking lot to be packed with cars. Instead, there were none. The mourners had likely already moved on to the cemetery, a place she knew well from visiting her parents' grave, at least in the days when she still used to make the effort.

Before Mary had set off to visit Darlene, she'd penned a sympathy note to Anicca's grandmother, Meg Ryder. It had been so humid the edges of the card curled as she wrote. When Mary licked the flap on the envelope and tasted the sweet glue, it hadn't seemed right somehow, as if envelope glue for sympathy cards should come in a different flavor, something gritty and sour, or, at the very least, flavorless. Before she sealed the envelope, she'd stuffed Dan's hundred-dollar bill inside the card and then, at the last moment, lost the courage to sign her own name and instead used the first one that popped into her head: Lavinia Rollwagon. That was her aunt's real name, though, with the exception of Darlene, no one Mary knew had ever called her anything but Lovey. Mary suspected the money might be better received if Meg Ryder thought she was some well-heeled local who'd heard the story and wanted to help out. Besides, Mary had no idea what Anicca might have said to her grandmother about the woman who ran the restaurant where she worked. Mary had a reputation for being a tough boss. Why dredge any of that up for the poor woman? As for Dan's money, she felt a tinge of guilt for not depositing it into the fund, which must have been his intention. But it was still going to the same place. Mary had just felt a sudden impulse to be rid of the phone number and the memories that went along with it. She'd move on in the same way he had fourteen years ago. Too much water under the bridge, as they say. Her life was complicated enough.

She had slipped the card into the wrought iron mailbox by her back door before leaving to see Darlene.

Now Mary drove on to the cemetery, a few dozen acres of rolling hills near the center of town. Chipped pre–Revolutionary War tombstones lined the cemetery's main street. Further back off the road, the shade-giving trees thinned out and the turf flattened. There, chunky new marble markers littered the grass haphazardly, crowded together in some areas and spread out in others, as people hadn't the decency to die in the order in which the plots had been sold. From the top of a hill, Mary saw the small gathering. She didn't dare drive any further for fear of disrupting the proceedings. She got out of her air-conditioned car and the heat hit her. She was overdressed, in long pants and a knit jacket. She wended her way down through the trees toward the group, careful to remain unnoticed. None of the mourners appeared to be looking anywhere but in the direction of the narrow white casket covered with flowers, mostly lilies and freesia. At the base of the stand were several other arrangements, including the rather over-the-top display that she herself had ordered from Thayer's Florist on behalf of the Clambake staff, and that now seemed garish in comparison to the rest.

She thought she recognized a few of the younger people there, including Hope, Megan, and the waitress Wayne had his crush on, whose name, Mary had finally learned, was Sage. The minister was reading. To his right stood a woman Mary estimated to be in her early sixties. She had short, thick salt-and-pepper hair, and she kept dabbing at the bottom rim of her too-big aviator sunglasses where the tears must have pooled. Mary recognized her as a cashier from Quanset Lumber. After she'd bought the new house, Mary had made a few trips there to pick up picture hangers, closet organizers, and other odds and ends. She remembered the cashier's name tag—"Hello. My name is Meg"—but hadn't since made the connection. Given her name, her age, and her proximity to the minister, and the fact that her hand was holding that of a toddler, she had to be Anicca's grandmother. The little girl had blond hair trimmed to her chin, with long bangs that fell into her eyes. A white eyelet skirt peeked out from beneath her purple fleece jacket. On her feet were white sandals, which she scuffed over the grass. The little girl's face was flushed. She was hot. *Someone should take off her jacket,* Mary thought. As the minister droned on, Mary felt the sweat dripping down her temples, down the back of her neck.

Aside from the people she recognized, there were only a handful of others. Mary expected there might be a grieving mother or father close to her own age, but there was no one in the front row who fit that description. Mary couldn't take her eyes off the little girl, who was now swaying gently on her great-grandmother's arm. Someone was passing around individual flowers to be laid on the casket. They gave a sprig of freesia to the girl and she put it in her mouth. When the grandmother noticed, she took the stem out the child's hand, causing her to wail. The grandmother's shoulders slumped and she pressed a crumpled tissue to her mouth. The minister paused and put his hand on the woman's back. Even though Mary and everyone there knew that the child was crying over the flower and not the body of her young mother in the white box, it didn't seem to matter. The grandmother picked up the girl. Mary turned away. Standing behind a wide oak, she had seen enough but didn't dare leave. She looked up though the branches of the tree to the firmament beyond and wondered if Anicca was watching from somewhere "up there," and if she was, what she might be thinking about her daughter and about Mary hiding behind the tree.

Eventually, the little girl quieted down. Mary pressed her head back against the tree. Her chest thumped. She felt her hair get caught up in the rough bark. When the minister stopped reading, Mary looked again. People were placing their flowers on the casket and dispersing. The kids who worked for her were already walking toward an SUV parked at the far side of the proceedings. The grandmother stood at the casket with her eyes closed and her hands clasped in prayer. No one was watching the little girl, who, having been set free, was climbing an ivy-covered tombstone adorned with a marble statue of an angel, its arms stretched toward the heavens.

The air conditioning in the kitchen had broken down and the giant fans they had blowing at high speed to cool things off made it impossible for the cooks to hear the waitresses and for the order line girls to hear the cooks, so that by the time Mary got there, the whole kitchen was in chaos and tempers were flaring. Fortunately, because of the heat, it was the kind of afternoon where most vacationers were at the beach. Nate was on the line, head down, going about his business, probably sensing he'd been a nuisance this past week and deliberately keeping a low profile. Maureen was serving a couple at the take-out window. Wayne and Sage were at it again.

"He sent it back. He said it tasted funny," Sage said to Wayne. She passed the platter of uneaten fish over the metal counter.

Wayne rolled his eyes. He took the plate, scooped up some fish with his fingers, and popped it into his mouth. It always amazed Mary how these kids could grow so comfortable with eating food off other people's plates. The fork that had been in the guy's mouth had touched the fish Wayne had just put in his. Sometimes she even caught waitresses snacking on uneaten fries or scallops from their customer's baskets before they emptied the rest of the contents into the trash. It turned her stomach.

Wayne set the tray down. He made a face. Mary knew he was tasting shapes when he reached both arms out in front of him and started to motion like he was fondling two small globes. He closed his eyes.

"What the hell are you doing?" Sage said. She kicked the bottom of the counter so that the metal shelves rattled. She put her hands on her hips.

Wayne jumped and opened his eyes. His arms dropped to his sides. "What? What did I do?" he said. He looked wide-eyed over at Mary. Did he expect her to rescue him?

"Is that supposed to be funny? Are you some kind of pervert?" she said. Sage was built in such a way that she'd obviously gotten her young life's share of teasing about her endowments. Who could blame her for being sensitive?

"I wasn't . . . It's just . . . ," he stammered. "It tasted strange, is all." The others had stopped what they were doing and were watching the two of them. "I mean *bad* strange—"

"I'm not putting up with your crap, Wayne Chen. You learn how to treat women with respect or it's going to be a long, hard summer."

One of the order line girls snickered.

"Shut up, Courtney," Sage said. "When you make it to an A cup we'll throw you a party." The order line girl's jaw dropped in horror. Sage stormed out the door.

"Nate, check the fish. And tell Sage to offer her customer something else. It'll be on the house. Wayne, go take a ten-minute break," Mary said.

Wayne reached into his pocket for his cigarettes and headed past the group of teens who were eyeing him like a rock star for his crude impropriety. He walked out the back door, letting it slam so that the springs vibrated their chords through the kitchen. Mary followed him out to where he was sitting on the stoop.

"What was that about?" she asked.

"It tasted bad. Way too soft, like it had gone funky. I could feel it." Wayne said. He held out his hand like he was holding a pool ball. Then he dropped it and shook his head. He lit a cigarette. "Now she hates me."

"If it's any consolation, I think she hated you before," Mary said.

What was the fish guy doing, bringing her bad fish? *Bad* fish were worse even than bluefish.

"Great. Thanks," Wayne said, dripping sarcasm. "You have this special talent for making people feel better."

"Oh, come on. I'm kidding. I actually think she likes you."

His whole being seemed to ignite. He turned to Mary. "Really?"

"Yeah. She just doesn't know it yet."

Wayne's shoulders slumped again. He knocked the ash from his cigarette.

"You've got five minutes. Pull yourself together and get back in there. And stop playing *air molester* or you'll get us both sued."

"Is there some kind of test you do to see if someone has Alzheimer's?" Mary said to the nurse on the phone. "I'm worried about my aunt. I think she might be imagining things." Mary fanned herself with a magazine. Her attic office was an inferno, but this was one call she didn't want to make downstairs.

"There are some mental tests the doctor performs. Do you want to set up an appointment for Ms. Rollwagon?"

"What if she has it?"

"There are some medications," the nurse said.

"But nothing to stop it, right? It just gets worse," Mary said.

Like most health care professionals, the nurse wouldn't be drawn down the what-if road. "Why don't we start by making an appointment?"

Mary marked Thursday's appointment in her calendar. She would have to think of an excuse to tell Lovey why they were going to the doctor. Maybe she'd bring her to lunch first, get some fish into her. Wasn't fish was supposed to be brain food? Mary'd eaten it all her life. Sufficient evidence that it was truly an old wives' tale. She was about to go downstairs herself when she heard the door at the foot of the stairs open, then footsteps.

"Jesus, it's hot up here." It was Nate. "Look, bad news. The entire shipment of flounder in the walk-in is bad."

"Bad. What does that mean, exactly?"

"The kids who dressed the filets for the broiler should have picked up on it. It smells and the flesh has gone to mush. Maybe the ice melted and it sat in water, or whoever gutted the fish let them sit too long. I don't know. All I know is, all the flounder Ernie brought over on Saturday has to be tossed."

"What about the haddock?" Mary dabbed the sweat off her upper lip with a cocktail napkin.

"It's fine."

"Okay, so drive down to the fish market and get enough flounder to at least get us through dinner. I'll get our pal Ernie Smith on the phone and straighten him out. Just thank God no one got sick."

A voice called up from the kitchen. It was Hope, the hostess. "Mary, there's a lady puking on the hydrangeas in the parking lot."

Mary looked at Nate. She shook her head. "I'm going to kill him."

Ernie tried to pin the blame on the temperature of their walk-in, but Mary wasn't buying it. She'd had Nate go down and check to make sure it was below 40 degrees. She calmly informed Ernie he'd have a new shipment of flounder to them by tomorrow and the fish had better still be moving. Or else. *Or else what?* What leverage did she have now that the season had begun? He had her. She'd used Ernie the last three years with few problems. Some seasons she got lucky. Others were one catastrophe after another. She could already see what kind of season this was shaping up to be. The fish made her think of Dan Bassett, who for two summers had taken care of everything, including Mary. And there'd been other seasons nearly as good since. But these days, reliable suppliers weren't so easy to come by. Nor were the fish. The industry had dwindled so much since she and Robbie opened the Clambake, it was a wonder all the fish didn't now come from off the coast of South America.

Mary often took a break before dinner, mostly just to get away from the commotion for a while. She liked to get in the car and drive someplace—anyplace, it didn't matter. Coming from the public beach parking lot now, she was heading back toward town when Robbie came to mind, and happier times, that very first day seventeen years ago when they opened for business. The weather had been like it was today, unseasonably hot. Robbie had taken a few hours off from the docks to help out in the kitchen for that first lunch shift, which had been enough of a success to finally convince him too that they were unstoppable. They'd made it through with no more than a few screwups—a customer who'd ordered tuna salad got lobster instead, though there were no complaints there. Once or twice the bar had gotten behind on drink orders. The fry cook had burned a few batches of onion rings and someone accidentally knocked the old chowder-burner switch to "off," so the chowder had to be heated in small batches on the stovetop. Otherwise, the shift had been indicative of the success that was to come, the dining room nearly half full that very first day.

After lunch, Robbie had gone back to his day job at the dock for a few hours and would return when he got off, in time for dinner. By the next season, Robbie would be working full-time at the restaurant, the two of them sitting at the bar at the end of each night with a few cold ones, tallying up receipts. One year later, he'd mostly be finding excuses to escape while Mary did all the work, or drinking his way through the cases of warm beer stacked outside the walk-in to hide how much he was consuming. By that time, all they ever did was take each other's heads off anyway. And then, by the following season, he'd be gone.

But there'd been more to that first day, another wave set in motion, one that Mary wouldn't even allow herself to acknowledge until after Robbie's death.

After Robbie and the last lunch customer had left, she'd gone down to the basement to cool off, welcoming the dim light and peaceful dampness after the first day's excitement. At the base of the stairs were two silver doors, so new no one had bothered to peel off the protective blue plastic film. To the left, the walk-in fridge, where cases of beer sat chilling on metal racks, live shellfish were piled high in wire buckets, and a slab of swordfish, she knew, was thawing for tomorrow's lunch. On the right was the freezer. Mary tugged on the heavy handle and a frigid mist greeted her. The cold air stung her skin. She switched on the light and saw the boxes of frozen shrimp and chicken nuggets, and a bag of fish heads, their glazed eyes staring through the plastic, causing a shiver to run down the back of her legs. The ice machine spit forth a batch of cubes and Mary jumped. She retreated, closing the door fast behind her.

She looked around at the new things, the oversized porcelain sink on the opposite wall (with the hose attachment that would eventually break off), and the maze of pipes leading up to the kitchen (one of which would freeze and crack in her seventh year, causing the basement to flood that winter). Next to the steps leading down from the bulkhead was a stack of gray milk crates that reached to the sills of two grimy windows, allowing in the only natural light in the room. In the center of the basement, directly above the floor drain, stood the old butcher block table Robbie had bought from an old-timer down at the dock for practically nothing. Above it, a high-wattage bulb dangled from the ceiling. Mary pulled the string and the room filled with eerie light. Next to the stairs was a single folding chair, which she brought over and set beside the table. She sat down and closed her eyes, reveling in the cool air and the afternoon's success. It was official. She and Robbie were restaurateurs. It was all theirs.

Mary opened her eyes and saw something sparkling on the ground beside one of the legs of the table, a dried fish scale, maybe. Upon closer examination it turned out to be an earring, a simple crystal bead on a silver wire. As she bent down to pick it up, the bulkhead door crashed open. The sound startled her, causing her foot to slip on the damp floor. She landed on her knees, ass in the air. When she scrambled to get up, she slipped.

"Don't move on my account." It was Dan Bassett, Robbie's best friend, who was then supplying some of the fish for the restaurant, mostly what he caught himself.

Dan, Robbie, and Mary had all gone to the local high school together, though Robbie and Dan were two years ahead and so Mary hadn't known them well then. They'd all gotten close only years later, one summer on the Outer Beach, at a spot some of their former classmates claimed each weekend with a tattered American flag, a caravan of four-wheel-drive vehicles, portable grills, and coolers filled with beer. Robbie drove an old brown CJ-7 Jeep, though he usually piled in with Dan and their friends in his painted green Chevy Blazer with the roof sawed off—a party on wheels as they bounced over the dunes on faulty shocks, fists pumping the air and Van Halen cassettes blaring. Mary became one of the weekend gang and, in no time, Robbie's girlfriend. She fell for his hippie demeanor and thick, dark hair. She'd never met anybody so laid-back. He was the most handsome guy in the group, with velvet brown eyes, chiseled features, and a long, lean body. Dan always seemed like the sidekick, good-natured but by no means as striking, still battling his adolescent baby fat. He had a prominent nose, wild hair, and eyes that always seemed to be smiling. After that summer, Dan went off to Alaska, where anyone who could stomach the rough seas could make a lot of money fishing king crab. He'd tried to talk Robbie into going with him, but by then, Robbie and Mary were a thing. And besides, Mary could never have imagined Robbie surviving those conditions. There had always been something fragile about him. And despite his aura of worldliness, the furthest west Robbie had ever been was Worcester, Massachusetts.

As Mary recovered from her spill and rose to her knees, she whacked her head on the side of the butcher block. Heat radiated to her face.

"You okay?" Dan asked. He stepped forward.

"I'm fine," she answered, holding him back with a wave of her hand. "You shouldn't just barge in on people like that," she said, rubbing her temple as she stood.

He was wearing dark green waders that came up to his chest, his muscles straining against the threadbare T-shirt with the weight of the wire buckets filled with oysters in each of his rubber-gloved hands. Mary hadn't seen Dan since he'd come back from Alaska and hadn't remembered him seeming so strong, or so barrel-chested. His hair had darkened and was trimmed close to his head, and his face had filled out some, making his nose seem smaller. He had what was probably a week-old beard and his cheeks were red from the sun and heat.

"Scorcher," he said. He set down the buckets, then stood and clapped the rust powder off his gloves. "There's a breeze on the water, but once we got inland, phew." He took a bandana out of his pocket and wiped his brow. "So, how've you been? Where's Robbie?"

The light from the open bulkhead made Mary's eyeballs twinge. "He went back to the dock. You must've passed him on your way here," she said.

"Gotta get those fish down here before they cook," he said. He walked back up the bulkhead steps. She folded up the chair and put it back by the stairs. She still had the earring in her hand.

A moment later, Dan returned, lugging an old-fashioned red Coca-Cola cooler. He set it down and lifted the lid. It was filled mostly with cod and a few blues. Mary came in for a closer look. She ran a finger along the sharp teeth of one of the bluefish.

"Careful!" Dan boomed. "Might not be all the way dead."

Mary jumped back. Dan started to laugh. "Gotcha, Sunshine," he said. It was the first time he called her that. She figured he probably called everyone that, but later she learned it wasn't the case. He slipped off a glove and reached into his waders, drew a pack of Winstons out of his shirt pocket. He shook the pack and pulled a cigarette out with his teeth. "So you gonna make me ask?"

"What?" she said. She was fixed on his cigarettes. He must have picked up smoking in Alaska.

"First lunch. How'd it go?" He pulled a lighter out of his pocket.

Mary beamed. "No catastrophes. We had a good crowd, and got some nice comments. Folks said they'd be back. What more can you ask, right?" she said. "Hey, can I bum one of those?" She didn't smoke.

Dan tossed her the pack. She accidentally let go of the earring to catch it. It landed by Dan's feet.

"Whatcha got here?" Dan said. He bent to pick it up.

"I found it under the butcher block," she said.

Dan's face seemed to darken. *Busted,* Mary thought. He'd brought a girl down here. She'd have to have a talk with Robbie about that. She wasn't going to have his friends acting like a bunch of schoolkids in her restaurant. This was a *business.* They had to keep the place sanitary. He handed back the earring and she snatched it away, tucking it into her pocket. He reached over with his lighter and lit her cigarette, then his.

She didn't inhale but coughed anyway. Dan had to be pretending he didn't notice, though there was a slight upward curl to his lips until he stuck the lit cigarette between them and carried the buckets of shellfish into the walk-in. He took a fish off the top of the cooler, setting it on the cutting board with the kind of thud only dead things make. Mary thought she should probably head back upstairs. She'd gone AWOL long enough. What if another customer had come?

But she had to at least finish her cigarette, which, after the coughing fit, consisted of letting it burn out between her fingertips. Dan plunged a knife into the fish's belly and ran it up to its gills. He opened the fish like a book and removed the stomach and guts. It was disgusting work, but Mary couldn't take her eyes off his hands, how fast they moved, how well he knew his way around the inside of a fish. She couldn't picture Robbie doing this, even though he worked down on the dock and, when he came home, his fingers always had that metallic smell.

"Never seen someone cut up a fish before?" Dan said.

Maybe she was bugging him. "I guess I should be heading upstairs," she said. She dropped her cigarette into a pool of moisture on the floor and it sizzled. Then she picked up the butt and dropped it into the metal trash can beside the table. She started for the steps.

"Hey," he said. She looked back at him. He took the cigarette out of his mouth and crushed it beneath his boot. "Congratulations."

"Thanks," she said. "Next time come upstairs and I'll buy you a beer to celebrate." As soon as she said it, she realized he might take it the wrong way. "When Robbie's around," she added.

Dan cracked a dark smile and got back to his fish. He never did come upstairs. Not once. Even after Robbie died and they started sleeping together.

In a few more minutes, Mary would have to head back to the restaurant for the start of the dinner shift. Without realizing where she was going, she had driven herself once again to the scene of Anicca's accident. The roadside memorial had sprawled as if the earth had blossomed with a groundcover of bright flowers and colorful tchotchkes.

Why had she come here again? Was she secretly hoping, now that the girl was in the ground, that the stuff would have been cleared away so things could get back to normal, as if it were just this profusion of memorabilia at the side of the road that was causing the feeling in her gut that wouldn't go away. If that were the case, why not just load it all into her trunk and cart it off to the dump? She pulled over to the side of the road and got out of the car. A motorcycle whizzed by and the flatulent sound rattled her bones.

Mary walked up to the tree, to the wound where the car had hit. She ran her palm across the bare wood. Its color had already darkened from the other day. The bark felt cool and the exposed flesh of the tree gave off the scent of autumn, though it was only June. Mary knelt down amid the leave-behinds. In addition to the Clambake T-shirt and the stuffed animals, there were notes, cards and song lyrics, candles, a white plastic cross, a small carved angel, a pink Red Sox cap, a page from a coloring book with a sloppily colored-in bumblebee, some faded plastic flowers, their stems stuck into the ground. Mary wondered whether all these people even knew Anicca, or whether some of these contributions had been made by complete strangers, a pastime for seniors maybe, something akin to quilting or scrapbooking, which not only got them out of the house but helped them dispose of the stuff they'd accumulated over the years in some meaningful way. Meaningful to them, at least. What good did it do Anicca? All the stuffed animals would have made better gifts for the toddler. Mary remembered having similar thoughts when Robbie died and his mother channeled her grief into a very public fight with the town to keep the white cross and candles at the side of the road for months after he was gone. For what? What difference did it make?

A stuffed red bear caught Mary's eye. She picked it up. Its fur was nubby and soft, and it had an expressive face—two black button eyes set a little too close together, making the bear seem vulnerable. The way the nose had been stitched, it looked handmade. The tag was still around the bear's neck. Someone had gone to a store, picked out a bear—by the looks of it, a pretty expensive bear—and then just deposited it here under this tree to get filthy. This afternoon they were forecasting thunderstorms, which meant everything that didn't get washed into the street and crushed under wet tires would be muddy and ruined by morning. Hadn't enough been ruined? Did this perfectly good bear have to be ruined too?

At that instant, Mary knew she wasn't leaving without the bear. She looked both ways to make sure no one was coming, then stuffed it under her shirt. When the road was clear, she dashed to the driver-side door. She imagined the person who'd left the bear, what he or she might think to come upon this spot in the road all of a sudden and find it gone. Or worse, find someone in the process of stealing it. What kind of person stole things from a roadside memorial? She wasn't *stealing*, Mary corrected herself. She was saving the bear from ruin, from becoming wet and soiled, and forgotten. She was saving it for the little girl, who if Mary ever got the nerve to actually send it, might one day appreciate the gesture. What was her name? A good boss would know the name of an employee's kid. A good boss would know the names of her employees, and whether or not they even had kids.

• • •

Mary set the bear in the passenger seat and started up the car. She knew where she was going next: home, to see whether, by some stroke of luck, the mail carrier had gotten his truck stuck in the sand as he often did, causing mail pickup and delivery to be delayed. Then the sympathy card would still be there in the box. She'd been a fool not to take down the phone number on the hundred-dollar bill. How many times after they'd broken things off had she tried to contact Dan? How may phone calls and letters had gone unanswered? And then she learned from an acquaintance that he'd gone back out west, this time to fish salmon, maybe for good. She thought she'd never see him again. And then last year, all of a sudden, there was word around town that he was back on the Cape. She kept expecting to bump into him at the market, or on the beach some evening, at the time they used to take their walks together. But she never heard from him or even saw him, which was hard to imagine given what a small place the Outer Cape was and how things slowed in the off-season. People who knew him said he just fished and lived on his boat, practically a recluse. He obviously wanted no part of her life. So, once again, she tried to let it go. But the thing that ate at her was, she never knew the real reason why he left. There had to be more to it than that one argument. Mary had always suspected another woman. But she never knew for sure.

First Robbie, then Dan, both men out of her life in eighteen months. And now, suddenly, Dan had shown up at the restaurant yesterday. He'd given her his cell phone number. *Given* it to her. And she'd let it slip through her fingers. No, worse. She'd gotten rid of it fast, as if her life depended on it. Maybe, in some way, it had. What person in her right mind would want to relive that kind of hurt? But she'd been acting on impulse and now she regretted it. Story of her life.

What was foolish too was that Dan was one of the few people who might be able to help her if Ernie Smith didn't clean up his act. What seafood restaurant could survive gossip that the fish was bad? If things didn't get better fast, she had no choice but to fire Ernie.

And then Dan might be her only hope, assuming he was still fishing. Regardless, he had connections at the pier, where Mary had burned a few bridges over the years. He might be willing to help out an old friend in a jam. He had to. He owed her that much.

As she pulled into her driveway, Mary convinced herself this was the real reason why the phone number needed to still be in the box. She threw the car into park. *Please be there.* She got out and ran up the back steps. The sun was low in the sky over the bay, casting the covered entrance at back of the house into deep shadow. She'd forgotten to turn on the outside light this morning and her keys were still in the ignition, so she couldn't unlock the door and flick it on. She opened the mailbox but it was too dark to see. She stuck her hand in and felt around, just in case. But it was no use. The card, the bill, and the phone number—they were gone.

Six

The coyote was back. Mary had found the bones of a rabbit in her driveway the day before last. Now she could see its grayish-red back weaving through the tall grass behind the old man's cottage.

Mary went out to the kitchen to warm up her coffee. A week ago today, Anicca Sutherland had been alive. People said it all the time: one minute you're here, the next minute you're gone. Dan was another story. One minute you're gone, the next minute you're back. And then gone again, at least as far as Mary knew. Since his visit to drop off the money, he hadn't returned or left any messages.

Mary looked to the sky. The weather had cleared. The thunderstorms from Tuesday had pushed the stifling heat out to sea. Now the sun was rising from behind her, casting its purple shadows. It was cool and the air was still. A beach day, which meant lunch would be slow but dinner would be busy as people went home, got cleaned up, and sought fresh air, to nurse their sunburns. Mary had always believed there was more to what fueled the seafood restaurant business on the Cape, a hunger in people that went beyond the quest for a satisfying meal. It was as if vacationers, even after a full day at the shore, were struck with a primal desire for a deeper communion, a hunger to ingest the rawness of the sea—to *become* it—as though slurping the quivering flesh of a mollusk or sucking the meat from a lobster claw allowed a return to one's aboriginal roots, to the dragons of the deep that we all once were, and the brine from which all human life began, the ocean of a mother's womb.

Anicca's obituary sat on the kitchen island. It had come out this morning in the local paper. Mary had hoped the listing would provide more insight into the girl's story, perhaps some mention of siblings or extended family. Instead, it only confirmed Mary's worst fears, that the grandmother was Anicca's sole surviving next-of-kin, which meant there'd be no one sweeping in to rescue the toddler whose name, she'd just learned, was Ariel.

Mary returned to the bathroom to get ready. She looked out the window. Rubbing circles of moisturizer into her cheeks, she watched the old man eat his cereal, only this time she noticed a subtle back-and-forth movement to the hand holding the spoon. Parkinson's? Mary was reminded of the tailor her mother and Lovey used to take her to see when she was a child, a small, bent man with spots on his face who used to alter her winter coats each season, taking the new ones in or letting the old ones out, and how his hand would move in a similar lateral rhythm with the tailor's chalk as he marked the fabric, and even as he drew it away, as if he were marking the air.

"Auntie, why does he do that with the chalk?" she'd asked when they got back into the car.

"He has Parkinson's, dear," Lovey had said. Back then Lovey drove a red Volkswagen Beetle that Mary adored as much for its sweet vinyl smell as for its whimsical shape, and the neat strap by the window that was intended for passengers to hold on to. The cautious way her aunt drove, though, never caused Mary to reach up and grab hold of the strap as if her life depended on it. Because it never had.

"What's Parkinson's?" Mary had asked.

"It's a disease that causes people to move in funny ways," Lovey said. Mary remembered thinking Lucille Ball must have Parkinson's. And Dick Van Dyke. And she remembered how, for a few weeks at least, she'd been very careful not to move in "funny" ways for fear of contracting Parkinson's and being destined to a life of drawing invisible chalk lines in the air.

Mary remembered, too, how much she loved those long afternoons with her great-aunt, who, after the tailor's, would take her to Fleming's for doughnuts and then to a movie at the tiny theater that used to be right in the center of town where the drugstore now stood. Together they'd seen Steve McQueen and Godzilla movies, and *Ring of Bright Water,* that British film with the lovable otter who, in the end, gets bludgeoned to death with an axe handle, a movie that resonated for Mary as a tangible marker for that first shift from childhood innocence to the idea that life was more complicated and scary than she could fathom, or sometimes bear.

In fuzzy slippers whose fuzz had worn off, Mary padded from the bathroom to the walk-in closet. She turned on the light. She'd never been one to fuss over clothes. Most days, a particular top or a certain color scheme would call out to her. Now, though, the clothes had lost their shape and distinction, colors blurring together to a smear of gray. Was it possible she'd contracted the opposite of synesthesia?

Or would anyone have a hard time choosing an outfit to take one's favorite aunt to the doctor, possibly to learn that her mind was slipping away?

"Nate, can you come up for a minute?" Mary called from the top of the stairs. She had a few hours before she had to pick up Lovey and had decided to catch up on inventory for Fourth of July weekend, which was almost upon them.

Mary had brought Anicca's obituary in to work. It sat on the desk next to the red bear she'd taken from the roadside memorial. She thought she would pack up the stuffed animal with some toys she'd picked up with the intention of shipping them to Meg Ryder and Ariel on behalf of their new benefactor, Lavinia Rollwagon.

Mary heard footsteps coming up the stairs.

"You wanted to see me?" Nate said.

"Any shellfish yet?" In the wake of the bad flounder incident, Ernie seemed to have gotten his act together—until this morning and the shellfish order that should have been delivered by nine but still hadn't found its way to the basement.

"Not yet," Nate said. "We're low. You should call."

"I have been. He doesn't pick up. That's because he knows it's me,

I'm sure." Mary turned around in her chair and looked at Nate. She smiled. "So how are things?" she asked.

"Good." His tilted his head down so that his blond hair hung in his eyes, giving him something to hide behind.

"I mean with Maureen. You straightened things out?" she said. "She knows nothing ever happened between us, right?"

"Uh-huh." He scratched a mosquito bite on his forearm.

"She hasn't been acting any different," Mary said. "I mean, she knows I know about the two of you, right?"

"She just wants to do her job and mind her own business. That's just how she is."

Mary smiled. "That's a good way to be. I'll mind my own business too," she said. "Did you see the obituary?" She tapped the paper and turned back toward the desk.

"Yeah," he said.

"Has anything more about Anicca's story surfaced since the accident? It just said in the paper her parents were deceased," Mary said.

"My dad told me her parents died in a boat accident. Up till then, they were summer people. My dad knew Anicca's father from softball. Right before they died, the grandmother had moved down here from somewhere off-Cape," he said.

"God." How could one family be visited by so much tragedy? Mary always thought she'd had it rough. "I just keep thinking about what kind of future the kid's going to have."

"People have been dropping off donations."

"That's not what I mean," she said. She felt that familiar vibration at the back of her nose. Her voice cracked. "I mean a kid needs *parents*." She was reminded of her own folks. After all these years, she still missed them.

Nate came closer. "You're doing what you can." He put his hand on her shoulder and let it rest there. Her flesh warmed to his touch. She missed being touched. "The girl will be okay. There are a lot of good people in this town."

She put her hand on top of his. He gave her shoulder a squeeze and slipped his hand away. That was it. She didn't want that to be it. He'd only touched her out of pity. If there was one thing Mary loathed, it was being pitied.

Her voice iced over. "You can go, Nate." She turned toward him. "Do me a favor. Send Maureen up."

Nate stepped back. He flipped the hair out of his eyes. He looked at her, as if trying to figure out her motive for wanting to see Maureen.

"Did I do something—?" Nate started.

"Don't be silly." Mary turned away from him and slid her reading glasses on. She closed the newspaper on her desk and folded it over.

A few moments after Nate left, she heard the door at the foot of the stairs open, then some whispers.

"Mary?" Maureen had never seen Mary's private office before, at least never while Mary was around. And when Mary wasn't around? For all she knew, Maureen and Nate might have had at it right on her desk. Mary shook some dust off a magazine. Then again, not likely.

"Come on up, Maureen." Mary took a deep breath.

Maureen lumbered up the stairs. She wore men's basketball sneakers. Mary guessed she'd been a tomboy most of her life, which is probably how she first caught Nate's attention way back in third grade. What boys liked girls for any other reason in third grade?

"How's it going down there?" Mary asked.

Maureen cocked her head and squinted at Mary. "Fine. I have some orders coming up in a minute, though." She looked around the room.

Mary decided to get right to the point. "I know you know I know about you and Nate. I just wanted to clear the air."

"Oh," Maureen said. Then an expression of horror swept over the girl's face.

"What is it?" Mary asked. That defensive tone took hold of her voice again. "Look, Nate and I *never*—"

The girl's forehead creased and she swallowed hard. "Where did you get *that*?" she asked. She pointed to the desk.

Of course, the obituary. Mary picked up the newspaper. She held it out to Maureen. "It came out today. I was going to tack it to the board downstairs for people to—"

"Not that." Maureen pushed the newspaper aside. *"That!"* She pointed at the bear Mary had brought up from her car. Mary felt a pinch in her abdomen. "That *bear*," Maureen said. "I bought one just like it for Anicca. I put it under the tree the day after she died. And then when I went back Tuesday, it was gone." Her eyebrows had sharpened.

"You mean this?" Mary picked up the bear. What were the odds? *Think fast.* "I bought it in town. For an elderly relative. See, my great-aunt might have Alzheimer's. I'm taking her to the doctor today."

Maureen crossed her arms and thrust out her hip, an aggressive move Mary'd seen her use with the waitresses a hundred times. *"Where* in town?"

"Brewster Crossing. Dr. Needleman."

"Not the doctor, the *bear*. Where did you get it?" Maureen shifted her weight from one foot to the other.

"Oh," Mary said. There was only one real toy store in town that would carry anything so nice. "Caribou Toys."

"That's impossible," Maureen said. "I bought the last one they had."

Mary shrugged. "They got more." She turned around and set the bear back down on her desk. The black button eyes seemed to glare at her.

"I wanted to buy another one. The clerk told me they were *discontinued,*" Maureen said.

Mary started straightening the things on her desk, squaring up papers. "Maybe they found some in the back. Who *knows*? Is it really such a big—?"

"What *day* did you buy it?" Maureen asked.

"Tuesday," Mary lied.

"Ha! Tuesday they were closed. They had a roof leak because of the thunderstorms. I know because I went back to get another one," Maureen said.

"Maybe it was yesterday, I don't know. You expect me to remember every little detail about when I buy what? Sheesh. Wait till you get to be my age. You'll be lucky if you can remember what you had for breakfast." The last two sentences had come directly out of Claire's cliché kit.

"Did you take other people's stuff too?" Maureen asked. "Or just *my* bear."

Mary turned to face her. The girl's eyes were blazing. "Okay, Maureen," Mary said. "Let's just settle down—"

"But *why*? *Why* would you—?"

Wayne's voice came from the kitchen. "Maureen! Order up!"

Mary jerked her chair back from the desk. "Fine. I took the bear. I'm not proud of it. And I honestly can't tell you why I did it. But the way I see things now, we're *even*."

"What—?" Maureen started.

"*You* got Nate. *I* got the bear," Mary said. Mary picked the stuffed animal up by the neck like she was holding it hostage. Maureen's eyes widened.

"Maureen!" came another voice from the kitchen.

Maureen thought about it for an instant. "Deal," she said.

"I knew you were a sensible girl," Mary said. "Now, go."

When the footsteps went away and the downstairs door closed, Mary dropped her head to the desk. With one eye, she looked up at the bear. It appeared to be satisfied with the arrangement as well.

Mary had asked to keep Lovey's drawing, but Dr. Needleman said they needed it for her aunt's file. From a design standpoint, there was something pleasing about the old woman's clock, something consistent in its inconsistency, like a thing that lay under water, shaped a bit like a thunderhead, or a beanbag resting on a hard surface and flattened at the bottom. And with not the usual two hands but three! The longest between the 12 and the 1, another somewhat arched, leaning suggestively a little more toward the 3 than the 4, and a short runt of a hand hinting somewhere between the 7 and the 10. (Numbers 8 and 9 had been left out entirely.)

Mary had seen a gag clock once where all the numbers had fallen into a heap at the bottom. Perhaps Lovey had been making some philosophical statement about time, sharing some insight the doctor couldn't pick up on because he'd been so fixated on his notion of an accurate rendering. "Draw a clock. Then place the hands at ten past eleven," he'd said. Dr. Needleman was probably the kind of man who taught his kids to color inside the lines—all science and no imagination. But Mary thought what Lovey had drawn was interesting, brilliant, even.

It was Lovey who'd taught Mary how to tell time on old Felix in the basement of her family home, the cat clock with eyes that scanned either side of the room with each tick of his tail. With his pointed ears, white bow tie, and mischievous smile, it looked like maybe old Felix knew something about time that Lovey and Mary didn't. Something that Lovey might be finding out now.

"I'd like her to see a neurologist," Dr. Needleman said. He pushed his glasses up higher onto the bridge of his nose. "The one I send my patients to is in Hyannis."

Mary's shoulders fell. "You think she has Alzheimer's," Mary said. "But she told you the year and the day of the week." Though Lovey had forgotten what town she was in. "And she remembered 'pen' and 'ball.'" Though she'd forgotten the third word he'd given her at the beginning: "ring."

"I suspect there's something going on here. When we get the results of the blood and urine tests, we'll be able to rule more things out," the doctor had said.

"What other things?"

"Anemia, vitamin deficiencies, electrolyte imbalances, even a brain infection," he said. "We'll call with the results."

"Can you leave a message on my machine if I'm not home?" She wasn't about to have them call her at the restaurant. She'd get nothing done until she heard from them. "If I have questions, I'll call you back."

A few moments later, Mary left with Lovey on her arm and a card imprinted with the name of a neurologist.

In the car on the way home Lovey asked how the doctor had liked her drawing.

"He said he'd never seen anything like it," Mary reassured her.

Lovey smiled so that Mary got a glimpse of the old woman's false tooth. The whiteness of it reminded Mary of Lovey, dignified, hopeful, and pure, and the teeth around it of everyone else in the world, weak, compromised, and yellowing. *Like Robbie,* she thought. She felt that old anger well up inside, an anger that hadn't touched her in years. Only now, thanks either to Anicca's death or to Dan's return, or both, it was back. How could Robbie have allowed his life to end that way? How could he have abandoned her, and let the drinking become more important than their marriage? To hit a tree and have it be the end, just like that, and to leave her, for all these years since, with no choice but to believe it was her fault. No second chance to take back what she'd said before he'd gone.

And there was the other thing Mary always wondered. Where had he been going? The car had been found wrapped around a tree on Route 28, heading *away* from their home, not toward it.

Robbie had died a month before the restaurant was supposed to open for the summer, which left Mary little time to grieve. There were menus to be printed, staff to be hired, new equipment to be installed and tested. Mary had thought about skipping the season entirely, keeping the Clambake closed and just going somewhere to be alone for the summer, maybe renting a cottage in Maine or driving cross-country, but Lovey had convinced her it would be best to remain close to home, and to keep busy. The restaurant was all she had now. Lovey didn't say it, but Mary understood. And Mary also understood how much Lovey had adored Robbie, and how she was secretly terrified that Mary might leave her too. Dan had supported Mary's sticking around as well, going so far that summer as to sacrifice his own fishing income to pick up tasks that would have fallen to Robbie.

During that time, Mary found Dan the easiest of everyone to be around, perhaps because of their history, how he'd known Robbie so well, and the problems she'd faced with him. And because he didn't blame her for what had happened, and had a way of reassuring her that none of it had been her fault. He had a way of saying the right things.

By June, they were business partners. By September, they were sleeping together, the first time as a threesome with a beauty named Iris, a category-three hurricane making her way up the coast from the Carolinas. After a three-day tango with the TV meteorologist, it had become enough of a possibility that Iris might make landfall on the Cape that Mary had no choice but to take action. The storm was supposed to reach Nantucket after midnight on Wednesday. On Tuesday, Mary had closed the restaurant and together with her inner circle of staff members spent the day securing things, moving tables and chairs into the back dining room, taking down signs and moving potted plants that might become projectiles in strong winds, backing up her computer files, boxing liquor bottles and bringing them down into the basement, testing the generator to make sure they'd keep the refrigerators going if the power failed, and taping up windows. She'd gone by Lovey's apartment to see that her aunt had everything she needed. In those days, Lovey still drove her car and had already made the trip to Stop & Shop for bottled water, bleach, flashlight batteries, peanut butter, and—since she was of the generation that venerated processed foods—her favorite: canned beef stew.

Dan had planned to come by that evening after he'd done what he could to secure his boat. He'd offered to pick up some sheets of plywood at Quanset's and meet Mary back at the house to board up the picture window in the living room.

Mary was upstairs changing her clothes when she heard the truck pull in. She'd slipped on her sexiest pair of jeans and a black tank top. While Dan was unloading the wood, she put on some lipstick and brushed her hair, dabbed some perfume on her wrists. She had a bottle of wine chilling in the fridge, a pot of kale soup warming on the stove, and a loaf of fresh bread from the farmers' market. If anything was ever going to happen between them, she knew, this would be the night.

The tension between them had escalated in recent weeks. She couldn't pinpoint precisely when she started daydreaming about what it would be like to have him in her bed. When she allowed herself to consider her feelings for Dan, she realized maybe they'd been there awhile, even before Robbie died. This made her feel guilty. Yet in these few short months, Dan had been there for her in ways Robbie never had. There was something so different about him, a rough, playful side to him that she found appealing, something rugged and "other" that made her breath quicken whenever she heard the sound of his heavy boots down in the basement. Robbie had never taken anything or anyone seriously. Dan knew how to be responsible and dig into life at the same time, tending to business with that twist of a smile on his lips that hinted there was always something more on his mind. She found him sexy in many ways, in his physical strength, in his knowledge about boats and fishing and the temperament of the sea, and in how she felt protected when he was around. There was something boyish about him too, which is why she'd taken to fixing meals for him herself and packing him lunches to take on the boat. When things upstairs were slow, she'd take a couple of beers down to the basement and watch him cut up the fish, for the thrill of seeing the knife in his sure hand as he artfully sliced his way through the luminous flesh.

And it wasn't just her infatuation. She'd seen him watching her too, one time when he'd come up to the kitchen for a knife sharpener and caught sight of her at the sink rinsing eggs out of a lobster hen. The way he'd looked at her. And there was what had happened in the basement most recently when the small talk between them ended and she asked him what he was thinking. He'd said, "You don't want to know." She'd pressed him and teased, but he wouldn't tell her. The thing was, she knew anyway. Because she'd been thinking, if not the same thing, then something close. She looked him in the eyes, defiant, almost challenging him. She slowly reached into his pocket for a cigarette she had no intention of smoking, deliberately brushing his chest with the backs of her fingers. She let her hand linger there until the hair on her arms stood on end, her eyes locked on his all the while. He kept his arms at his sides but she knew he was feeling it too, a shift in time and molecules, a movement of the mind from linear to horizontal, to a surface that was smooth and polished and went on forever. And then the moment passed. She said good night and went back upstairs. But later that night, she'd lain in bed staring at the ceiling, feeling an ache deep inside. Someone had to make the first move. But she was his best friend's widow. Part of the reason she was so attracted to him was that she'd been able to trust him all these weeks. So she'd have to be the one, and she'd have to do it soon. The summer was almost over and, after that, who knew how often they'd see each other. He'd even mentioned something about going back to Alaska.

From the upstairs bathroom, Mary listened to the hammering and gathered her courage. By the time she came down, the plywood had been affixed to the window, casting the living room in eerie darkness. She got some candles out of her sofa-table drawer and lit them, then went up to the picture window as Dan continued to sink nails into to the frame. She put her hand on the glass to feel the vibrations. The pane was cool and the heat of her body fogged the glass, creating a halo around her fingers.

She held her breath and listened, not just for the hammering but for the other sounds too, the creak in the stepladder as he shifted his weight from one foot to the other, his grunts as he strained to reach the top of the window frame, even the steady in and out of his breath. It was amazing how much she could hear if she really listened, and how the sounds alone could create a picture in her mind's eye. She imagined the body separated from hers by a mere quarter inch of glass and a thin piece of wood. She could almost feel the heat of it, see the tension in his shoulder has he drew back the hammer, the trapezius muscles in his back as they tightened, and the power uncoiled as he struck the nail.

She wondered if it was possible to communicate with him like this, using just her mind. With all her concentration, she focused on the hammering, willing it to stop. She wanted him to think of her instead, and tonight and where it might lead for the two of them. A few more blows and then, to Mary's surprise, the hammering did stop. And there was nothing. Startled, Mary drew back from the glass. And then Dan sneezed. "Bless you," she said. He blew his nose. "Hay fever," he replied. She smiled and went out to the kitchen to set the table and wait for him.

Moments later, he knocked on the kitchen door.

"Come in. For God's sake, you don't have to knock," she said. "Thanks so much for taking care of that. What do I owe you for the wood?"

He looked around the room, at her, then at the pot of soup on the stove and the set table.

"Looks like dinner," he said. He was wearing jeans and a flannel shirt with the sleeves rolled up to his elbows. The soft muted grays and reds of the faded plaid suited him. She was used to seeing him in T-shirts and waders, so this was a welcome improvement.

"Can you stay?" she asked. "I brought home soup."

"Why not," he said. He took off his marina logo cap and mussed his short, wavy hair. "Mind if we turn on the weather?" He had to be nervous about his boat. He didn't wait for an answer, just switched on the portable TV on the kitchen counter.

"How does one *turn on* the weather, exactly?" Mary said in an absent way, her back to him as she stirred the soup. It was a funny expression when you thought about it. She lowered the flame under the pot.

At first she thought she was still imagining things when she felt his hands on her hips. She dropped the lid down on the soup pot but didn't turn around. She caught her breath and froze.

"Why don't *you* tell me?" Dan said. He planted his lips below her right ear. She felt his eyelashes brush her cheek. Her knees went soft and something electric pulsed up her body from her toes. While they were on the subject of weather, a lightening bolt, maybe. He breathed into her ear. His hot breath tickled her neck.

"Does this have anything to do with the TV?" she asked. Her voice had cracked. She turned around. She noticed the tan line on his neck and forehead from where the cap had sat all summer. She could see he'd shaved. His eyes, which until that evening she would have sworn were brown, now suddenly appeared the gray green of the sea after a storm, with ten-foot seas still roiling.

"Nothing to do with TV," he said. He brought his lips down onto hers. She tasted the salt on them. He'd been out at the marina, after all. Or maybe this was how anyone who spent so much time on the sea ended up tasting. His kiss was long and hot. She felt his hand pressing on the back of her head, holding her, and she was grateful, for she might have otherwise toppled onto the stovetop with the weight of his embrace.

She was taken by his bulk and strength, so different from Robbie—and others since. They kissed again; then he picked her up in his arms and carried her out to the living room, where the candle-light flickered caramel on the walls. And she had thought *she* was going to have to seduce *him*. He laid her down on the wide sofa and hovered over her. He ran his palm over her forehead and brushed away the bangs she wore back in those days. He ran the back of his finger down her cheek.

"What would Robbie think?" he asked. Mary saw points of pain in his eyes. It was something he obviously wrestled with.

Rather than answer, she pulled him near and began to unbutton his shirt. His chest was tan and muscular, with coarse brown hair that bisected his abdomen in a dark, narrow line and disappeared into the top of his jeans, just maybe the sexiest thing she'd ever seen. Why hadn't she noticed it when they were teenagers on the beach? Maybe because he was self-conscious then about his extra pounds and never took off his shirt? Could that be the reason? Because she would have remembered. With her fingers she traced the trail of hair down to his belly button, down to the button on his jeans, then undid it.

He pulled her tank top up over her head and pressed his flesh into hers. There on the sofa, cushions thrown on the floor, they made love till the wind came, and on into the night as it howled through the trees outside. In the morning, as the voice on the television in the other room confirmed that Iris's eye had passed miles offshore, leaving minimal damage, a few power outages, and some moderate beach erosion, they knew they'd been spared one tempest for another.

As Mary lay in his arms, her legs intertwined with his, listening to his soft breath, she remembered about the earring upstairs in her dresser drawer, the one she'd found in the basement the day that she and Robbie opened the restaurant, and she wondered about the girl Dan had been with. What did she look like? Had she been a serious girlfriend or just a fling? It wasn't the first time she'd wondered. Only now, as Dan lay beside her, Mary had more to wonder about, like how she measured up in Dan's mind to the earring girl.

"You're in luck," the neurologist's secretary had said. "There's been a cancellation and the doctor can see Ms. Rollwagon tomorrow." What Cape Cod doctor worth his or her salt could book an appointment the very next day, let alone the next month? At least, having to wait for a decent practitioner had been Mary's experience, though she was now on a different planet entirely from that of mammograms, eye doctors, and gynecologists. She was in a new world, one of gerontologists, proctologists, and neurologists. And so she figured she'd better take the first appointment she could get, for Lovey's sake. Not to mention that she didn't want to be anywhere near the restaurant when Ernie Smith showed up a day late with the shellfish or she might rip him to pieces herself. As it was, she'd left that task to Wayne. Last night they'd known they were running out of oysters by six o'clock and hadn't gone to the market to buy more because Ernie had assured her he'd be there in time for dinner, and then he didn't show up and didn't return her frantic cell phone calls the rest of the night. By the time they ran out of oysters, the markets were closed. And so they only had littlenecks, and those only until seven fifteen. And by then customers were so annoyed—some even getting up and walking out upon hearing the news—that Mary was forced to hand-letter a sign for out front that read: "Sorry, No Shellfish Tonight." And then she had to watch potential customers get as far as the front door only to turn on their heels, get back in their cars, and drive off. She was seething. To everyone's relief, she finally went upstairs and became absorbed in paperwork, until she noticed the flashing blue light on her cell phone. A text message from Ernie, who didn't even apologize but said he'd be there with the shellfish first thing in the morning.

If only she could remember Dan's cell phone number. Directory assistance hadn't been of any help, though that didn't surprise Mary. Dan had never listed his phone number. She remembered the area code was 508, which meant it was a local number, and the first three digits had to be either 240 or 255. She assumed, because he'd come back to town within the past few years, it was probably a 240 number, the newer exchange. And she knew there'd been a 9 in there somewhere at the beginning, and possibly a 4. How hard could it be to come up with four numbers, one of them a 9 and one of them maybe a 4? Impossible, it seemed, given the many attempts she'd made. If only she'd had the kind of synesthesia where people attribute colors to numbers. Then she might have seen Dan's number as a striped beach towel, snazzy wallpaper, or a scarf. She'd always been good with color schemes.

Yet even if she managed to get hold of him, what in the world would she say? This didn't stop her from visualizing the numbers, formulating sequences in the shower, in the car, on the register downstairs, on the backs of her eyelids that night when her head finally hit the pillow.

And as if her obsession with re-creating a phone number weren't troubling enough, it seemed Mary could no longer go anywhere in town without driving down Bridge Street, no matter how out-of-the-way, to spy on Meg Ryder and Ariel, just hoping to get a glimpse of either. Now, on her way to pick up Lovey for her second doctor's appointment, she slowed as she approached the old Cape. There was no sign of anyone. It had been a week since Anicca's death. Where did people go to commemorate a thing so terrible?

Mary came to a stop in front of the house, this time really taking the time to notice the shape it was in. The homey wreath on the front door had fooled her into believing the house was in better condition. Now she saw peeling paint on the shutters and on the door, where Ariel might pick off a chip, put it into her mouth, and end up with lead poisoning. There was lichen growing on the roof, and the shrubs clearly hadn't been trimmed in years. Mary pulled a note pad out of her pocketbook and made a list. When she got home, she'd call her Brazilian maintenance guys and asked them to swing by and take care of the work. How could Meg Ryder object to getting hundreds, maybe even thousands, of dollars' worth of free repairs to her house? And the toys would have arrived yesterday or today at the latest, though at the last moment, Mary had taken the red bear out of the box, setting it in the passenger seat of her car. It didn't seem right to give it away. It hadn't been hers to give. She felt bad about upsetting Maureen, and about taking it at all.

Seven

Mary was waiting in the doctor's private office as directed by the attendant at the front desk. The exam was over and Lovey was out in the waiting room with a nurse.

Mary shifted in her seat so she could reach into her jeans pocket to make sure the paper on which she'd written Dan's phone number was still there, that she hadn't just imagined she'd gotten it back. She pushed the slip deeper into the pocket so it wouldn't fall out. Later, she'd figure out what to do about it. Right now, her mind was on Lovey.

Mary wasn't accustomed to being invited into a doctor's private office. It made her uneasy. Mary's doctors never even revealed the clothes under their white coats, let alone invited her into their personal space. That's the way she liked it. She didn't need to see a doctor's sailing trophies or pictures of his wife and kids (this one had none). She didn't need to know his taste in furniture, in this case standard mahogany fare with a high-gloss finish. No fingerprints or dust. No personality either, save for an interesting finger labyrinth centered just beyond the blotter. Was that for him or for his patients? Mary reached over and ran her finger through the sand-filled grooves, causing some grains to spill out onto the wood surface. She blew them away.

To the left of his desk, the obligatory wall of diplomas, Harvard among them, though even they couldn't change the fact that, for one thing, he was considerably younger than she was, and that his name was *Green*. But she'd read a newspaper story that said younger doctors weren't necessarily any worse than older, more experienced physicians. In fact, many were better. They were more on top of the latest research, less set in their ways, less apt to make inaccurate calls based on past experience. She couldn't hold that against him. So, what was it that made her dislike him? Aside from the fact that he was probably about to come in and tell her something that would break her heart.

And then she found what she was looking for, directly behind the desk, a framed lithograph, one of those inspirational corporate posters. It depicted the image of a wave, more of the "tsunami on Maui" variety than anything that might tumble onto New England shores. The color photograph was set against a black ground with a word below it, reversed out in aqua: CHANGE. Of course. That's why people came to him, after all. Because they'd undergone some change. A woman who'd lost her words, another who could no longer recall how to tie her shoelaces. A man who'd forgotten where he lives. A truck driver who'd suffered massive head injuries in an accident and didn't recognize his wife. Change, in most cases—the kind that brought people to Dr. Green anyway—was not a good thing.

Beneath the word "change" there were two lines of smaller type. Mary got up and walked behind the doctor's desk to read the rest:

IF YOU'RE NOT RIDING THE WAVE OF CHANGE . . .
YOU'LL FIND YOURSELF BENEATH IT.

She realized the poster wasn't speaking to Dr. Green's patients or their families at all. It was speaking to him, and to his peers in the medical profession, about the importance of staying on top of his research, keeping an open mind, continuing to learn, never becoming stale or staid. But what of the poor people who sat in this office, the patients and loved ones who faced becoming engulfed? Dragged under. There was no cure for brain damage or Alzheimer's disease.

Mary had been fortunate enough to experience very little change over the last fourteen years. Or *un*fortunate, depending on how she looked at it. But this morning after she'd picked up Lovey, she knew there were things about their lives that would never be the same.

Mary had pulled her car into the cul-de-sac, a practice that was frowned upon by the busybodies in the apartment complex. But Lovey had a bad knee and didn't need to be walking all the way down the long sidewalk to the parking lot. At the main door to Lovey's building, Mary noticed that one of the neighbors on the ground floor had given up on her window boxes and had stuck some red plastic geraniums and yellow mums into the dirt. Mary might not have known except that mums wouldn't be in bloom for another two months. She pressed the buzzer button next to the name Roll-wagon on peeling tape. Mary always tapped the button with a special rhythm so Lovey would know it was she. It usually took Lovey a while to get up and make her way across the room. This time, Mary waited longer than usual. She tried again. Nothing. Maybe her aunt had the TV volume up too high. After a few more tries, Mary used the key Lovey had given her for emergencies. She went upstairs and knocked on Lovey's apartment door. The first thing she noticed was that there was no sound coming from the apartment, no TV. And, again, no answer.

Mary began to worry. Using her second key, she let herself in. As she pushed the door open, she came upon some resistance. Mary cracked the door open enough to squeeze through. The lights were off. She looked around the back of the door and saw that one of the end tables had been pushed up against it. And there was some contraption of string and tape and bent coat hangers that had been affixed to the doorknob.

"Auntie?" Mary called.

She felt a sense of dread. She'd always wondered how it would happen, whether she'd be the one to find her aunt one day cold on the floor. Mary turned on the light.

"Auntie, it's me, Mary. I'm here to take you to the doctor."

No answer. Mary made her way across the room to the kitchen. She touched the teapot and felt it was cold. She was stalling, she knew. Afraid of what she might find. She switched on the overhead light and continued to the bathroom, which was also empty, the sink dry. The bedroom door was slightly ajar. As Mary got closer, she heard Lovey's soft snore. She was alive, at least.

She went to her aunt's bed. The old woman had the covers up to her chin. Her mouth was agape and her flesh was pale. Bobby pins crisscrossed at her temples. Mary placed her hand on her aunt's forehead.

"Auntie, wake up. It's me, Mary."

Lovey stirred. Her eyelids fluttered. Mary nudged her arm and Lovey's eyes opened. A look of distress came over her face; her eyes widened.

"It's okay, you just overslept," Mary said. "I'm sorry I had to come in, but we have a doctor's appointment this morning. Did you forget?"

Lovey drew her arms from under the covers and examined one hand, then the other. Mary thought it strange. Was she still asleep?

"You're not Dorothy," Lovey finally said.

Dorothy was her sister, Mary's grandmother. "No. I'm *Mary,*" Mary said. "You must've been dreaming."

"Of course," Lovey said. She smiled a sad smile. "Dopey me." She seemed to be coming back to herself. "I thought you were Dorothy." She lifted herself up on the pillow. "She's been dead thirty years."

"I'll put on some hot water and wait out here while you get ready," Mary said.

"Should we call and tell them we'll be late?" Lovey asked.

"No, take your time. We'll be fine." Mary left the room. She heard the bedsprings creak. Her aunt was getting up.

"I'm sorry, dear," Lovey called out.

"Don't worry about it," Mary said. "I oversleep all the time." Though she'd never known her aunt to oversleep for an appointment ever in her life. Not once.

Mary put on the water, then went back out to the living room and turned on some lights. She pushed the end table back into the depressions in the carpet and replaced the doily and lamp that were on the floor. Her aunt shuffled out to the bathroom. The fan came on and the door closed.

Mary picked up the coat hanger contraption and noticed the

strings and tape that hung from it. It must've been affixed to the wall and come undone when she pushed her way in. She set it back down on the floor, then clicked on the TV for some background noise. She sat in her aunt's chair, which held the chemical residue of her inexpensive toilet water. On the table beside the chair was an ashtray, which hadn't been used for cigarettes since Lovey quit smoking decades ago. It was filled with quarters for the washer and dryer downstairs. Next to the ashtray were a *TV Guide* and a stack of mail that had already been opened. Mary took it for granted that her aunt had been managing her finances adequately. She'd never asked Mary for help. Now, with all that was going on, Mary wondered how she was really faring. She put aside the feeling that she was invading her aunt's privacy, picked up the pile of mail, and began to thumb through it. There were a few bills—Lovey's electric and cable—which, based upon the balance, must have been paid on time last month. There was a solicitation from the Humane Society thick with cloying kitten and puppy dog mailing labels that had been imprinted with Lovey's full name and address, an attempt to guilt her into sending them a check, particularly if she planned to use them. Mary pulled off a small pack and dropped them into her purse, thinking they might come in handy, making her mailings to Meg Ryder look legitimate at least, since it was likely she'd continue to send the woman cash on Lovey's behalf. As it was, she knew she'd have to write a letter to explain why the workers would be show- ing up at Meg's door with paint and landscaping supplies. The next few envelopes informed Lovey that she had won ten million dollars. *Predators,* Mary thought. *Capitalizing on the unfulfilled dreams of the elderly. They should all burn in hell.* Mary took those three envelopes and dropped them in the trash basket beside the chair. She returned to the pile. That's when she saw the note.

It was a simple, white, card-sized envelope addressed to Lavinia Rollwagon. It had been opened. Mary turned it around and saw the return address. Another Humane Society sticker, this one in the name of Margaret Ryder, with a Bridge Street address.

Mary'd been so engrossed with the envelope that she hadn't even heard the teakettle start to whistle. Lovey came out of the bathroom in a cloud of Jean Naté and hair spray. She already had on her tan stretch pants and navy short-sleeve sweater with the hidden zipper up the back.

"I'll get it," Lovey said. She disappeared into the kitchen.

Mary scrambled to return the pile of mail to the table. While her aunt was fixing tea, she pulled the card out of the envelope. As she opened the card, Dan's hundred-dollar bill fell out onto her lap. There was the M and the sunshine. Mary traced it with her fingers. And there was the phone number. She pulled a pen and a pad of paper out of the table drawer, scrawled down the number, then stuffed the page in her pocket. She read the note:

Dear Mrs. Rollwagon

(She'd gotten the "Mrs." part wrong.)

> *Thank you so much for your kind words and generous gift but I couldn't possibly accept such a large sum of money from someone I don't even know. Please don't be offended or think that I have been in any way. Your outpouring of compassion for a complete stranger is heartwarming. Just understand I'm a woman with little left except my beautiful granddaughter and my old Yankee pride.*
>
> *Sincerely yours,*
> *Meg Ryder*

Mary was dumbfounded. The woman was hardly in a position to be turning away money. She had a little girl to raise without any help. In some way Mary not only understood but admired that she'd returned the gift. After all, her ancestors and Meg's had probably come over on the *Mayflower* together. They had a tradition of stubborn pride to uphold. Yet as happy as Mary was to see the bill returned, she wondered whether Meg might eventually come around. Should Mary go on trying to help the family, or should she let this setback discourage her from doing so? By today, the box of toys would arrive. What kind of grandmother could return those? Though Mary would have to reconsider sending the workers to her house. Meg would probably shoo them right off her property. All this meant was that from now on Mary would need to be more creative, so that Meg didn't feel like a charity case.

Speaking of creative, somehow Meg had found out Lavinia Rollwagon's post office box number, which Mary hadn't included on the sympathy card envelope.

Lovey came from the kitchen carrying a cup to tea. It was made the way Mary liked it, with a little milk. Her aunt was almost ready.

"I just need to finish taking my pills," she said, about to head back to the kitchen. Then she saw the note in Mary's hand. "You know, I think I *must* be losing my mind. I have no recollection of ever sending that woman money."

For another thing, Dr. Green had too much hair. He had what Wayne called "football hair," after the phenomenon of thick-maned coaches like Jimmy Johnson and Mike Ditka. Maybe because Mary didn't like football, her aversion for the hair extended to this neurologist who now sat across from her with his hands folded on the desk. She also couldn't help but notice he'd carried a box of tissues in with him and set them on the desk before he started talking. Not a good sign.

"Of course we don't have all the blood work yet, but I've seen many of these cases, Ms. Hopkins," he said.

"Call me Mary," she said.

"Mary." He took what appeared to be a theatrical breath, one that might signify the deliberate transformation from one character to another, brilliant neurologist to compassionate humanitarian. Or maybe it was part of the whole meditative-labyrinth-as-a-stress-reducer-deep-breathing thing. She tried to take a deep breath herself but couldn't get the air past her throat. "Based on the tests we did today, my diagnosis is midstage Alzheimer's."

"Fuck," Mary said.

He seemed unshaken by the profanity. He reached into a desk drawer. Mary thought she heard bottles clinking, but it was probably just wishful thinking. He pulled out a brochure.

"Start off by reading this," he said. He ran his hand through his hair. "It tells what you need to know about the disease and some of the treatments, and there's a list of Web sites with more information." He pulled out a blue piece of paper. "And here are some local resources." He handed it to Mary. She read the first one: Lower Cape Alzheimer's Caregiver Support Group. This was no club she wanted to be a member of. She folded the paper and stuffed it into the brochure.

"Is that it?" Mary said.

"Here are a couple of prescriptions." He pulled a slip of paper out of his shirt pocket and handed it to her. "We'll start her on these. An antidepressant and another for a drug that reduces the breakdown of acetylcholine in the brain. For some, it slows down the progression of the disease. It might give her more time."

Since he'd brought it up: "How much time does she have?"

"Given that she's eighty-six, my best guess is about three years." He tilted his head. He must've learned that move in compassion class.

"Three years. So this will eventually kill her?"

"At her age, anything could kill her. This is just assuming the disease is allowed to run its course," he said.

"But Alzheimer's *kills* people? I just thought it turned their brains to mush."

"You can find all that information on those Web sites." He tapped the desk.

"But you're her doctor and I'm sitting here in your office, so why don't you tell me?"

Maybe he wasn't used to being challenged. He drew the labyrinth toward him and started running his finger through the sand. He spoke over the crunching sound. "In advanced cases, it can lead to pneumonia, blood clots, malnutrition, infection. Sometimes treatment for these things prolongs life, but by then, the patient is already gone." He looked up at her and tapped his temple, leaving a residue of labyrinth sand on his skin. "You'll need to talk to your aunt about what her end-of-life wishes are. You should do this sooner rather than later."

"I believe her end-of-life wishes are for her life not to end," Mary said.

Mary and Lovey didn't say anything for the first five minutes of the ride home. Mary thought Lovey might be nervous about hearing what the doctor had said. But as she kept driving, Mary realized it was as if her aunt had already forgotten where they'd been, and was now merely engrossed with flattening the ears of the red bear against her knee with her palms.

"Guess what," Mary finally said.

"What?" Lovey said.

"You get another couple of pills to take in the morning."

"That's all?" Lovey asked.

"That's all," Mary replied.

"And what about the break-ins? What does he plan to do about those?"

Mary looked over at her. Lovey's expression had soured.

"This morning when I let myself in the apartment," Mary said, "I noticed the end table had been pushed up to the door. And there was that hanger thing—"

"When nobody believes you, you have to solve problems for yourself." Lovey sat the bear squarely on her lap, like it was just she and the bear against the world. Mary had been lumped into the category of nonbelievers. "That's my burglar detector."

Mary felt terrible. "How does it work?"

"Simple. If I wake up and the tape is unstuck or the table's been moved, I know someone's been in the apartment."

"Has it ever been moved when you got up?"

Lovey looked down at the bear. "They're clever, is all I'll say. They seem always to be one step ahead."

Mary reached over and squeezed her aunt's hand. It was cool and veiny. "This morning you called me Dorothy. Do you remember?"

Lovey gave her a blank look. Then her face lit up. "I dreamt your mother and I—"

"You mean my *grandmother.*"

Lovey looked confused. Then her face relaxed. "Of course. Your *grandmother* and I had been given a nickel by our father to go down to the neighborhood tavern. He sent us down there all the time to pick up a cold beer from the tap. Back then children were allowed to do such things. Dorothy was the oldest, so she always got to carry the stein. Usually when we got to the top of the stairs to our apartment, Dorothy would open the metal lid and draw some of the foam off the top; only, in the dream, this time she let me do it. And she was laughing at my white moustache." She stopped and looked wistful. "And that's when I woke up. I can't explain it but I felt like I was right there, like I was young again. I get those dreams sometimes. They seem so real I have to check myself when I wake up to see if it's true." She pinched the skin on her forearm. The skin stayed pinched even after she took her fingers away.

A few moments went by; then Mary asked. "Do you think about dying, Auntie? Are you afraid of it?"

"I used to think about it all the time. And then I made my peace with it. And that was that."

"How did you do that?"

"I've lived a good long life." Lovey had raised her finger to emphasize each syllable. "Most of the people I've known and loved—Dorothy, your grandfather, Claire, Tom, old friends, relatives—they're long gone. I think what it might be like to see them again. And I know they've all gone through it, and that it's part of nature. So, no, I'm not afraid. You never need to feel sorry for me when the time comes," she said. She put her hand on Mary's wrist.

Mary felt the tear-making twinge at the back of her throat. Did those words sound like they'd come from a person who was losing her mind? Did Lovey sound like someone with Alzheimer's disease?

Hardly. At that moment, she had sounded more sane and enlightened than anyone Mary had ever known. To hell with the Darlene and the doctors. What if they were wrong? What people Lovey's age didn't get a little forgetful now and then?

With renewed hope, Mary drove on. They rode the next few miles in silence. Then, as the exit sign approached, Lovey said, "Will Robbie be meeting us at the apartment?" She reached down for her purse. "We'll get some Chinese. My treat."

Mary looked at her aunt, who'd begun humming. A skip in the tape. A scratch in the DVD and fourteen years erased. As they drove through town, Mary almost let herself believe Robbie would be waiting there in his truck with a bottle of schnapps for his favorite girls, flashing his handsome smile. She had no choice but to believe it.

"You . . . have . . . seven . . . new . . . messages. . . . Thursday, nine sixteen a.m." Beep.

"I'm calling for Mary Hopkins. This is Darlene Snow from Nauset Senior Housing. I'm just following up on our conversation over a week ago to see if you had the opportunity to take your aunt to the doctor. (Have a seat, Mrs. Deschamps, and I'll be right with you. Here, have a Tic Tac.) Her calls to me about the break-ins haven't abated and—(No, Mrs. Deschamps, there *hasn't* been a break-in. Just hang on.) Anyhow, it seems she's now got it into her head that our maintenance man is coming in and— (No, no. Bruce did *not* break in to anyone's—Mrs. Deschamps, where are you going?) Oh, for heaven's sake. I have to go, but please call me back. As you can see, she's disrupting the whole complex. This can't continue." *Click.*

"Thursday, nine forty-two a.m." Beep.

"This is Amy from Dr. Needleman's office calling to let you know we have the results from Miss Rollwagon's blood tests. Everything came back normal. If you have any questions, please call the office." *Click.*

"Thursday, ten twenty a.m." Beep.

"It's me, Ernie. Goddamn refrigerator truck broke down on 93 on the way home from the Sox game last night. But don't worry. Got my buddy, Gus, coming by with some nice top-haul tuna this afternoon. And don't let the dreadlocks fool you—he bathes! (*Guffaw.*)" *Click.*

"*Thursday, ten thirty-three a.m.*" *Beep.*

"Mary, this is Sage. Hope wanted me to call you because she's afraid you'll kill her. ['Don't say it like *that*!'] Your fisherman friend came back this morning when we were setting up and she gave him your home phone number. It was a stupid thing to do, everyone here agrees, but just don't kill her, okay? Bye. ['Omigod, Sage. I cannot *believe* you—']" *Click.*

"*Thursday, eleven oh four a.m.*" *Beep.*

"Hey, Sunshine. Must seem strange hearing from me after all this time. When I learned about the kid and how she died, I just thought you might be reliving some stuff. Guess I'd been thinking about you anyway. Always do this time of year. Well, I'll stop harassing you. If you wanna talk, you got my number." *Click.*

"*Thursday, eleven sixteen a.m.*" *Beep.*

"Ernie again. Gus's goddamn brother fell off a ladder and broke his collarbone. So he won't be dropping off the fish. But I'll figure something out, don't worry." *Click.*

"*Thursday, eleven thirty-six a.m.*" *Beep.*

"Mary, it's Maureen. Wayne wants to know if you're ever coming in. And he's swearing at us in Chinese again."

Mary had had every intention of being at the restaurant by nine that morning. But driving through town on her way to work, she'd made her routine detour past Meg Ryder's house only to find, for the first time, both Meg and Ariel out on the front lawn. The actual sight of the two of them took her by surprise.

By the time she turned into the parking lot at the end of the street, her hands were shaking. She pulled into a spot in front of the medical supply store—in its window, a display of three-footed canes, wheelchairs, and plastic raised toilet seats. She thought of Lovey, and wondered when the medication Dr. Green had prescribed would kick in. Mary wondered whether she'd even notice a difference. He'd said the stuff worked on *some* patients. Not all. Mary just hoped it would ease her aunt's paranoia and give her a little more time in her apartment. Then again, they hadn't heard back on those blood tests yet. Maybe they would pick up on something else entirely, something treatable, reversible. Mary could still cling to that. In the meantime, she just had to stall Darlene. And pray that Lovey's brain wasn't like a tire with a slow leak, words, memories, and faces seeping out until one day there'd be nothing left.

Mary pushed Lovey out of her mind. She got out of the car and started walking down Bridge Street. She didn't have a plan. She'd worry about that once she got there.

A canopy of trees darkened the sidewalk. Honeysuckle and roses filled the breeze with their perfume, the sea air mingling with the sweetness, the scent permeating her flesh, ushering in a sense of well-being. Here she was, just enjoying her town on a fine summer morning without any ulterior motive at all.

The sidewalk was buckled and badly in need of repair. Mary had to watch not to trip on the chunks of concrete. Further down, a colony of ants swarmed the surface. Navigating the sidewalk and avoiding the insects kept her from worrying about what she might say or do when she got to the house. What was it that fueled the compulsion to get out of her car? What morbid curiosity? Was she just doing this to punish herself for never really knowing Anicca? Or was there something more to it? All she knew was that it had felt good sending the money to Meg and the toys to Ariel, better in some way than when she sent donations to the Lower Cape Outreach Council, the Animal Rescue League, the Wellfleet Harbor Actors Theater, and the Audubon Society, all worthy recipients. It wasn't as though she was unaccustomed to giving. She'd bought her share of Girl Scout cookies, veterans' poppies, and brightly colored rubber band bracelets in her lifetime, and made generous contributions on behalf of the restaurant to the fire department, when they were funding the new firehouse, and to the Cape Cod Museum of Art, the Provincetown Center for Coastal Studies . . . The list went on. But this was different, more personal. Actually choosing the toys and packing them up for the little girl, imagining what she might like to play with, imaging her delight in opening the package had made Mary *feel* something—just the littlest *something*—which was a welcome change from the usual emptiness in her heart, the blanket of *nothing* she wrapped herself in on the nights she didn't try to fill the void with work. But nothing ever filled it completely; there were always gaps and fissures that let the *nothing* back in.

Fourteen years ago, Mary's husband had died the exact same way Anicca had, on the same road, even, wrapping his Jeep around a tree after having too much to drink. His death had left so many unanswered questions, things Mary had nearly come to accept she'd never know. And now here was Meg Ryder, just setting off on this same journey with her own questions and her own set of regrets. In some way now Mary felt drawn to the pain, the rawness of it, which over the years for her had morphed into something different and flat, more chronic than stabbing. How would Meg handle this? How would she deal with those feelings of anger and abandonment?

For Mary, losing Robbie had been so different from the deaths of her parents. Robbie's end had been senseless; he'd brought it upon himself. This time, Mary couldn't even blame God. There was no one to blame but Robbie, which seemed cruel considering the price he'd paid for his mistake. And so she'd blamed herself. Maybe she'd been too hard on him. She should have recognized his addiction and tried to help instead of just chastising him. She shouldn't have let him go that night.

What about Meg? Did she bear the weight of some responsibility too? Was she tormented by it? How would she grieve? Would her age provide some insight? Was there some important step toward self-forgiveness that Mary had missed? Some cathartic session of screaming into a pillow? Some symbolic ritual of release?

The closer Mary drew to the house, the more selfish and voyeuristic the intrusion seemed. There was the child on a white blanket on the lawn, stretching a bracelet of pink beads around her toes. Meg had her back to the street and didn't see Mary approaching. There was still time to turn around.

Just as Mary was deciding to retreat, one of her low heels caught a crack. She saw the ground move closer, time stretching out before her in slow motion. She let out a cry. She held out her hands to break her fall, felt the raw heat on the heels of her palms as they scraped the concrete. Her right knee connected with the ground, then her left. There she was, sprawled on the sidewalk. For how long? Seconds? Minutes? She scrambled to her feet and looked up. Meg was approaching. She had the baby on her hip. Mary felt blood oozing from her right knee.

"Are you okay?" Meg asked.

"I'm fine, thanks," Mary answered. She brushed some grit from her hands. There was a tear at the seam of her jean skirt. "Just clumsy."

"You're bleeding," Meg said. "Come, let's get that cleaned up." Meg's hair was only partly gray, but when Mary got up close she could see the flesh around her eyes scored from years of sun, and the skin above the cheeks hanging in pouches, as if tears might have collected there. There were broken blood vessels all around the woman's nose and cheeks, and her eyes were bloodshot. She had on a yellow T-shirt tucked into a pair of pleated khaki shorts that came belted high to her waist, accentuating the breadth of her abdomen—a comfortable lap for a toddler.

"No need. I'm fine, really," Mary said.

"Nonsense. In another second you'll be bleeding into your sandals. Let me at least get you some paper towels and a Band-Aid," Meg said. Then she turned toward the house. "Come," she directed.

Mary followed. They walked across the lawn toward the door at the side of the house, where a rhododendron bush had burst into cheery purple blooms, as if no one had suggested it might tone it down this year, given the circumstances. Mary noticed some rotting wood at the base of the door, and the chain at the top of the screen door that was broken. Meg pulled on the door handle.

"I can wait out here," Mary said. "I hate to bother you."

"Don't be silly," Meg said. There was a curtness to her tone. Someone who didn't know what the woman had endured these last two weeks might have taken it the wrong way, perhaps attributing it to her feeling put-upon.

Mary stepped inside. The shades on the front windows were drawn, so it took a moment for Mary's eyes to adjust to the dark. The kitchen opened onto a dining area furnished with a round oak table and chairs. There was a small living room to the right. And then there were the flowers, at least seven or eight baskets and vases of half-dead blooms on the kitchen counter and table, giving off the cloying scent of decay.

"Don't mind the flowers," Meg said. She offered no further explanation. She set Ariel down on a blanket near the table, then went to the kitchen, pulled some paper towels off the roll, and handed them to Mary.

"Thanks," Mary said. "I really appreciate this." She pressed them to her knee.

"Have a seat and I'll get you something to clean it out with," Meg said. She pointed to one of the chairs at the table. Mary stepped around the little girl. As she did, she recognized the toys on the blanket as the ones she had sent, a pyramid of colorful plastic doughnuts and a toy beagle with a red pull cord. Ariel picked up the dog and held it like a baby in her arms.

"She's beautiful," Mary said to the child.

Meg must have thought she was talking about Ariel. "She's a good girl," she said from the sink, where she was wetting another wad of paper towels, adding a little soap from a Walt Disney Little Mermaid dispenser. Mary made the connection. Ariel had been named for the cartoon mermaid. Anicca would have been a young girl when the movie first came out. "Her name is Ariel. And mine is Meg. You look a little familiar. Think I've probably seen you around town."

"I'm sure," Mary said. She almost offered her name and then thought better of it. She didn't want the woman to know she'd been Anicca's boss. "I'm Hope," she said, with no idea what had possessed her, out of the infinite possibilities, to choose that one.

"Another Hope," Meg said. "Unusual name. You're the second I've met these last couple weeks." *How stupid,* Mary thought. Hope had gone to the funeral. Meg brought the bunch of wet towels over to Mary. "Let's take a look."

The two women examined Mary's knee. It was a deep scrape but nothing too bad. "Just clean it out good and then apply a little pressure," Meg said. "Those damn sidewalks. I keep writing letters, trying to get the town to fix them. Of course, Bridge Street isn't such a priority, if you know what I mean. We're zoned commercial. But there are still children living on this street. They ride their bikes on the sidewalk. It isn't safe." Meg took an arrangement of wilted irises off the table to make more room for Mary. "Where do you live?"

Mary cringed. "On the bay side," she said.

"Pretty there," Meg said, rather absently. "I'll go get some Band-Aids. Just keep an eye on the baby, will you?"

"Sure thing," Mary said.

As soon as Meg started up the stairs, the little girl stood up. She looked at the stairs, then at Mary, and decided to stay and take her chances. She took a step toward Mary and pointed to her knee and the bloody paper towels.

"A boo-boo," Mary said.

Ariel nodded. She was a lovely little thing, with a crown of blond wisps. Her cheeks were full and pink and her nose had a slight up-turn to it. Her fingernails had at one time been painted pink, though now only chips of color remained. Mary wondered if Anicca had been the one to paint them and perhaps the grandmother now couldn't bring herself to take the nail polish off.

Ariel stared at the strange lady in her kitchen. The crotch of the child's pink tights dipped below the light blue cotton skirt. She turned, knelt down on the blanket, picked up the dog pull toy, and handed it to Mary. Mary noticed teeth marks in the black vinyl ears.

"Can you show me how it works?" Mary said. She handed the toy back to Ariel.

"Where are those Band-Aids? I know I bought a new box," Meg said from upstairs.

Ariel put the dog on the blanket, grabbed hold of the cord, and pulled. She looked at Mary for approval and so didn't notice she was headed for the corner of the dividing wall between the dining and living areas.

"Watch out, honey," Mary warned. But it was too late. Ariel bumped her head and fell. She began to cry, reminding Mary how the toddler had cried at the funeral. Mary flew up and took her in her arms.

"What happened?" Meg called from upstairs.

"She's fine. She was just showing me her pull toy and she bumped into the wall." Ariel had already stopped crying. She put her thumb into her mouth and nestled into Mary's lap. Mary smelled the top of her head, a mingling of baby shampoo and maple syrup. Mary wiped a tear from beneath the girl's eye with her thumb. Ariel put her hand on Mary's forearm. Mary felt the heat rise to her face. She had no business here. What right did she have to be holding this beautiful child while her poor mother was in the ground? Mary felt an incredible urge to run out of there, and an equally strong opposing force to sit there with the girl in her arms for as long as she possibly could.

A door opened upstairs. "Okay, *here* they are," Meg said. "I'll be right down, Hope."

Mary looked down at the toddler. The neckband of her shirt was stretched in such a way that Mary could see the birthmark on her neck. Not a whale like her mother's, a shape much less distinct, but in exactly the same spot. An angel kiss.

Meg came down the stairs. She took the child and handed Mary a Band-Aid. The bleeding had almost stopped. Mary applied the strip and stood to go.

"Would you like some coffee?" Meg asked.

Mary assumed she was just being polite. "No, thanks, I should get going."

"It's no trouble, really. I was going to put on a pot myself," Meg said.

Mary got the sense that the woman wanted the company. And Mary was in no hurry to leave. Something about being in this house, the peaceful dimness of it, with its stained window trim and kitchen cabinets, gingham curtains, stenciled wallpaper boarders, and spider plants hanging from the ceiling made Mary feel at home, as if this would have been an interior she could have pictured herself in had she seen it advertised for sale at the back of the local paper. And so she stayed and the two women talked until Ariel fell asleep on her blanket and Meg eventually got around to explaining the flowers and sympathy cards lined up like holiday greetings on the mantel. She talked a little about Anicca, who Mary learned had dropped out of Pine Manor College two summers before Ariel was born, and how Anicca's own parents had died in a boating accident as well, confirming Nate's story. Meg talked about her son, Anicca's father, and how she herself had grown up outside of Worcester and lived there most of her life, and how her family had owned a lumber company that went under, which was why she ended up working at Quanset's when she moved down to the Cape for good after her son and his wife died. And she told about the enormous outpouring of support from the community, both this time and when the first accident happened while she was still living off-Cape, and how it had gotten no easier to be on the receiving end of that kind of generosity. Mary tried to convince Meg it was okay to accept help from others, for Ariel's sake at least, though deep down she understood the woman's reluctance.

At some point, Mary looked at her watch and realized she'd spent her whole morning there at Meg's table. Back at the restaurant, lunch was under way. Mary needed to go. First she needed to go home and change out of the torn skirt. People were probably wondering where she was, though the sad thing about her life—one of the sad things—was that it was likely no one particularly cared.

"Thanks for dropping by, Hope," Meg said. "Literally, I mean. I'm pretty sure today was going to be one of those days where the mind just spirals. I'd felt it from the moment I opened my eyes. The distraction was what I needed."

"Happy to oblige," Mary said. "And I still have a fresh knee to donate to the cause next time you're feeling down."

The two women looked down at Mary's knees and laughed. Ariel stirred on her blanket.

"I mean it. Drop in anytime," Meg said. "No bleeding necessary."

"Thanks, I will." Mary liked her. "And in case there's anything I can do for you, let me give you my number. She picked up the pen on the kitchen counter and scrawled her home phone number. She handed it to Meg. Then she took another look at Ariel, how her eyes were moving under their lids and her breath came deep from her belly.

"Bye, sweetie," Mary whispered. Then she left.

Eight

Now Mary stood in her bedroom in her torn skirt listening to the long string of phone messages, the pounds per square inch of pressure in her jaw intensifying with each. She felt a migraine coming on. And then there was Dan's voice. When he stopped, she played it again. And again.

Twelve years hadn't changed the sound of his voice at all, except that maybe there was a little more gravel to it, and a little more bass, as if the body that voice now came from had grown larger, as he had in her mind, taking up even more space, as any of the ghosts of one's past loom large.

Dan had heard about Anicca's death and had thought of her. He said he thought of her *every* year at this time. All he did was *think*. He'd never bothered to do anything about it. Sure he cared, just not enough. By the third playback, Mary felt the anger stirring up the coffee and soggy vanilla wafers in her belly. And then there was Ernie again. It seemed as if she might have to call Dan whether she wanted to or not.

She had Dan's number tacked to the fridge with the "Jesus loves you, everyone else thinks you're an asshole" magnet one of her employees had given her a couple of summers ago. (As a joke, she hoped.) But every time she thought about calling, she had no idea what to say. She didn't want to talk about Robbie or waitresses or car accidents or even fish. So then what was there to talk about? She could have thanked him for the money, which now sat in Lovey's wallet, Lovey having made the reasonable assumption that the money had been returned to her and therefore must have been sent by her.

And then there was that last message about Wayne, who was evidently having a meltdown. She had to get to the restaurant.

• • •

In the end it was this that made her fall to pieces: not that their marriage had been a failure, or that Robbie's death seemed senseless, or that he'd died at all. It was his ashes.

After a long, happy life together, when one of them died, the ashes were to be saved to be mingled with the ashes of the other, and then sprinkled out at sea in a symbolic gesture of the two becoming one for all of eternity, impossible to tell where one ended and the other began. A molecule of his ankle and a bit of her lip. His cheek and her heart. His eye and her hair. Together in one final testament to their union before being scattered to the wind.

But when Robbie died, his mother begged that he receive a "decent Christian burial." She needed a place to visit her son, just as she'd needed the roadside memorial and the candles that she kept lit until the town eventually lost patience. In the end, Mary didn't have the heart to deny the woman. But it scared Mary, the idea of being sprinkled alone. And it scared her even more, the idea of being stuck in the cold ground next to Robbie.

Robbie was late. He was supposed to meet her at the restaurant at six with a couple of lobsters from the pier. They were going to have dinner together for the first time in weeks. Mary had turned the heater on in the dining room and lit a few candles for atmosphere. After two hours, one had already burned through its wick. This was exactly the kind of thing she'd planned to have out with him that night. She'd be damned if this season ended up like last. Here it was only May second and, from the looks of things, Robbie was well on his way to picking up where he'd left off, already shirking his responsibilities, avoiding her, not telling her where he was going, staggering into the bedroom at ungodly hours, comatose till noon.

This afternoon, he was supposed to meet with a restaurant supplier about a new grill, then get a wholesale price from the farmers' market on their corn, and, finally, swing by the pier for the lobsters before heading back. How much was she willing to bet he'd never even made it to see the supplier? Mary was seething. Unless he had some fantastic excuse, this was it, the last straw. A familiar place, "the Last Straw." She had been here countless times before. She knew the menu, the sawdust on the floor, the initials carved into the tables, and the shape of the bar stools, all of which by now were molded to the shape of her own seat. She knew all the words to the songs on the jukebox by heart. The bartender always knew what to pour. At the Last Straw she could feast on self-pity, maybe with a side of worry to satisfy that pressure behind her sternum and the buzzing in her ears. It was here where she could rehearse her script for the upcoming scene where he came home late or intoxicated or both and she threatened to walk out on him. The Last Straw. It had certainly become one of her haunts.

Well, what if this really was the last straw? Why did she always renege on her threats? How much of it was love and how much fear? Fear of everything, of being alone, of having to run the place by herself, not that she wasn't doing that already. It was her fears she was contemplating when his Jeep pulled into the parking lot. He parked in his usual spot and even remembered to turn off the lights. Then he got out and walked a straight line to the dining room. He seemed sober. So if he hadn't been off drinking, what was his excuse?

"I'm sorry," he said. "I was in the shower when I remembered I was supposed to meet you here."

"You were at the house?" she said. She tried to keep her voice from shaking.

"I was watching the game. Fucking Sox. Lost in the tenth." He went behind the bar and took a cold beer out of the case. His hair was still wet, brown waves spinning to the base of his neck. Mary had always loved the look of his hair wet. "Want one?" Then he must've seen the wine bottle. "Never mind. You got a head start, huh? So what's for dinner?" He came up and gave her a peck on the cheek.

Mary was dumbfounded. "Where are the lobsters?" she asked.

"Lobsters?"

"The ones you were supposed to pick up at the pier after you talked to Edna across the street about the corn."

"Man," he said. He sat down at the table with the candles and shook his head.

"You did talk to Edna, right?" Mary said.

"Want me to go get some takeout?" he said. He started to get up.

"Don't even think about going anywhere," she said. "We've gotta talk, Robbie."

He slid back into the seat and put away the first beer in a few long gulps. "In that case, I'll need another." He got up and revisited the cooler, pulling out another long-necked bottle and snapping off the cap under the bar.

"What the hell's wrong with you, Robbie? I mean, do you happen to see what's been going on around here? I do *everything*. I ask you to take care of a few simple things and you fuck up every time." She paced.

"You own a seafood restaurant, Mary. You can have lobster whenever you want. You can have it every night all summer," he said. He wrapped his lips around the bottle and took a swig. "What's the big deal?"

"That's not the point." She glared at him.

"Yeah, what *is* the point?" He glared back.

"You're a shitty partner, Robbie. And I don't just mean at the restaurant." Mary turned and walked toward the back of the dining room. The silence followed her.

"What are you saying?"

Mary heard the chair screech against the concrete floor. She stopped and turned. "What do you think I'm saying?"

He was standing. "I guess you're saying I'm a piece of shit all the way around."

"Look," she said, "you drink too damn much. You drink all the time now, every night, just about." Mary straightened a chair under one of the tables.

"Look who's talking." He nodded toward the open bottle on the bar.

It was true. She had been drinking more lately. But she didn't *need* it. It was something she enjoyed at the end of the day, something that helped her deal with Robbie. If anything, it was he who'd gotten her started.

"We're not talking about me," she said. "I'm talking about you and how each year it gets worse. Who wants a husband who passes out on the couch and snores his head off, when he comes home at all? Who wants a guy who can't string two sentences together half the time, but just sits there with that shit-eating smirk on his face?" She looked at Robbie. He had that smirk on now, and had his arms crossed in defiance. So she lashed harder. "You're no good to me here either. I can't count on you to do anything. No one around here has any respect for you." *Except Dan,* she thought. And why in the world was that? Robbie treated him like garbage too. Sometimes she wished she'd gone into business with Dan instead of Robbie. Sometimes she wished she'd never married Robbie at all.

"Fine." He smiled. His voice was calm. "So I'm no good." He reached in his pocket and pulled out his keys, then finished the rest of his beer. Mary watched his Adam's apple dip and rise. "I guess I'll be going." He tossed his second empty toward the trash bin by the waitress station at the bar and missed. The glass hit the floor and shattered. "Shit," he said. The smile was gone.

"That's just great," Mary said.

"Relax. I'll clean it up. Where's the broom?"

Mary reacted like someone had stuck her with a pin. "*See?* You don't even know where the broom is! This is *your* restaurant. You should know where the fucking broom is, Robbie." She was practically shrieking.

He put his hands up to his ears, "For Christ's sake, chill out," he said. "You're acting like some kinda psycho."

"*I'm* psycho? Because I expect my husband and business partner to pull his weight around here? That makes me *psycho*? This is the last straw, Robbie. I mean it. I've had it." Mary marched behind the bar and retrieved a dustpan and brush. "First thing tomorrow, I'm calling a lawyer."

"Right, sure." He started for the door. "Do what you need to do. I'll see you later. Sorry about the bottle. And about dinner. I truly am."

"Where are you going?" Mary said.

"Out," he said as he opened the screen door. He let it bang shut behind him. She heard his feet crunch the shells on his way to the car. He was practically jogging to get away from her.

"When are you coming back?" she called after him.

"What difference does it make?" The Jeep door opened. She heard the vehicle settle with his weight as he got in.

"You didn't have dinner," she called from the door. "At least eat something."

"I'll get something out," he said. He started the engine. The lights turned on. She heard the radio. The song playing was "Hot Blooded," by Foreigner.

"And another thing," she yelled out the door, though she knew he couldn't hear her anymore. "We never throw bottles in the trash. There's a deposit, you shithead." She knelt down and starting picking up the large shards.

And those were her last words to her husband. She'd called him a shithead.

"You call this top-haul? Will somebody please tell me how this can be considered top-haul tuna?" Wayne was standing in the middle of the kitchen waving a cleaver over his head when Mary walked in. There was a slab of tuna meat on the counter. It looked like a chunk of torso. Like maybe Wayne had finally snapped and filleted a waitress.

"What's going on?" Mary demanded. She set her purse down on her stool. She'd come back wearing long pants to hide the Band-Aid on her knee. "Wayne, how many times have I told you not to wave the knives?"

"Well, look who decided to show up." Wayne said. He was the only one who dared say it.

"Wayne, your face is all screwed up like a monkey's ass," Sage said. She was standing by the chowder pot. Mary noticed she was wearing lip gloss.

Wayne looked at Sage and his face unfurled. He set the cleaver on the counter.

"The tuna came?" Mary asked. "Ernie left me a message saying he had trouble with his—"

"It came, all right," Nate said. He was standing by the basement stairs.

"What does 'top-haul' mean anyway?" one of the order line girls asked.

"It's supposed to be the last catch before the boat comes ashore. The stuff at the top of the hold. You pay more for it 'cause it's supposed to be fresher," Nate said.

"Look at this," Wayne said. He slid the raw meat toward Mary. Maureen leaned in. "It's practically gray. And it stinks."

Maureen stuck her nose down near it and sniffed. "It doesn't *stink*."

"If I can smell it at all, it stinks," Wayne said. He was rotating his wrists, like he was loosening them up, getting ready to knock someone out. Mary figured it had something to do with his synesthesia and the smell.

"Who dropped it off?" she asked.

"Nobody saw," Nate said.

"I'm not serving this. Forget about it," Wayne said. He went back behind the counter. Mary saw him look up to see if Sage was still there, but she'd gone.

"Nobody's asking you to," Mary said.

"What are you going to do?" Nate asked. Like he was nervous she might overreact or do something crazy.

"I'll handle it," she said. Mary grabbed her handbag.

She stepped around Nate and went up the stairs to her office. The pile of mail on her desk had grown. Between doctors' visits with Lovey and stalking the Bridge Street house, she'd been neglecting her bookkeeping. She picked up the phone and dialed.

"Hello?"

"Ernie, this is Mary."

"Hey, doll. Did you get your fish?" he asked.

She took a deep breath. "What we got this morning wasn't top-haul, Ernie."

"Sure it was. I seen it come off the boat."

"Not only do we pay a premium for top-haul, it's the only thing we've ever served here at the Clambake, which is why customers keep coming back year after year." *The ones who don't end up puking in the hydrangeas.*

"I hear you. You want me to see what I can do?" Ernie said.

"No thanks, Ernie. I've *seen* what you can do. This is it. Our business relationship is over. That was your last shipment. Bill me and we're done," she said. And she hadn't so much as raised her voice.

She couldn't say the same for him. "Are you out of your mind? It's Fourth of July weekend."

"Yes, I'm out of my mind," she said. "But I'd rather serve hamburgers than the crap you bring us. Good-bye, Ernie." She hung up.

There, it was done. Mary felt good. That wasn't so hard. The feeling good lasted three or four minutes. She shuffled a few papers on her desk. Opened a few envelopes. Then reality set in. Fourth of July was upon them and she had no fish. This was one of her biggest weekends. Not only that, but it was the beginning of the summer crush of tourists. If word got around about her troubles, she'd be poison all summer.

She knew what she had to do. It didn't matter that Dan's number was still on the fridge back home. When she'd gotten it back, she'd committed it to memory. Now she knew if she gave herself too much time to think, she'd chicken out. So she picked up the phone and started dialing. It was early afternoon; he was probably still out on the boat, out of cell phone range. She hoped she'd just get his voice mail.

"Hello," the voice said.

Shit. "Dan?" She blanked. *What should I say?*

"Who's this?"

"It's Mary."

He chuckled. "I was beginning to lose faith."

"Lose faith?" What kind of thing was that to say? "Lose faith in *what?*"

"Old friends, I guess. So how've you been?"

"You heard about Anicca," she said. "Thanks for stopping by. I appreciate that. And the money for her fund." She was all over the place. "Thanks for that too."

"Felt sorry about the girl. Just thought it might've dredged up some stuff for you too."

"I suppose it did." *All kinds of stuff. And people too.*

"I think about him a lot, even still. It's weird. All these years later. He was like a brother," Dan said. "Always felt like I should've done something more to help him."

"There's nothing you could have done that you didn't try," she said. "Remember, I'm the one who drove him to drink that night."

"You're not still thinking about it like that, are you?"

"Sometimes," she said. "I can't help it."

"Spent a lot of nights trying to talk you out of it."

Mary thought about those nights, maybe not in the way he was referring to them. She shivered. "Is Robbie all you think about?" She couldn't believe those words had escaped her lips. She felt herself flush.

He didn't answer right away. "I think about you too, if that's what you mean."

"That's not at all what I meant," she backpedaled. "What I meant was, we used to have fun, the three of us."

He laughed. "Nice save," he said.

"It wasn't a *save,* I'm in a bind."

"Really?" His tone changed.

Nice save, Mary, she thought. "You know Ernie Smith?"

"'Fraid so."

"I fired him."

"He's your fish guy?" Dan said it like he knew what a bad choice it was.

"Not anymore." Mary took a breath. "I just got off the phone with him."

"You fired your fish guy on the Thursday before the Fourth?"

"Well, like I said. I'm in a bind."

He laughed. "Oh, Sunshine, that temper of yours. You haven't changed a bit."

She felt her spine straighten. "I didn't yell at him at all. In fact, I didn't even raise my voice."

"But you fired him."

"Well, yeah."

"A little impulsive, don't you think?"

"Maybe."

"And now you're wondering if I can help you out?"

"Look, I don't even know what you do for a living anymore. But you were the best fish guy I ever had. If you can help me, great. If you can't, no hard feelings." He didn't say anything. Mary took it as a no. "Just forget it. I'm sorry I even bothered you."

"Hey, slow down," he said. "I was just thinking what I could do. And for the record, I was the one who bothered *you*."

"That's right. How come?"

"I told you *how come*."

"I suspect not *all* of 'how come.'"

Now he was the one at a loss for words. "Why don't we pick a place to meet and let's talk about what you need to get you through the weekend. I can meet you after six."

"Tonight?" Mary said. She panicked.

"It's *Thursday*, darlin'," he said. "Weekend starts tomorrow."

"Okay, sure. Where do you want to meet?"

"You want me to come there?"

She thought about all the busybodies in the kitchen who knew there'd been some history with Dan that they'd have no trouble embellishing. It would be all over the joint. "Not here." And she didn't want to invite him over to her place. Might give him the idea this was something more than business. "I know. How about the bar at the Triple Pagoda?"

"Ever wonder how many multimillion-dollar deals are struck over scorpion bowls?"

"If it's multimillions you're looking for, you're in trouble," she said.

"It'll be nice to see you again."

Mary had three hours. Just enough time to send Nate to the fish market before dinner, for her to check in on her aunt, and then to figure out how the hell she was going to erase twelve years from her face.

Wayne's truck smelled like smoke and fryer grease. A jade ornament in the shape of a bat hung on a red cord from the rearview mirror. There were fishing lures on the dashboard and a half-eaten bag of potato chips on the seat. The rugs were so sandy she could barely tell what color they were. Still, she was grateful he'd let her borrow it. The last thing she needed was for Darlene to spot her car in the parking lot. What would Mary say to her? The blood tests coming back clean pointed even more definitively to the Alzheimer's diagnosis. To the inevitability that her aunt was losing her mind. If that was the case, Darlene had made it clear she wanted Lovey out. Mary needed to buy some time to figure out what to do next.

Once Mary had thought of asking Wayne for the truck, she found him out back on a cigarette break after the lunch shift had finished.

"Sure, take it. Keys are under the seat," he said.

"Thanks," she said. She turned to go.

"Hey," Wayne said. "If you don't mind my asking, what's up with you these days? You've been AWOL. Is it the Anicca thing?"

Or the *Dan* thing? Or the *Alzheimer's* thing? Or the *fish* thing, which she didn't dare bring up. "It's my aunt," Mary said. She sat down on the granite step beside Wayne. "She's losing her *points*."

"Huh?"

"They think she has Alzheimer's."

"That's awful."

"Let me bum one of those," Mary said.

Wayne pulled the pack of cigarettes out of his pocket and shook one out. Mary put it between her lips and he lit it for her. The door behind them opened. It was Nate. He seemed startled to see Wayne and Mary there.

"Oh, hey," Nate said.

"Hey," Mary said. "Maureen's not out here."

"Okay, thanks," Nate said. He closed the door.

"What's up with you two?" Wayne said. "Don't tell me it's over already."

"What are you talking about?" Mary said. "There was never any *it*." She flicked the cigarette, even though there was no ash yet. "He's half my age."

"He was making progress," Wayne said. He grinned.

Mary's face felt hot. "Puh-leeze." She glanced toward the door. "Did you know he's been going out with Maureen on and off since they were in third grade?" Mary said.

"*Kitchen* Maureen?" Wayne said. "Think you've reached a new level of hallucination."

"It's *true*," Mary said. "He told me. And they're on again, by the way. I caught them in the basement."

Wayne turned to her. His eyes opened wide, wide for him. "You're serious."

"Completely."

"Fascinating." He rubbed the whiskers on his chin. "And you're okay with this?"

Mary grabbed a handful of pebbles and sifted them through her fingers as she spoke. "You mean that policy I have about coworkers not dating? As if anyone has ever paid attention to it. *Wayne?*" She tossed a pebble and it hit his shoe. "To be honest, I think there's something kind of sweet about it. Like they've gotten past all the exterior bullshit and just see each other for who they are. After all these years, they understand each other." Mary thought of Dan. *"Anyway."* She crushed the cigarette under her shoe and started to get up.

"Hey, you always do that. You barely even smoked it," Wayne said.

"Quit whining. I'll buy you a pack. And a tank of gas. Okay if I bring the truck back in the morning? You can take the Lexus. Keys are in the top drawer of my desk."

"No problem," Wayne said. She could tell he was trying to contain his joy.

"Just don't wrap it around a tree." As soon as it came out, she felt a chill. The smile slipped from the corners of Wayne's lip. He fixed on a dandelion pushing up between the white pebbles. "Where are you going now?" he asked.

"To see my aunt. She wanted me to bring her a table I have at the house and it won't fit in the trunk," she lied. "Then I have a business meeting." *Keep shoveling, Mary.*

"A *what?*"

"Never mind. Make sure Nate gets enough fish for tonight. I'll see you in the morning." She got up to go.

"I'll hold my breath."

Nine

That brother of mine had a fine head of hair," Lovey said. She sat in her recliner and rubbed at a new bruise that had cropped up near her bracelet.

"What was that?" Mary asked.

"Dorothy and I always said it wasn't fair. What does a man want with hair like that?"

"What made you think of Joe?" When Mary had arrived, she noticed the door contraption had been dismantled. The shades were up and the windows were open. Lovey had been watching a rerun of *Matlock* with a plate of saltines and small squares of American cheese on her lap. Business as usual.

"Right here." Lovey tapped the bruise. "I woke up and he was right here."

"What do you mean?" Mary asked. She felt a squeeze in her gut. She got up off the couch and looked at Lovey's arm. It was one hell of a bruise, ranging from dark purple-brown to almost bloodred, that must have been caused by the medical bracelet.

"Look." Lovey traced the colorations. "Here's his nose and his heavy brow. Here are his thick curls."

"Oh, Auntie." Was she cracking up? Could it happen this fast?

"Where's your imagination? Remember how you used to see ships and dragons in the clouds?" Lovey said. "That's all I meant." She sat back in the recliner and let her arm dangle off the rest. "Fifty-two years old. Cirrhosis."

"I never knew him."

"Of course you didn't. You weren't even born yet." Lovey's face lit up a bit. "You know, he's the one who came up with the name 'Lovey.' When he was a little, he couldn't say 'Lavinia.'" She smiled.

"Years later he said it was just as well, that I'd always seemed more like a Lovey to him than a Lavinia. I knew what he meant. I never really lived up to the name. I think my mother hoped I'd grow up to be a glamourpuss." Mary hadn't seen Lovey this talkative in a while. It warmed her heart. She'd always loved the old stories. She had since she was a little girl. Lovey sighed and shook her head. "A real troublemaker, that Joe."

"How so?" Mary had hoped to find the right moment to broach the topic of moving. But maybe she was being too hasty. There seemed no reason the woman couldn't be on her own. Not today, anyway. What right did Darlene Snow have to threaten eviction?

"'Lovey! There's one behind the dresser!'" Lovey said. She pointed to the opposite side of the room.

Mary looked around. *"What?"*

Lovey waved her hand. "Dominickles. Imps. Gremlins. Or some such thing. Don't ask me. I never saw one. My mother had brought them with her from the old country. In her head, at least. They were very superstitious, the people who lived out in the Vienna countryside. Near the end, she saw the creatures everywhere. It wasn't funny, but that brother of mine used to have me in stitches anyway. He was so bad." She cackled. "Ma was in the next room. I was in the kitchen, wrist-deep in raw hamburg. Joe was reading the paper. When she cried out, I told him it was his turn. He just winked. 'I'm all greasy. You go,' I insisted. He set the paper down. He said, 'Wash your hands. We'll *both* go.' He grabbed a broom out of the closet. We could hear her sobs before we got halfway down the hall. Understand, we weren't being cruel, it's just that by then, her crying had lost its effect on us. We entered the room and she was in the bed, her body pressed up against the headboard, the sheets gathered around her neck." Lovey paused. She smiled and shook her head. "Poor Ma." Lovey put her hands on her cheeks. "'Shh. Right there. Behind the dresser,' Ma said. She shivered and pointed to a dark corner. Joe stepped in front of me. He raised the broom. 'Lovey, get back!' he said. I went over to the bed to comfort Ma.

"'All right, you devil,' he said. 'You get out of here or else!' By then I knew my part. 'Look, Ma. There he goes! See him?' I pointed. Then Joe swung the broom and stomped toward the door to chase away the imaginary intruder. 'I see you. You'd *better* run,' he roared." Lovey laughed. "Then Ma asked, 'Is it gone?' 'It's gone,' I said. But by then I was on the verge of tears. I had to get out of there. 'You're so brave, Joe,' I heard Ma say."

Lovey drew a deep breath. She caressed her bruise and smiled. "Those were the bad days. With Ma, I mean. I think the good days were even worse, for me, anyway. When the sparkle came back into her eyes and there was something left of the woman she'd been. She'd come from Austria with her sister at sixteen and found a job cooking for a wealthy family all on her own, found a husband, raised three kids, all from nothing. I think those good days were harder because that was when *she* knew there was something wrong with her mind." Lovey sighed.

Mary looked out the window. A truck had stopped in the circle to make a delivery—the Milk Man, as it said in large, old-style lettering along the side of the vehicle. Many of the people here still believed the best milk had to be delivered to the home. Mary recalled another time the Milk Man truck had been in the circle.

She had been sound asleep in her own bed when the phone call came.

"Mary Hopkins?" the voice said.

"Yes."

"There's been an accident. An officer is on his way to your home. He'll explain everything. In the meantime, you need to get up and dressed."

Before Mary could protest, there came a rap on the front door. She flung her arm to the other side of the bed. It was empty, the bedding still tucked. Robbie hadn't come home. She threw off the covers and grabbed one of Robbie's old sweatshirts from the chair. She stepped into a pair of jeans she found on the floor, not knowing if they were hers or his. She ran downstairs and unlatched the front door. Two officers stood before her, a man and a woman. She looked between them to see if Robbie was standing behind.

"Mrs. Hopkins?" the male cop said. He had thin lips. "I'm afraid we have bad news. There's been an accident."

"Robbie?" Mary said.

"Yes. We're going to need you to come with us."

It was as if the earth had shifted and jagged boulders had started tumbling down into the valley of her mind. She had to think fast to dodge them.

"How bad is it? Is he at the hospital? Can I speak with the doctor?"

"Mrs. Hopkins, I'm afraid—"

"Is he conscious? I need to see him." Mary turned her back to the two cops in her doorway and went to the hall closet to grab her sneakers. She sat down on the floor and put them on, talking all the while. Dodging boulders. "See, we got into an argument before he left last night and he never came home, which isn't like him, I mean not usually though he's done it before but you know how it is. He said some things and then I said some things and I'm sure he must've had too much to drink. That's it, isn't it? Of course it is. That's why you're here. And now he's in trouble with the police. I knew this would happen one—"

The female cop knelt down beside Mary and took the sneaker from her hand and set it down. She put her hand on Mary's knee. Mary felt the rumble of one enormous rock. It was heading right for her. The cop gave Mary's knee a squeeze. She had thick bangs that were still flattened to her head from the police hat.

"Honey," she said, "he's gone. He died at the scene. By the time the emergency crew got there he was— Look, is there someone we can call to come with you to the . . . " Her voice trailed off. "We need you to identify him."

The next thing Mary remembered was sitting in the back of the police car on her way to Lovey's. They pulled into the circle and came to a stop behind the Milk Man truck. Mary stared at the letters while one of the cops went up to ring the buzzer. It had struck her how people could still be getting milk on the morning Robbie had died. He was just thirty-two.

The cops had called ahead and explained to Lovey what had happened. She'd no doubt still have been in her nightgown at that hour. Mary recalled the male cop growing impatient as he waited in the car. Mary knew the time it took to undo the bobby pins Lovey slept in each night to give her hair some curl. Not even death could derail certain morning rituals. When Mary buried her head in her aunt's neck on their way to the funeral home, she smelled the Aqua Net Lovey used to cement her hairdo in place.

It was Lovey who identified Robbie. Mary would never forget how she looked as she came back into the waiting room, her hands gripping the strap of her purse as though she were wrestling with gravity, her hair too in place for the occasion. Her face was red and her skin puckered in places. She pressed a tissue to her nose and looked up at Mary. No words had been necessary.

In the days leading up to the funeral, Lovey moved in with Mary and took care of everything. She cleaned the house, packed up Robbie's clothes, and filled the freezer with things Mary used to love to eat as a child. Homemade macaroni and cheese. Frozen waffles. Pints of butter pecan ice cream. She kept track of who sent cards and flowers and knew who to let in to see Mary and who to keep out. During the bad times, Lovey had been there for Mary in ways no one else ever had.

"What do you say, Joe? Am I losing it like Ma?" Lovey tapped her arm.

Mary was startled back to the present. The milk truck was gone. Lovey was talking to the skin above her wrist.

"You're not losing it, Auntie," Mary said. "Everything will be fine."

Lovey got up from her chair and shuffled over to the bookcase, the shelves filled with colorfully bound volumes of Reader's Digest Condensed Books. She ran her finger along the spines and stopped at one. *"Hawaii,"* she said. "I remember reading this." She pulled the book off the shelf and brought it back to her chair. "Reading is good for the mind," she said. "I think I'm going to read all of these again. That's a good idea, isn't it Mary?"

Mary pushed though the gold beads at the entrance to the lounge of the Triple Pagoda, a small red room with a bamboo bar down one side and Naugahyde booths on the other. The walls were papered in crimson embossed with a bamboo tree motif and decorated with neon beer signs: Budweiser, Sam Adams, and Tsingtao, the latter draped with multicolored Mardi Gras beads. Faded holiday garland and Christmas lights festooned the mirror behind the bar and wrapped around a wood carving of a Chinese dragon. In the top-right corner above the bar, a dusty gold Buddha rested on an old television set tuned in to Court TV. Bamboo flute music wafted through the air.

"What'll it be?" the bartender said. The woman set a white paper napkin on the bar in front of Mary. Mary recognized her, a German gal in her early fifties who'd worked for Wayne's father since he opened the place. Despite her heavy accent and overprocessed platinum blond hair, her upper eyelids were thickly lined in black and she wore a Mandarin-collared red silk shirt embossed with Chinese characters, as if the costume and makeup might trick someone into believing she was fresh off the boat from Shanghai.

"I'll have a mai tai," Mary said, and eased onto a barstool. She was early. She wanted to get a drink under her belt to settle her nerves before Dan got there. The bar was empty, except for the waiters in Hawaiian print shirts who bellied up to the side nearest the dining room to fill their drink orders. By two in the morning, the place would be packed. They were the only restaurant in town that catered to the last-call crowd.

"Is Raymond here?" Mary asked one of them.

"Can I tell him who's asking?" the waiter responded. He had a heavy Chinese accent.

"Just tell him Wayne's boss," Mary said.

The bartender set the highball glass in front of her. Mary plucked off the cherry, the orange slice, and the purple paper umbrella. Opening an umbrella indoors was bad luck. Mary thought Chinese people were supposed to be superstitious. She drew the umbrella closed and set it down on the corner of the napkin, then took a sip from her drink. The rum had settled at the bottom of the crushed ice.

Mary looked around. She was glad she'd suggested they meet here. This was neutral territory. They had no shared history here. Even so, that didn't stop the memories from coming. These last two weeks it was as if someone had opened a Tupperware container in Mary's brain—one that had been safely sealed for twelve years—and now things were sloshing and spilling out all over the place.

Earlier, she'd taken a long, hot shower. She'd pulled on a pair of khakis and a tailored white blouse (leaving one more button undone than might be considered businesslike). Then she'd sat down on the bed to slip on a pair of leather flats and found herself in a different bedroom, a different decade entirely.

The September after Robbie died was the first time she and Dan had slept together. By November, after some coercing, Dan had given up his musty studio apartment above a local fisherman's garage and moved what few belongings he had into Mary's place. That first winter, they'd taken a trip to Florida over Christmas—Dan's idea, so Mary wouldn't have to be on the Cape that first holiday season without Robbie. At the time, Mary thought the proposed change of scenery had been as much for Dan as it was for her. After they returned, for the next three months, he went back to Alaska to recoup some of the money he'd forgone to help Mary out over the summer. But when he returned, they'd picked right up where they'd left off. He spent the spring helping her ready the restaurant, and that summer he supplied her seafood once again.

Their relationship had raised a few eyebrows. Those Clambake employees who'd been around long enough to remember Robbie aired some resentment. Their expressions would sour when Dan's truck pulled into the back alley. He sensed the animosity and kept his distance from the restaurant when the season was in full swing. But it wasn't just people at work. Robbie's mother had caught wind of their relationship and made it clear through a series of histrionic missives that she thought it too soon for Mary to be with someone, Robbie's best friend of all people. Lovey, on the other hand, was happy that Mary had found someone to share her nights with. "Life is short," she would say. "Enjoy." It was the simplest of advice, but Mary was grateful and took it to heart.

For the first time in a long while, Mary was happy, perhaps happier than she'd ever been during her marriage to Robbie. Life was simple. Her relationship with Dan felt comfortable, like a sexy pair of flannel pajamas, if there was such a thing. He made her feel safe.

That second November, Dan had been offered the opportunity to double his money by going to Alaska before the holidays. Mary had tried to talk him out of it. The restaurant had been pulling in a decent profit and she argued that they didn't need the money he'd make fishing that winter. But Dan protested. He said he couldn't let her pay his way. So it was settled. He would leave for Alaska in mid-November and come back a little earlier, in February, so they could take another trip down south together before preparation for the summer season began.

For years, Mary would wonder what might have happened if she hadn't let her curiosity get the better of her the day he left. Would they still be together? How was it that an earring could have been her undoing?

The day before Dan's flight out, Mary had helped him pack. In the process of clearing out his things, she'd gotten ambitious and decided to tackle a few of her own overstuffed drawers. She had found the earring in a cardboard gift box that held some other costume junk, some cat earrings Robbie had bought her when she first got Seventy-Eight, an old mood ring, a papier-mâché tropical fish pin, and some broken chains. Mary took the earring out the box and held it up to the window, watched how the light danced through the crystal bead. She recalled that day she'd found it on the floor of the Clambake basement, the first day they'd opened for business and Dan had come down to make a delivery. She remembered Dan's reaction when he saw it, how his face had gone dark. It had belonged to someone Dan was involved with. *What was she like?* Mary wondered. *Had he been in love with her?*

Dan and Mary rarely brought up the past. Because of Robbie, it was difficult for both of them. Mary believed Dan felt guilty for stepping into his best friend's life, which was why he tended to venerate Robbie. When they did talk about Robbie, it was only about the good times, and the talk centered on Robbie's brazen antics when they were in school or fun times out on the beach, never on those years when Mary suffered through her marriage. Never about his addiction and the pain it had caused.

Mary got the feeling Dan was one of those people who didn't like talking about the past in general, something she could relate to herself. The past was the past. What hold did it have on the present? Her own father had been that way too. And yet Dan seemed to take it to the extreme. When she asked about his time out west, about the conditions, being on the boat, the people, Dan said the work was work. He made it seem like there was nothing to tell. But there had to be stories. Sometimes Mary wondered if things happened out on the boats that were hard for Dan to relive. When Mary asked Dan about Alaska, she usually got a three-part answer. The work was hard, the winters were unbearably long, and, of course, the money was great.

But there were other things Mary wanted to know, the things any girlfriend would want to know. Had he been in love before? Had he had a serious girlfriend? Had he had his heart broken? The earring brought up all these questions. Now, suddenly, because he was leaving, there was an urgency. Mary couldn't bear the thought of waiting three months. That morning, she decided to come right out and ask.

All Dan's bags were packed and had been brought down to the

front door the night before so he and she would have time together in the morning. They were lounging in bed with minutes to go before Dan had to get ready to leave. His jeans, black turtleneck, and a heavy knit sweater were laid out on top of Robbie's old dresser. A cab would be coming soon to pick him up to take him to the airport in Boston. Mary had offered to drive, but his departure the year before had been so tearfully traumatic that this time she agreed to say her good-byes at the house.

"I have something important to ask you," Mary said.

"Important, huh," he said. He groaned and put a pillow over his head.

She yanked it off. "I'm serious."

He looked over at her, no doubt trying to read whether she was, in fact, serious. He lay on his back with his hands under his head. "Suppose you better ask, then."

Mary sat up. She was wearing one of his white undershirts. "You remember that first day Robbie and I opened the restaurant? I found an earring under the chopping block." Mary gathered the covers around her waist. "It turned up yesterday when I was going through the drawers."

"I don't remember any earring," Dan said. He closed his eyes. Mary could tell he was lying.

"You had that look men get on their faces when they're busted. Kind of like the look you have now," she said. "So fess up." She swatted him playfully on the arm. "Who was she? Tell me about her."

He opened his eyes and raised himself on one elbow.

"Don't play coy with me," she said. "I suspected something was going on, so I asked Robbie and he *told* me."

Dan raised his eyebrows. "He did?"

"He told me he'd given you a set of keys so you could bring some girl down there who was visiting from Alaska. Hell, I don't even care that you used the basement. I just want to know about her. What was she like? Was she someone special?"

"Robbie told you that?" Dan said.

"What was her name? Was it serious? I always wondered how come you didn't ask for the earring so you could give it back to her. I took that for a sign it wasn't serious. Was I wrong?"

Dan sat up. He started for the edge of the bed. Mary panicked. *Why this reaction?* She grabbed his arm and pulled him back. "Okay, none of my business. If you don't want to tell me, that's fine."

Dan sat with his back to her.

"Come on," she said. "I didn't think this would upset you. I know there had to be plenty of women before me. I'm fine with—"

"Robbie shouldn't have said that to you," he said.

What's the big deal? Mary thought. "If there was one thing about Robbie, he was lousy at keeping secrets." She forced out a half-hearted laugh. "But I was his wife. Spouses trump best friends, you know. At least *he* wasn't sneaking around with women in base-ments." She pinched his hip playfully.

He recoiled a little.

"Come on, I'm *kidding.* I said we don't have to talk about her if you don't want to. You should get in the shower. I'll go make us breakfast." She'd never seen him like this. She wished she'd never asked.

"It's not that," Dan said.

Mary crawled closer to him. "Then what?" She could sense he was withdrawing. It was happening right in front of her eyes, like he was backing down a long, dark hallway. And then it struck her. A wave of horror washed over her, leaving her soaked in jealousy. Her throat went dry. "There's someone else," Mary said. "The ear-ring girl. She's in Alaska." She shot off the bed and paced the room. "You're planning to see her." Mary knew she was taking this to a bad place but she couldn't stop herself. Dan was supposed to tell her she was wrong. He was supposed to tell her she was the only one for him.

Instead, he didn't tell her anything. He just stared at his feet over the edge of the bed. Incriminating silence. "Too complicated," he said under his breath.

"You're the one who's making it complicated. Robbie was supposed to be your best friend. What would he think about you doing this to me now? I can't believe this is happening." Like the earring, it was all crystal clear. "You've been stringing me along all this time. Does she even know about me?" Mary felt sick to her stomach. "I never pegged you as a womanizer, Dan Bassett." She fled to the bathroom. "He may have been a lazy drunk but that's one thing Robbie never did to me." She slammed the door.

"Don't say that," she heard Dan say.

Mary didn't know which part she wasn't supposed to say. That he was a womanizer or that Robbie was a lazy drunk. Either way, she wasn't about to ask Dan another question. Not ever. For the first time in over a year, she missed her dead husband. The *old* Robbie. For all the bad, at least with Robbie she knew where she stood, even if it was behind a bottle.

Ten minutes later, she sat at the kitchen table listening to Dan get dressed upstairs, listening to the rain pelt the gutter above the picture window. The cab was already idling in the driveway. Dan came down with his travel kit and kissed her wet cheek before he brought his bags out to the cab. She didn't offer to help. She didn't even look up at him. Part of her wanted to run up and throw herself into his arms. But the other part was glued to the chair. How could she have been so blind?

By as early as that afternoon, Mary started to second-guess herself. He'd never actually confessed to being involved with a woman in Alaska. She'd done all the talking, hadn't she? She'd pieced the whole thing together. But he hadn't denied it either.

Mary thought she'd give him a day or two to get settled. If she didn't hear from him, she'd make the call and they'd talk things through. She'd apologize. If it came down to it, she'd fight for him if she had to. She'd track down this other woman. But when she tried to call the place where he was supposed to be staying, she got no answer. Maybe the boat had taken off ahead of schedule. Maybe he was with *her*. Once he shipped out, there'd be no way to reach him.

The holidays came and went. Three months passed and she never once heard from him. The more time that went by, the more she believed her suspicions had been warranted. He'd gone out there and forgotten all about her. February passed, then March. Finally in April she heard rumors that he was somewhere on the Upper Cape, but then that he'd left again to fish salmon through the summer. She didn't give up. She kept trying to reach him, making phone calls and writing letters. Eventually, after a year, her pride told her enough was enough. One day it sat her down and said, "Look, honey, it's either me or him. You're going to have to pick." She did. She let Dan go. But letting go of the pain wasn't so easy. It had found a home, a place where it could fester and thrive, and keep her from ever truly being happy.

"Mary Hopkins." It was Wayne's father. He had on a white business shirt and a tie with an apron over it. Mary suspected that when dressing that morning he hadn't planned on spending time in the kitchen. Wayne said he was a hands-on kind of guy. Mary knew it took that kind of dedication to be successful in this business.

"Hey, Raymond." They shook hands. "Hate to be the one to break it to you, but Christmas has been over for over six months." She pointed to the tinsel.

"People want festive," he said. One of the waiters handed him a covered serving dish. "Tinsel is cheap." Maybe all restaurant owners had a miserly streak.

"I suppose." She took another sip of her mai tai. It was strong. "Good drink," she said. She winked at the bartender. Raymond set the serving dish in front of Mary. A waiter appeared with a red cloth napkin, a fork, and a small white plate. "What's this?"

"A new dish." Raymond lifted the silver lid. "Taste and tell me how you like it." Local restaurant owners were always trying to impress one another. He slid onto the bar stool beside Mary. "How's that boy of mine? I saw his truck in the parking lot. Is he here?" Raymond looked around.

"He loaned it to me for the night. I needed it to haul something." Mary unfolded the napkin and laid it on her lap. "Let me ask you something, Raymond. There are these words he says in Chinese. I don't understand him. Maybe you can help me out." Mary spoke one of them. "What does it mean?" She tried to keep a straight face.

Raymond's cheeks turned red. He looked to the beads to make sure no one out in the dining room had heard. A waiter who was retrieving his drinks from the bar almost dropped his tray. The bartender smiled. She raised her eyebrows and shrugged at Mary as if she didn't know what it meant either. Mary was guessing she knew damn well.

"Never mind," Raymond said. He smoothed down a cowlick in his thick hair. "You tell that son of mine I'll come down there myself and wash his mouth out with soap I hear he says that again." He dabbed at his brow with a cocktail napkin.

Mary picked up the fork. He knew better than to give her chopsticks. "Seriously," she said, "you should be proud of him. He's a hard worker. And he's talented." She took a scallop and some lobster sauce and ate. "Delicious," she said. "I'm sure it pains you that I get to have him." She rested her hand on Raymond's sleeve. "But I'm grateful. Really." She took another bite, some onions and a piece of fish. "That's the way the fortune cookie crumbles, I guess."

He shook his head. "'Fortune cookie crumbles.' That's original." He rolled his eyes and slid off the stool. "Great to see you, Mary Hopkins. Keep your eye on that kid of mine. Make sure he doesn't get into any trouble." Mary thought of Sage. From the look of things, the kid was already in over his head.

"Thanks for *this*," Mary said. She pointed at the serving dish with the back of her fork and gave him the thumbs up sign.

"Enjoy your evening," he said. He went back into the kitchen.

Mary took another bite and closed her eyes. She held out her hand in front of her, twisted her wrist and tried with everything she had to imagine how this might possibly feel like razor blades to Wayne. All it took for Wayne to feel pain were some bamboo shoots and hoisin sauce. For Mary, it had taken a broken marriage, the death of her husband, the loss of a sweetheart, and, most recently, an ailing aunt and the tragic death of a young employee.

Mary felt something warm and rough clamp down on her outstretched hand. She opened her eyes. He wasn't smiling, exactly, though his lips were slightly curled at the edges, mostly hidden beneath days' worth of unshaven moustache and beard. His hair had grown long, to the base of his neck, and so curly, with gray mixed in, that she might not have recognized him at all if not for his eyes, which now seemed to search hers for something—for what?—for too uncomfortably long, that was for sure. And yet she couldn't break away. Such familiarity in that gray-brown gaze and yet something different too, some added weight to the eyelids, a certain heaviness in the brow.

"Mary Sunshine," he said in hoarse whisper. He smiled.

"Dan," she said, like a gasp. She looked down and realized he was still holding her hand. He had on a blue T-shirt that said "Dreamland Bar B Que," faded jeans, and work boots. His body was still strong and lean, though he was more sinewy through the forearms. Mary noticed a long scar just below his elbow.

He tugged on her hand and yanked her off the barstool and into his arms. She buried her head in his chest. He smelled like butter, spice, and salt air. She felt the urge to cry.

He gave her a squeeze, then let her go. Still holding her hand, he gave her the up-and-down once-over. "Can it really be twelve years?" he said. "You haven't changed a bit."

Get a freakin' grip, girl. Mary withdrew her hand and took a step back. She smoothed down her blouse. "Has it been that long?" she said, as if she didn't know down to the month.

"Sorry for the way I look. Just came off the boat," he said. He rubbed his whiskers. "I'd of taken care of this too if I knew—"

"Don't be silly. I kind of like it," Mary said. She reached up and touched a curl. "This too." She let her hand drop. "When you came in to the restaurant that day the kids thought you were a pirate." *Not like Johnny Depp or anything. He was a ton older.* "Since when did you have curly hair?" He'd always worn it so short she couldn't tell.

"One too many winters in the Bering Sea, I guess." He seemed self-conscious. He pointed to her stool. "Want to sit here?"

"Let's grab a booth," Mary said. She nodded in the direction of the bartender, who had her back to them, mixing something in a blender. "Walls have ears." The last thing she wanted was for it to get back to Raymond and the locals that she was having trouble with her fish supplier.

Mary lifted her almost-empty glass off the bar and took it over to one of the red booths. She slid into the seat. All the red made her feel like she was inside a kidney.

Dan ordered a beer. "Can I get you another?" he asked.

"Sure. Mai tai."

Mary watched him from the back as he stood at the bar. *Dan Bassett.* She couldn't believe it was really him. He'd changed. But in a good way.

Dan brought the drinks over. He slid into the seat opposite Mary. He was looking at her again.

"What?" she finally said.

"Those pretty blue eyes," he said. "I'd almost forgotten."

She took a sip of her drink. He'd forgotten, all right. For over a decade. Mary felt a wave of anger rising within her. *Don't let it break,* she thought. *Dive into it, let it pass, or you'll get pummeled.* What she had to do now was navigate this conversation out of hazardous waters. She had to remember her objective for this meeting: fish. "Are you hungry? Raymond Chen gave me a dish to try and—" Mary looked to the bar but the dish had been cleared away. "Or we could just order something. It's on me," she said. Upper hand.

"Thanks, darlin'. Had a late lunch," Dan said. "But you go on and order something if you want. Beer tastes perfect about now." He stretched out his legs under the table.

Mary had begun dismantling the toothpick spokes of the drink's paper umbrella. This one was pink. "So you're still fishing," she said.

"Doing mostly charter trips. More tourists to be caught than fish these days," he said. "But I think I'll be able to help you out. Have a buddy at the dock who'd be willing to negotiate as long as I do the legwork. He doesn't deliver."

"Oh, Dan, that's great." Mary slumped back in the booth. *Thank God.* "You were my only hope." She poked the straw through the crushed ice in her drink. "Guess it'll cost me, though. Can't say I have much leverage for negotiating."

"Don't worry. He'll be fair. He's a friend." Dan took a long swig off his beer. "And he owes me a favor."

Mary reached forward and rested her hand on his forearm. "You always came through for me. I appreciate that, now especially."

His gaze met hers, then he dropped his head. After a while, he spoke. "Must've been rough when the girl died," he said.

"That too." Mary realized she was running her finger along the scar on his arm. She drew her hand away and went back to shredding the umbrella.

He smiled. "What do you mean, *too?*"

"It's Lovey. She's sick. They think it's Alzheimer's. Maybe that's not *sick*, just old, I don't know." Mary's eyes welled up. "I just found out last week."

"Oh, honey," he said. He reached for her hands. "I'm so sorry."

"You remember her, right?" Mary sniffed.

"Of course I do," he said.

"I've been lucky to have her this long. It's just that some days she seems perfectly fine and other times it's like she's only halfway there. She forgets things. The other morning she thought I was her sister. She talks to a bruise on her arm that looks like her brother. And she thinks people are breaking into her apartment."

"Breaking in?"

"And using her pots and pans." Mary looked up at Dan. He was frowning and wide-eyed at the same time. His expression made her laugh. "It's ridiculous, I know. But when you're there, it's not funny. She gets so upset." She felt the tears coming again.

Dan handed her his bar napkin. He didn't say anything. She was glad for that. She just wanted someone to listen.

"And the worst part is, the lady who runs the apartment complex wants her out. If Lovey gets any worse, I'm going to have to put her in a nursing home."

The bartender came around and Dan ordered another beer. Mary ordered club soda. She was exhausted and she still had to get Wayne's truck home in one piece.

Ten

Mary lay in bed. It was two in the morning. Tired as she was, she couldn't sleep. Her head was churning from all that had gone on that day. She tried reading. She tried counting backwards from a thousand. She tried gently nudging the thoughts from her mind as soon as they appeared. Nothing worked.

Finally, she grabbed her reading glasses from her bedside table, got up, and threw a terry cloth robe over her pink pajamas. She flicked on the light and went across the room to her dresser, to her jewelry box. She opened the lid.

Mary's collection was a far from impressive. She'd never been the sparkly type. There were few family pieces, a good watch that had been her mother's, a strand of pearls, some diamond stud earrings. But most of the stuff was costume junk given her by Lovey over the years. A long gold chain with a broken watch pendant, elaborate brooches that were losing their gold plate, and old-lady earrings Mary knew she'd never wear, even when she was an old lady, but didn't have the heart to get rid of. There sat her engagement ring, a small square diamond in simple gold setting that Mary had loved wearing, and a shiny gold band for her wedding ring, just like Robbie's, which sat above it in the ring holder. She took out his band and put it on her ring finger. It almost fit. Robbie had such long, thin fingers. His mother always told him he should play the piano.

Mary took the ring off and put it back in its slot. She lifted off the top tray and rummaged through the tangle of loose earrings and bead necklaces in the bottom compartment. She knew it was there somewhere. Then she saw the crystal bead, its wire hooked around a sterling chain bracelet. Mary carefully undid the tangle. She set the earring on the dresser, put the top compartment back in the jewelry box and closed the lid, then picked the earring up and brought it to her vanity. She set it down on a black powder box. The thin wire had tarnished. Mary turned on the lamp and examined the crystal bead as if she might learn something new this time. It was the kind of earring that would look lovely on a young girl; how it would catch the light and hold it at the nape of her neck. Mary slid the earring into the hole in her earlobe. She pulled a hand mirror out of the drawer and looked at herself. What if she'd shown up today wearing it? Would Dan even have remembered?

Dan. How he'd changed. And not changed.

A dozen years ago, he'd left her for another woman, or at least that's what she had no choice but to believe. He'd never denied it. Obviously it hadn't worked out with Earring Girl either. He'd come back to the Cape alone. Today, he'd acted like those twelve years had evaporated into the mist. He'd tried to kiss her when they left the Triple Pagoda. She'd turned her cheek at the last moment. It would be a challenge having him around the restaurant now. Happy as she'd been to see him, she wasn't looking to rekindle an old romance with her new (old) fish guy. The restaurant came first. It had to. The Clambake was the only thing in her life that had lasted. Fourteen years ago she would have let it all go. If not for Lovey, she'd have sold and started over somewhere else. But over time, the place had seeped in and settled into her bones. It had become part of who she was. In spite of the monotony, the years that all seemed to spin together into one indistinguishable sphere of her existence, she couldn't imagine living without it. The Clambake, a wooden box filled with transients, fish, and fryer grease, had turned out to be her greatest love of all.

Mary set the earring down and went into the bathroom. She splashed some cold water on her face. The light was still on in her neighbor's cottage. Had the old man just forgotten to turn it off, or was he up too? Too bad she didn't know him. It would have been nice to have a fellow insomniac to talk to. From the bathroom window, she saw him at his kitchen table, not him but his striped pajama arms. He was holding a pencil above a pad of paper. The hand with the tremor kept time like a metronome as he sketched.

This gave Mary an idea. There was no use trying to sleep. And there was a letter she'd been meaning to write. There were two of them, in fact.

She returned to her vanity and pulled paper and a pen from the drawer. She sat down on the wicker bench and began:

Dear Darlene,

(No. Be more formal.)

Dear Ms. Snow,

I'm sorry it's taken me so long to get back to you. As you may have heard, we lost a young staff member in a tragic accident and there's been much to deal with at the restaurant these past few weeks, not to mention we're approaching the high season.

(As if she cares. Never mind. Leave it.)

I did, however, have the opportunity to bring my great-aunt to her doctor and then to a neurologist in Hyannis who detected some mild cognitive impairment but nothing that should in any way threaten her ability to continue on in her apartment. The neurologist prescribed some medication that should help with any behavioral issues and improve her general sense of well-being.

(All Mary's eggs were in that basket.)

I thank you for your patience and concern, though I see no immediate need to pursue alternate living arrangements at this time. Feel free to contact me if you have any questions.

Sincerely,
Mary Hopkins

(When has she ever remembered who I am? Better add . . .)

> *Great-niece of Lovey Rollwagon*

And the second letter:

Dear Ms. Ryder,

I was disappointed though not surprised that you thought it necessary to return my gift. I hope you'll forgive my persistence, for I do respect your position. I too came from modest circumstances and only quite recently have come to understand what it's like to have more than enough, thanks to my late husband's business success.

Now I am a wealthy widow who lives alone with no dependents and no immediate family. When I learned of your predicament, it resonated with me. You see, I too lost my mother at an early age.

(Brilliant.)

It is for these reasons that I hope you will allow me to provide assistance, if not for you, then for the sake of your great-granddaughter, who certainly deserves a well-cared-for home and certain niceties (Niceties! Was that a word Mary had ever used in her life? In any event, it was a sufficiently "old" sounding, something Lovey might say. And open-ended too. It could mean anything.) *that may provide comfort as she comes to terms with the loss of her mother. For this opportunity, it is I who will be indebted. I will be in contact soon. And again, please accept my condolences. My heart goes out to you and the child.*

> *With humble gratitude,*
> *Lavinia Rollwagon*

Mary faked her aunt's signature and used one of the address stickers she'd taken from Lovey's apartment. A kitten pouncing on a ball of string. She contemplated including some cash and then decided against it. She'd give Meg the chance to digest the letter. Then she'd hire the workmen.

"What's that noise?" Wayne said. He brushed some butter on a piece of swordfish on the grill.

"What noise?" Maureen said. She sprinkled some paprika on a tuna roll and nestled a small bag of potato chips beside it. She slipped in a pickle spear.

"The rain," another order line girl said. "It's coming down harder."

Mary was at her window ledge. She was busy assigning waitress stations for the dinner shift, writing names on a photocopied diagram that the girls would see posted beside the time clock when they punched in at four.

"Are you *humming*?" Wayne said.

Mary looked up. "Me?" she said. Had she been? She never hummed.

"You were," Wayne said. "You were humming."

One of the steam cooks grinned.

"Never mind. You get this kitchen humming," Mary said. "It's going to be a zoo in here in a few minutes. The parking lot is filling up fast."

It was the Friday leading into Fourth of July weekend and the skies had opened up. The weather was supposed to be "a mixed bag" all weekend, which basically meant the meteorologists didn't have a clue. Ambiguity over inaccuracy was their creed. Wayne said they had ample seafood to get them through the lunch shift. Dan had said he'd be by in the early afternoon with his first delivery. Might that be why she was humming?

One of the Jennifers came into the kitchen and slammed her empty tray on the counter. "Nobody says please. 'The tea's too cold.' 'The chowder's too hot.' Is it my fault the weather gods decided to fuck up everyone's beach day?" She was a callback from last season. Her blond hair was cut short and spiked, a bit punk for the Clambake, but only in that benign-rebellious prep school way.

"Watch the language, Jennifer," Mary said without looking up.

There was a no-swearing (in English) policy in the kitchen that inevitably went to hell by the end of the night. But it was too early to start with the "fucking."

"My customer wants to know what spice is in the macaroni salad," Megan said.

Wayne smashed a clove of garlic with the side of his knife. "Basil," he said.

Mary looked up at Wayne. There was no basil in the macaroni salad.

Sage came into the kitchen. "Where are the lobster bibs?" she asked. She opened up the metal storage bin beneath the chowder warmer and rummaged through the paper supplies. She found the last two. "We're out."

"I'll get some," Maureen said. She wiped her hands on her apron and ran upstairs to the storage closet.

"Why did you tell Megan there was basil in the—?" Mary started.

"Where's the other Jennifer?" Wayne said. "This tray has been up here for five minutes." It had really been more like thirty seconds.

Maureen came back down to the kitchen in time to call an order that had just come up. She leaned in to the microphone. "Jennifer B.," she said, kittenish. Then, "We're out of lobster bibs" in her regular voice.

"Give them extra napkins," Mary said. These were the kinds of fires she put out a hundred times a day.

Megan came back into the kitchen. She went to the chowder station and grabbed two cups. "My customer said it's not basil. I told her it was and she said, 'No, honey, you must be mistaken. I know what basil tastes like.' Come on, Wayne. Don't fuck with my tip," she said. She lifted the lid. "We need more chowder," she yelled to the back of the kitchen.

"Don't swear," Mary said.

"Coming up," a voice came from the back of the kitchen.

"What do you want from me?" Wayne said. He dropped a handful of frozen shrimp into the fryer.

"Yeah, thanks a million," Megan said. She left with her chowder, almost colliding with Jennifer B., the nicer Jennifer, who was wide-eyed and red in the face.

"Where the hell have you been?" Wayne said. "You can't let my food sit around like that."

"I know. I'm sorry," she said. She was shuffling order tickets in her hands. "I've got a table of guys who had to cancel their fishing trip because of the weather and they keep sending me to the bar for more beers."

"Tell Todd to keep his eye on them," Mary said. She didn't ever want to see another accident associated with the restaurant.

"Hot soup!" A kid who was all knuckles and knee caps threaded his way thorough the kitchen carrying a large vat of chowder. He set it down on the counter, lifted the old vat out of the warmer, and slid the fresh batch in, dripping hot water all the way back to the dishwasher station.

"Wayne," Mary said. "Why did you tell Megan there's basil in the—?"

Wayne slammed a pan on the stove. "Am I the only one who gives a shit about the recipes around here? You want to tell everyone our secrets?"

Mary was tickled. It was as if he were safeguarding something precious, like McDonald's special sauce or the secret recipe for Twinkies.

"Mary, there's a guy delivering stuff outside," Maureen said.

Mary jumped off her stool. She smoothed her hair and started for the basement. She almost bumped into Nate, who was coming up with a bucket of steamers.

"No one down there," Nate said.

"Out front," Maureen said. She pointed. Mary looked out the window. It was the paper goods guy. "Lobster bibs," Maureen added. "Finally."

Megan came back into the kitchen. She folded her arms, seemingly ready for a brawl. "She wants to see the spice bottle."

"Tell her we only use fresh—" Wayne started.

"It's celery seed," Mary said.

Wayne turned around. "Why did you do that?"

"If we piss off enough customers, we won't have to worry about guarding our secrets, will we?" Mary said. She headed out the door to greet the paper goods guy. He had all the boxes lined up at the end of his truck bed. Mary counted them to make sure they corresponded to what was on the packing slip, then signed it. This time she would show him where they went, in the upstairs closet, so he didn't just dump them in the hall. While she was up there, she checked that box of salt and paper shakers Nate had roughed up during their storage room encounter. (The shakers were fine; none had broken.) Two weeks seemed like two million years ago. Then she wrote the delivery guy a check from the business checkbook. She was about to go downstairs when she saw the light on her answering machine blinking in her office. She pressed "play."

"Ms. Hopkins, this is Darlene Snow." There was no way Darlene could have gotten the letter Mary had written last night. She'd only just put it in the mail this morning. "All morning I've been trying to call your aunt and I'm getting no answer. The rent check was due yesterday. If you like, I can use the master key to check on her. Besides that, we really do need to talk."

Mary wasn't overly concerned. The old woman's alarm clock was probably just on the fritz again. Mary imagined she was fast asleep, dreaming of a brother and sisters and happier times. As for last night, lots of people saw faces in clouds. Why not in bruises? Mary wondered whether she was beginning to believe her own lies about her aunt's condition. Maybe things weren't so bad. After all, doctors made mistakes. It wasn't as if she'd failed any definitive test for Alzheimer's. There really was no such thing. It was one doctor's opinion, two at the most. Regardless, if Darlene used her key to let herself into Lovey's apartment and saw the crazy burglar contraption by the door, it would only make things worse.

Mary dialed the office. Darlene picked up. "Darlene, this is Mary

Hopkins. . . . I appreciate the call, but I'm sure she's just resting. I saw her last night and she was fine. . . . You must've missed me. In any case, I'll go check on her. . . . No need, really. . . . I sent you off a letter this morning explaining things. . . . The doctors say it's nothing that should progress to any . . . Yes, but . . . No, but . . . Look, I'm sorry but I can't talk now. I'm at work and the kitchen is . . . I'll see to it you get the rent by tomorrow. But thanks for your concern."

Mary hung up. Why did that woman make her so nervous? She grabbed her handbag and headed down the stairs like Darlene might be chasing after her.

She walked in on a conversation in progress.

"I think he looks like one of those old rock stars. You know, from the eighties," Jennifer B. said.

"I think he's scary," Hope said. "He should cut his hair. Or wash it or something."

"Not a lot of dudes like that walking the streets of Darien, huh, Hope?" Maureen said. She hacked into a cucumber.

"Shut up, Maureen," Hope said. She left the kitchen with a handful of lobster bibs.

"Who are they talking about?" Mary said.

"The new fish guy," Nate said. He was back in the cooking line.

"He's here?" Mary said. She looked out the window to the back alley.

"Just left," Wayne said. "Saw the truck pull out." With the back of his hand, Wayne adjusted the bandana that kept the sweat out of his eyes. "Where'd you find this one?"

Damn. She'd missed him. At the very least, she had wanted to say thanks. She gathered up the papers on her window ledge. "Known him since high school. He fished crab off the coast of Alaska for a lot of years."

"No way," Maureen said. "I just saw a show about guys who do that. It's insane."

"What do you mean?" Mary said. She pressed the papers to her chest.

"It's freezing and miserable and they're out on these boats where the waves come and wash them right off their feet," Maureen said. She grabbed some parsley out of the fridge. "And when they're not slipping overboard or puking from seasickness or getting frostbite they sometimes get caught up in lines and lose fingers. I saw this guy with a stump—"

"What channel?" the gangly chowder kid said.

Mary shivered. She'd always suspected things out there were rough. No wonder Dan's hair had gone curly.

"Okay, everyone. Let's get back to work," Mary said. "Wayne, I'll go down and check out the delivery. Then I have to run an errand. I'll be back as soon as I can."

Mary opened the door to the basement and started down the stairs. It was especially damp from the cool nights and rain. There was no sign that Dan had been there, yet she could somehow sense his presence. She unlatched the door to the walk-in fridge. There she saw hunks of fresh fish wrapped in clear plastic. Mary brought her nose down to the fish. It was completely odorless. *Just like the old days,* she thought.

Mary exited the walk-in and started back for the stairs. That's when she saw a note on the cutting board. It had been written on the back of a gas station receipt.

Sorry I missed you today.

Mary took the note and put it in her jeans pocket. On the way up the stairs, she caught herself humming.

Lovey used to complain that sometimes the fan in the bathroom was so loud that she didn't hear the phone ring. Or sometimes she'd hear the phone ring but now moved so slowly because of her bad knees and general aches and pains that by the time she got to the phone to answer it, the ringing would have stopped. For these reasons, Mary had bought Lovey an answering machine last Christmas. By now,

Mary figured, Lovey had gotten up, seen the messages from Darlene, and returned her phone call. Still, she'd been a day late on her rent, which wasn't like her. Maybe it was time for Mary to help Lovey with her bills. Lots of old people needed help with such things.

Mary arrived at the outside door to the apartment complex. She pressed the buzzer, then riffled through her purse for the keys, just in case. But before she had the chance to find them, Lovey buzzed her in. The lock clicked and Mary pushed the door open. Her aunt was up. *What a relief.* Mary climbed the stairs to the apartment and heard Lovey fumbling with the lock. The door opened.

Instead of a welcoming smile, Lovey stood there with a furrowed brow. "I overslept," she said. She hadn't put in her tooth. She was wearing a blue long-sleeve shirt under her housecoat, which was mis-snapped, the hem from one side hanging down three inches below the other.

Behind Lovey, Mary noticed one of the bookshelves in the hutch had been cleared of its books. On the floor was a lumpy white plastic bag with holes where the book corners had popped through. Was she planning to throw them away?

"I'm sorry to barge in on you," Mary said. "Did you get Darlene's messages?"

Lovey didn't answer. She didn't have to. Mary could see the light flashing on the machine. Lovey hadn't listened to her messages. The old woman smoothed out her hair and stuffed her hands in her pockets. There was a vacant look to her eyes.

"Auntie, what are those books doing in the trash bag?" Mary asked. "I thought you said you wanted to start reading them."

"I've already read them," she said. She waved off the idea.

"I thought you were going to reread them. That's what you said last night."

Lovey seemed agitated. "I was up all night reading them. And then I realized he's gone."

Mary felt her stomach bottom out. "Who's gone?"

"Who do you *think*?" There was a harsh, impatient tone to

Lovey's voice that Mary had heard her use with Claire and Mary's grandmother years ago. Lovey had never used it with Mary.

"Are you talking about your brother?" Mary looked to the arm with the pacemaker bracelet. The bruise that had been there yesterday, the one that had somehow captured Joe's profile, had faded some. "Auntie, he died years ago. You remember that, don't you?"

"No, he was right here." Lovey pinched at the yellowing bruise. "That good-for-nothing sonofabitch." Lovey spit a little when she said it. "It's a wonder Eleanor never left him." Her eyes seemed to have sunk deeper into their sockets and her face had turned the color of a pomegranate. To Mary's horror, her aunt closed her arthritic fingers into a gnarled fist and hit herself hard just below the shoulder. Then, with the other hand, she did the same, this time hitting herself on the forearm.

Mary didn't know what to do. She grabbed both her aunt's hands in hers and turned them palms-up toward the ceiling. "What are you *doing*?" she asked.

Lovey started to sob. "He's left us again. I don't know how much more I can take."

Mary let go of Lovey's hands and they dropped to her sides. The old woman went limp. Mary thought her aunt might topple onto the floor.

"Come, let's sit down," Mary said. She sniffed back her own tears and guided Lovey to her chair. Mary knelt on the floor in front of her. That's when Mary noticed more purple at the base of her aunt's left sleeve. A new bruise. Mary pushed the blue fabric up her aunt's arm. Lovey winced.

So did Mary. The entire arm was covered in bruises. Some looked like purple roses, others like bad tattoos that had bled into the surrounding skin. Mary lifted the other sleeve and found the same thing. "My God," she said. "Did you do this to yourself, Auntie? *Why?*" Mary felt sick to her stomach.

"He's not coming back. This time he's gone for good. Don't ask me how I know, but I do." She was staring at the air above Mary's head and speaking loud, as if for the benefit of some third party in the room. "I'm losing him. I'm losing everything."

"Auntie, we need to take you to the doctor," Mary said.

There were some tense moments in the doctor's office. When the physician on call saw all the bruises, he assumed a case of elder abuse. It wasn't until he saw Lovey hit herself again, until they pulled up her chart with the neurologist's Alzheimer's and dementia diagnoses, that he believed Mary's account of what was going on.

"Just minor contusions," the doctor had said. He gave Lovey a sedative and some pills that would help her sleep. He strongly recommended Lovey not be left alone, especially this evening. The medicine might further disorient her. And then he asked Mary if she'd given any thought to the idea of moving Lovey into a nursing home.

Eleven

D id I do something wrong? Did Vanessa tell you I was stealing her tables? Because that's a big fat lie. Hope wasn't out front so I seated the deuce and then right away they asked me to get them drinks. What was I supposed to do?" Prep School Punk Jennifer, fast becoming *Angry* Jennifer, sat, arms folded, in the chair across from Mary's desk.

"Jennifer, it's not—," Mary started.

"And if it's about the swearing thing, I'm sorry, but I just can't help it." Then it was as if Jennifer finally realized where she was, in Mary's private office. The girl started looking around, at the stuff on the desk, up at the bookcases, at the wilting pink roses in the vase. "In case you didn't notice, the guys in the kitchen swear all the time. It's like you have a double standard. It's sexist."

This was harder than Mary thought it would be. "You're not here because of that."

"Then what?" Jennifer crossed her legs and started picking at the rubber at the back of her sneaker.

Mary took a breath. "It's just that this is your second season here and I barely know anything about you."

Jennifer didn't look up. She just kept picking. "I get it. This is about Anicca. In that meeting you said you wanted to get to know us better. Is this how you meant?"

She made it sound so lame. "Well, yes, actually."

With Anicca's death, Mary realized not only that it wasn't right for her to know nothing about the people who worked for her, but that even *she* had been missing out with the distance she kept between herself and her employees. She'd told her staff in that meeting that she would make an effort to learn more about them. They'd all rolled their eyes. Here it had been over two weeks and she knew no more about most of them than she had the day Anicca died. And so she'd set July Fourth weekend as the official start date for her new initiative and she intended to keep to it, despite everything else that was going on. Because she knew it was the right thing to do. And because she'd never forget the way the cop had looked at her that morning.

Jennifer fidgeted in her seat. The idea that she wasn't going to be reprimanded didn't seem to relax her any. "What do you want to know?"

Mary folded her hands and leaned in. "Let's start with where you're from."

"My mother lives in Boston. My father's in Orange County. I've spent summers here with my grandmother at the family house since I was a kid."

"Where's that?" Mary asked.

"The Heights."

Mary was starting to feel like an interrogator. "And you go to college?"

"Hampshire. I'm a sophomore."

"Do you like it there?"

"Sure." Now Jennifer was looking around again, only this time like she was trying to find an escape hatch.

Mary thought people were supposed to like talking about themselves. Not kids, she concluded. "What's your major?"

"Women's Studies."

Here was some common ground. They were both women. "You know, I've always been curious what one studies as a Women's Studies major. I mean, I always thought it was the men who should be studying women, right?"

Jennifer looked at her like she was from Mars. Or Venus?

"That was a joke," Mary said.

Jennifer nodded. She took a deep breath. "We study feminist thought as it relates to economic and cultural imperialism, gender, class, race, sexual orientation. We look at how gender inequalities affect us." Jennifer looked up from her sneaker. "Like, I could go on for days about what goes on here."

"Really?" Mary said.

"I mean, look at the women out on the floor, who you call *girls* by the way—a pejorative term—and *waitresses*." She scrunched her nose like the word smelled bad.

"Well, that's what you are." Mary hated the way her voice sounded when she got defensive.

"The politically correct term is *server*."

Good grief. "Like 'flight attendant' as opposed to 'stewardess.' I get it."

Jennifer rolled her eyes. "I mean it's pretty clear there's a class division here based on physical appearance, on cup size, even. I'll just leave it at that." Mary couldn't help but look at Jennifer's ample chest. So they were on to her. All these years she thought she'd been subtle. "Plus we're encouraged to *flirt* with customers." Another smelly word.

"I ask you to smile. Is that flirting?" Mary asked. She started shuffling some papers on her desk, as if there might be one buried there with the right answers written on it.

Jennifer seemed to forget she was talking to her employer. "You ask us to 'smile at the *husbands* because they pay the bills.' A sexist assumption. And never mind that." She slid up to the edge of her chair. "Look at these tight shirts we have to wear"—she pinched the Lycra-infused cotton clinging to her bosom, pulled it away and it snapped right back—"while the guys behind the bar get to wear loose polo shirts. And that's *another* thing. And how come there are no female bartenders? And how come the head cooks are all guys? Like I said, I could go on and on." She slid back in her chair and started picking at the shoe rubber again.

The girl was right. Mary had never given much thought to feminism. She was too busy running her business. "Hey, at least the owner's a woman," she said, trying to charm Jennifer with a warm smile. "Top of the food chain." She smoothed down her hair. "Let's talk about something else, shall we?"

Jennifer ran her fingers through her blond spikes. "Fine."

A few moments of awkward silence passed while Mary tried to figure out what to ask. "I know. What do you do for fun?"

"I'm into sports. I windsurf." Jennifer put her foot down again. She started tapping it. "I read."

This was good. Mary liked to read. "What are you reading now?"

"Karl Marx."

Okay, then. Cut to the girl talk. "Do you have a boyfriend?"

Jennifer looked up, eyes wide. "You're kidding, right?"

Here it was, so obvious it was a wonder Mary could have missed it. Beneath the edgy exterior was a girl who obviously had never come to terms with her own feminine beauty, which was why she cut her hair in this short punk style and wrapped herself up in this militant feminist persona. She was insecure. Maybe it had something to do with her parents' split. Or maybe she'd had a bad experience with a man, and developed low self-esteem as a result. Mary could take this opportunity to mentor the girl. Boost her confidence. "I don't know if you've looked in the mirror recently but you're a lovely girl, Jennifer. *Woman,*" Mary corrected herself. "I'm sure if you just softened those hard edges a bit there'd be busloads of men waiting in line for the chance to—"

Jennifer shook her head. She leaned in. "Mary. I'm a lesbian." She slapped her palms on the table and leaned back. "I can't believe you didn't know that. *Everybody* knows that."

Everybody but Mary, as always seemed the case. "Oh, hell, I'm sorry," she said. "Not sorry that you're a lesbian." *Oh, Jesus.* "I just mean I'm sorry I didn't know sooner." Even worse.

"I already *have* a girlfriend," Jennifer said. She picked at her fingernail.

"She doesn't work here, does she?" Mary asked, now making it sound like she didn't want lesbians working for her, when in fact this was something Mary really had no opinion on. What did she care as long as they worked hard and were good at what they did? All she had meant was, how many other employees was she as clueless about?

"No, she doesn't work here," Jennifer said, a little hostile.

The door downstairs opened.

"Mary, you've got to come down and see this." It was Nate.

Mary had followed the doctor's advice, taking Lovey home to stay with her the day she'd discovered the bruises. He'd given Lovey a sedative, and on the way back from his office, the old woman had slept as Mary stopped by the apartment to pick up some of her things—her tooth, some housecoats, and those scary, amorphous white undergarments she'd kept in a drawer since Mary was a kid that could only be purchased in one particular store in Province-town. Mary'd written a check for the amount of Lovey's rent and slipped it into the tin box at the door to the office with a note for Darlene, saying Lovey had a touch of the flu and would be staying with Mary for the next few days.

The next morning, Lovey had awakened in a confused state, not knowing where she was or how she'd gotten there. When Mary looked at her aunt's face, it was as if a shadow had slipped down over her eyes, a vagueness, reminding Mary of those veils her aunt and mother had worn in the 1960s. She wondered what Angry Jennifer might have to say about those.

With the help of the local Council on Aging, Mary arranged to have a home health care worker stay with Lovey so Mary could go to work. She couldn't afford not to be at the restaurant during Fourth of July weekend. That night, when Mary came home, Audrey from Home Health Services said that Lovey had slept most of the day but had asked where she was each time she woke. Each time, Audrey told her she was at her niece's home, but it hadn't seemed to register. Mary understood how that might be the case. Lovey rarely left her own home. She'd only stayed with Mary one weekend close to when Mary had first moved into the new house. And even then, before she became ill, the experience had been confusing. She'd told Mary that at one point she'd left her room in the middle of the night to use the bathroom and had ended up out on the porch.

Audrey said that Lovey had eaten well and the bruises seemed to be giving her no trouble. And there'd been no mention whatsoever of brother Joe. Hopefully, whatever that had been about had passed. By the time Mary got home, Lovey was asleep. Mary quietly entered the room and kissed her aunt on the forehead, then went to her own room to sleep herself, and was out as soon as her head hit the pillow.

The second day, Mary awakened early to the smell of coffee and cinnamon. Had Audrey arrived and started fixing Lovey's breakfast? Mary looked at the clock. It was only 6:30 a.m. Audrey wasn't expected there till 8:00. Mary threw on her bathrobe and slid her feet into her slippers. She made her way out to the kitchen, then stopped.

"What a lovely kitchen this is, dear," Lovey said. There she was beside the stove, wearing a crisp yellow seersucker robe, having taken the time to style her hair as best she could without the bobby pins Mary had neglected to stuff into her overnight bag. There were two place mats out on the kitchen island, set with plates, mugs, and utensils. A bowl of eggshells and a bag of sliced bread sat on the counter. Lovey was tending to two slices of French toast in the fry pan. "Coffee's ready. And breakfast will be a minute," she said. Lovey slid the spatula under a slice of bread to check for doneness.

Mary looked around to see if Audrey was hiding around the corner, though it would have been hard for Audrey, weighing in at close to three hundred pounds, to hide anywhere. Her weight was probably why she'd given up her job at the hospital as an RN. Still, without Audrey, how could Lovey have pulled this off, especially given her condition the day before?

"Do we have any maple syrup?" Lovey asked. "If not, butter will do. You always liked yours buttered, with a sprinkle of sugar."

She even remembered that. "It's in the cupboard to the left of the sink," Mary said. "So you're feeling better this morning?"

"Of course, I'm fine," Lovey said. "But I seem to have developed some kind of affliction." She held out her arms for Mary's inspection. The purple welts had faded some. "It doesn't hurt at all."

"You don't remember?" Mary said. "About Uncle Joe?" she added.

"Funny how he's been on my mind lately. I had a dream he was right in my apartment." Lovey waved her hand in dismissal. "Unfinished business. It's how we all felt when his liver gave out. So young. We were angry with him." She shook her head. "Such a waste."

Mary felt that her aunt knew more about the bruises than she was letting on. Like she was playacting to see what she could get away with. Or perhaps it was just a defense mechanism produced by her own psyche to spare her the pain of facing her deficits. Not only that, but Lovey seemed perfectly at home in Mary's place, not asking why or how it turned out she was there. Not asking when she'd be going home.

Before Mary could probe any further, Lovey changed the subject. "Come. Sit. I'll pour you a cup," she said.

Mary started for one of the stools beneath the place settings. Lovey took Mary's mug and filled it, then poured her own.

"How did you figure out where everyth—?"

"Did you know you have a coyote, dear? A handsome, well-fed devil." Lovey drew a sip from her mug. "Saw him right in the driveway this morning. Right *there*." She pointed. "And then he ran off behind the house."

"There's a cottage right behind—," Mary started.

"Don't I know it. I had to pull my bedroom curtains shut this morning or I might have seen that old codger's arse. I wonder if he was being fresh with me. Started yanking off his pajama bottoms for all the world to see. He should really get some shades," Lovey said. She brought the fry pan over to the plates and deposited a slice of toast on each.

Mary felt bad for the old guy. He didn't have shades because he'd never needed shades before her house was built on top of his. Now he was probably too old to deal with installing them. "I'm sure he didn't do it on purpose," Mary said. "I think he has Parkinson's."

"Remember Mr. Snyder had Parkinson's? He was that nice tailor we brought you to when you were a little girl." Lovey said

"I remember," Mary said, her mouth full of French toast.

Lovey went to the cabinet for the maple syrup, then came around the island and took the stool next to Mary's. She unfolded her napkin and set it on her lap. "Such a terrible disease," Lovey said. "One of the women downstairs had it. Betty. She's dead now."

"Hmm," Mary said. What voodoo made Lovey's French toast taste so good?

The two of them ate side by side, just like they used to when Mary was a child and would sleep over her aunt's house. Mary felt her heart grow warm. It was nice having the old woman here.

"You know, tomorrow's the Fourth of July," Mary said. "You can see the whole fireworks display from right here. That's Rock Harbor right out there." Mary pointed.

Lovey's face lit up. "I haven't seen fireworks in years."

Mary felt bad about that. She should have taken her aunt at least a few times in all these years, but the Fourth was always too busy a night to leave the restaurant. "Well, you'll see them tomorrow," she said. "And then we can think about getting you back home."

"Speaking of fireworks, dear, who's 'sorry he missed you'?" Lovey asked. She pulled the note out of her robe pocket and set it on the table between them.

Mary nearly choked on her toast. She must have left the note lying around. She finished chewing, then cleared her throat. "Remember Dan Bassett? He was the guy who supplied my fish after Robbie died."

Lovey grew taller in her seat. Her back stiffened. "He supplied more than *fish*, as I recall." Her voice had gone cold in that old movie-star way, like Ethel Mertz when she was pissed off at Lucy.

"That's the one," Mary said. She smiled. "Don't worry, he's just supplying the fish this time."

"Hmm." Lovey drizzled some syrup on her toast.

"'Hmm' yourself," Mary said. She laughed. "Mind your own

beeswax, old woman. And thanks for breakfast." She leaned over and planted a sticky peck on her aunt's cheek.

As she ate her French toast, it struck Mary that things could be falling apart around her, but given one positive sign, one scrap of cinnamon French toast, it was so easy to slip into the feeling that there must be some mistake, that things were all right after all. As she watched her aunt enjoy her breakfast, delighting in each bite, Mary thought how Alzheimer's disease forced its victims and even their loved ones into living in the present moment. With all the meditation classes Mary had taken, all the times she'd tried to quiet her mind in those days after Robbie died, and again after Dan left, she simply couldn't manage to stop the tape from replaying the past or stop worrying about what lay ahead. She'd been a miserable failure at living in the present. Yet now, somehow, everything came down to this bit of buttered toast on her fork. The scent of cinnamon. A yellow robe. Warm coffee on the lips. A seemingly contented loved one on the stool beside her.

As Mary started to leave her office, she saw the small pile of rubber shoe bits on the floor beneath the chair Jennifer had fled when Nate called for them. When Mary reached the bottom of the stairs, he grabbed her by the elbow.

"What is it?" Mary asked. She checked the parking lot and it was about half full. Not bad, given that the sun was out, even for the Fourth of July.

"Your aunt," Nate said. He led her through the kitchen. He was smiling, so Mary knew Lovey couldn't have gotten herself into too much trouble. Still, what had Mary been thinking? She'd all but forgotten she'd left her aunt down at the bar folding lobster bibs more than forty minutes ago.

Because Lovey had seemed so well this morning, Mary decided it might be fun for her to get out and be around people. What harm could it do? She knew business wouldn't be too brisk until later, when people left the beach and returned to their rental cottages to rinse off the day's salt and sand in their outdoor showers, maybe take a nap before dressing for dinner and hitting the town.

Nate led Mary out the screen door.

"Check it out," Nate said. He pointed to a table at the center of the main dining room.

Lovey was seated at a table beside a young male customer. She had a red-white-and-blue pinwheel stuck into a buttonhole of her blouse. She held a pen in one hand and a green pad in the other. A young woman across the table from them was laughing.

"She just told him to scoot over so she could sit down," Sage said. She picked up her drink order at the bar and headed out to one of her tables.

"That's great," Nate said.

"What is she *doing*?" Mary said.

"I guess she got tired of folding lobster bibs," Chuck the bartender said.

"I don't mind as long as she splits the tip," Jennifer said. The other girls had covered for her while she'd been upstairs. Now, ready to take over, she tied the short apron around her waist and tousled her hair. "I mean, it is *my* table." She glared at Mary as if all this was Mary's fault, which Mary supposed it was.

Mary watched her aunt get up from the table, flatten the shirt around her belly, and hobble to the bar, grinning from ear to ear. Her eyes were bright. "Move over, dearie," she said to Mary. "I have an order for this handsome young fella."

Chuck blushed.

She continued, "One Budweiser and one *Virgin* Mary." She winked at her niece. One of the waitresses saw the gesture and guffawed.

"What do you think you're doing?" Mary said. She couldn't wipe the grin from her own face.

"Making myself useful," Lovey said. She licked her arthritic thumb and used it to separate the top sheet on the pad, then tore it off and skewered it on the order holder. Waitresses weren't supposed to do that, only bartenders were, their way of knowing an order had been completed.

Jennifer said to Nate, "How come she doesn't have to wear one of these?" She once again snapped the clingy fabric of her uniform shirt. "*Age* discrimination," she said. Nate rolled his eyes.

"Never mind," Mary said. Then she turned to Lovey, who'd started to lift the tray with the beer and the drink, then no doubt finding it and herself too wobbly, had decided to just take the two drinks, one in each hand. "You can bring those out. Then come with me. I have a better idea."

"Phew. Those girls work hard," Lovey said. "Just watching them was enough to make me want to take a nap."

The two women stood in the front door alcove of Mary's house while Mary unlocked the door.

"You *should* take a nap," Mary said. She opened the door and flicked on the lights in the hall. "I won't be back until at least eleven. Besides, you worked your butt off today. I was proud of you."

They walked down the hall and Lovey stopped at the door to her room. It was strange for Mary to see her aunt in one of the restaurant uniforms, even if it was one of the bartenders' polo shirts—a long-sleeve one to cover the bruises, which had nearly faded—and not, thank the Lord, one of the clingy waitress tops, as Angry Jennifer had suggested.

"I'm not sure sitting on a comfortable stool by the entrance and smiling at people can be considered *work*," Lovey said.

Mary knew there was no way Lovey could keep up the pace in the dining room, so she'd set her up at the entrance, where she could greet diners, then let Hope lead them to their tables. At one point there'd been a short wait and Lovey had entertained customers with stories about Cape Cod in the old days. They loved it.

"Smiling all day *is* work," Mary said. God forbid Mary ever had such a vocation.

"Don't worry about me, dear," Lovey said. "You go on back now.

I'll make myself something to eat if I get hungry." Lovey took the hanger with the white shirt she'd worn to the restaurant out of Mary's hand.

"There's chowder in the fridge. You just have to heat it up." Mary looked at her watch. The dinner shift would be arriving soon. "Are you sure you don't want me to have the girl come keep you company this evening?"

"Nonsense. I've lived alone the last forty years." Lovey seemed tired and eager to lie down.

"Okay, fine, but the number for my red phone is upstairs on the island. And my cell phone number is on there too. If you need anything at all, don't hesitate to call."

"I'm fine. Later I'll come up and make some dinner, then watch the fireworks, and then go to bed. No need to rush home. Now, shoo."

Mary gave her aunt a hug, then headed for the door.

"Call me if you need anything."

Lovey stuck up her crooked thumb. "Will do."

When Mary returned to the restaurant, Sage and Wayne were out back, sitting close together on the top step, taking a well-deserved break. Nevertheless, Mary didn't want her employees to think she'd gone soft.

"What's this, a coffee klatsch?"

"Don't get your knickers in a twist. There are four customers in the restaurant and they all have their food," Wayne said. He had a cigarette going.

Laughter came from around the side of the building. Mary jumped.

"Haven't heard that expression in ages." Dan came around the corner with a big cooler balanced on his shoulder. He was wearing green waders and a navy blue T-shirt. He had his hair pulled back off his face and knotted at the back of his neck, making him look more like the old Dan.

"Where's your truck?" Mary asked.

"Around front. There was a propane truck in the driveway when I got here."

"He just left," Wayne said.

"Dan, this is Wayne," Mary said. Her voice was a little higher than usual. Wayne and Sage seemed to pick up on it. They looked at each other, then at Mary, then at Dan. "He's our head cook. And this is his . . . Sage."

Dan set the cooler on the ground near the bulkhead. He came over and shook their hands. "Wayne. Sage."

Wayne nodded. "Fish has been great. Wicked fresh." He stamped out his cigarette and started to get up. "For a change," he added, and looked at Mary.

"If people can have fresh fish in Kansas, shouldn't be too hard to get it a couple miles from the docks, right?" Dan said.

"You'd think," Wayne said. He opened the door for Sage.

"So long," Sage said, and went in. Wayne followed. Mary noticed how Wayne put his hand on the small of her back. They were already lovers, Mary guessed. An unlikely pair, Mary had to admit. This year the kitchen was full of them.

Now Dan stood between Mary and the door. She walked over to the side of the building, pretending to inspect the paint trim around one of the kitchen windows. She hoped he'd pick up his cooler and go down through the bulkhead. She'd wanted to see him. Now she didn't know what to say. Was he nervous too?

"So—," he said.

"Know a good painter? This trim is a disaster," she said. She chipped off a chunk of paint with her thumbnail. "I never noticed."

"Did you get my note the other day?" he asked.

She looked up at him. "Note? Oh, *that*. Sure I got it. Funny how we kept missing each other. But that's what it's like around here, you know. Busy as hell sometimes. People coming and going." *Shut up, already.* She shoved her hands into her jeans pockets.

He eyes smiled. "How's Lovey?"

"She's staying with me for a few days. I think it's been good for her. I had her here all afternoon. Just brought her home, actually."

"How's that been, having her around?"

"It's nice. Reminds me of when I was a kid. Only now in some ways it's like she's the kid. But it's nice having the company. The big house gets lonely." Why did she say that? She sounded like some pathetic spinster.

"Heard you sold the old place," Dan said. He ran his hand along his graying whiskers.

Images of a younger, naked Dan on the sofa at the old house immediately came to mind. Mary blushed. "It was about time," she said. "The new place is great. It's just spacious by comparison, which is hard to get used to. Know what I mean?"

"I live on a boat," Dan said. He winked.

"Right."

"So you live alone, huh?" he asked. "I mean when your aunt's not there. No boyfriend?"

Let's not mince words. Let's get right to the point. Jesus. She could put this whole thing to bed right now. So to speak. All she had to do was say she had a boyfriend. "No boyfriend," she said.

The way he was looking at her, it was coming back to her, how much she used to like it. Sirens were firing off in her brain. *Mayday. The ship is going down.* She didn't give him a chance to talk. "So thanks again for bailing me out this weekend. I don't know what I would have done if you hadn't." She started for the door. If he wouldn't move, she'd walk around him.

"No problem." He grinned, apparently amused by her feeble attempt to escape. "Me either."

She stopped. "You either *what*?" What had she missed?

"No girlfriend."

Sirens at full blare. The ship is taking on water. "I should get going," Mary said. "Dinner prep. Staff's coming on. Fourth of July. You know how it is." She made it halfway around him when he turned and touched her arm.

"Have dinner with me," he said.

She looked into his eyes. It took a minute to register what he'd said.

He laughed and looked down at himself. "Don't worry, I'll clean up this time."

"It's Fourth of July. I can't just leave."

"Still stop serving at nine?" He remembered. She'd always been one of the earliest places in town to stop serving food. In the early days, it had been so she could try to track down her husband before he got into any trouble. Later, it was because she just didn't want to deal with the late-night crowd. Thankfully, she earned enough with her business model that she didn't have to rely on late-night liquor sales to keep her afloat, and all that they entailed—the bouncers, the permits, the entertainment, the cleanup, the sloppy stragglers, the property damage.

Mary nodded. "But we don't get out of here till at least elev—"

"I'll pick you up at nine."

"But—"

"Let Wayne be in charge." He winked and nodded toward the kitchen. "Don't get your knickers in a twist." How come when he said 'knickers' it sounded different? A little dirty.

Mary looked at him. "You really think this is a good idea?" She was just aping the little voice inside her head.

"Wouldn't've suggested it otherwise." He finally stepped out of her way and moved over toward the bulkhead.

She looked down to the gravel. "I just think—"

"I miss you," he said. Like he was talking about the weather. Twelve years. He turned the latch and pulled open the doors to the bulkhead. The hinges squeaked so loudly she wondered if she had heard him right. He hoisted the cooler up on his shoulder. "When I saw you the other day at the Pagoda, reminded me how much." He started down the stairs.

Mary felt a flash of anger. *What nerve!* She clenched her fists. "I've been right here the whole time."

Dan rested the cooler on the edge of the bulkhead. He looked up at her. "I know," he said. He looked sad. All the confidence seemed to have left him. He rested his head on the side of the cooler and looked at her. He was that nice kid from high school.

"Nine," she finally said. "But park across the street at the farmers' market." She half-smiled.

"Don't want people to think you're fraternizing with the help," he said.

"Something like that."

He laughed. "I'll be there." He started down the stairs.

Mary called out, "Where are we going?"

"Beats me."

Twelve

Around seven thirty, Mary made a quick trip home to check on Lovey and grab some clean clothes for her "date." When she got to the house, Lovey's door was closed. Mary put her ear to the panel and could hear her aunt's soft snore. She was fast asleep. Mary went upstairs and left Lovey a note saying she'd be a bit later than she'd first planned and that Lovey shouldn't wait up for her. Mary decided too that she'd call Audrey, the home health care worker, who lived less than a mile away, and invite her to watch the fireworks with Lovey. She'd brought home dessert for them, two slices of New York–style cheesecake that she left in the fridge. Audrey lived in an old saltbox just a couple of streets inland. She agreed to come, though she said she had grandchildren visiting and wouldn't be able to stop by until the after fireworks display was over. Mary told her if the old woman was still asleep when she arrived, to let her be. Mary was wondering now whether being at the restaurant today had overtired her aunt.

With minutes to spare, Mary flew to her room and yanked off her T-shirt. She pressed it to her nose and smelled the fryer grease. No good. If the shirt smelled this bad, she must too. She jumped into the shower for a rinse, then slid on a clean pair of jeans and a cute black top, a little low-cut, that tied in the back. She threw her makeup, silver hoop earrings, and a bottle of perfume into her purse so she could freshen up right before Dan came to get her.

She was standing in front of the sink when she noticed bright lights coming from her neighbor's house. Maybe the old man was using a sunlamp. Or growing hydroponic weed—reason enough to make friends. More than likely he'd accidentally bought an overly bright set of lightbulbs at the market. She hoped the lights wouldn't disturb Lovey's rest. Mary grabbed her stuff and had started for the door when she saw the answering machine flashing. She ran over to the side table and pressed "play."

There was a pause, then: "I'm sorry, I'm not sure if I have the right number. I'm looking for Hope but the answering machine gave a different name. But I'm sure I dialed . . . Well, in case I do have it right, this is Meg Ryder. Hope came by one morning and we talked and she gave me this number. Anyway, Hope, if you could please call me back sometime, I'd appreciate it." She left her phone number.

Mary's empty stomach lurched. She picked up the phone and dialed.

"Hello."

"Meg, this is Hope. I got your message."

"I thought I had the wrong house," Meg said.

"Mary's my . . . sister. She gave me her answering machine and I haven't gotten around to changing the message." More lies. She'd have to start writing them down to keep them straight.

"Well, thanks for calling back so soon."

"How are you?" Mary asked. "How's Ariel?"

"We're doing okay," Meg said. "Look, I hate to bother you—"

"No bother at all. I enjoyed our talk last week—you were so kind—and, well, anything I can do."

Meg hesitated. "I just had a question for you. I don't know many people around here, except for the ones from the lumber company. But I've asked all of them and none of them know . . . I'm wondering if you know a woman by the name of Lavinia Rollwagon."

Mary's heart jumped. "Good old Lavinia. Of course. I've known her for years."

"You do?" Meg sighed. "It's just such an usual name and, of course they're mostly kids at Quanset, but no one I asked seemed to know who she—"

"Well, that's no wonder. She's a widow. And a bit of an agoraphobe, I've heard."

"Really."

"How did you come to meet her?" Mary asked.

"I haven't met her. She wrote to me after the accident, and again last week. She wanted to offer her financial support to Ariel but I couldn't accept help from someone I don't even—"

Mary forced a laugh. "That's Lavinia. Always looking for ways to help people. And Lord knows she's got the means."

"In her letter she said her husband had left her—"

"A small fortune, to put it mildly. She's loaded. If I were you I wouldn't hesitate to accept her generosity. Her heart's in the right place, believe me."

"She said she lost her mother when she was a young girl—"

"Hmm. I didn't know that. All the more reason to let her help. A lonely old woman reliving her childhood, her husband gone. You'd probably be doing *her* a favor," Mary said.

"Well, thank you, Hope. I appreciate your candor. From that first day I felt like you were someone I could talk to. It's as if you dropped out of the sky and landed at my door. Like an angel."

Mary felt a little ashamed. "Lavinia's the angel," she said, though she understood what Meg had meant. Their connection had been effortless, even given the circumstances. "As for you and me, maybe we knew each other in a past life," Mary said. She half-believed in the possibility of such things. "Would you like to get together for coffee sometime?"

"That would be nice. Maybe one day next week?"

"How about Thursday?" Mary suggested.

"Thursday would be fine if you could come by the house. Ariel does better at home."

"I'd love to see her too," Mary said.

"Is eight too early? She has me up at dawn these days."

"Perfect." She'd still make it to work before most of the crew. "And if you want me to speak to Lavinia on your behalf, I'd be happy—"

"Oh, no. I'll think about it and get back to her myself in the next few days. But thanks."

Mary panicked. "I'm not sure her phone number is listed."

"She didn't give a number, so I'll just write her back. She seems like a kind woman." Mary thought she could detect hopefulness in Meg's voice. She'd done a brilliant sales job.

"Oh, she is," Mary said. "One of the kindest I've had the pleasure of knowing." She looked down the hall to where her aunt slept. The funny thing was, if her aunt were healthy and well off, she might very well have reached out to Meg and Ariel. Mary believed that with all her heart, and it somehow made her feel less of a liar.

Mary sat in the cab of Dan's pickup. They were almost in Wellfleet when a blast of fireworks flashed above the tree line.

"Look!" Mary said. She felt like a little kid. She realized she sounded like one too.

Dan smiled. "When I get to the clearing up ahead, we can pull over."

"Yes, do," she said. She looked over at Dan. She could hardly believe she was actually riding in Dan Bassett's truck on the Fourth of July, on her way to a late dinner. She felt a strange sense of déjà vu, not so much of reliving the past but of living one of the countless dreams they'd starred in together over the years.

And, true to her dreams, he looked handsome, maybe more handsome than ever, despite the lines in his face from a lifetime on the water. As promised, he had cleaned up. He'd shaved and was wearing a simple black cotton boatneck sweater with the sleeves bunched up at his elbows, and jeans. He wore his hair down and had put some kind of gel in it that tamed and defined his curls. It smelled citrusy.

Once again, she noticed the wide scar on his forearm, just below the elbow. She was looking at it when she got caught.

"You're wondering about my beauty mark," he said.

"No, I was just—"

"Happened in Alaska. Every day it reminds me how lucky I am to be alive."

Mary wanted to hear the story, but they had come to the place on the highway where the view opened up across the marshes to the bay beyond, to where the fireworks were being launched at the end of the town pier. Other cars had pulled up along the shoulder and people were sitting on the hoods. No cars were coming in the opposite direction, so Dan accelerated across the oncoming lane and onto the far shoulder, near the marsh. He stepped on the brakes. Mary felt a rush of adrenaline.

"Let's get out," she said. Before the truck had come to a full stop, Mary was out the passenger-side door. Dan killed the headlights. Mary jumped onto the tire rim and rested her feet on the guardrail.

A bowl of red, white, and blue stars lit up the night sky and then spilled out over them.

"Wow," Mary said. She felt goose bumps migrating up her arms and rubbed them down.

"When was the last time you saw fireworks?" Dan asked.

"Not since before the restaurant opened. Seventeen, eighteen years." *Not since we were together,* she wanted to say.

"No kidding." He disappeared around the back of the truck.

Another flash erupted into fiery corkscrews. Then an unearthly boom. People around them oohed and aahed. Mary felt a mosquito pierce the flesh of her arm. She swatted at it.

As if he'd read her mind, Dan came around the front of the truck with an itchy blanket that smelled like clams that have dried out in the sun. He draped it over Mary's arms. Some sand spilled onto her jeans.

"Thanks," she said. "Come up." She tapped the fender.

Dan hopped up beside her. The front end of the truck sank. She lifted up one end of the blanket so he could come underneath.

"When was the last time *you* saw fireworks?" Mary asked.

"Last Fourth of July." Mary felt a pang of jealousy. She wondered who he'd been sharing the blanket with then. "I usually take the boat out and watch them offshore," he said.

"It must be nice to see from out there," she said.

A series of flashes erupted in hot white diamonds that seemed to hover in the air above them. With each burst of light Mary saw plumes of dark smoke echoing the previous display. With each flash, the smoke grew thicker, something she'd never noticed when she was a kid. With every flash, shadows of smoke could be seen hanging in the sky, like memories.

Dan fished for her hand beneath the blanket and she forgot all about the flashes and smoke. He found it and gave it a squeeze. She shivered.

"You warm enough?" he asked.

"Sure," she said, then leaned into him a little as if it had been an invitation. "I'm just thinking about Lovey. I left her to watch the fireworks by herself."

Dan looked at her like she might be nuts.

"Someone's coming to check on her in about a half hour. She was sound asleep when I left." Mary looked up at the sky, which cracked into a thousand flaming tongues. "But I hope she's watching them. She hasn't seen them in years either. I feel bad I never took her, but the Fourth is so busy and— I probably could have taken her. I managed to sneak away tonight, didn't I? She used to take me when I was little. We used to pack dinner and lay out a blanket on the beach." Mary sighed. "I wonder if she'll even be here to see them a year from now."

"Nice memories," Dan said. "The kind you can keep with you always."

Bittersweet, like the smoke, Mary thought.

"Why don't you give her a call if you want?" Dan asked.

Mary reached into her back pocket for her cell phone, just to check that there'd been no messages. "If she's asleep, I don't want to wake her. Plus the phone's on the second floor in the kitchen and I wouldn't want her to rush up the stairs and have a heart attack or break her hip or something."

"The kitchen is above the bedrooms?"

"It's an upside-down house, more or less." Mary said. "My bedroom's upstairs, though."

"I can't wait to see it someday."

Mary didn't know if he meant the house or her bedroom. She looked at him. He was watching the sky. She could see the flashes of light reflected in his eyes.

"You will," Mary said. She squeezed his hand.

Mary leaned back from the table. The only things left on her plate were a few cherrystone shells, a little broth, and a couple of cooked leeks. "I can't eat another bite," she said. "That was incredible. This place deserves the hype."

"Almost as good as the Clambake," Dan said. He brought the napkin to his mouth.

"Don't patronize me, Dan Bassett. I know I've never been worthy of hype. Thanks only to Wayne, we're one or two rungs above your average fish-and-chips joint, but always a few rungs below the 'happening' restaurant scene."

"The 'happening' restaurant scene is fickle."

Mary raised her glass of white to his red. "Hear, hear," she said. They clinked glasses. "I have regulars who've been coming since the day we opened."

"I believe it," Dan said. Now when he smiled, the dimples Mary remembered cracked into deep grooves that ran up and down his cheeks.

"How was your chop?" Mary asked.

Dan had devoured a huge pork loin chop and all the fingerling potatoes that came with it.

"Terrible." He winked and pushed the empty plate away.

Mary leaned back. "You never told me how you managed to get a last-minute reservation here on the Fourth of July. Don't tell me you're *their* fish guy too."

Dan pushed out his chair and stretched his legs. "I'm a one-restaurant man, Sunshine," he said. All night they had managed to steer clear of any touchy subjects. Dead husbands. Awkward partings. Long absences. Cheating. "One of the guys down at the dock lives with the lunch hostess."

"Hmm." Mary studied him. Maybe it was the liquor she'd consumed, or that the awkwardness between them had given way to old comfort and familiarity, or that a few elephants had suddenly plopped themselves down in the middle of the table, but Mary felt as if there were things she wanted to get off her chest. For whatever this was to proceed further, she would eventually need some answers.

"What was that 'hmm' for?" Dan asked.

The waiter appeared and instructed the busboy to clear the plates. He whipped out a plastic card and scraped the crumbs from the table and into his hand. Mary's waitresses didn't have plastic cards. They barely wiped away crumbs. "Can I get you any coffee or dessert?"

"Coffee sound good?" Dan asked.

"Sure," Mary said.

"Cute kid," Mary said when the waiter left. "I should offer him a job at my place next year when this 'happening' place goes under."

Dan cleared his throat. "So you surround yourself with 'cute kids,' I hear."

Mary leaned back from the table. Had she heard him right? "What's that supposed to mean?"

Dan raised his hand. "Sorry. None of my business."

What had he heard? Mary had an idea how the story of Nate staying at her house might have gotten around town. She blushed and looked down. "Let me guess. Ernie Smith has a case of sour grapes."

Dan laughed. "Guess he didn't like getting canned right before the Fourth," he said. He shrugged and finished his wine. "So he's full of it. That's what I thought."

Mary bristled. Why should Dan just automatically make that assumption? Was it too far-fetched to think a guy Nate's age could actually want to be with her? She carefully folded her napkin. "Well, I wouldn't necessarily jump to that conclusion."

Dan looked a little surprised. "You mean you actually messed around with one of those *kids*?"

"If I were a man, you think anybody'd be talking? What about Higgins at the Salty Dog, who despite being married keeps a string of them going all summer? He's not even discreet. Last year he bought one a car, for God's sake."

Mary was starting to sound like Angry Jennifer. The idea of it made her smile. If Dan was jealous, what harm would it do to prolong the agony a little? Payback.

Dan frowned, then folded his arms and sat back.

Mary laughed and lifted her bottle of white out of the cooler beside the table. She poured the last drop into her glass. "Okay, so nothing happened." Then, to save face: "He had a girlfriend I didn't know about and, unlike some people, I'm not the cheating kind." As the ribbon of words unspooled from her lips, she wondered how they'd even found their way there in the first place. One minute she'd been talking playfully about an imaginary tryst. And now suddenly this.

The silence was an ocean, the Atlantic and Pacific combined. Mary rolled her napkin into a floppy tube. She looked up at Dan, his forehead pinched at the brow, like he didn't know how he was supposed to respond.

The waiter returned with the coffee. He set down their cups. "Cream or sugar?"

Dan looked at Mary. She shook her head. Tears had formed at the corners of her eyes that made the waiter appear blurry.

"No, thanks," Dan said. The waiter left.

Mary leaned in. If she could just keep up the charade that she was still talking about Nate. "He goes out with one of the kitchen girls," she said. "Since third grade." Her voice cracked.

Dan reached out and grabbed her hand. He pressed it between both of his palms. He leaned over the table and looked into her eyes. Mary felt her heart thumping in her chest. "I never cheated on you, Sunshine. I know you thought that all these years. I let you think that. But I didn't."

Mary's throat had gone so dry she couldn't utter a sound if she wanted to. And then her cell phone went off in her purse. "Brick House" by the Commodores wafted through the dining room as people lingering over their wine at neighboring tables glared at her. *"She's mighty mighty, just lettin' it all hang out. . . . "* Mary reached into her bag. Her own home phone number appeared on the screen.

"Hello."

"Mary? This is Audrey from Home Health Services. I'm at your house and your aunt's not here."

Thirteen

Unlike Wayne's pickup with sand and junk everywhere, or even her own car, seats piled with overdue library books, food magazines, and old restaurant ledgers, Dan's truck was immaculate. Mary hadn't taken notice on the way up. She'd been too swept up in the magic of the fireworks. Now, as they headed back down the highway, even in the dark, Mary could see that the floor mats were clean and there was no debris, no empty cans. Nothing dangling from the rearview mirror. No sand in the cup holders. Just the faint smell of boat grease and leather, which now somehow comforted her, as though she were occupying a safe zone.

"You okay?" Dan asked. He reached for her hand and gave it a squeeze.

"Where could she have gone?"

"Maybe you should give the police a call," Dan said.

Mary had just gotten off the phone with Audrey again to ask if she'd checked the basement. Audrey said she had checked everywhere.

"Why did I leave her alone?" Mary scrolled for the town police on her cell phone. She had them on speed dial in case of trouble at the restaurant. "What was I thinking?"

It was just after midnight when she and Dan arrived at the house. A police car was already in the driveway. Dan pulled up behind. The cop met them at the back door, the same tall Officer Boyd who'd shown up at the restaurant the day after Anicca died. He'd had the graveyard shift then, too.

"Ms. Hopkins," he said. He had a candy in his mouth again.

He shifted it to the other cheek. Mary wondered how his teeth withstood the nightly abuse. "Hey, Dan." Mary wasn't surprised they knew each other. Most locals liked to fish. "Already took a look around inside. The health care worker gave me your aunt's description."

"Have you checked down by the water?" Dan asked.

"Was just about to," Boyd said. Mary half-expected him to scold her for losing her aunt. But he didn't.

Mary looked out to the water and saw the moon reflecting off the flats. It was low tide, though she could hear the water coming in. "What if she got lost out there? What if she can't find her way back?" *What if she's cold and afraid?* Mary thought. *What if she drowns?*

The moon slipped behind a cloud and the landscape darkened. Dan put his hand on the back of her neck. "Do you have a flashlight?" he asked her. "I'll go with him. We can cover more ground."

"In the hall closet, I think. I'll get it." Mary ran up the steps and through the back door. In the hallway, she met Audrey's formidable silhouette.

"Mary!" Audrey said. "Thank goodness."

"I'm sorry about all this, Audrey," Mary said. "Let's turn on some lights."

"I couldn't find them."

Mary reached behind a plant in the foyer that obscured the switch. She flicked on the light, half-expecting to discover Lovey standing in a dark corner. But the dark corners were empty. Mary went to the closet. "What time did you say you got here?" she asked. She reached up on the shelf above the hanging coats, feeling for the flashlight.

"A little after ten thirty. By the time my daughter got the kids packed up it was a little later than I thought."

"It's not your fault, Audrey. She was fine today. She was sleeping when I left. I thought she'd be okay."

"It's not uncommon with these folks, you know. They tend to wander," Audrey said.

Mary's hand found the flashlight. She pulled it down off the closet shelf and pressed the button. A circle of light hit the opposite wall. "I'll be right back." She ran out and met Dan on the porch. Mary saw the beam from Boyd's flashlight heading over the dune. "Do you remember what she looks like?" Mary asked. "She's a lot older now."

"Probably won't find many folks out there to confuse her with," Dan said. He took the flashlight out of her hand and pressed his cheek to the top of her head. "It'll be okay. If she's out there, we'll find her."

"I hope so," Mary said. She tried to believe him. She watched him go, then went back into the hall. Audrey was sitting on a low bench by the closet, fanning her face with her hand.

"What do you mean, they *wander*?" Mary asked.

Audrey seemed out of breath. "Alzheimer's patients. Sometimes noise triggers it. Maybe the fireworks startled her and she felt like she had to get away."

"Get away from *what*?"

"That, together with being in a new environment. It's all disorienting." Audrey stopped fanning and looked up at Mary. "They just feel as though they have to *go*. They start moving."

"Moving," Mary repeated. In some way it made sense. Like they were trying to escape their bodies, their minds, sensing their illness and impending decline. She looked at Audrey. There were dark circles under her eyes. *She must be exhausted,* Mary thought. "Audrey, you should go home."

"I can't just leave."

"There's nothing you can do. I'll call you the minute we find her. I promise," Mary said. She took hold of Audrey's arm and helped her up. "Maybe go slow on your way up the street. See if she wandered out that way."

"That's a good idea," Audrey said. "I'll drive around a bit."

"Thanks. I'll call you, I promise."

Mary wasn't sure Audrey had done such a thorough job searching. Her size would have prevented her from getting into small spaces. Even though Boyd had been through the house, Mary just needed to see for herself. She went upstairs and checked her room, the bathroom, the closets. She went out onto the roof deck. She went to the kitchen. The chowder and cheesecake in the refrigerator hadn't been touched. From the windows she saw the two flashlight beams on the flats about a hundred feet apart. She ran downstairs and checked the bedrooms on the lower level. She entered the room where Lovey had been sleeping. The bedcovers were slightly rumpled but it was obvious she'd never gotten inside them. So maybe Audrey was right. Maybe she had still been napping and the fireworks had startled her.

The shades were drawn. There was a glass of water beside the bed, and a saucer. Lovey's white tooth glistened on the blue porcelain. She never went anywhere without her tooth. She thought she looked like a hillbilly without it.

With no sign of Lovey in the house, Mary decided to go outside and help in the search. She thought there might be an extra flashlight in the bathroom closet off her bedroom. When she got there, from the bathroom window, she saw the same bright light coming from her neighbor's cottage that she'd seen earlier. He was still up. Or maybe all the commotion had woken him.

Then again, what if Lovey had seen the light and gone over there? Maybe she'd seen the coyote and decided it to follow it. Mary had a hunch the old man was feeding it, because it always seemed to be heading in that direction.

Mary took the flashlight and left by the back door. A voice bathed in static was coming from the police radio in the cruiser. The night air was sweet with wild beach roses. She made her way through the tall grass between the two houses and picked up the path that brought her to the old man's door. A few wood steps led up to a small porch. A towel hung over the railing. There beside the door was an empty steel bowl that must've once contained scraps for the coyote. There was nothing in it now, just the shine from Mary's flashlight.

"Please be here, Auntie," Mary said to her neighbor's door. She raised her hand to knock on it.

• • •

The old man's eyes were the color of dried seaweed. As he emerged from the brightly lit cottage, his pupils were tiny and she could tell he was having a hard time making her out. His eyebrows were a tangle of black and gray bristles, like the beards pulled from a mussel shell. A cluster of skin tags on his chin looked like crumbs he'd neglected to brush from his face. His eyes were heavy-lidded, with bladders of skin hanging beneath. He had no upper lip, just a long straight seam that met his lower teeth. As he struggled to see her, the furrow of his brow took the shape of a flattened letter *m*, like those seagulls Mary drew as a child.

"I'm sorry to bother you at this hour. I'm Mary Hopkins. I live next door."

He raised his right hand. Mary watched it sway back and forth. He took her by the sleeve and the motion stopped, like a pendulum caught.

"Come. She's here."

"Oh, thank goodness," Mary said. Relief washed over her. Mary squinted as she entered the bright cottage. She felt a twinge at the back of her eyes. The strong smell of some solvent—turpentine— caught her in the throat. He led her through the living room, which was furnished with an old brown sofa, a lobster pot for a table, and a worn wood chair. In the middle of the room, an easel was set up with artist lamps around it. There were unframed oil paintings on the wall, mostly loosely rendered views to the water in misty blues and aquas, heavily layered. A larger painting over the sofa displayed the old target ship, used in the early 1950s for bombing exercises, which had long ago given up her hollowed-out skeleton to the bay and could no longer be spied from shore, even at low tide. It would have been easily seen from the old man's cottage decades ago. Another painting showed his former view to the north, Lieutenant Island and Wellfleet Harbor. The view Mary's house had stolen. The easel held a canvas washed in orange underpainting, with some black markings on it, just the beginnings of a sketch.

"Where is she?" Mary asked. She didn't mean to sound impatient, but he moved so slowly.

The old man turned off one of the bright lamps by the easel and walked toward the kitchen. There, at the table where Mary had watched him eat breakfast in his pajamas, sat Lovey. She had a cup of tea in front of her, which seemed like it hadn't been touched, and a soft blue blanket around her shoulders. She was staring out the window at the side of Mary's house.

"I saw her coming through the grass. She might have been following the coyote. She hasn't spoken. What's her name?"

"Lovey!" Mary flung her arms around her aunt.

Lovey seemed startled. "Dorothy!" she said. "Where have you been? I've been waiting."

Mary's heart sank. "I should be getting her home," Mary said. She guided Lovey up out of the chair. Lovey didn't resist. "I'm so sorry about all this," Mary said.

"Don't be," he said. "I was happy to have the company." *Some company*, Mary thought. "I knew she came from the big house," he said. "I had seen her in the window this morning. I came over to tell you she was here, but there was no one home."

Audrey must not have heard him knock. Maybe she hadn't arrived yet, or had been upstairs.

"She's my great-aunt. She's been visiting." Mary felt her throat tighten. This wasn't her great-aunt. This was someone else. An impostor. Mary led Lovey to the door. "I'm sorry. I didn't get your name," Mary said when she reached the threshold.

"Carleton Dyer. Pleased to meet you." He bowed slightly and raised his hand in a belated greeting.

"Nice to meet you, Mr. Dyer." Mary said. "And thanks again for your kindness."

"Carleton, please," he said.

"Carleton."

Mary led Lovey out the door and down the steps. Carleton Dyer flicked on a porch light so they could see where they were going.

The moon had disappeared completely, but the white sand of the path was still discernible.

"Why in the world did you wander off like that?" Mary scolded. "You scared me half to death."

Lovey didn't answer. As they approached the dune, Mary saw a flashlight beam in her driveway.

"Mary?" It was Dan.

"I'm here. I found her. She was at the neighbor's house. She's fine." Mary looked at Lovey and realized they'd left with the old man's blanket. And she'd left her flashlight there too.

"Great," Dan said. "I'll go tell Boyd."

Before Boyd left, he actually told Mary he was sorry if he'd been hard on her the day after Anicca died. He said he'd seen too many kids die like that on the roads during his career. It never got easier. Mary understood. Dan offered to call Audrey while Mary got Lovey back to into bed. It was almost two by the time Mary came out of Lovey's room with the blue blanket over her arm.

Dan was sitting in an uncomfortable Windsor chair at the end of the hall. His eyes were closed. When he heard her come out, he rose to his feet.

"She went right out," Mary said. She walked over and dead-bolted the back door, then came back. "Can I make you some coffee?"

Dan stretched his arms. "Forget coffee. You should try to get some sleep," he said. He took the blanket from Mary and wrapped it around her shoulders. "I can stay if you want."

Mary looked up at him. There was sand on his cheek. She brushed it away. As much as she wanted him to stay, she knew the time wasn't right. Not with Lovey there and all that she faced the next morning. "We're okay. But thanks. And thanks for dinner." A few sprigs of dried grass had lodged in his sweater from when he'd gone through the brush. She picked them off. "I really had a nice time."

"I did too," he said. "A little like the old days."

"Except for the AWOL aunt," Mary said. She patted his chest.

"Back in those days, we had AWOL Robbie," Dan said. Mary looked up at him, surprised that he'd brought him up. He cast his eyes down. "I'm sorry—"

"No, you're right. Those days were hard. Sometimes I thought you put him too much on a pedestal." She tightened the blanket around her. "He made my life miserable. And I never forgave him for dying."

Dan walked to the window at the end of the hall. He traced the bottom sill with his thumb. "I never forgave *myself*," he said.

Mary followed him to the window. "For what?"

He turned around. He didn't look her in the eye. "Nothing, I—I just thought I should have tried harder to stop him."

Mary took another step closer. "Stop him from what? Drinking? You couldn't stop that. No one could."

He shook his head, as if he were shaking off the night. "Listen, I should get back to the boat. I have a charter at dawn."

A minute ago, he was offering to stay the night. Now suddenly he had to leave. Before she had a chance to ask why, he took her hand and pulled her toward him. She felt the strength in his arms as they tightened around her. She buried her face in his neck. Whatever his regrets over Robbie, that was fourteen years ago. Tonight, she was just grateful for his help with Lovey, with the restaurant, grateful even to just have him back in her life at all. If nothing more, they had history, which was something she shared with no one but Lovey. And she finally accepted now how that was slipping away.

She drew back. "I'm sorry to keep you up half the night," she said.

"Like the old days," he said. Mary heard the smile in his voice. She felt the hot points of his stare on her skin.

She laughed, a little shrill. "*Not* like the old days, I'm afraid."

"We'll see what we can do about that," he said. Without taking his eyes off hers, so there could be no mistake whether or not this was what she wanted too, he leaned in and pressed his lips to hers, to a place they'd been sorely missed since the day he left for Alaska and didn't come back. Mary closed her eyes and drank in the warmth of his body, his unhurriedness. She threw her arms around his neck so that this moment—this kiss—might never end, so that he might never leave her again. Through a lifetime of soul searching, at that instant she knew she hadn't truly learned a thing about the futility of clinging, about the illusion of attachment. How every moment brought change. Just as the bad times passed, so would the good. The key to life was to go with the flow. She could write a book of aphorisms for the ages, Eastern wisdom and spiritual platitudes. But none would uncurl her fingers just now. None would loosen her grip.

Mary lay awake in bed with her door open, listening for the slightest sound that might indicate Lovey was awake and on the prowl. A creak of the floorboards. The squeak of a door hinge. Tomorrow—later *today*, actually—she would bring the old woman back to her apartment and arrange to have Audrey and others visit her three, four, maybe even five times a day to prepare her meals, help her in and out of the tub, do whatever was necessary to keep her aunt safe and comfortable in her own home. Even if it meant having someone babysit her through the night so she didn't wander off. Because the idea of putting Lovey in a nursing home was just too awful. And there was still a chance the medicine might help. They just needed to give it a chance. Meanwhile, as long as Mary could pay for the care her aunt needed, even if it was round the clock, how could Darlene object? Surely they could come to some agreement.

The sky was tinged with violet. It was already lightening. Mary thought of Dan on his boat, cutting up bait, checking the tackle, stocking the cooler with ice and beer for his fishing party. She shut her eyes and imagined him there. A bird sang outside her window. Through all the commotion, she'd almost forgotten what he'd said at the restaurant before the call from Audrey came in. She'd forgotten entirely until her head had hit the pillow. And then she'd remembered, and all night whenever she almost found sleep, it jarred her awake.

I never cheated on you, Sunshine. I know you thought that all these years. I let you think that. But I didn't.

So then why had he left her?

Fourteen

Mary pulled into the circle and Audrey parked right behind. It was already midmorning. Mary had wanted to get Lovey home earlier but her aunt had slept in. Mary might have gone into her aunt's room to wake her, but she had been a little fearful of which "aunt" she might find. Mary hoped, almost superstitiously, that allowing Lovey to wake up on her own might increase the odds of having the original Lovey appear, as if some as yet undetermined ritual might bring her true aunt back.

When Lovey did wake up, she was neither her old self nor the uninhabited shell of a person she'd been the night before. Rather, she was someone in between, a spaced-out, addled version of the old Lovey, but at least one who recognized Mary as her great-niece and not as her long-deceased sister.

Mary had called Wayne to let him know she wouldn't be in until later. She'd had another conference scheduled with one of the servers that she had to postpone. Today's victim would have been Sage. Wayne's relief wasn't lost on Mary.

She threw the car in park and got out. She and Audrey met at the passenger side, where Lovey was sitting. Audrey looked better today. Sleep seemed to have softened the circles under her eyes. Earlier, over the phone, she and Mary had discussed the options for managing Lovey's care.

"Thanks for meeting me here," Mary said. "You said Darlene knows you and I thought it might help—"

"I'm still not sure she'll go for it," Audrey said. She picked at a cuticle. She seemed a bit on edge.

Mary opened the passenger-side door. "Sure she will."

"Go for what?" Lovey asked. Her hearing was still sharp as ever.

"Auntie, you remember Audrey. She's going to help you around the apartment, fix your meals, help out with the cleaning, shopping, the medicine—"

"I don't need any help," Lovey said. She swung her legs out of the car and planted her feet on the grass.

"Everyone needs a little help now and then," Mary said. As she faced the car, she saw someone coming up the drive from the direction of the administration building. It was a woman, and Mary guessed she was moving a little too fast to be a tenant. "Watch your head." Mary helped Lovey out of the car. Audrey offered her arm to the old woman. "Wouldn't it be nice having someone wait on you hand and foot?" Mary said.

"No," Lovey said. She took Audrey's arm anyway.

The woman had already made it as far as the parking lot. And there was something around her neck . . . a wide band of mint green . . . a yoked sweater. It was Darlene.

"Audrey." Mary discreetly nodded in Darlene's direction.

Audrey jumped. "Oh no," she said. She proceeded to guide Lovey with a little more urgency, looping her arms under Lovey's for added support. Evidently Mary wasn't the only one afraid of Darlene.

Mary tried to remain calm. "Why don't you take Lovey on upstairs." She handed Audrey the keys. "This one is for the outside door and this one is for the apartment. It's at the top of the stairs. There's a macramé wall hanging on the door." The one Mary had made in Girl Scout camp the summer of 1974.

"Come, Ms. Rollwagon," Audrey said. "This way."

Lovey looked around. "My *mother's* here?" she said. She sounded annoyed. "Who called my mother?"

"Auntie, she means *you*," Mary said.

Audrey had Lovey by the arm and they began walking over the grass to the paved path that led to the door.

"Hello there," Darlene called.

Mary turned to Audrey. "Can't you take her any faster?" she whispered. She felt like a kid playing hide-and-seek in that moment when it becomes clear you're about to be found. That same panicky flip-flop in the gut.

"We're practically sprinting," Audrey said. They had gone three feet.

Darlene raised her arm. "Hold up," she said. She was at the mouth of the circle. Mary could sense the neighbors' stares. She turned around and caught a flash of gray hair in the window. In another apartment, curtains swayed.

Mary decided to run interference or block the tackle or whatever they did on football fields. "Darlene, great. I was hoping to have a word with you." Mary looked back. Lovey and Audrey were almost to the door.

Darlene stopped behind Audrey's car. The two women stood face to face. Mary had a good three inches on her but it didn't seem to matter. Forget power ties and business suits—maybe the secret to commanding authority was simply an optimally colored, high-contrast yoked cardigan. Maybe preppie women had been on to something all these years.

"Yes, indeed," Darlene said.

"As you can see," Mary started, "Lovey's recovered from the flu but she's still a bit wobbly." She pointed to her aunt. "So I've arranged to have some help—"

"I'm afraid I can't allow that, Ms. Hopkins." Darlene's chin jiggled a bit as she spoke.

"Please, call me Mary."

"I've been very clear from the beginning that if it were determined that your aunt had Alzheimer's, we could no longer have her here."

"Whoa," Mary said. She poured on the incredulity. "Who said anything about Alzheimer's? She just had the flu. But the good news is, I've arranged for her to have round-the-clock care for however long . . ." Mary's voice trailed off.

Darlene folded her arms under her formidable green yoke. She cocked her head. "You're not being straight with me, Ms. Hopkins."

"*Mary.*"

"One of our tenants was tuned in to the Orleans police radio frequency last night."

"Police radio?"

"They find it on the Internet."

More fun than reruns of Matlock, Mary imagined. *Don't old people sleep?*

Darlene continued, "Evidently, just after midnight, a call came in reporting a missing woman, a senior, who it was feared had wandered off. Does that ring a bell?"

"Should it?" Mary knew her face was betraying her guilt, even if her words weren't.

"The officer who made the call—Officer Boyd it was, I've known him for years, our sons played hockey together—he gave her name over the radio. Lavinia Rollwagon. And not only that, the missing person was identified as an Alzheimer's patient." Mary had never actually told him that. Then, as if Darlene had read her mind, "That is, according to the health care professional who was also on the scene. I'm guessing that might be Audrey McGinnis, who just took Lavinia upstairs?"

Mary felt like she'd been punched in the gut. She looked down at her shoes, blue espadrilles splattered with cooking grease. "It was the fireworks. They startled her. And then there was this coyote—"

Darlene tightened her arms across her chest. "Ms. Hopkins—"

"Mary." It came out more like a question.

"We both know what's going on here."

Mary raised her arms in frustration. "Yesterday she was at the restaurant waiting tables, for heaven's sake. How sick can she be?"

Darlene stood her ground. She pressed her lips together.

"She's not used to sleeping anywhere but her own bed," Mary went on. "Surely you can understand how an eighty-six-year-old might have awakened confused."

Darlene shifted her weight. Mary wished that by some act of God the green wreath would begin to tighten around the woman's thick pink neck.

"I'm willing to pay for an arsenal of people to look in on her," Mary said. "I can arrange to have someone move in if I have to." In the end it had to be about money, right? Wasn't that always the case?

"It's a hard-and-fast policy, Mary," Darlene said. "No Alzheimer's patients. It's right in the lease. It's for the safety of the other tenants. *And* for your aunt's. She simply can't live on her own in this condition. You need to understand that. We had a tenant once who left a pot on the stove and nearly burned the residents out of their homes. Lavinia needs to be in a place where people can care for her."

"It'll kill her," Mary said. She was talking more to herself.

"You mean moving or the disease?" Darlene unfolded her arms. Her jaw softened.

"Both," Mary said.

"Where am I going now?" Lovey asked.

"To a rehabilitation facility in Yarmouth," Mary said. That sounded better than "nursing home," though this place was both. They had just passed the bend in the road where Robbie had lost his life. Mary always held her breath when she passed that spot. This afternoon, she'd forgotten.

"What am I rehabilitating from?"

Of course, the cloud that engulfed her aunt's mind had to dissipate now, as Mary was transporting her to her temporary home. Darlene had already made calls and secured a bed for Lovey at a local nursing home and rehabilitation facility with an Alzheimer's wing. But there was a waiting list for a bed in the wing itself, and the bed Darlene had reserved was just for short-term patients. Mary would need to make other living arrangements for Lovey until a bed in the wing became available.

Mary pulled over at the first clearing at the side of the road. Lovey seemed small in the seat beside her. She had the stuffed bear on her lap and was tapping its button eyes with her fingernail.

Mary waited until a bicycle passed them. "Auntie, you have a condition that causes you to forget things. The doctors I took you to confirmed it. I don't know if you even remember, but last night I left you alone and you wandered off from my house in the middle of the night. We had to call the police. Do you remember?"

Lovey kept her eyes fixed on the bear. She shook her head.

Mary continued, "You just walked over to the neighbor's cottage—no harm done, but Darlene found out and now she won't let you go back to your apartment." *Make Darlene the villain.* Mary was willing to bet Darlene got a lot of that.

"I see," Lovey said.

Mary reached for her hand. She gave it a squeeze. "This is just temporary until I can figure out what to do next." Mary felt the twinge of tears on the rise. She rubbed her nose with the back of her hand and took a breath. The last thing she needed now was to fall apart. She threw the car in drive and pulled back onto the road.

"Can I ask you a question, dear?" Lovey said. "And I want a straight answer."

"Of course."

"Is it Alzheimer's disease?"

Mary gripped the steering wheel until her knuckles turned white. "I think so," she said.

Lovey let out a long sigh.

"What?" Mary said. She looked over at her aunt, then back at the road. She braced herself for her aunt's tears and realized she'd never actually seen the old woman cry, except once, at Mary's mother's funeral. But when she looked over at Lovey, she saw she wasn't crying at all. Her eyes were fixed on the road ahead.

"What a relief," Lovey finally said. "I thought I was losing my mind." And a moment later: "Did you remember to pack my tooth?"

Mary would never forget the look on Lovey's face when she left her in the charge of that overly chipper West Indian nurse in yellow scrubs with pink strawberries on them. Lovey was allergic to strawberries. "My name is Sherril," the woman had said. "Come," which sounded like "comb." Before she took Lovey by the arm and led her

down the hall, the old woman had looked up and Mary saw helpless-
ness and resignation in her eyes. It was as if she'd utterly given up.

"Should I go with her?" Mary had asked the administrator with
the name tag that said "Hello. My name is Suzie." The woman's
bangs were too long and she wore feather earrings that looked like
fishing lures.

"Why don't you let us get her settled," Suzie said. "You can come
back tomorrow and we'll talk about what else she needs. We can fill
out the rest of the paperwork then."

Mary reached into her handbag and pulled out an old black ring
box trimmed in gold.

"This is her tooth," Mary said. She held it out to Suzie. "I'd appreciate it if you'd keep it somewhere safe. She always wears it out in
public. She hates to be without it." Suzie seemed reluctant to take it.
"Please." Mary thrust the box toward her.

"I can't guarantee it won't get lost," Suzie said. She took the box
and set it on the table. She took a yellow Post-it and wrote *L. Rollwagon,* then Scotch-taped over the sticky note, securing it to the felt
bottom of the box. "We really discourage keeping any valuables in
the patients' rooms."

"This isn't valuable to anyone but her," Mary said. "Call me if
there's any problem, if she calls for me or gets upset or can't sleep,
even if it's the middle of the night."

"We'll talk with her doctor and hopefully be able to give her
something to help her sleep tonight. It tends to take our residents
a little while to get used to the noise, though most of it's over in
the Alzheimer's wing." As soon as she said it, Mary saw her wince,
as though for a moment she'd forgotten that was where Lovey was
eventually headed, if not at this facility, then another.

"I'd like to see that wing."

"Certainly," Suzie said. "We'll show you around tomorrow."

Mary left the woman's office and walked out into the hall where
residents were lined up in wheelchairs waiting to be taken out into
the warm sun. Some smiled at Mary. Others just stared. When Mary

got out to the car, she crumpled over the steering wheel and finally allowed herself to fall apart. She didn't know whom this was harder for, herself or Lovey. Mary had been coming to that apartment for the last thirty years. Now suddenly, in a matter of hours, Lovey had been kicked out, discarded like a piece of trash. Darlene had given Mary till the end of the month to pack up her aunt's things. *And do what with them?*

Mary wondered whether it would have made her feel better if Lovey had protested or made a fuss rather than just accepted her fate. Maybe there wasn't any fight left in her. Or maybe, on some level, it was a relief for the old woman to know she'd now be cared for. Maybe, unbeknownst to Mary, she'd been struggling for a long time. Regardless, it was the day Mary had dreaded for years, the beginning of the end, a life in decline, a chapter closing. How could Mary be expected to just accept and let go?

After all that had transpired over the last twenty-four hours, there was no way Mary could go in to work. She felt too fragile, too brittle, like the dried bones of a fish in sand. *Bury this with the bones: Lovey is fading, receding, ossifying. Lovey is becoming something else. Lovey is returning.*

The coyote stood in the driveway. Mary stopped the car to see what it would do. She imagined watching through the eyes of an old woman who has spent the last decade of her life holed up in a tiny apartment, who suddenly comes eye to eye with a wild creature, frozen in its tracks—its long, sinewy body and thick, dappled coat, alert ears, and white-rimmed eyes, its legs and the tip of its tail dipped in black. Mary held her breath, as if that might hold him there. But moments later, he slipped through the tall grass.

Mary climbed the stairs, realizing that some of her weariness was a result of her not getting much sleep the night before. She let herself in to the hall, then entered the room Lovey had slept in. What was Lovey doing right at that moment, she wondered. Was she resting in her new bed, one that adjusted to a sitting position with the push of a button, and with bars on the side to keep her in? Was she disoriented, or scared? Mary squeezed her eyes shut. When she opened them, she saw the old man's blue blanket draped over a chair by the window.

Mary hadn't even had time to process her encounter with Carleton Dyer last night. She went to the window and peered out from behind the drawn shade. He was an artist, which explained the eerie glow of the artist lamps. At least he wasn't cultivating melanoma with a sun lamp. She took the blanket and wrapped herself in it, then lay down on the guest bed, closed her eyes, and drifted off to sleep.

Moments later, she was awakened by a call from the Clambake. It was Nate, wondering if she was coming in. He wanted to talk to her about the fund-raiser for Anicca's daughter. Mary told him some of what had transpired and said that she just needed to rest. She put him in charge of whatever needed doing regarding the event. Then she hung up and tried to go back to sleep. But this time, her mind kept racing.

Finally, she hoisted herself from the bed. She folded the blanket, then went upstairs to the refrigerator to retrieve the uneaten cheesecake from the night before. She took them both and headed out the back door.

There were dark brown smudges on Carleton Dyer's face, and if Mary hadn't known better, she'd have thought she had caught him in the midst of changing the oil in his car. He had on heavy work pants and an oversized blue dress shirt, paint-spattered, with a frayed collar. The clothes seemed to weigh him down.

"Hi," Mary said, as soon as he opened the door. "I hope I'm not bothering you. I just wanted to return this." She held out the blanket. The old man took it. "And thank you again for your help last night." Mary raised the cake box in her left hand. "I brought cheesecake."

"Why, thank you," he said. "And how is your aunt today?"

Just a simple question. The polite thing to ask, really. But no sooner did the words escape his lips than Mary felt her eyes fill with tears, which then began to spill out onto her cheeks. Her shoulders started to heave.

"Come inside," Carleton Dyer said. He took her by the forearm and she could feel the tremor contained in his limb, like a bird trapped in a box. "Sit for a minute," he said.

"I'm so sorry," Mary said. She sniffed and wiped her face with her hands.

Carleton gestured toward the chair in the living area. Mary set the cheesecake on the lobster trap table. Most lobster trap tables had glass tops, but this one didn't. It was just a lobster trap made of wood and rope.

Carleton took the blanket and draped it over Mary's legs. He picked up the box and said, "I have some water on the stove. I'll make tea." Before she could protest, he shuffled off to the kitchen.

Mary pulled a tissue from her pocket and blew her nose. What was wrong with her, breaking down like that? Never a crier, she'd cried more these last couple of weeks than she had in all the years since Robbie died. Mary heard the teakettle whistle. She took a deep breath and looked around. She felt something of the equanimity she'd felt riding in Dan's truck the night before, which she realized now had more to do with the lack of clutter than with the presence of anything in particular. There was a dignity to the space itself, a clean, modest functionality, was the best way she could explain it.

"You like lemon?" Carleton called from the kitchen.

"Please," Mary answered. She looked at the paintings on the wall. It was eerie in a way to have the view from her own home captured here on the walls of this tiny cottage. The view she'd worked so hard for all her life now felt as though it didn't rightfully belong to her. At least he'd done something with it when it was his. More important, now that her house stood between his and the water, what did he paint?

Mary got up from the chair and went to the easel. Since last night some progress had been made on the sketch, though Mary still couldn't quite tell what she was looking at, a box of some kind, or a structure. A group of canvases rested against the wall beneath the window. Mary took a step in the direction of the kitchen and peered around the corner to make sure Carleton wasn't coming. Then she knelt down beneath the easel and drew back the first canvas.

Though it was a loose rendering, she immediately recognized the structure in the painting. It was her outdoor shower! Mary stood and looked out the window. Precisely the view he now had from this vantage point. She crouched back down and flipped back the second canvas, a depiction of her rusty bulkhead and some weeds that were shooting out from the ground beside it.

Mary felt sick to her stomach.

The next painting was another version of the outdoor shower in different light, with sharp shadows, perhaps in the early morning sun.

"Would you mind coming for your tea?" Carleton called from the kitchen. Mary jumped up. "If I try to carry two cups, I'll end up giving myself a hot shower."

Mary's heart was still beating hard in her chest as she entered the kitchen. Last night, it had been too dark and she had been too distracted by Lovey to get a good look at what Carleton saw from his kitchen window. Now it was clear—just a wall of gray cedar shingles with some windows up above, Mary's bathroom window, and below, Lovey's drawn shade.

Carleton handed her a mug. "Feeling better?" he asked.

"You must hate me," Mary said. "I know I didn't build the house, but what difference does it make? Your view was stolen from you. Now it's mine and I can't give it back."

Carleton laughed.

Mary looked at him. She wanted to laugh too. There was a warmth emanating from his face, a light like the one that shone from his cottage at night. "What's funny?" she asked.

"You saw the paintings," he said. He picked up his own mug from the counter and blew across the surface.

"Of the bay. They're lovely. It must have been beautiful to live here once," Mary said.

Carleton took a long slurp of his tea. "I mean the ones on the floor."

Mary's face reddened. She contemplated denying her nosiness, then said, "I'm sorry. I was just curious—"

"Come," he said.

Mary followed him out to the easel. He set his mug down on a small side table covered with tubes of paint, then began unscrewing the knobs on the easel to release the canvas he'd been working on. He carefully set the canvas down on the floor beside the others. Then he took the first painting, the one of Mary's shower, and propped it up where the work in progress had been. He directed the light from the lamp toward it.

"What do you see?" he asked.

"A really accomplished painting of a rather ugly outdoor shower." She could fix that, at least. She could change out the rusty hinges and bleach away the mildew.

"Now, take away the label," Carleton said. "What do you see?"

"What do you mean, *label*?"

"The word. Just look. Better yet, look *there*." Carleton pointed to the real shower stall outside the window. Mary had no idea how late it was—she'd lost all track of time—but the sun was already low and the shower was cast in shadow. "What do you see?"

Mary set her mug on the radiator. "I see a dark box made of wood with a door and a handle."

"Let me tell you what I see," Carleton said. "I see shapes of light and dark. I see texture in the wood, knots from where branches once reached out for sunlight, and the knots themselves, like eyes. I see life emerging from slats in the floor—"

"You mean weeds." How embarrassing. The least she could do from now on was keep up the back of the house.

"I see the vibration of life." He took a sip of his tea, closing his eyes.

Mary wondered if they were looking at the same thing. "But

Carleton, *that* view"—she pointed to the painting over the couch—
"the one you had when you painted *those*"—she pointed to two
other seascapes on the wall—"was *beautiful.*" Now pointing to the
painting of the shower. "*This,*" she said, "is *ugly.* Not that you haven't
done a brilliant job rendering it. But by comparison—"

"What is *ugly?* For there to be beauty, there has to be ugliness.
Why do we need to judge? Maybe it's all part of the same thing, eh?"
He winked at her over his mug.

Mary looked at him. She never thought like that. It made sense
on some elusive level, like something that you know is floating out
there on the horizon but there's a good chance you'll never lay your
hands on it or even see it up close. "But some things are universally
beautiful," Mary protested. "The ocean, the beach, the sky. People
come here from all over the world to experience such beauty, because it makes them feel happy or peaceful, or even a little closer
to God." Mary knew a thing or two about what motivated tourists,
after all. "They don't flock here to view the outdoor showers."

She had him. At least she thought she did.

Carleton's lips twisted into a smile. Intuitively, she braced for
what he'd say next. "You would say a spider is ugly. But what is the
beauty behind its creation? The same beauty you find in the sea or
the beach or the sky."

Evidently, Carleton was the Zen master of turning lemons into
lemonade. Mary knew of locals who'd pitched fits when so much as
a tree limb marred their view. Homeowners were constantly fighting with the town and dragging each other to court for the smallest
infractions. And here she was supposed to believe Carleton didn't
harbor even the slightest resentment toward the ones who came and
put walls in front of his windows? Mary didn't buy it.

"So the day that wall went up, are you telling me you didn't experience some sense of loss or regret?" Mary folded her arms. She
wasn't sure what was driving her questions anymore. Was she trying
to get him to admit he was secretly heartbroken? Did she want to
make him hate her?

"Of course I felt the loss," he said.

Mary released her arms. "What did you do about it?"

Carleton looked out the window. "I sat with it."

"You *sat* with it," Mary repeated.

Carleton continued, "I sat with my discomfort for days, weeks, even months, and looked at it from all possible angles in all possible lights, much in the way I look at that shower." He grinned.

Mary let out a sigh of frustration. "And where did that get you? I mean, you probably could have fought the construction. Half the town would have turned out in your defense."

Carleton set down his cup. "I was sad to lose the view. The same way I'm sad to lose control of my own body." He held up his hand and in its back-and-forth tremor, Mary saw the irony of a wave good-bye.

"So how can you be okay with that?" Mary said. "How can you get past having precious things taken from you?"

Carleton raised one of his caterpillar-on-acid eyebrows. "You're not talking about my view anymore," he said.

Mary stood there with her mouth open. He was right.

"Trees resist brokenness by bending. Your aunt is yielding to what is happening to her. You need to let her do that. You'll only make it harder for both of you if you fight it." Carleton walked to the kitchen and came back out with Mary's flashlight. "It's getting dark."

"Yes," Mary said. Her head was spinning but she felt some sense of relief as well, as though something had been lifted. Some weight or fog. "Thank you," she said. She took the flashlight from him. "For everything."

As he escorted her to the door, she noticed another painting, one she hadn't seen before, of the coyote.

"I saw him today in my driveway," Mary said. "He's beautiful."

"And a little bit ugly too," Carleton said. He winked. "Know what I mean?"

She smiled. "Good night."

"Good night, Mary."

• • •

Mary was almost to the back door when she heard the phone ring-ing inside the house. She scrambled to unlatch the door. *What if it's the rehab facility? What if Lovey had a problem and they've been trying to reach me all this time?*

Mary dropped the flashlight on the chair in the hall and ran up-stairs. She heard the answering machine click on and her own voice: "Hello, this is Mary—"

She grabbed the receiver. "Hello? Sorry, I'm here."

The person on the other end waited for her message to stop play-ing. Then: "Hey, Sunshine."

Mary let the air out of her lungs. She slid her back down the wall until her bottom hit the floor. "Hey," she said, relieved just to hear his voice. Something more than relieved.

"How'd it go today?" he asked.

Mary's exhaustion from the sudden sprint up the stairs and the events of the day now caught up with her. She was wiped out. "She can't go back," Mary said.

Dan waited for some further explanation and then must have real-ized there wasn't one coming. "None of us can, I suppose," he said. "We can only go forward."

Fifteen

They were shells, with chalky surfaces and hair bleached white, their faces smoothed and polished from the disease's relentless pounding. Some were intact, others were bent over their dinner trays or rigid in wheelchairs, eroded and washed up after a long life's journey. Some had clearly been discarded. Others, though, were still very much cherished, hands clasped in the palms of loved ones who wouldn't let go.

A few still echoed the sounds of their lives in the way an empty conch might produce a song when the wind blows over its opening, or the way a shell brought to the ear still hums the ocean's music.

In every case, the meat—the viscera—was gone.

When the tour of the Alzheimer's wing was over, Suzie invited Mary back to her office, where they could discuss how long Lovey might have to wait for a bed to open up.

"Take her off the list," Mary said.

At least Lovey had been in good spirits. She seemed to be enjoying her breakfast and had already made friends with the nurses on the floor. Mary couldn't figure out how much Lovey understood about her situation. She seemed like a well-adjusted kid who'd been sent away to camp. "I have my own television" was the first thing she said when Mary entered the room. She produced a remote control with six enormous buttons. "On." "Off." "Channel up." "Channel down." "Volume up." "Volume down."

It wasn't until breakfast trays were delivered that Mary realized Lovey had a roommate. The nurse pulled back the accordion divider to reveal a very old, very frail-looking woman. Lost in the covers, her tiny frame appeared like something precious and fragile on a bed of cotton.

"You're going to behave today, aren't you, Helen?" the nurse said. She had an Irish accent and wore blue scrubs that were too tight in the thighs. Her dark hair was pulled back into a shiny ponytail.

As soon as the curtain was drawn, the old woman in the bed looked around the room with eyes like a bird's. Mary could see the pain behind them.

"Hurts," she complained to the nurse.

The nurse looked at Mary. "She broke her hip. She was on a chair dusting the top of the refrigerator." The nurse hit a button and the back of the woman's bed hinged to 120 degrees. "She's five two in heels. Who's she dusting for?"

"My boyfriend," the woman said without missing a beat. "He's six two." She looked at Mary. "I'm Helen."

"I'm Mary. Lovey's niece." Mary pointed to her aunt, who was absorbed in the act of eating her toast.

"That can't be her real name, is it?"

"Lavinia."

"Hmm." Helen adjusted and grimaced.

"Have you met her?" Mary asked. Lovey had changed the channel to a diet show for overweight celebrities. Marsha from *The Brady Bunch* was stepping on the scale. The volume was up too loud.

"We met last night," Helen said. The nurse swiveled the table around, then set the food tray on it. Helen winced.

"Painful, huh?" Mary asked.

"Like a bastard."

"Watch your mouth," the nurse said. "She's got the biggest potty mouth on the floor," she said to Mary. "Such a little thing too. Makes the most racket of them all." She fixed the covers at Helen's feet and tucked them in. "Thrives on the attention. Napoleon complex."

"Come closer, Colleen, and I'll tell you what you can do with your pancakes."

Colleen smiled. This was obviously a game they both enjoyed. "It's scrambled eggs. And you're going to eat them."

"I'm not hungry."

"I'm not listening. Eat them or I won't help you pee."

"See the abuse? Do me a favor and call the authorities when you leave." Helen unfolded her napkin and set it at the bottom of her chest. "You should take your aunt somewhere else." She started to peel the foil lid off her fruit cocktail.

"Never mind." Colleen produced a cup of water and some pills. Helen took them in her bony hands. She squeezed two red capsules between her fingers and put them on her tongue, then washed them down with the water, some of which trickled down her cheek. Colleen wiped it away. Then she brushed the stray hairs from Helen's brow.

"A bit of a drinking problem, this one has. Keep your eye on her," Colleen said before she left. She winked.

Minutes later, Mary left for work feeling that Lovey was in good hands. And there was some relief in having made the decision not to exile her aunt to that chamber of horrors known as the Alzheimer's wing. There had to be some alternative.

There was an arrangement of irises and roses on Mary's counter by the window when she arrived at the Clambake. *That Dan,* she thought. There was a delicious warm feeling in the space around her heart. All the kids had stopped what they were doing and stared at her as she pulled the card from the bouquet.

"Go back to work," she scolded. "Bunch of busybodies."

Some heeded her words, some didn't.

She pulled her reading glasses out of her purse, then drew the note card from the white envelope.

We're sorry to hear about your aunt. Hang in.

The Kitchen

The writing on the card was in Nate's hand. Mary looked up. He was standing beside Maureen, who offered up a sympathetic smile. Mary looked at Wayne. He winked and turned back toward the grill. She nodded to the steamer cooks and to the dishwasher, who raised a dirty spatula in a bashful wave. The other two order line girls smiled at her.

"Like I said"—Mary cleared her throat—"back to work." She buried her nose in the bouquet and took in the scent of the roses. "And thank you."

Still a little shaky in the knees, Mary took her handbag and the bouquet and brought them up to her office.

When Sage arrived at the top of the stairs, she saw the flowers. "We wanted to chip in but they wouldn't let us. We're sorry about your aunt too." "We" meaning the wait staff, Mary assumed.

"I appreciate that, Sage." Mary said. She had Sage's folder containing her job application on her lap. "I suppose we should get started before the lunch rush. This won't take long." It was overcast, and unless the sun broke through the clouds in the next half hour or so, people would be heading their way instead of to the deli for sandwiches to take out on the beach.

Sage was probably the prettiest of all the girls, and in a natural way. She had thick blond sun-streaked hair that curled into ringlets on hot days. She had big blue eyes, a sculpted nose, and full lips. Not only was she attractive, she was shaping up to be a solid head waitress. She had that elusive balance of work ethic, smarts, honesty, and an unwillingness to be pushed around. It also didn't hurt that she was going out with Wayne, who still terrified most of the girls. They were a power couple. Mary still didn't fully understand what a girl like Sage would be wanting with a guy like Wayne. Mary thought it might have something to do with the novelty of dating a guy with some quirky affliction. Sage could have all the football players and lifeguards she wanted, but how often did you meet a guy with synesthesia?

Mary scanned Sage's application. "So you grew up in Newton and you go to BU. And your Dad is a ophthalmologist."

"Yep."

"And your mom?"

"She stays home. I have an autistic brother."

"That must be tough."

"Sam is fourteen. He goes to a special school," Sage said. She took off her hair elastic and redid her ponytail.

Mary wanted to let Sage know she knew about her and Wayne and that it was okay with her. "Has Wayne met him?"

Sage looked down at her hands. She seemed a little embarrassed. "Sam thinks he's great."

"Wayne's a special guy." Mary closed Sage's folder and set it on the desk. Time for some girl talk.

"Yeah." Sage smiled. "He's really sweet. And he cracks me up."

"And how often do you meet a guy as 'talented' as he is?" Mary said. Mary wrapped the word in finger quotes.

"You mean the cooking, yeah," Sage said. "It comes so natural. He's one in a million."

"Actually, one in *ten* in a million," Mary corrected. "But who's counting, right?"

"Huh?" Sage raised an eyebrow.

"The synesthesia thing," Mary said. She leaned back in her chair and crossed her legs. "When I first found out, I looked it up and learned the kind he has, where you *taste* shapes, is even more rare than the kind where you hear colors or—"

Sage scooted to the edge of her seat. "Whoa. *Taste* shapes? What do you mean?"

"He didn't—?" *Shit.* Mary had just assumed . . . "It's not a big deal. Forget I mentioned it." Mary uncrossed her legs and sat up.

"No, tell me. I don't understand. How can you *taste* shapes?"

Mary's shoulders slumped. She'd gone from cool confidant to royal screw-up in a matter of seconds. "I'm sorry. I thought he told you. He's got this condition where when he tastes something, he actually experiences the sensations of shapes and textures in his hands. Like when the fish has too many points. Or not enough." Wayne had done a lot better job explaining it than she did.

"*Points* on a *fish*? I don't get it," Sage said. Her face flushed red.

"That's why he couldn't work for his father at the Chinese restaurant. Because Chinese food gives him a really painful reaction, like a sharp stabbing—" *Was that how he put it? Or had he said something about razors?*

Sage stood up. "He just told me he and his father didn't get along."

"Well, maybe that too." Mary buffed her fingernails on her shirt. Wayne was going to kill her. "You should talk to him about it."

"Oh, I will," Sage said. Her ears were the color of the candy apples that garnished the broiler plates.

"You should probably be heading back down—"

But Sage was already halfway down the stairs before Mary could finish her sentence.

Mary spent the rest of the afternoon avoiding Wayne. The pace of the kitchen never let up, so she knew she was safe at the far corner of the bar, where she caught up on paperwork and finished off the next week's schedule. A few times she'd looked up to see Sage snapping at the girls for not wiping off their drink trays or letting customers sit too long with empty plates and baskets in front of them. Sage probably hadn't had the chance to confront Wayne yet. Next week Mary would slip a little more into his paycheck and hopefully that would appease him.

Mary's stealth paid off. She managed to slip out the front door before the kitchen started breaking down for the night. Last night on the phone, she and Dan had made plans to meet down at the beach parking lot. He was bringing the blankets. She was bringing the wine.

Mary and Dan lay flat on their backs looking up at the night sky. The air was warm and buttery, with a mist that left a slight stickiness on the skin.

"When you think about it, nothing's really changed since we were kids. Same stars in the sky. Same beach. Maybe a little more of it in places, a little less in others," Dan said.

"Except then we were drinking Boone's Farm, not Château Margaux." Mary raised herself up on her elbow and refilled Dan's glass, which wasn't nearly as empty as hers. She was waiting for the right moment to bring up what he'd said at the restaurant the other night about not cheating. Waiting for the wine to kick in.

"And we were drinking it out of the bottle, not fine crystal." Dan raised his glass.

"Food Service Warehouse premium stemware, but definitely a step up."

Dan laughed. A few moments passed.

"There's one," Mary said. She pointed to the sky. "Did you see it?"

"Missed it. You know, we always thought they were stars. Turns out they're just chunks of rock colliding with Earth's atmosphere," Dan said.

"Really? Somehow that's not as romantic as the idea of having just witnessed the extinction of a trillion-year-old star."

"Not nearly," Dan said.

More moments passed.

"I wonder what Lovey is doing right now," Mary said. She grabbed a handful of cool sand and sifted it through her fingers.

"Sleeping, hopefully," Dan said.

"I need to find a new place for her."

"I thought you said she could stay where she is."

Mary didn't want to talk about what she'd seen in the Alzheimer's wing. She didn't even want to think about it. "They have no permanent beds," she said.

"Have you started calling places?"

"I will tomorrow. I also need to pack up her apartment. That's one thing I really dread," Mary said. All those things countless tchotchkes and ephemera she'd been around since childhood, worthless to most people yet precious to her and her aunt.

"I can help if you want," Dan said.

"We'll see." Mary had a feeling this was something she needed to do alone. She sipped her wine, then rested her head on Dan's stomach. He draped his arm around her waist and she felt the weight of it. Her head rose and fell with his breathing. She imagined she was lying on the bow of a boat. She rubbed his forearm and felt the deep gouge of his scar. "Tell me about this," she said. "You said it happened in Alaska."

"Pretty much put an end to my illustrious crabbing career."

"Really?"

"Still have to look the other way when I see them on ice at the fish market."

Mary traced around the scar with her finger. "Never served them at the restaurant. 'Only fresh and local fare at the Clambake,' so the ads say. Except for the fried shrimp. Come to think of it, I should probably take those off the menu."

"You want to hear the story or you want to talk about shrimp?"

Mary laughed "Like they say, you can take the girl out of the clam bar but you can't take the clam bar out of the girl. Sorry. Tell me what happened."

Dan stretched out his legs. Mary felt the vibration of his muscles lengthening.

"That season I was working one of the smaller boats with just a three-man crew. About two in the morning we hit a patch of rough seas. We were getting tossed around pretty good, rising and falling eight feet between waves so at the trough you'd see nothing but a wall of black."

"Just the thought of that makes me seasick. How could you function?"

"You got used to it. You had no choice. That night, the deck was slick with ice and we were dropping seven-hundred-pound pots over the rail. It was only about eighteen hours into the season and we hadn't had more than a few minutes' rest since we left the harbor. But I doubt that had anything to do with it."

"To do with what?"

He took a deep breath. "Out of nowhere, a rogue wave hit the boat and washed me right overboard."

Mary jumped to her knees. "In the pitch dark? In the middle of the Bering Sea?"

"The crew acted fast. One of the guys threw a tube and it landed right in my hands. I slipped my arm though and they used the crane to pull me out. When I hit the deck, I sliced my arm on the corner of a pot. Cut clean through the foul-weather gear. Good part was, my arm was too frozen to bleed. For a while, at least."

"Oh, my God. How long could you have survived in that water?"

"Without a survival suit in thirty-seven-degree water? Minutes. The body shuts down fast. All the blood goes to the heart and brain, so within a matter of seconds, you can't move your limbs. Then you slip under."

"Does that happen a lot? I mean, do guys get washed overboard?" Mary asked. She lay back down.

Dan closed his eyes. "All the time," he said.

"Do most of them survive?"

"Hardly any."

Mary couldn't believe what she was hearing. He could have died out there. Just like that, it would have been over in minutes. For what? Money? No amount was worth that kind of risk.

A few moments later Dan opened his eyes. "You okay?" he asked.

"You never told me how bad it was," she said. She squeezed her hand around his scar.

"You never would have let me go."

"I'll never let you go again." She moved on top of him and her hair fell around his face, obliterating the stars. She leaned in and brushed her lips across his. She kissed his cheek, then his chin, then his eyelids—one, then the other, like something precious. She felt the heat rising off of his body. Then Dan put his hand on the back of her neck and in one swift motion rolled them both over so that he was on top of her, bearing his weight in his forearms. His lips seemed to melt into hers like warm wax, as though there was no longer any separation between them. For a few moments they kissed in long, slow, rolling waves.

Flustered, Mary pushed him off her and came up for air. "So, why don't you tell me what you meant the other night?"

"What?" He buried his face in her neck and started nibbling her ear.

Mary shuddered. She pushed him off and laughed. "You can't just tell a girl who thinks her guy cheated on her that it never happened and expect she'll want no further explanation."

Dan rolled off and landed on his side. "There is no further explanation." He put his arm around her hips and pulled her close.

"There has to be. Listen to me." Mary untangled herself and sat up. "Everything had been going great. We had one little fight that morning you left." Her voice had thinned. For these past few weeks, she'd managed to swallow the hurt and anger she'd carried through the years because it just felt so good to have him back in her life. Now the pain had resurfaced, like bones trapped in a pocket of air beneath the sand. *Breathe,* she told herself. She took Dan's hand in both of hers and spoke slowly. "You walked back into my life after twelve years. And you have to know I'm happy for that. You not only saved the season at the restaurant, but you came at a time when kids were dying and beloved old women were drifting away. I didn't ask questions. But for us to go any further here, Dan, I need you to be straight with me." Her voice cracked a little. "I need to know why you left that morning and never came back to me, never called, never even answered my letters."

Dan squeezed his eyes shut. "Lie beside me and I'll tell you."

Mary nestled into the crook of his arm. She felt her heart thumping in her chest. It was as if she'd set something in motion and now suddenly wanted to pull the brakes.

"Remember the earring?" Dan asked.

"I still have it," Mary said.

"You thought it belonged to a girl I'd met in Alaska. If you knew how crazy the idea of that was. First of all, there were never any women on the boats. It's bad luck. And second, there are no women in Alaska."

"But Robbie told me you'd met a girl out west. And that you'd been bringing her down to the basement. Why would he lie?"

Mary felt Dan's body tense up.

"You found it that first day you opened," he said. "You remember that?"

"Right before you came down through the bulkhead."

Dan sucked in a breath. "It belonged to a girl named Katy Hanson. She and Robbie were having an affair."

Mary sat up. "Whoa. Wait a minute. That's impossible. I mean, Robbie was a lot of things. He was a drunk and a lazy son of a bitch. But he wasn't a cheater."

"He told me." Dan rose up on his elbows. "But he didn't even have to. I knew. He was my best friend."

"But he—"

Dan pressed his forefinger to her lips. "It's *true*," he said. "He was having an affair."

Mary closed her eyes. Robbie's face appeared in her mind. She knew it was true. "For how long?"

"It's where he was headed the night he died. She lived on the Chatham line."

"But that would mean he was seeing her before the restaurant opened up until— That's more than three years. That's our whole marriage."

"You never suspected anything?" Dan asked.

"Never." Mary's felt like *she'd* been washed out to sea. She felt a chill. And then the next obvious question: "You knew about this the whole time and didn't tell me?"

"I was Robbie's best friend."

"What about *after* he died? What about when we were together? You could have told me then. You should have."

"I wanted to—"

"You wanted to. Why *didn't* you?" Mary scooted back to the edge of the blanket. "All those years you let me suffer, believing I'd sent my own husband to his grave because I yelled at him that night. I thought it was my fault. Meanwhile, he was just off to see his girl-friend." Mary hopped to her knees.

"I must have told you a thousand times it wasn't your fault," Dan said.

"Who was she? Does she still live here? Do I see her in the super-market? Does she come and eat in the restaurant?"

"She moved away years ago," Dan said.

"Jesus." Mary was shaking.

"I'm sorry I didn't tell you. I had my reasons but they don't matter now."

Mary wasn't hearing him anymore. "I just need to go home," she said.

"Don't." Dan sat up. He reached for her hand.

She pulled it away. "No, really. My head's a mess. I don't know what to think."

"Come on, Mary," he said. "You know how I feel."

"I feel like I've been betrayed by two men in the same night. Both ghosts."

"I'm not a ghost."

"You've haunted me for years. And now this will. I have to go." Mary stood up. She grabbed her bag and left everything else, every-thing except the pain brought on by this new knowledge, there on the sand.

It was a little past six in the morning when Mary unlocked the back door to the kitchen. She loved being at the restaurant in the early morning hours when no one else was around. When no food was being prepared, no chowder simmering on the stove, no dishes being watched, no burgers on the grill, no bodies milling around, the kitchen had its own scent, a mellow mix of cleaning products and cooking oil. At these times, Mary felt an intimacy with the place, a communion she occasionally needed to renew over the course of a busy season, when the frenetic energy of the business seemed to take over. Here in the stillness, she was reminded that everything her eyes could see was there because she'd put it there. It was all her design, her planning, her vision.

With the car still idling in the alley, she opened the door to her attic office and climbed the steep stairs. On her desk, the flowers given to her by the kitchen staff yesterday were at their height of beauty. The roses and had fully opened and released their sweetness into the room. Now would be a great time to sit down and make some headway on the piles of paperwork she'd been neglecting. But after a sleepless night, she didn't trust her mind for anything that required her full attention. Besides, she had something more important to take care of. Mary pulled the chain on her desk lamp. She sat down and scrawled a note to Wayne saying she wouldn't be in until midway through lunch. In a P.S. she added *I'm sorry about yesterday,* and assumed he'd get that she was referring to her big mouth blunder with Sage.

There on the windowsill was what Mary had come for. She picked it up and put it in her pocket, then switched off the light. She tore a piece of tape from the dispenser, took the note, and headed downstairs, where she stuck it to Wayne's grill. Then she opened the fridge and pulled out a two-quart tub of the chowder they sold to customers at the take-out window. She put it in a white bag along with a handful of chowder-cracker packets. Then she left the kitchen, locked the door, and headed out to the car.

Mary was surprised to see there were already people walking the ocean beach at that hour. The sun had risen but was low in the sky. The air had grown stickier since last night. Mary hadn't heard the forecast, but she suspected they were in for a scorcher.

Mary kicked off her shoes and left them at the foot of the white-washed lifeguard stand. She walked down the beach a ways to where she and Dan had lain the night before. Mary believed she was standing in the exact spot where the blanket had been, and she found further evidence: the cork from last night's wine bottle. She picked it up and held it in her fist. She knelt down, then sat cross-legged in the sand. She took a deep breath, closing her eyes and just tried to allow herself to melt into the scenery. She wanted to sink into the sand, seep down between the grains. Wasn't it simply a matter of aligning molecules with the sand in just the right way? Mary opened her eyes and looked at the cork. She set it on the sand, as if it were one of those coins golfers place down in the grass to mark where their balls have landed. Then she got up, brushed the sand off her pants, and walked down to the water's edge.

A white streak left by a jetliner bisected the sky. A plane bound for Europe, Mary guessed. She pulled the stone from her pocket and held it in her palm. It too had a white streak, a stripe of quartz, which Mary now lined up parallel to the one above.

They'd honeymooned in Provincetown. After dinner at an inn, they'd gone for a walk on the beach. The tide was low and each wave's undertow rattled the rocks so that it sounded like a million teeth chattering all at once. Robbie had gotten his pants wet trying to retrieve the stone. He'd found it, then lost it, then, to Mary's amazement, found it again. When he'd presented it to her, he'd said it reminded him of the two of them, how they'd been two separate entities who'd joined together to become one. And how, with eyes closed, by just feeling, it would be impossible to tell where one began and the other ended.

It had always been Mary's intention to return Robbie's stone to the sea to symbolize her acceptance that he was now part of something greater even than the sea itself. It was to be her grand gesture of letting go. Over the years, she'd forgotten about her intention and left the stone on her windowsill to gather dust. Maybe, too, it was that they hadn't been together long enough to amass a lifetime of things. Of the few belongings from him she'd kept, the stone was really her greatest treasure.

With last night's sea change, Mary was now ready to hurl the cold, lifeless hunk of minerals into the sea. Her whole marriage had been a lie.

A wave was cresting. Mary squeezed the stone in her palm, then gathered her strength, drew back her arm, aimed for the belly of the oncoming wave, and launched. Her aim was off and the stone skimmed the top of the wave, then hopped a few times more before being swallowed up. Something she couldn't have done if she'd tried. Mary remembered reading once about a French physicist who'd worked out a mathematical formula for successfully skimming stones. Evidently it was all in the spin. One of the kids who worked in the kitchen a few years back had reported that in *The Guinness Book of World Records,* the record for skips was thirty-eight.

Feeling strangely devoid of emotion, she brushed the sand from her palms. "Goodbye, Robbie," she said. She walked back to where she and Dan had been the night before and picked up the cork. Then she retrieved her shoes from beneath the lifeguard stand and headed back up to the boardwalk. At its end was a blue garbage pail. Mary tossed in the cork.

"Goodbye, Dan," she said.

Why she was driving to Meg's house, Mary really had no idea. Sure, they'd made a coffee date for Thursday, but under the circumstances, given that she hadn't slept, that she'd just found out her dead husband had cheated on her, and that this secret had been kept from her for over a decade by the only man she'd ever truly loved, and given that she had just three weeks to move her aunt from the rehab unit to a permanent bed in a nursing home before the insurance company gave her the boot, and that she'd done something to piss off her head cook at the busiest time of the season and had no idea what the fallout might be, and given that she had enough pain in her life that she should have it compounded by the grief of a woman whose granddaughter had recently died, Mary really could have justified canceling.

And yet something other than a sense of duty drew her to Meg Ryder's home.

• • •

With the fading flowers from the funeral home cleared away, the inside of the house on Bridge Street actually looked sadder, if that was possible—a little more empty, unkempt, and neglected. The babies on the spider plant hanging in its macramé sling by the sliding door had become desiccated, presumably from lack of water. The sympathy cards on the mantel remained, though some had curled at the edges, others had fallen over. Several of the lightbulbs in the dining room fixture had blow out.

Meg had lost weight, but not in a good way. Her clothes were loose in the wrong places and her face was drawn. There were deep circles under her eyes and her hair had become striped like Robbie's stone, with a narrow band of gray at the part.

Ariel sat on a blanket near the dining room table, a vision in her white sundress, her blond hair clipped back in a yellow plastic barrette shaped like the sun. It was obvious that everything else had taken a back seat to her care. Mary imagined what it might be like for a woman Meg's age, overcome with grief, to be chasing a toddler around. Ariel saw Mary and pointed.

"Excuse the place. It's a bit of a mess," Meg said.

"I brought you some chowder," Mary said.

"Thank you." Meg took the white bag, unrolled it, and looked inside. "From the Clambake." Mary had forgotten to peel off the label. "I just got a basket of stuff from them too." Nate must have sent it. "They've been so good to us since the accident. They're even having a fund-raiser in August to help pay for Ariel's college."

"It'll be a long time before she needs it," Mary said.

"Oh, but she'll need it," Meg said. "Come. Coffee's ready." She motioned for Mary to have a seat at the table, where the cream and sugar had already been set out, along with two teaspoons placed on folded paper towels.

Meg filled two mugs from her Mr. Coffee machine and brought them to the table. "I hear the owner of the Clambake is rolling in it, though Anicca said you'd never know it. I guess she's a bit of a tightwad." She set the mugs down and returned to the kitchen.

"Really," Mary said. She cleared her throat. "Speaking of women who are rolling in it, what have you decided to do about Lavinia?"

"I sent her a note," Meg said. Which was probably sitting in Lovey's post office box. Mary realized she needed to retrieve her aunt's mail. "I invited her over for tea, and we'll see what happens from there." She returned with a plate of Stella D'Oro anisette toasts. A favorite of Mary's and Lovey's as well.

"I have a confession to make," Mary said. She'd thought through all possible scenarios. "After you told me she'd contacted you, I called Lavinia. It reminded me that I hadn't talked to her in a while and I just wanted to catch up. I told her I had met you and that I was coming over here today and she insisted on having me deliver this." Mary pulled a sealed while envelope from her purse. "I don't know what's in it, but I assume it's a little something to help fix up a few things around the house, you know, a little paint in the right places, some landscaping, and so on."

Meg took the envelope. Mary had made sure it was enough but not so much that Meg would feel obliged to return it.

"How could she know what the house needed?" Meg said. "She's never been here."

"All right." Mary leaned back in her chair. "She asked me, so I gave her an idea of how she could help. That first day I dropped by, so to speak, I noticed the peeling paint and thought it might be dangerous for the baby."

"Oh, Hope." Every time Meg used that name, Mary felt like a fraud. *False* Hope. Meg slipped the envelope under the empty napkin holder on the kitchen counter. She seemed like all the fight had drained out of her. "Tell her I said thank you. And I still want to have her over for tea. Maybe she'll come if you're here too?"

"Maybe." That would be the day. Mary went over to the little girl. There were a few books laid out on the blanket. "Hi, Ariel. What a pretty dress you have on today!" Ariel was chewing on her forefinger. She looked down at her dress and smiled. "I see you have a lot of books. Which one is your favorite?"

Ariel took the finger out of her mouth and pointed to *Pat the Bunny*. She ran her wet finger over the patch of fur peeking through the cutout.

"I can certainly see why."

As if suddenly overcome with bashfulness, Ariel jumped up and went to her toy box.

Mary returned to the table. She picked up her teaspoon and looked at her own upside-down reflection. She looked a little wind-blown. She smoothed down her hair. "I didn't sleep much last night."

"Welcome to the club." Meg raised her mug in a toast.

"I found out I wasted fourteen years feeling guilty about something I shouldn't have," Mary said. In her mind's eye, she saw Robbie's rock skimming across the surface of the wave.

"There's something I know about. Guilt."

Mary looked at Meg. She appeared stricken. "What is it?"

"I just can't get it out of my head. The scene just plays over and over." A chickadee landed on the empty birdfeeder outside the sliding doors. Meg stared at it. "The night Anicca died, that morning, we had an argument." The bird flew away.

"Do you want to talk about—?"

"She was still in love with Ariel's father. She had this fairy-tale idea of the three of them living together as a family. I told her it was time to let go of the fantasy and get on with her life. I told her she had a baby to raise and what she needed to do was take him to court to get him to pay her the child support she and Ariel deserved. It was the first time I'd ever spoken to her that way. I could tell she was really upset. She went up to her room."

Meg brought her gaze back inside, to the table. She smoothed out her paper towel. "Later that morning, he called to tell her he was going away, leaving the country on some backpacking trip. He told her he wasn't ready to be a father." Meg gathered up the paper towel and squeezed it in her fist. "I'd have given anything not to be right. Her heart was broken. I told her to call in sick. You know what she said?" Meg looked up at Mary.

Mary shook her head.

"She said, 'I can't. I have a baby to raise.'"

No wonder Anicca had dropped the tray. She'd been a strong kid to make it through that day.

"Then she kissed Ariel good-bye and she left. That was the last time I saw her." Meg's body crumpled over the table.

Mary got up and put her arms around the woman while she quietly sobbed.

"Meg, you have nothing to feel guilty about. Anicca knew you loved her. You just told her the truth. It was the right thing to do. It's when people lie or keep things from others, that's when they deserve to feel guilty." At that moment, Mary realized she'd done precisely the same thing with Robbie. She'd felt guilty for telling him the truth the night he died, that he'd been a bad husband. And it must have resonated with him on levels she had no idea of at the time. The truth was something he couldn't bear to hear.

"Nana."

Mary and Meg looked down. Ariel had brought a half-clothed doll and placed it on her great-grandmother's lap.

"Baby," she said.

Mary pulled back and watched the child, fascinated. Meg took the doll by the arm so it wouldn't slide off her knee.

"No. *Baby*, Nana," Ariel insisted.

Mary watched as Meg took the doll up in her arms and held it like a baby. She rocked it back and forth.

"Nana cry."

"It's okay, Ari," Meg said. "It's okay."

Mary reached for the doll. "Go upstairs for a minute," she said to Meg. "Take as long as you need. I'll tend to her."

Meg didn't argue. She got up. "Not what you expected when I invited you over for coffee."

"I don't mind. You've helped me too. You have no idea," Mary said.

Meg started for the stairs. "I can't see how."

"Someday I'll tell you."

Ariel watched her great-grandmother go up the stairs. As on that first day, Mary could see she was weighing whether to go after her or take her chances with the new lady.

"What's the baby's name?" Mary asked. She took the doll and sat it on her lap. She bounced it up and down on her knee.

Ariel giggled. "Me," she said.

"*Me?* Your baby's name is *Me?*"

"No." Ariel knew she was teasing. She knocked the doll out of Mary's hands.

Mary pretended to gasp.

With a wicked smile, Ariel pointed to Mary's lap.

"Oh, I see. You want to go bouncy." Mary lifted Ariel onto her lap. The child weighed practically nothing. Mary started bouncing her up and down on her knee to the rhythm of a silly song Lovey used to sing to her in German. She had no idea what the words even meant, just how to sound them out. By the end of the song, Mary's leg was tired. She stopped.

"Again," Ariel said.

Mary started up again. At the end of the song, she swept Ariel up into her arms. Ariel looked as though she was trying to figure out who this strange lady was. Mary put her finger on Ariel's button nose and the baby smiled. Mary saw the birthmark on her neck.

"I knew someone who had a pretty mark on her neck just like yours," Mary said.

"Anicca had one like that," Meg said. Mary jumped. She hadn't heard Meg come back down. "It looked just like a whale. I can't figure out what Ari's looks like. A flower?"

"A bug," Ariel said.

"Not a *bug*," Meg said. She wrinkled her nose and grabbed Ariel's toes.

Ariel reached both arms up to Meg, who lifted her out of Mary's lap.

Mary smoothed down her rumpled clothes. "Know any good nursing homes?"

"You're probably a little young yet," Meg said. "I'm the one who should be looking." Ariel fidgeted to get down. Meg set her on the ground and Ariel picked up her baby doll.

Mary laughed. She appreciated that the woman could still have a sense of humor after all she'd been through. "It's for my great-aunt," Mary said. "Turns out she's got Alzheimer's."

"I'm sorry, I didn't mean to make a joke."

"I'm glad you did. It's the only way to get through life sometimes." Mary smiled and reached out for Meg's hand. "Though I should probably get home and make some calls."

"There's one in Hyannis I heard good things about. One of the guys at the lumberyard has his mother there."

Mary gathered her handbag and took an anisette toast for the road. She kissed the top of Ariel's head. "Bye-bye, darlin'," she said.

Meg walked Mary to the door. She took Mary's face in her hands and squeezed. *"Hope, Hope. Hope."* Mary took it as a mantra, a poem, a prayer. "Thank you," Meg said.

"Thanks for the coffee. Call me if you need me, okay?" Mary said. "I mean it."

"I will. And please thank Lavinia."

"You bet."

Wayne hadn't looked up when Mary entered the kitchen. Under normal circumstances, he'd have announced her late arrival with some snarky remark. That's how she knew she was in for it.

Mary walked to take-out window to assess the lunch crowd. The dining room was nearly full. There were two waitresses at the chowder station who had their backs to Mary. She couldn't help but overhear their conversation.

"I'd do him. In a heartbeat."

"Megan, he's *old,*" Vanessa said, as if the word had an unpleasant taste. She ladled out her fourth cup of chowder while Megan waited her turn.

"But he's hot," Megan said. "In an aging bad-ass kind of way." She dug two packs of oyster crackers out of the basket at the station and tossed them onto her tray, then plucked out two plastic spoons.

Vanessa dropped the ladle back into the vat and handed the lid to Megan. "He's not *that* hot," she said.

At the same time Vanessa exited the kitchen, Angry Jennifer entered. "*Who's* not that hot?" she asked. An order was waiting for her. She checked her ticket to make sure it matched the food on the tray. A step most of them forgot, Mary acknowledged.

"That new fish guy who was just here. *I* think he's hot. Vanessa thinks I'm nuts." Megan ladled out two cups.

Mary felt her own cheeks grow hot.

Angry Jennifer lifted the tray up on her right shoulder. "I think *Vanessa's* hot," she said.

"Gross," Megan said. "Chowder's low," she yelled to the back of the kitchen. "Thanks," came a voice down the line. She left.

Mary went to the back door. She'd parked out front and was probably pulling in just as he was leaving. There was no sign of him.

"He was looking for you," Nate said. "He left an envelope for you by the phone. Said it was just a bill."

Mary went to retrieve it.

"Nate," Wayne called. "Come take over. Burgers medium well. They need another minute."

Mary slipped the envelope out from under the phone. She looked up to see Nate tying on his apron.

"Can I talk to you for a minute?" Wayne said. He had sneaked up behind her. "Outside," he added, like he wanted to rumble.

"Sure," Mary said. Thank goodness Sage was off today.

As she followed him out the back door, she ran her thumb under the seal of the envelope. She pulled out the slip of paper, not a bill, just a handwritten note: *I feel terrible about last night. You left before I could tell you the whole story.* Mary didn't think she could stomach more of that story. She folded the note and stuffed it in her pocket.

Once they got outside, Wayne turned to her. His eyes were so crazed and wide she could actually see whites.

He launched right in. "Where do you get off telling people my personal business? I confided in you. I *trusted* you." He had a wide stance and hands at his waist like he was about to pull a pistol.

"Wayne, I never meant—"

"Now she not only thinks I'm some kind of nut, but she's pissed that I didn't tell her sooner." Wayne walked over to the screen door to make sure no one was listening.

"I just assumed you'd already told—"

"You *know* this is something I've struggled with my whole life. And it's not up to you to decide when and how I let people know." His nostrils were flaring.

"Wayne," she said. She pulled him by the apron strings further away from the door. "No wonder Sage is angry. You're acting like an idiot." Maybe it was that Mary's dearest relative happened to be losing her senses while this kid had been blessed with an abundance of them, or that Mary felt she'd been walking around like a zombie herself for the last dozen or so years, unable to feel real emotion, real love, real pain. Whatever it was, something inside her snapped. "What you have is not an *affliction*. So for God's sake stop pitying yourself. What you have—this ability to experience things in a way no one else in the world can—it's something special."

Wayne looked over to the door. Mary noticed sweat at his sideburns. "Keep it down, will you?" he said.

Mary whispered as loud and with as much urgency as could still be considered a whisper. "You're one of the best cooks in town and I'm willing to bet it's not because you win any personality contests. You have a gift. And if your girlfriend is pissed off, it's not because she thinks you're a *freak*. It's because she thinks you're a *jerk* for keeping something like that from her. Because when you don't tell people things, it's as good as lying. And when the truth finally comes out years later, it *hurts*. And it's too damn late."

Wayne scratched his head. "We've only been going out a couple of weeks."

"Never mind. My point is this. Admit that you're a fool for not telling her the truth. Tell her you're sorry. For God's sake, Wayne, tell her what shape you feel when you kiss her. She'll swoon, I promise. Now get back in the freaking kitchen." Mary used her palm to wipe away the sweat that had beaded up on her own brow.

Wayne stood there a second, stunned. Mary could see he was digesting her words. Then he shrugged. He turned and headed for the door.

"And, Wayne," she said.

"What?" he said in his normal voice.

"I'm giving you a damn raise." Mary felt like she needed to go sit in the shade somewhere. "Only because you've earned it."

Sixteen

Across the Cape, the roses had already begun to fade. For Mary, it always seemed the summer no sooner got under way than the lushness and vibrancy of the foliage started to slip away. At least the hydrangeas were in their full glory and this was a good year for them. Nature's cheerleaders, Mary thought, with their big white and blue pom-poms encouraging the perennials to kick out a few more blooms before the August drought. It was a subtle shift that happened midsummer, but Mary was all too sensitive to the passing of the lilies, the wilting of the bulb greens, and the blossoming of the black-eyed Susans. Sometimes she could look at her entire life and see it marked by the rising and falling of nature, in the storms that forever changed the beaches, in the migration of birds, in the cycles of the seasons.

Dan's phone messages seemed to mimic the roses, at first coming daily, so hardy and hopeful, and then, as the weeks went by, growing more sparse as he must have gradually come to accept that Mary wasn't willing to forgive him for his misplaced loyalty.

Dan kept up his seafood deliveries to the restaurant and Mary made sure he was paid on time. She assigned the dishwasher to keep a lookout for when his truck pulled into the back alley so she wouldn't have to endure any awkward encounters. When he came, she usually manufactured some reason to be out on the floor, where she knew she was safe. Dan had never set foot in the dining room. For some reason, perhaps because of Robbie, or because he was always coming straight from the dock and felt self-conscious about his appearance, he must have felt the front room was off-limits.

"What's up with you and the fish guy?" Wayne asked her about a week after her night on the beach with Dan. Wayne and Sage had patched things up almost immediately after Mary had her talk with him, which was probably why Wayne seemed to forgive her on the spot. Or it might have been the extra money in his paycheck. Now, evidently, he felt his role as kitchen Casanova made him an expert on matters of the heart.

"I don't know what you mean," Mary said.

"I mean I thought you were *old friends.*" Wayne slathered butter on some buns and tossed them on the grill. "Some of us thought more than that."

Mary picked up some mail on the counter and started flipping through the kitchen supply catalogs. "Never more than that," she lied.

"Right. Which is why you make for the dining room like a busboy on crank every time his truck pulls in." Wayne turned back around. "What gives?"

Mary set down the mail. "Nothing *gives.* He's a vendor. I'm the client." She pointed an envelope at him. "And *you're* on thin ice."

Wayne shrugged. The order line girls looked at each other. When Mary was almost to the stairs to her office, Wayne yelled to her, "Better watch it. I hear a couple of the waitresses wouldn't kick him out of the sack."

Mary stopped but didn't turn around. "They have my blessing."

Plans at the Clambake were under way for the benefit to raise money in Anicca's memory for her daughter's college fund. Nate and Maureen had orchestrated the whole event, which was to take place the second week of August. Posters with a beautiful black-and-white photograph of Anicca holding Ariel when she was an infant had already been plastered all over town. Meg had given Nate the photo, one that Mary had seen in a frame at Meg's house. In the fuzziness that resulted from its poor-quality mass reproduction, mother and child look almost luminous, like the Virgin and the Christ Child. Mary imagined that's what people thought when they looked at the image. She suspected that had been Nate and Maureen's intention.

Mary had offered to donate the entire day's food proceeds to the cause. If she was being completely honest, part of the reason was to counteract Meg's perception, and probably the whole town's, that the owner of the Clambake was a tightwad. There was a difference between being a frugal businessperson and a generous soul, and deep down Mary believed a person could be both. She wasn't the only one with generosity in her heart. The servers and bartenders had pledged to turn over their tips. All the kitchen workers volunteered their time that day as well, so that their pay could go toward the fund. The idea was to get as many people into the restaurant as possible, with brisk turnover. On their way out, customers would have the opportunity to buy quart containers of "world-famous" Clambake chowder. And there was to be a raffle for a grand prize, which had yet to be been determined.

Mary hadn't been to visit Meg since the day Ariel had sat on her lap, though they spoke regularly on the phone. Mary still took the long way to work, driving past the Bridge Street house, and was happy to see the fresh coat of paint on the doors and the window trim, and the landscapers busy mowing the lawn and pulling out the old, grim-looking yews. She'd sent another box of toys and clothes for Ariel in Lavinia's name. In one of their conversations, Meg informed Mary of the benefit at the Clambake, as if she didn't know. Mary felt bad about keeping up the charade of being someone named Hope, but by now it had gone on for too long and her connection with Meg had grown too deep. But the hypocrisy wasn't lost on Mary. Here she was, furious at Dan for having kept a secret from her, and yet she was doing the same thing to a woman she'd grown to consider a friend. But then again, it wasn't truly the same. Mary and Dan had been lovers. He should have told her what had been going on. He should have told her why he left, instead of letting her stew in her abandonment. Mary's intentions with Meg had always been simply to find a way to help.

"Do you think you'll go?" Mary had asked over the phone when Meg brought up the benefit.

Meg didn't answer right away. "I probably should, seeing that they're doing something so nice for Ariel. This is going to sound awful, but I don't think I could bear to see all those young people Anicca's age, those girls enjoying their lives the way she should have had the chance to." Meg cleared her throat. By now, Mary had grown used to the pauses in their conversation. She gave her friend the spaces of silence without feeling the need to rush to fill them with words.

"I understand completely," Mary said. "I'm sure they would too. You don't need to be there." Mary was relieved; if Meg had decided to go, she'd have had to concoct some reason to disappear during the event.

"You really think it's okay?" Meg asked.

"Absolutely," Mary said. "I'll speak to the owner about it on your behalf if you'd like. I'll make sure she understands."

"Hope, you're an angel."

Lovey had accepted her new surroundings, though her condition seemed to worsen under the care of others. What Carleton Dyer said had been true. She was surrendering to her illness, letting go.

After touring every nursing home with an Alzheimer's wing on the Cape, Mary found Lovey a permanent bed in the small, residential-style home in Hyannis that Meg had mentioned. There, Lovey had her own private room with a peek at the harbor. Because the place had no Medicaid beds, and Lovey had no other insurance, it was costing Mary a fortune, but at least Lovey was comfortable and able to retain some sense of dignity. There was still a woman down the hall who moaned something incoherent to anyone who passed by her room. Every nursing home had at least one, it seemed. And while the place was clean, there were still times when the stench of fresh urine hung in the air. But unlike the other facilities Mary had visited, this felt more like a home. There was a parlor with a piano, and the choir director from the local Congregational church came every Tuesday to lead the residents in singing hymns, which, to Mary's amazement, most of the patients—including some who couldn't even remember the names of their own children—were still able to do.

Another comforting thing about the Harbor House was that the earlier-stage patients were separated from the ones who were close to death, who no longer ate without help and were mostly confined to their beds. Those patients, the "empty shells," resided on the second floor.

Mary secretly hoped her aunt would one day slip away in her sleep before she ever became bad enough to have to make that move. At the moment, though, there was still enough of Lovey left to be enjoyed. Mary just had to learn how to lower her expectations. The medicine the doctors had prescribed had given Lovey a sense of well-being so that the awful fits of fear and paranoia she'd been experiencing had all but vanished.

Mary was even able to take Lovey for occasional day trips to the restaurant, where she sat contentedly at the bar. While she no longer tried to wait on tables, there were still days when Lovey could converse with the crew and customers. Mary thought the outings did her good, even if they wore her out a bit.

The day before the move, Mary had gone to Lovey's apartment to gather some clothes and select a few pieces of furniture. She'd rented a U-Haul van and paid one of the kids from the kitchen to help her bring over Lovey's bedside table and a carved Chinese chest that reeked of mothballs (which was better than reeking of urine, but not by much), and, of course, Lovey's green recliner. There wasn't room in her Harbor House bedroom for much else. Mary brought some framed photographs and a hooked rug wall-hanging she had made for her aunt of an orange-and-brown lion, the astrological sign for Leo, that Mary had chosen not because there were any Leos in the family but because Mary had been going through her cat phase, which fit in somewhere between her obsession with horses and her brief fascination with snakes.

• • •

Left uneaten, the dog food in the bowl had hardened in the sun; flies chased each other from the cracked surface. Mary shifted the bag of food to her left arm, then rapped on Carleton's screen door.

Carleton appeared. He had a red streak on his cheek that some-one might have mistaken for blood or war paint. The color of it made Mary hopeful.

"Have you seen him at all?" she asked. She nodded in the direc-tion of the food bowl. "I wonder if he was hit by a car."

"Come in, come in." He led her inside. "Not for a week and a half. Every day I put out fresh food, but nothing."

"You must miss him," Mary said.

"It was probably just time for him to move on. I understand."

Mary got the sense Carleton had done something similar in his life. He'd once mentioned something about a woman that he'd left behind, and there'd been a child, though Mary didn't know if it had been his. She figured he'd share it with her if he ever felt so inclined.

Carleton sniffed the air. *He must smell the fried clams,* Mary thought. She'd learned they were his favorite.

She saw the canvas set up on the easel. She set the bag down on the lobster pot table. "Oh, I love it," she said. She clapped her hands.

There was a new painting of the outdoor shower. Unlike the others, this one had a bright splash of color, a large red-and-white-striped beach towel hanging on the wood door. Two days earlier, Mary had snuck out in the middle of the night and tapped a nail into the door, then draped the bright towel over the nail in hopes of surprising Carleton the next morning when he came out of his bed-room. If this went well, she had other surprises in store, a colorful beach pail and shovel she'd picked up at the Christmas Tree Shops that she planned to set up like a still life on the ground. And she had found an old Adirondack chair in the garage that had been painted so many times, in layers that had cracked and peeled, that it was no longer any one color. Since meeting Carleton, Mary had begun to see objects differently, observing them in space, seeing them for their texture, and for their potential as subjects—their color and form—and how light might pool in places and bounce off others.

"It was quite a surprise," Carleton said.

"A good one, I hope."

"I'll leave that up to you," he said. But he already knew how good the painting was. He put his hands on his hips; he was practically beaming. He'd managed to capture the weight and texture of the towel. It even looked damp. There was a truth to the shadows trapped in the folds, not just darkness, so that it seemed Mary could pass her hand there and expect to feel it fall into the coolness of shadow.

She turned and noticed he was hovering over the bag on the lobster pot.

"Fried clams. Come eat them while they're still hot," Mary said. She gathered up the bag.

"Will you join me?"

"They're for you. I can't stay. But I'll sit for a minute." They went to the kitchen. Mary set the bag on the table and pulled out two cans of beer, one for each of them. Carleton's eyes lit up. A man after her own heart.

"Sorry, they got a little warm from the clams," she said. "I should have put them in a separate bag."

"Nonsense." Carleton sat. "We'll pretend we're in Europe."

Mary wondered where and under what circumstances Carleton Dyer had been in Europe. She pulled out the box overflowing with clams, cupping her hand over them so they wouldn't scatter, and then she drew out the plastic cup of tartar sauce and an ear of corn wrapped in foil. She flattened out the bag and placed everything on top of it. She pulled the lid off the tartar sauce, then slid the bag toward Carleton, who wasted no time. He lifted a fat clam from the box and shook it free from the others. He popped the belly in his mouth, biting off the strip. Breading crumbled to the bag. Some of it stuck to his shirt.

Mary tore a paper towel from the roll on the counter and brought it over. She sat down and snapped open both beers, sipping hers as Carleton dredged his clams in tartar sauce with his steady hand, his right exiled to his lap. From as far up as the muscles in the shoulder, Mary could see the arm protested its exclusion.

"So how has your aunt settled into her new home?" he asked.

"Quite well, actually," Mary said. "She seems to accept it. I would have thought she'd be more upset."

Carleton nodded. "That's good." He ate another clam.

"I have to pack up her apartment and move everything out by Sunday. Darlene already has a tenant lined up for next month," she said. "Which is in four days."

Carleton took a long draw off his warm beer. "I imagine there's a lot of transience there, people moving in and out."

"People dying right and left," Mary added.

"I'll stay where I am, thank you very much." He slid the packet of butter toward Mary. "Would you mind?"

Mary peeled open the foil. The butter had already gone creamy from sitting beside the hot corn. She slid the open packet back to him. Carleton rubbed the pat over the kernels.

"I thought impermanence was a good thing," she said.

"It's not a good thing or a bad thing. It just is. Acceptance is the key. We all tend to grow attached." By the look of him, Carleton had grown attached to that ear of corn. "If you need some help moving her things, I'm at your service, though I don't know how much help I'd be." He had a couple of pale yellow kernels stuck to his chin.

Mary smiled. "Thanks for the offer, but this is something I need to do on my own. In a weird way, I'm almost looking forward to it. It'll be interesting going through all those things. Her apartment is like a time capsule of my family."

Carleton wiped his face with the paper towel. "Just don't let the past overwhelm you," he warned. "Try to stay present."

Mary knew what he meant. Some of it was bound to be painful.

"I will," Mary said. "I should get going." She was about to get up, then remembered what she'd come to ask. "The kids at the restaurant have organized an event to raise money for the family of the girl who died in that car accident at the beginning of the summer. You remember I told you about that?"

"I'd read about it too. Terrible," he said.

Mary waited for him to pop another clam in his mouth. Then she said, "It's on Tuesday, the eleventh, and I want you to be my date."

Carleton looked up. Mary had timed her invitation well. He had too much food in his mouth to protest. He shook his head and his eyes widened a little.

"It would do you good to get out and be with people," Mary argued.

All he could do was raise his finger.

"I knew you'd resist—" "resistance" was one of his terms—"but it's for a worthy cause. And of course I don't expect you to pay for anything. But I might ask you to donate a painting for a raffle they're holding at the restaurant."

Carleton swallowed. "I'd be happy to give you a painting, but—"

"But what? But you have other plans that day? Come on, Carleton. Just say yes. It'll be fun. All kinds of people will be there."

Carleton's face darkened. His wiry brows drew together like two caterpillars facing off. He brought his bad hand up onto the table. Mary couldn't be sure he wasn't exaggerating the tremor as his arm suddenly hit the paper bag and the ear of corn shot off onto the floor. He just looked at Mary with defiance as if to say, *See?* As if the flying ear of corn had said it all.

Mary leaned back in her chair and waved him off. "You think that's bad, you should see what some of the brats at the restaurant toss on the floor. I'll never forget I had one spoiled kid dump a whole lobster, drawn butter and all, which caused another little kid to slip and crack his chin. Would have had a lawsuit on my hands if the kid who slipped hadn't been the little wild man's brother. And another time a little monster poured an entire glass of milk down a waitress's back. Your hand isn't *that* naughty, is it?"

Carleton rolled his eyes.

"Just keep Mr. Jitters on the down low"—Mary moved her hand to her lap to illustrate—"and no one will get hurt." She got up and went around to the back of Carleton's chair to pick up the corn. She put it in the sink in case he decided to wash it off and eat it. "So I can count on you coming, then?" She slung her purse over her shoulder. "You wouldn't stand a gal up, would you?"

He smiled and slumped back in his chair. "I'll think about it," he said.

Mary headed for the door. "Remember, Carleton. 'What we resist persists.'" She'd gotten that from a yoga class. In this case she didn't think it was entirely apropos, but she improvised. "Which means I'll keep bugging you till you say yes, so you might as well give in."

It was a suitably cloud-filled sky that Mary could see from her aunt's apartment windows. She would have found the whole task more difficult had the sun been streaming through. Mary sat on the floor surrounded by Lovey's things, with concentric circles of moving boxes just beyond. Much of the furniture was already gone, either moved to the nursing home or given to some of the kids who worked in the complex. Where those pieces had sat, only deep depressions in the carpet remained. In another day, these marks would be all that was left of her aunt in this place. Nearly thirty years. In some way it comforted Mary to know that no amount of cleaning and steaming would ever lift her aunt's impressions from the cheap synthetic pile.

Mary had already packed up the kitchen in cartons designated for the Goodwill. Most of the pots, pans, and utensils were in decent shape but of lesser quality than the ones Mary already had at home, with only a few exceptions, a heavy cast iron griddle and a large Le Creuset covered casserole dish. Just seeing the fry pans brought Mary back to those painful days earlier this summer when she first learned something was terribly wrong. What a difference a month could make in someone's life. What a difference a moment could make, thinking now of Anicca and Robbie, and how even Dan had nearly lost his life in a random mishap on that fishing boat.

Mary had already thought of Dan plenty today. All the memories of her life seemed to jumble together in this room. When Mary had taken down the photo collage that still held Robbie's photo, she'd wanted to rip out his picture and tear it to shreds. Then she thought of Carleton and how he might frown on such reactivity. *Just let him go,* she heard his voice in her ears. She slipped the frame into a box filled with old, heavy plastic holly wreaths from the days when plastic holly wreaths were a novelty, superior to traditional holiday greens for their practicality. (No sap. No needles or loose leaves. No muss.) Mary knew she wouldn't be reopening that box anytime soon. It would be relegated to the hot purgatory of her attic. If the holiday greens melted a bit onto Robbie's face, well, *c'est la vie.*

Mary set a few more things aside for herself from the kitchen, her aunt's heavy metal ice cream scoop with its wide, flat spoon that had come over on the boat with Mary's grandfather from Germany. Why he'd come to this country with an ice cream scoop was a question Mary had never thought to ask until today. To a child, an ice cream scoop must have seemed a perfectly normal thing to take, a necessity. Mary also took the old kitchen shears her great-grandmother and great-aunt had used to cut chickens, recalling how it used to fascinate her to see Lovey drive the sharp blade through the bird's rib cage, along either side of the spine, as if she were snipping paper dolls. It was as much the sound of the fine bones crunching that awed her, like the sounds made when Dan cleaned the fish, the scraping of scales and crunch of cartilage.

Mary had also worked her way though the bathroom, which hadn't taken long. Some of the things Lovey no longer needed, like the cleaning products, toilet paper, and cakes of soap, she planned to bring home and use herself. Other things she would take to the nursing home: the tin of bobby pins, the Noxema, Jean Naté, and Pepsodent. And some things she had discarded, the Pearl Drops tooth polish—a whiter smile just didn't seem like a priority for someone in a nursing home who was missing a tooth. Mary had been crushed to learn that Lovey's false tooth had accidentally been thrown out the very first day at the rehab facility. But the old woman didn't seem to miss it anymore.

In the medicine cabinet, Mary had found an old jar of Dippity-doo, from when Lovey used to set her hair each night. As a kid, Mary had always loved the smell. She lifted it down from the shelf, unscrewed the cap, pink flakes of dried gel falling to the sink, took one final sniff, and then tossed the jar in the trash. She did the same with the ancient bottle of Mercurochrome, redder than blood, her mother and Lovey used to swab over Mary's scraped knees. Mary had always secretly liked the way it exaggerated the wound so the next day at school she elicited more sympathy.

Now Mary was busy emptying out her aunt's desk and side table drawers, which were deep and held a surprising large amount of stuff. Having lived through the Depression, her aunt had always been a pack rat, though a neat one. Everything seemed to be organized in tidy packets of random things that had been grouped together and painstakingly Scotch-taped into bits of saved plastic or bubble wrap. If there was some greater order to the organization of Lovey's belongings, some sophisticated system, it was lost on Mary.

She found a cluster of cassette tapes her aunt had saved even though she'd long ago give up her cassette player and made the switch to CDs. The Mormon Tabernacle Choir. The sound track to the movie *Titanic*. Pachelbel's Canon. *Christmas with Mario Lanza*. Mary wrote down the titles so she could try to find some of them on CD to bring to Lovey or even just play for herself when she was missing her aunt.

Another packet contained old letters and holiday cards from dead friends, a recipe for tuna casserole, and a yellowed magazine article on warning signs of illness in cats. Lovey's cat had died six or seven years ago. There were marbles; a hole punch; a good-luck coin her aunt had pressed in a machine at an amusement park in Rye, New York; and one of those tomato-shaped pincushions into which round-headed straight pins, organized by color, had been stuck in equidistant rows. Mary could remember when she was a teenager watching TV with Lovey one night as her aunt had first organized them. And there were so many other things: a bracelet Mary had made her aunt out of clay beads in grade school, pens, pencils, staplers with more staples than a person could ever hope to use in her lifetime, an old dagger-style letter opener, packets containing scraps of gift wrap. It went on and on.

Lovey had a footstool with a vinyl cushion that flipped up to reveal a storage compartment. Mary had forgotten all about it until she lifted the stool and felt things shift around inside. It was here Mary discovered the secrets Lovey had been keeping, the evidence of her struggle to keep it together in the face of her decline. Inside the stool, Mary found the calendar she'd given her aunt for Christmas. Each day had been crossed off, with a heavy black slash, up until the end of May, when it seemed Lovey had lost her place. There was a slip of paper with the definitions to words Mary knew her aunt knew, or had known at one time. A corner of an envelope on which she'd written: *Perry Mason, every Thursday, 7 p.m.* It had been her favorite TV show. Even Mary knew when the reruns were aired. Lovey had planned her weeks around them. How could she forget? There was a schedule for her daily medication and a list of what the medicines were for. So Lovey had known something was wrong with her, that things were slipping away.

Mary was nearing home stretch and feeling proud of herself. After the footstool, only the dresser drawers and bedroom closet remained. Most of Lovey's clothes would be given away, as Mary had been instructed by the nursing home about the kinds of clothes she now needed, mostly elastic-waist pants and tops and sweaters that could be thrown in the wash, and were put easily on and taken off. Lovey needed things that would keep her warm in the chilly halls of the facility. So she wouldn't be requiring the umpteen lightweight snap-front housecoats anymore, or the zipper-back sweaters and wool slacks that had to be hand-washed or dry-cleaned.

So there wasn't much else. Throughout the day, whenever she'd felt a sense of loss, she'd reminded herself that it wasn't as though

Lovey had died. She could still visit her at the nursing home anytime she liked. *Just get through this damn footstool,* she told herself. Then she could give herself a gold star for maintaining her composure during one of the most dreaded days of her life.

All day Mary had been waiting for the one thing that would catch her off guard and send her over the edge. She imagined it might be the old Hummel figurines, or the family Bible, or the cross that her grandmother had made of palm fronds. But it hadn't been those things. It hadn't even been the photo albums containing images of Lovey with Mary's mother as a young girl. None of those things had tripped the switch.

Instead it was something that had rested at the bottom of the footstool, in an unassuming pad of unlined paper. On the first page, a grocery list organized by supermarket aisle so Lovey would re-member where items were found. On the second page, in her aunt's fine though less confident cursive, these words, obviously written there so she wouldn't forget:

> *Amazing grace, how sweet the sound*
> *That saved a wretch like me.*
> *I once was lost, but now am found,*
> *Was blind, but now I see.*

With that came the tears. For Lovey. For herself. For Robbie, An-icca, Meg, Ariel, Dan. For all of them. All wretches. All lost. Where was the grace in such a horrible disease? Where was the grace in any of it?

It was Tuesday night at the Clambake. Still emotionally drained from the weekend, Mary just wanted to go home. Tomorrow she planned a visit to the nursing home to deliver the few things she'd set aside from Lovey's apartment, in addition to some clothes and toiletries, a few tchotchkes to make the place feel more like home: a shell on which Lovey's mother had painted a red rose, a jar of

"Pickled People" made out of nylon stockings that Mary had given her aunt in the early 1970s, and Lovey's bedside table lamp.

Mary went up to her office and then, as happened so often, saw a pile of mail she had missed earlier. In it were things that needed her attention, inquiries to be answered, subscriptions to be renewed, bills to be paid. The next thing she knew, she was still sitting at her desk, buried in paperwork, two hours after she'd told the kids downstairs that she was going home.

It was almost nine and Mary could tell by the scrubbing and slamming of pots that service had stopped in the kitchen. The night had been slow. Just one more check to cut for the landscaper and she could put the rest off till tomorrow.

That's when she heard something. A scurrying sound that seemed to be coming from down the hall. She raised her reading glasses up on her forehead and listened. Nothing. A moment later, she heard it again, only louder this time, and another sound, as though something had fallen over in the storage room. She hoped the squirrels from last year hadn't found their way back into the attic. She'd paid a small fortune to have a roof guy seal up the eaves where the pest guy had been certain they were getting in. And the pest guy had assured her the family of squirrels caught in the Havahart traps had been relocated to the National Seashore park two towns away. So what if he'd missed an uncle? Or maybe the whole clan had found their way back.

Mary pushed back from her desk. The last thing she needed at this hour was a rodent encounter. Because she'd seen too many old horror movies, she scanned the room for something to use as a weapon. With Robbie's rock on the floor of the Atlantic, she was left with few options. At last she took a bottle of wine from the cooler beneath her desk, noting, in the random firing of synapses in her brain, that the store of bottles seemed to be diminishing at a slower rate than in past summers. Lately, she'd simply been too distracted to drink.

With the bottle poised above her head, Mary tiptoed down the narrow hall so as not to upset the brittle floorboards. As she approached the door, she heard more shuffling. Whatever it was, it was too big to be a squirrel. If one of the girls had come upstairs to get something, why had she closed the door?

Mary heard a voice. Then another. She pressed her ear to the door and heard heavy breathing. She dropped the bottle to her side. *Oh, for God's sake.* She wrapped her hand around the door knob. *Let me guess. Wayne and Sage,* she thought. *Maybe Jennifer and Vanessa. Or how about Vanessa and Dan? Wouldn't that be a kick in the nuts?*

Just the thought of the last pairing reinvigorated her so that she yanked open the door and flicked on the light.

Just Nate and Maureen.

"What the—?" Nate started.

Blinded from the light, they tugged at their clothes.

"Damn," Maureen said, yanking down her shirt with one hand and shielding her eyes with the other.

"Mary!" Nate said. He squinted at her, then looked down on the floor, where he'd apparently lost a sneaker.

Maureen still couldn't see. "You said she went home!" she said through her teeth.

Mary smiled. "You seem to like it up here, huh, Nate?"

"What's that supposed to mean?" Maureen said. She didn't wait for an answer. She just punched him in the bicep, hard. He winced. Suddenly Mary saw them as third-graders. Or a couple that had been married thirty years.

"Ouch," he said. "What'd I do?"

"You *know* what you did," Maureen said. "Even if I don't." In a huff, she smoothed down her hair, adjusted the waistband of her Bermuda shorts, and shot off down the hall. "And I don't want to know either," she called from stairs.

Mary cringed. "Sorry," she said. "I'll talk to her if you want."

Below them they heard the door slam.

Nate sunk down onto a carton and put on his shoe. "She'll cool off." He wiped his hand over his face. "Look, I'm sorry. I shouldn't have—"

"Here," Mary said. She handed Nate the bottle of wine. "Tell her I was just having fun."

Mary backed out of the storage room. Nate started over the threshold, then leaned back and turned off the light.

Good kid, Mary thought. She felt a pang of guilt for having even fleetingly entertained the idea of being with him last summer. "Hey, I almost forgot. I got a local artist to donate a painting for the raffle."

Nate's face brightened. "That's awesome. What's it of?"

She wasn't about to tell him her outdoor shower. "Not sure. Something Capey."

"That's great. Wait till I tell Maureen."

"Go on," Mary said. Then she remembered what she wanted to ask. "Hey," she called after him. "Do you have a grand prize yet?"

"Not yet," he said. "But we're close to figuring out something."

Seventeen

I t was only a little past twelve and already the Clambake's lot was full. Mary pulled the car up as close as she could to the entrance. Audrey got out of the back seat and went to the trunk to retrieve Lovey's collapsible wheelchair. Lovey could still walk, but in the last few weeks her wobbles had worsened and the last thing she needed was to end up like her old rehab roommate, Helen, with a broken hip. Mary had since learned from the obituary in the local paper that Helen had passed away.

There was a time when Lovey would have put up a big stink at the idea of having to be wheeled around in public. That Lovey seemed to have been packed away like the boxes Mary had the kids move from the old apartment to the attic at One Skaket Drive.

Mary had invited Audrey to join them, partly to make up for the hellish night of the Fourth when Lovey had disappeared, and partly because she didn't want to leave Carleton alone with Lovey. Mary anticipated she herself wouldn't be able to sit with them for long stretches without having to leave occasionally to play host, which was probably why she now felt the hum of tension in her jaw on this day of the fund-raiser to benefit Ariel.

Mary had tried to prepare herself for the fact that she would likely face more customers today than she had over the last ten years combined. Early this morning, she must have tried on seven or eight outfits, finally settling on a sleeveless navy jersey dress with an empire waist and a wrapped V neckline, plus a white cropped sweater to provide a little cover-up. Against her better judgment, she'd slipped on a pair of tan wedge sandals that made her calves look great but would probably have her nursing blisters by the end of the day.

Mary got out of the car and walked over to the take-out window.

She put her face up to the screen. "Maureen, get Nelson. I need him to park my car someplace." She deposited the keys on the window ledge. "When did all this start?" she asked.

"You mean the busyness?" Mary noticed that Maureen was wearing small gold hoop earrings. She'd never seen her wear jewelry. This was a big day for the kids. Maureen and Nate had worked hard to put this together. "Like a half hour after you left," Maureen said.

Mary had gone to pick Lovey up at the Harbor House in Hyannis, then had to swing back to get Audrey and Carleton. He was just now emerging from the front passenger side. He had on khaki pants and an old brown twill blazer that smelled a bit musty, and beneath it, a crisp white shirt and a vintage hand-painted necktie featuring an elaborate illustration of a female nude crossing a stream, stepping from stone to stone, her long hair covering her nether regions, at least. Mary had complimented him on it. He'd said it was a gift from a "lady friend" a few years back. She'd looked at him and raised an eyebrow. He'd just smiled. With the tie, the sparkle in his eye, and his hair slicked back with Vitalis (or some equally noxious grooming agent), he looked the part of an artist.

A table had been set up near the entrance and decorated with a dozen or so white balloons. It was unmanned at the moment, but on the ground there was a cooler that Mary assumed contained the quarts of chowder the kids had stayed late to ladle out last night. On the table were rolls of raffle tickets, stubby blue pencils, and a foil-covered restaurant-sized mayo jar most likely intended to serve as a place for people to deposit their tickets.

"Shouldn't someone be sitting here?" Mary asked Hope as the young hostess whizzed by on her way to bring menus to a table.

"Megan's on her way in," she called.

"What's the grand—?" But Hope was long gone before Mary could get the rest out. As of last night by the time Mary left, the grand prize had yet to be nailed down, though no one had seemed too worried. The second prize, however, was displayed prominently at the entrance to the restaurant—Carleton's painting of Mary's outdoor shower, the one with the candy-striped towel hanging on the door. Mary hadn't told anyone the particulars about the subject, though secretly she felt proud that the painting had been a collaboration of sorts. She'd expected Nate to be a little disappointed when he saw it wasn't a beach scene or seascape, but he'd thought it was great. Everyone loved it, in fact. Mary liked how it looked there on the wall near the door so much that she thought she might have to commission Carleton for another. Or maybe just buy enough tickets to win this one.

On a tripod at the far end of the table was an enlargement of the photograph of Anicca and Ariel, mounted on a foam board.

Nelson came out of the kitchen. His white apron was stained, he had a red bandana tied around his head, and the crotch of his jeans hung down below the hem of the apron, practically down to his knees. For an instant, Mary had the panicky feeling that customers might lose their appetites at the sight of what creatures lurked in the kitchen. Nelson grabbed her car keys and headed for the driver-side door. Hope was already greeting a new party of three. Audrey had Lovey in the wheelchair and was bringing her around the back of the car, struggling to keep the wheels from digging into the gravel. Carleton was standing with his hands behind his back, looking at the sea of people in the restaurant like someone who, having gotten up off the sand, suddenly realizes he's nowhere near hot enough to want to jump into the Atlantic. Here was a man whose biggest excitement while dining during the past few years might well have been having a hummingbird pass his window.

While everyone was otherwise engaged, Mary dug into her handbag and pulled out the red stuffed bear she'd taken from the site of the crash. She set it near the tripod, below the picture of mother and child, and felt a whale like the one on Anicca's neck rise inside her own throat. *Did this kid really have to die?* Mary swallowed hard. She straightened out the bear and pulled up its ears. Just then, she heard a waitress's name called over the loudspeaker. She looked up to the take-out window and saw Maureen, who was watching her and had probably seen the whole thing. Maureen smiled. Mary nodded.

"Are we all here?" Hope asked.

"I believe we are," Audrey said.

"Right this way," Hope said.

Mary couldn't remember the last time she'd eaten in her own restaurant. In the early days, she used to come out to a table and sip wine with old high school girlfriends whenever they'd stop by, friends who had all since moved away and whom Mary never bothered to replace. Now she tried to see the Clambake through the eyes of someone who'd never been there before. What would her first impression be? The place had a friendly feel to it. It was quaint and casual, though she still thought she'd gone a bit overboard with the nautical motif, perhaps one too many fishnets floating in the rafters, one too many painted lobster buoys. Even Robbie's big red plastic lobster had remained through the years, despite her initial protests. After he had died, she'd never had the heart to take it down. But in general, the decorations all worked and made for a welcoming environment. The shellacked pine tables warmed the room, particularly against the marine gray concrete floors, which got a fresh coat of paint each season.

When Mary had come in earlier, she'd seen Angry Jennifer stuffing white hydrangea blooms into tiny white vases she must have hauled down from the supply closet. Jennifer said she'd clipped the flowers from her grandmother's shrubs. When Mary asked if her grandmother knew this, she'd simply shrugged.

Hope led the party to a table at the back of the dining room, one of the few that accommodated wheelchairs. Mary felt the eyes on her as she made her way down the aisle. She recognized some of the locals. They were the ones who came out for events like this. *That's Mary Hopkins, the owner,* she imagined them saying, and she saw herself through their eyes as part of a parade that included an old man with a naked woman on his necktie; an old woman in a wheelchair, wearing a bright pink sweat suit and matching Keds; and, pushing the wheelchair, a morbidly obese woman in a Mexican peasant dress. An interesting ensemble, to be sure.

Hope gave them a chance to settle into their seats, then set the menus down on the table and plucked off the card inscribed *Reserved*. "Enjoy your lunch," she said. No sooner had they picked up their menus than Mary saw someone at the door she needed to greet.

"I'm sorry, I have to run up and say hi to someone. I'll be right back. Will you order me a diet ginger ale?" Mary started to get up.

Lovey raised her finger. "I'll have a glass of Chablis," she said.

Mary turned to her aunt in surprise and smiled. "We haven't had Chablis in ten years," she said.

"I don't think you can drink with the medications you're on," Audrey said.

"Order her a chardonnay," Mary said. "If the lady wants a glass of wine today, she's getting a glass of wine. You have one too, Audrey." Mary turned to Carleton. "Hope you don't mind. I told you I'd probably be a bad date."

"I just wouldn't leave me alone for too long in the company of these lovelies. You never know what might happen," Carleton said. He winked.

Audrey blushed.

Lovey looked at him like he was an annoying little brother.

"I'll keep that in mind," Mary said.

She got up and headed for the entrance, where Raymond Chen now stood. On her way, she touched Vanessa on the arm and whispered, "Tell Wayne his father's here."

"Raymond, thanks so much for coming," she said when she got to the entrance. Mary held out her hand and Raymond took it.

He brought it to his chest and bowed, then nodded toward the poster of Anicca and Ariel. "When you have kids of your own, you can't imagine—"

"I know," Mary said. *Even when you don't.*

"Mary Hopkins, this is my wife, Huan, Wayne's mother," he said. He stepped aside. The woman took a step forward and bowed. She was dressed a bit like Raymond, in a dark blazer with tan pants. Her hair was cut blunt to her chin and had begun to gray at the top, casting a milky veil over the black hair beneath. She had a warm smile, and Mary saw Wayne in it.

"Pleased to meet you," Mary said. "Can I buy you both a drink at the bar while you wait for a table?"

"No, thank you," Raymond said. "Too early." He reached in the breast pocket of his blazer and produced a small tan envelope. He handed it to Mary. "For the girl," he said.

Mary saw Wayne's mother wave to Sage, who had a tray of food balanced on her shoulder but managed to smile and nod. He'd already brought her home to meet the folks. What if this thing was serious? Mary was stung with a sudden thought. What if Wayne left next year to be with Sage? What would Mary do then? Find another cook, she imagined. What else could she do? The fact that things kept changing was another of the things that didn't change. Why had it taken her forty-four years to figure that out? Sometimes she felt as if there was nothing to hold on to, like an old person in the shower, feeling herself slipping, grabbing for the handrail only to realize there wasn't one there, and trying as her body moved closer to the cold porcelain to somehow be okay with that.

"Would you like me to get Wayne?" Mary asked. "I'm sure he'd like to say hi."

"Oh, no," Huan said. "He's busy. We see him later."

"Wouldn't want the kitchen to grind to a halt," Raymond said. He smiled.

"On most days, you probably wouldn't mind," Mary teased. "More customers for you."

Raymond laughed.

"Enjoy your lunch, and thanks again," Mary raised the envelope over her head. She headed for the kitchen so she could slip it beneath the money drawer in the take-out cash resister.

She got as close as the "in" door when she heard a familiar string of Chinese syllables.

"Jeez, Wayne. Put a lid on it. You're mother's out there," Mary said. Wayne's moon-shaped face went slack; his jaw dropped. "They didn't hear me, did they?" he asked, looking like a little kid.

Mary turned to Angry Jennifer, who was ladling soup. "Jennifer, do me a favor and take out three cups of chowder to my aunt's table, the one with the wheelchair. I'm not sure whose station it is."

"Sure," she said. "It's mine anyway."

Mary turned to Wayne. "Didn't Vanessa tell you your parents were here?" she asked.

"Wayne was too busy screaming at her, so she blew out," the nice Jennifer said. She was loading a tray onto her shoulder.

Wayne looked from one Jennifer to the other. "Make sure I know which order is theirs," he said.

"Yup." Angry Jennifer left with eight cups of chowder on her tray.

Wayne turned to the grill and tended to the steaks already there. He checked an order ticket and threw on two hamburgers.

"Should tell him his mother's here more often," Mary said to Maureen, out of Wayne's earshot. "Shuts him right up."

"We have our new secret weapon," Maureen said. She grinned and nudged Courtney.

Earlier that morning, Mary had gathered the crew outside the entrance to the dining room. "I just want to thank each of you for coming in today, and for all your hard work to this point," she said. "It's really a great thing you're doing and it's going to make a very big difference in a little girl's life." She felt goose bumps erupting on her arms. "Of course, you don't need me to tell you that. So . . ." Mary felt herself swept up in a current of emotion.

Wayne was standing between Sage and one of the order line girls, among the first shift of servers and bartenders. He dug his heels into the gravel. "Is there something else?" Just as he pointed his thumb in the direction of the kitchen, there came a crash, as if on cue. He winced. "I kinda need to go."

"Well, actually, there is," Mary said. "You know how I've been trying to get to know you all a little better, and how, despite my best intentions, I've only managed to offend some of you or stir up trouble for others." She glanced at Wayne. "But I'm not ready to give up, because I believe it's important for me to know who you are. So today, for a few minutes this morning, while I have you all here— Wayne, if you could gather up the kitchen crew and get them out here—I'd just like to ask you all to form a big circle—"

"Yeah. Nice concept but got a few things to do, like—oh, I don't know—*cook*," Wayne said. "Let's go, Court." He started for the door. Courtney was already ahead of him.

"Come on, Wayne," Mary said.

"Not gonna happen," he said. He dismissed her with a raised hand.

She'd had a feeling from the start he wasn't going to go for it. The screen door slammed behind them and she heard him bark out orders to the kids doing prep.

"Okay, fine," Mary said. She shrugged and took a breath. "It'll just be us. This'll be easy, I promise. All I want is for you to get into a big circle."

The kids who remained let loose with heavy sighs and groans.

"That's it," Mary encouraged. As they lumbered into something circle-ish, Mary dashed past them into the restaurant and swiped a bottle of ketchup off a table. It was sweating a little from having just gone from the refrigerator to the warm air. She came back out. "So what we're going to do is pass this ketchup bottle around the circle. When it's your turn, all you have to do is tell us one thing about yourself that we don't already know."

"Do we have to sit down? I don't want to get my skirt dirty," Hope said.

"We don't have to sit down," Mary said. "Okay, I'll start." The morning sun was shining in Mary's eyes. She had no idea what she was going to tell them. She squinted so that she could see their faces. Finally something came to her. "I was an only child."

Vanessa and Hope looked at each other. "Big deal. Me too. Tell us something *good*," Vanessa said.

"Yeah," "Come on," "Dish," others added.

The red-haired bartender who jumped at any opportunity to assume the role of clown chimed in with a bad impersonation of Dan Rather: "Tell us, Ms. Hopkins, is it true you don't wear underwear?"

"Knock it off, Chuck," Mary said. "Okay, here's one. I've officially given up men."

All the kids looked at one another, then at Nate, who looked to the kitchen for signs of Maureen. Then he grinned and launched into an elaborate bow. The others applauded.

Mary was dumbfounded. They *all* knew he'd crashed at her place earlier that summer? "Okay, just for the record, *nothing* happened that—" she started.

"Nate has that effect on women," ribbed bartender Todd, who stood beside Mary.

"Nate, would you please *tell* them—," she said.

"I did," Nate said. "A million times."

"This giving-up-men thing, would this be for the summer, or the rest of your life," Chuck asked. "Or were you just talking about today?"

"I haven't figured that out." Mary said. She passed the ketchup bottle to Todd, then wiped her palms on her dress, glad her turn was over.

"This is gonna hurt," he said. He looked at Mary. "I. *Hate.* Seafood."

There were chuckles. Mary frowned.

"But in spite of it all, I *love* working here," he added. "And did I mention you look lovely today? Love the dress."

Mary rolled her eyes. He passed the bottle to Nice Jennifer.

"I have a dog named Rocket. He's a black lab and he likes to eat toilet paper," she said.

"Unused, I hope," Angry Jennifer said.

"That's gross," Nice Jennifer said. She passed the ketchup bottle to her left.

"I have a crush on Vanessa," Angry Jennifer said.

"You're supposed to tell us something we *don't* know," said Hope.

Vanessa shook out her long, straight reddish-blond hair. "Jennifer, you're starting to creep me out," she said.

"I'm kidding," Angry Jennifer said. "The real thing I wanted to say is that I'm totally over Vanessa and now have a crush on someone else."

Mary looked over at Vanessa. She appeared crestfallen.

"Who?" Hope asked.

"I'm not saying."

"Maybe you have a shot with Mary. She's given up men," Todd said.

Nate wrested the ketchup bottle out of Angry Jennifer's hands. "I want to run my own restaurant someday," he said.

Mary studied him. "Really? I never knew that."

"I know," he said. "That's the point of this, isn't it?"

She smiled. "Looks like I might have some competition." She winked at Nate.

He passed the ketchup bottle to Chuck.

"I have a third nipple," Chuck announced.

The guys laughed. The girls groaned.

"No way," Hope said.

"He does," Todd said.

"That's gross," Angry Jennifer said.

"Do you *really?*" Nice Jennifer asked.

"That's for me to know and you to find out," Chuck said. He handed the bottle to Sage.

"Okay, here goes," she said. "I probably won't be back next year. I got accepted to grad school at Stanford."

"Sage, that's incredible," Mary said. She let out a sigh. By now she knew the drill. The good ones never stuck around for long. "Congratulations."

"Does Wayne know?" Hope asked.

"Yeah," Sage said. She twisted her lips and looked down at the gravel. *Poor Wayne,* Mary thought. The good ones never stuck around for him either.

"That's awesome," said Shawn. He was the "quiet" bartender.

"Thanks," Sage said. She handed the bottle to Hope.

Hope turned the bottle in her hands a few times and picked at the label. Then she looked up and said, "I used to have an eating disorder."

"No way," Angry Jennifer said.

"It started when I was fifteen and lasted about two years. My parents sent me to a place where I got help. But it's still hard sometimes," Hope said. Tears had pooled at the corners of her eyes. She wiped them away with her fingers.

"I bet," Vanessa said.

Mary didn't say anything. She just walked over and put her arms around the girl.

With Hope's confession, the atmosphere had changed, becoming thicker, like the stuff inside the bottle. Hope handed the ketchup to Shawn, who shifted his weight back and forth from one foot to the other.

"It's okay," Hope offered. "It's not that bad once you just say it."

"I had a thing for Anicca," he said. He looked up to the sky, to a robin that swooped from a tree to the power line. They all looked up. It was as if they all at once remembered why they were there.

Now as she exited the kitchen, Mary couldn't help but notice the attractive blonde in a floral sundress Nate had his arm around. She looked to be about Mary's age too, maybe a little younger. A man came around the side of the building, where the restrooms were. Before he joined them, Nate let the woman go. Mary looked to the take-out window. She wondered if Maureen was catching any of this.

Nate waved. "Mary," he said, "come meet my folks."

When Mary was little, in the same way she believed she could breathe underwater, she also imagined she possessed the power to make herself disappear, to scatter her atoms so infinitesimally that they could be cloaked behind molecules of air. Perhaps it was Lovey who used to encourage her when they played hide-and-seek, pretending she couldn't find Mary even when Mary wasn't trying very hard to hide, her feet sticking out from behind a curtain or her head popping up from behind a chair. Mary looked into the restaurant and saw the wheelchair with its pink occupant at the back of the room. If only Lovey could make her disappear now.

Mary walked toward Nate and his folks. "Hi," she said. She reached for the woman's hand.

"This is my mom, Linda, and Walter, my dad," Nate said.

"Pleased to meet you," Mary said. Did they know she'd harbored their fugitive son earlier that summer?

Walter put his hands on his hips. His brow wrinkled. "I have a bone to pick with you, Mary Hopkins," he said, wagging his finger.

Mary felt her face flush.

"You don't remember me?" he said. "Wally Chisolm? You sat next to me in World History and used to make me pass notes to Tessie Robinson. I never realized you were the same Mary Hopkins until today." He held his hands out at his sides. "Have I changed that much?"

Of course he had. He was forty-four. "Wally Chisolm." Mary said. Now, come to think of it, she could see the resemblance. Who would have thought in their high school days that almost thirty years later she'd have a crush on her classmate's son? "I thought you looked familiar, but you know how it is—I see so many people in this place who remind me of other people. After embarrassing myself enough times, I learned I'm better off just keeping my mouth shut." She forced a laugh.

"I'm just kidding," Walter said. "You never gave me the time of day back then either." He seemed to be only half-kidding there.

Mary was almost starting to relax when Nate's mother started in.

"I don't know *what* you did to this boy"—Linda Chisolm looked up at her son and rested her hand on his back—"but we've seen a big change in Natey this summer."

Mary winced and looked at Nate. "I really didn't do *anything*. You can be assured of that." Nate seemed to be enjoying it all.

Linda continued, "He's so much more responsible at home. And he's been so involved in planning all this . . ."

They all turned toward the poster on the table where people were lining up to buy chowder and raffle tickets.

"I think all the kids grew up a little this summer," Mary said. "You should be proud. Nate's smart, and he's a hard worker. He's a special kid." With that, she reached over and pinched "Natey" on the cheek, perhaps a little harder than was necessary. "If you'll excuse me, I have to get some food into my great-aunt before she polishes off any more chardonnay. So nice to see you again, Wally. No hard feelings, I hope. And great meeting you, Linda."

When Mary returned to her own table, there was a woman standing beside Lovey's wheelchair talking to Carleton. Evidently he *was* a lady's man. Lovey and Audrey weren't paying either of them any mind. They were focused on eating their chowder.

"Hi," Mary said. "I'm Mary Hopkins."

"Celia Brandeis." The woman held out a limp hand, as some women did. "I was just enjoying my lunch when I spotted Mr. Dyer over here and wanted to pay my respects."

"You know each other?" Mary winked at Carleton.

"We do now," he said. He smiled.

"I should explain," Celia Brandeis said. "I own an art gallery in Truro and I'm familiar with Mr. Dyer and his work. No one had heard from him for so long, we thought he must have moved on."

"More like kicked the bucket," Carleton said. He chuckled.

"You didn't tell me you were famous," Mary said. She nudged his arm.

"Ms. Hopkins, may I have a word with you?" Mary looked at the woman and sensed some agitation. Celia Brandeis was a bit older than Mary had originally thought, probably in her mid-sixties. She had her hair cut short and spiked at crown. Over a long, shapeless gray cotton jumper, she wore a silver chain from which hung a large white Lucite tile that had been silk-screened with a human eye. Flash-forward forty years to Angry Jennifer.

"I'll be right back. I promise," Mary said to Audrey, Lovey, and Carleton. She looked to see that they all had their drinks. "And then we'll order."

"Don't worry," Audrey said. She held up her white plastic chowder spoon. "We're fine."

Mary guided Celia Brandeis to a quiet corner near the bar, out of the path of customers and oncoming servers.

"Do you have any idea who Mr. Dyer is?" Celia asked. She pursed her lips.

"He's my neighbor," Mary said.

"That painting you have out there?" She pointed toward the entrance. "Have you any idea what it's worth?"

"No."

"Mary. Carleton Dyer is one of the last of a cluster of famous local artists. If memory serves, I believe he's originally from upstate New York and he studied at the Art Students League in Manhattan, where he befriended Edwin Dickinson." She seemed to be searching Mary's eyes for some spark of recognition. No luck, so she continued. "Edwin recognized Carleton's talent and took him under his wing." She dropped her hands at her sides and let out a sigh. "You have no idea who I'm talking about, do you?"

"No."

Celia rolled her eyes. "One of the Provincetown painters—Henry Hensche and John Whorf, who studied under Hawthorne; and Dickinson; and abstract expressionists Leo Manso, Robert Motherwell . . ." She rattled off the names, assigning each one a finger. "There was a whole colony of important painters living and working in Provincetown in the middle of the twentieth century."

Mary shrugged. Maybe she'd heard something about all that. But Provincetown to her had always been a place to eat, people-watch, and disco dance.

"Dickinson's work hangs in the Fine Arts Museums of San Francisco, and in the Smithsonian. Come to think of it, Carleton may have work hanging there as well."

"*The Smithsonian?*"

"That's what I'm trying to tell you. This man is a national treasure," Celia said.

Mary knew as much, though for other reasons.

Celia continued: "About thirty years ago, he just disappeared from the art scene. There've been different versions of the story, but the one I've heard most often is that he was living with a woman at the time who'd given birth. She'd told Carleton that the baby was his. A few years later, he learned it wasn't true. It crushed him and he just vanished. People thought he'd gone back to New York. The gallery that represented his work tried for years to track him down, to no avail. They had a lot at stake. His work had been selling well even back then. As the years went by, people just assumed he'd died. And now to find out he's been living right here under our noses all the while!" Celia shook her head in disbelief. She seemed to have to gather herself for the next question, clasping her hands as if in prayer. "Do you know, has he been painting all this time?"

"He has an easel set up in his cottage and there are paintings four or five deep on the floor against the walls."

Celia grabbed the edge of the bar. Her thick plastic bracelet and long fingernails clicked against the surface.

"You should know he's not well. He's got Parkinson's," Mary said.

"I noticed the tremor in his right arm," Celia said.

"I guess he's always been a lefty, because he seems to do pretty well—"

"Just so you know what you're giving away here, that painting on the wall would probably fetch about forty grand at my gallery. Or anyone's." Celia fumbled in her purse. She produced a business card and handed it to Mary. "Please have him call me, for his own sake. Or have him contact someone at one of the art museums, either in Provincetown or in Dennis. Call them yourself if you still have any doubts about what I'm saying. He could be sitting on a great deal of money. And I'm sure he could use it."

Celia zipped her purse. The sound reminded Mary of that needle-scratch sound effect that signals, *Hold on. Back up. What did you just say?* Carleton could be "sitting on a great deal of money." Knowing Carleton, would he even care? What mattered to that man anyway?

Mary had a pretty good idea it wasn't money, especially considering the career he'd walked away from.

"I'll talk it over with him and see what I can do. But no guarantees. I've found he's got a pretty unorthodox way of looking at things."

"I think he always has. That's what made him great," Celia said.

When Celia returned to her table, Mary sat down beside Carleton. He needed to know what he was giving away. So Mary just came out and told him what Celia Brandeis had said, that the painting he'd donated might actually be worth forty thousand dollars. Carleton seemed surprised at first; then he realized Mary was asking if he still wanted to give it away. He smiled and said, "Maybe we can get a little more for the raffle tickets?"

Oh my gosh! Mary rushed to the entrance, to the table out front where Megan sat with the metal cash box on her lap. Thank goodness there was a lull in the activity.

"I just counted," Megan said. "We already collected a hundred and twenty-six bucks. That's including the chowd—"

"Megan, how much are you selling those raffle tickets for?" Mary asked.

"Five bucks a pop," the girl answered.

"Make it a hundred," Mary said. "There's been a change of grand prize. I just learned that painting's worth forty grand."

"Holy crap!"

"Tell Nate. Tell him we need a new sign. Tell him to get the yellow pages and call all the galleries from Boston to P-town to let them know what we're raffling off. An original by the Provincetown art legend Carleton Dyer."

"Yeah," Megan said. She tucked the metal box under her arm and ran into the kitchen.

Mary looked over at Lovey, who was fishing chunks of lobster meat out of her lobster roll with her fork. She seemed quiet today, and most days now. Mary had read that passivity was a symptom of Alzheimer's disease, and when she thought about it, she realized there had been a marked shift in Lovey's demeanor over the last six or eight months, maybe longer. What she had taken for lack of interest in the goings-on in Mary's day-to-day life and the restaurant had really been the first sign of Lovey's illness. Now Mary wondered how much her aunt understood about what was happening. Even before Lovey had become ill, Mary knew it was sometimes overwhelming for the old woman to be out in crowds. Her aunt had once described how it was the activity that took place at the periphery of her vision that was particularly unnerving. All she could detect was the movement; her ability to determine what was actually going on around her had diminished. She told Mary how it was sometimes just better for old people to stay home where they had control of their surroundings.

Audrey was making a pretty good dent in her Fisherman's Special, an enormous basket of fried clams, oysters, cod, and scallops on a bed of French fries. Carleton—who was apparently full of surprises—had forgone his beloved fried clams for Wayne's special of the day, pecan-crusted haddock drizzzled with pesto. He seemed pleased with his choice.

Lunch for Mary's table had been delayed further when people from the town newspaper came to take pictures of Carleton and his painting of the outdoor shower. While Mary had declined to pose for the camera, Celia Brandeis had wheedled her way into some of the shots. Carleton seemed to handle the attention well. Mary would have expected that someone who'd made a conscious choice to step out of the limelight thirty years ago would feel some agitation at suddenly, unexpectedly being thrust back into it again. But Carleton seemed adept at handling whatever life threw at him. Even his meddling neighbor. Mary had the feeling she had much more to learn from him, assuming he could find a way to forgive her for bringing all this upon him.

When it was time for them to give up their table, Lovey, Carleton, and Audrey moved to their VIP seats at the bar. Lovey needed a little help out of her wheelchair and into the tall captain's chair, but once in it, she was comfortable.

Carleton had his nose buried in an art magazine Celia Brandeis had given him. Mary stood beside her aunt. She felt a tap on her shoulder.

"Hi, Mary."

Mary turned around to see Darlene Snow flanked by Officer Boyd and a woman Mary didn't know. For a moment, she thought she was caught in the middle of a bad dream. They'd come to take her away. Where? To the jail? Or a nursing home?

"Darlene," she said. "Officer Boyd."

He nodded. Thank goodness he wasn't wearing his gun in her restaurant.

"Bet you're surprised to see me, huh?" Darlene said. She turned to Lovey and rested her hand on the old woman's arm. "So good to see you, Lavinia." Then she turned back to Mary. "How's she doing at the new place? I think about her all the time." Before Mary could answer, Darlene again turned to Lovey and, louder, in her talking-to-old-people voice, she said, "You were always one of my favorite tenants."

Mary bristled. If Lovey had been one of Darlene's favorite tenants, Mary would hate to be on the list of those Darlene didn't "adore." Now Mary just hoped Lovey would keep it together. There was still some part of Mary that wanted to prove to Darlene that she had been wrong.

"Hello, Darlene," Lovey said, in a voice reserved for people she didn't like.

Darlene turned back to Mary. "I think I mentioned to you that Charlie Boyd and I go way back."

"You've done a great job here," Officer Boyd said. Mary assumed he was referring to the fund-raiser and not to her taking her aunt to a nursing home.

"Thanks," Mary said.

"This is Charlie's wife, Candace," Darlene said. "Candy, I'd like you to meet Mary Hopkins and Lavinia Rollwagon."

Mary wanted to correct her and have her aunt introduced as "Lovey," but if Darlene hadn't managed to breach that formality in all the years they'd known one another, what difference did it make now? The officer's wife and Audrey seemed to know each other. They were already in deep conversation. At the introduction, Candace smiled and raised her hand, then returned her attention to Audrey.

"As you can see, my aunt's doing quite well," Mary said. She felt her spine stiffen.

At that moment, Lovey raised her finger and flagged Todd. "I'll have a glass of Chablis," she said.

The bartender looked confused.

"House chardonnay," Mary said behind her hand to Todd. "Just a little."

"Look, I want you to know I feel terrible to see people go," Darlene said.

"No offense, but you sure have an interesting way of expressing it," Mary said, against her better judgment. This was neither the time nor place.

"People think I'm some kind of monster." Mary smelled a bit of chardonnay on Darlene's breath as well. "But you don't know what it's like to deal with these folks all day. Mostly, they're like a bunch of children, always trying to bend rules and get away with things, sneaking cats and snakes and candles into the apartments." Darlene smoothed out her pastel pink, short-sleeve yoked cardigan. "I learned a long time ago I'd be better off if I didn't get too attached. You can't run a tight ship if you're everyone's best friend." Mary had employed the same philosophy herself, at least until recently. "It's easier that way when you have to say good-bye." Darlene put her hand on Lovey's. "How many years have we known each other now?" she asked the old woman.

Lovey waved her other hand. "At least three or four."

Mary stifled a laugh.

"More like eighteen," Darlene said. She turned back to Mary. "All I'm saying is, it isn't easy being misunderstood all the time. I hope you don't judge me."

Mary felt herself soften toward the women. She looked up at Officer Boyd, who'd joined in the conversation with Audrey and his wife, and remembered how it felt when she thought she was being judged. As Lovey's second glass of wine was set in front of her, Mary reached out and gave Darlene a warm embrace.

Mary was needed in the kitchen for a while; then, out on the floor, she ran into a woman who worked at her bank. The whole while, the line at the raffle table hadn't let up. Already gallery owners from as far away as Sandwich had come to get in on the action. Then at last she had a moment to see how her "guests" at the bar were faring.

Lovey was watching Todd fill an order for three strawberry daiquiris. Mary had to admit it was remarkable how these guys could eyeball the ingredients for any number of drinks without wasting a drop. He filled the third glass to the rim with the last of what remained, raising the blender jar high in the air for dramatic effect. Mary noticed bubbles clinging to the inside of Lovey's glass. Someone had replaced her wine with ginger ale.

"We've got to see about getting you home," Mary said to Lovey.

"Let me take her," Audrey said.

"Audrey, I couldn't ask you to do that," Mary said.

"I don't mind at all. You're needed here. When you're ready, just drop off Carleton and me, and I'll buzz her back to Hyannis. I've nowhere to be this afternoon."

Hyannis wasn't exactly a "buzz," especially this time of year. Traffic could be a nightmare. Mary started to protest. Audrey cut her off. "You've given me a lovely day. I'm happy to, really. And I'd like to see the Harbor House. I've heard nice things about it but have never been there myself."

"That's a huge help, Audrey." Mary also didn't feel comfortable leaving for too long with an uninsured, forty-thousand dollar painting hanging out in the open.

Mary thought Carleton must be getting tired, but he showed no signs of it yet. People kept coming up to him and introducing themselves, probably the same people who'd seen him around town the last thirty years and just thought he was no one special. Suddenly, he was a celebrity.

As Mary turned from Audrey, she noticed another commotion brewing outside, a flurry of activity, perhaps another group of art lovers who'd converged on the Clambake, more gallery owners or someone else from the press.

"I should probably go see what all that is about," Mary said. "I'll be right back."

Eighteen

As Mary drew closer to the entrance, she realized most of the participants in this outbreak of commotion were members of her own staff.

"Hey!" Mary clapped her hands. "What's going on? There's still a dining room full of customers."

As the last angled rays of sun came over the top of the kitchen roof, they clipped the fair hair of a toddler who, from the arms of her great-grandmother, pointed to the poster on the table. "Mama," came the child's voice. The kids dispersed, some of them with tears in their eyes. "Mama," she said again. With the child still in her arms, Meg walked over to the image. She sipped in some air, then through the exhale became smaller, as though something vital had been drawn out with her breath.

Mary put her hand on the woman's back. "Meg," she said.

Meg turned. It seemed to take her a moment to process what her eyes were seeing. "Hope!" she finally said. She pulled a tissue out of her pants pocket and pressed it to her nose.

The real Hope had just emerged from the kitchen with a large tray under her arm, presumably on her way to help bus the tables of several parties that had cleared out all at once. Upon hearing her name, she swung around, "Have you changed your mind, Mrs. Ryder? Would you like a table?"

Meg turned to the girl. "No, dear," Meg said. "I really can't stay." She shifted the child from one arm to the other.

"Sure, okay," Hope said, likely confused then as to why her name had been called.

"What are you doing here?" Mary asked. "I thought you weren't coming."

"At the last minute I just"—she stuffed the tissue back into her pocket—"I don't know. It's good to see you. I didn't know you'd be here."

Ariel pointed her finger at Mary. The little girl was wearing a pink crocheted dress with ribbon pulled through the bodice. A matching pink barrette held the blond hair back from her eyes. For the first time, Mary could really see Anicca in the child.

"Hello, sweetheart," Mary said. She grabbed hold of the tiny finger and Ariel smiled.

The screen door to the kitchen slammed and Mary jumped. Maureen was headed their way. She scooped up the stuffed bear from the table.

Mary felt the panic rise from her chest to her throat, a tightening.

"Mrs. Ryder." Maureen held out her hand. Meg took it. "I'm Maureen Donovan. We talked on the phone a few times."

"Of course, *Maureen*. You're one of the ones responsible for all this. I don't know how to begin to thank you—"

"I'm glad you decided to come after all," Maureen said. "It's been like this all day." She nodded toward the crowd in the dining room. She looked at Mary.

Mary felt the urge to run. All Maureen had to do was say one wrong thing and Mary's cover would be blown right here, right now. How in the world would she be able to explain that she'd been lying to Meg about who she was all these weeks? How could she make her understand? She didn't understand it herself. Mary finally mustered the nerve to look up from the gravel as Maureen held the bear up to Ariel. "Is it okay?" Maureen asked Meg. "I want her to have this."

Wayne's voice came from the kitchen. "Maureen!"

"How nice," Meg said. Ariel's eyes were bright with anticipation. Maureen handed her the bear. Ariel looked to her great-grandmother to make sure it was all right.

"Say thank you to the nice girl," Meg said.

Ariel took the stuffed bear and crushed it to her neck. She smiled and squeezed her eyes shut.

"Gotta go," Maureen said. "I'll be in touch in the next few days." She ran back to the kitchen.

"Such a thoughtful girl," Meg said. She and Mary both looked at Ariel. "I was home thinking about all the trouble Maureen and the rest of these folks had gone to on our behalf, and not showing up just didn't seem right. I was having a good day, so I thought, Let's just go." Meg wiggled the bear into Ariel's neck. The little girl laughed. "And so here we are." Meg looked around. "Also, I really wanted to say thanks to the owner."

On her way to the kitchen, a flustered Sage stopped beside Mary. "Condiments are running out," she said. "We need five ketchups. And a lady just complained that the kale soup was lukewarm, so someone needs to check the burner." Sage looked at the toddler, then apparently made the connection. "Oh. Mrs. Ryder. I didn't realize it was you. I'm glad you could make it."

"Hello, honey," Meg said.

"My name is Sage. I met you at the—" Sage's cheeks caught fire. Mary realized Sage was about to say "funeral" when Maureen's voice over the loudspeaker called her name.

"Sorry, that's me," Sage said. She hurried off.

"Why was she talking to you about ketchup?" Meg said. "You never did say what you were doing here."

"I'm just helping out."

"Oh, Hope," Meg said. She smiled and shook her head. "You really are too good to be true."

At that moment, Hope passed by with a tray full of dirty broiler plates, baskets, and silverware that she was bringing around back to the dishwasher. She must have heard her name again. "Can I get you something, Mrs. Ryder?"

"I'm sorry, dear," Meg said. "I was talking to the *other* Hope."

Hope wrinkled her brow and looked at the woman, then at Mary. "Okay," she said, and walked off. Mary caught her shaking her head.

"So, now you can help me," Meg said. "I have no idea what the owner looks like. Do you see her?" Meg shifted Ariel to her other arm. The kid must have been getting heavy. "Anicca described her as 'good-looking for an older woman.'" Meg looked around. "Is that her there?" Meg pointed to a gray-haired woman in a white sweater with scalloped edging and kelly green knit elastic-waist pants standing by the take-out window. She had to be in her late sixties. "Older" was clearly a relative term.

"No," Mary said. She pretended to look around. "I don't see her. Why don't I get you a table and we can get a high chair for Ariel."

"No, really. I don't want to stay," Meg said.

A waitress whizzed by, her tray coming too close to Ariel's ear. "Oh, sorry," Angry Jennifer called back over her shoulder.

Mary guided Meg away from the high-traffic dining room entrance. No sooner had they moved than Vanessa came by and dumped a tray of ketchupy cardboard containers and paper trash into the bin beside them. This wouldn't do either.

"Compliments on the special from table six," Vanessa said. "And a customer wants to know if she can mail in her donation when she gets back home. Where should I have her send it?"

Another waitress came by and emptied a tray of clear plastic cups filled with ice and mangled lemon wedges into the bin. Some liquid splashed up. Meg took Ariel away from the trash and over to the bar. She sat the toddler on the edge, right beside Lovey.

Mary froze.

"Mary?" Vanessa said, trying to get her attention.

"Give them a take-out menu. The P.O. box number's on there," Mary said.

"Okay," Vanessa said. She was off.

Mary went to the bar to catch up with Meg.

"What can I get you?" Todd said. He set a white napkin in front of Meg. "Hi, there, adorable," he said to Ariel.

The toddler pointed to Lovey, then to her own dress. "Pink," she said.

Lovey's face lit up, as though she'd been given back a long-lost word. "Yes, *pink*," she said. Ariel's white patent leather Mary Janes were dangling near Lovey's hand. Lovey reached up and gave one of them a jiggle. She had always loved little kids.

"Dorothy," Lovey said, "I remember you had shoes just like these."

Meg looked at Lovey and smiled. Then she turned to Todd. "Nothing for us, honey. I was just wondering if you could tell me where I might find the owner."

"Remember them, Dorothy?" Lovey said to Mary.

Mary felt her heart racing. She looked from Lovey to Todd.

"You're in luck," he started to say, "she's right—"

Mary's eyes grew wide. Behind Meg's back, she waved her hands and shook her head no. Ariel was faster on the uptake than Todd. She started shaking her head too.

"Dorothy!" Lovey said. "The *shoes*." She waved her hand in irritation and turned away, as though she'd had enough of all of them.

"She's right here *somewhere*," Todd said. Mary's flailing must finally have registered. He picked up a bar cloth and started swabbing the surface. "Yes, I do believe I just saw her. I'll ask around." He set the cloth down under the bar, walked over to Chuck at the far end of the bar, and started whispering in his ear.

"Thank you, dear," Meg called after him. She leaned back toward Mary, just as Mary's arms fell to her sides. Behind her hand, Meg said, "I think that woman has you mistaken for someone named Dorothy."

"Appears that way." Mary grinned, then noticed in horror that her aunt had begun to turn around. *She must have the hearing of a twenty-year-old,* Mary thought. Lovey started to reach her hand out to Meg. The rest seemed to go down in slow motion.

"Lavinia Rollwagon," the old woman announced, enunciating each syllable. "How do you do? And this *forgetful* one here is my sister, Dorothy."

Meg's mouth fell open.

Mary clapped her hand over her forehead.

Ariel presented her bear to Lovey.

"Why *thank* you, dear." Lovey sat the bear on the edge of the bar. "Now *you* look familiar," Lovey said to the bear.

Meg's face had lit up. She put her hand on Lovey's forearm. "Mrs. Rollwagon. I'm Meg Ryder. What a pleasure to meet you. I can't believe I just ran into you like this." Meg turned to Mary. "Hope, you should have—"

Mary let her shoulders drop. "Meg, allow my to introduce my aunt, Lovey. Also known as Lavinia Rollwagon. Auntie, this is my friend Meg." Her friend, but for how much longer?

"Your *aunt*?" Meg said.

"Great-aunt, actually," Mary corrected herself. "My grandmother's sister."

Meg looked from Lovey to Mary. "So who's *Dorothy*?" Meg asked.

"Dorothy is—*was*—my grandmother. She's been dead for over thirty years," Mary said. Her throat felt like it was squeezing shut. She called down the bar. "Chuck, can I get a glass of water?"

Chuck nodded.

"I don't understand," Meg said. The look of confusion on her face broke Mary's heart.

Lovey turned back to the woman she'd just met. "Do I know you?" she asked. She looked to Mary for some help. "Mary?" she said.

Suddenly, she was no longer Dorothy. Or Hope. Just Mary.

"She called you Dorothy, and then Mary. I thought Mary was your *sister*. Remember that time I called and the machine picked up?"

"I know, Meg. We need to talk," Mary said.

Chuck deposited the glass on the bar and Mary gulped some of the cool liquid. Time slowed for an instant as Mary stared at the ice cubes in front of her nose. If only she could stay right here in this cool, clouded world.

Hope approached them on her way to the waitress station with a stack of newly folded lobster bibs.

Mary set down the glass. "Hope," Mary said. The girl didn't look up. "Hope!"

"You mean me?" she asked. "I thought you were talking to the *other* Hope."

"I need you to do me a favor," Mary said. She took the lobster bibs out of Hope's hands and set them on the bar. "Take Ariel outside and show her the flowers. Just for a few minutes." Mary put her hands on the toddler's knees. "You want to go see the flowers with Hope, Ari?"

Maybe Hope reminded Ariel a little of her mother, because without hesitation, the toddler launched herself off the bar so that Mary had to catch her, then reached both arms out and locked them around Hope's neck.

"Just keep her entertained for a few minutes. Maybe take her around to meet some of the customers. Okay?" Mary said.

"Sure," Hope said. She started chatting with Ariel right away. "What a pretty dress. You know, pink is my favorite color," she said to her. The two of them went off.

"Meg, come with me." There were a couple of empty seats at the far end of the bar. "Auntie, we'll be right back," Mary said to Lovey, who seemed relieved to have just the bear to contend with.

Mary led Meg to the quiet corner.

"I don't understand any of this," Meg said. She ran her hand though her hair, then eased herself onto the bar stool.

"I don't expect you to. And when I'm through explaining, you'll probably never want to speak to me again." Mary took Meg's two hands in hers.

Meg looked so stricken and vulnerable.

"My name isn't Hope," Mary said. "It's Mary Hopkins. I'm the owner of this place. I was Anicca's boss." Mary dropped her head in shame. When she looked up, Todd had reappeared.

"Excuse me, ma'am," he said to Meg. "I checked around and I guess the owner had to take her dog to the vet—"

"Forget it, Todd." Mary said. "She knows."

"Oh, okay," Todd said. He shrugged and moved away.

Meg watched him go, then she withdrew her hands from Mary's. "Why did you lie to me about who you were?"

Mary figured it might all make more sense—even to her—if she started from the beginning. She sat down.

"I was married once," she said. "Fourteen years ago, my husband died the same way Anicca did. He drank too much and then drove his car into a tree on Route 28, just about a quarter mile from where Anicca . . ." Her voice trailed off. She cleared her throat. "We had gotten into a fight before he left. For years, I carried the guilt around with me." Mary looked up at Meg but found the woman's face too painful a place for her eyes to rest. She floated her gaze down to her lap. "I'd always worried whether what I'd said to him had been the reason he drank too much that night." She flattened the bottom of her sweater. "I recently learned there were other things going on that I had no idea of at the time." Mary felt her face grow hot. "But none of that is important.

"When Anicca died, it brought back a lot of the pain from Robbie's death." Mary suddenly felt unbearably warm. "I wanted to see how someone else coped with it." Mary looked up. Meg had tears in her eyes. "I thought I might learn something that could help me." Mary hung her head. "See, even after all these years, I still hang on to that pain. But that's not the only reason I lied to you."

Mary took off her sweater and draped it over her lap. She took a deep breath, then continued. "When I learned Anicca had a child, that just floored me. How could I not know something like that about someone who worked for me?" Mary frowned and looked down at her hands, which where clasped in a knot. "Because I'd never bothered to ask. I just assumed they were all the same, an endless sea of good-looking, privileged young kids who kept me in business, whose faces and personalities all blended together over the years. I couldn't even keep their names straight. I treated them like they owed me something. I suspected they knew it and hated me for it." Mary paused. "It took Anicca's death for me to even care. Then it became so clear. I'd been living life focused on the wrong things." Mary looked up. "I was ashamed for you to know who I really was. I didn't know what Anicca might have said about me." Besides the parts about her being a decent-looking tightwad.

"She never said much," Meg said.

"That's a testament to her," Mary said. She tried to gauge Meg's expression. The woman's jaw was set, though Mary detected a quiver in her chin.

"What about Lavinia?" Meg asked.

Mary looked down the bar at her aunt. The old woman had her eyes closed. *She must be tired,* Mary thought. Audrey had her purse on her lap, like she was finally ready to go. Mary needed to take them to Audrey's house so that Audrey could pick up her car and drive Lovey home. Carleton too, though he'd gone off somewhere again. "I learned this summer that my aunt has Alzheimer's disease," she went on. "I had to move her to a nursing home a couple of weeks ago. She's the only family I have left and I adore her. For the longest time, it's just been me and her."

"This hasn't been an easy summer for you either," Meg said. In the middle of the sentence her voice cracked and compassion poured out. Mary wanted to wrap her arms around the woman's neck and plant a kiss on her cheek. But she didn't dare. There was more to tell.

"When I learned about you being left with Ariel, I wanted to help. At first, maybe some of it was to relieve my own guilt. But then, the more I got to know you, the more I truly cared. I wanted to send you some money. I had that hundred-dollar bill all set to go in an envelope, then at the last minute I scribbled that note and signed Lavinia's name instead of my own. I thought the money might be easier to accept from a generous widow."

Meg rested her hand on Mary's knee. "I suppose that's what you are," she finally said.

Mary felt her emotions well up in her throat. She hadn't seen herself as a generous *anything*. Certainly not a widow. Not for years. "I'm so sorry I lied to you, Meg. I really value our friendship. I know this sounds crazy, but the closer I got to you, the more I felt like we'd been brought together for a reason."

"Hope," Meg said.

Mary looked at her, confused, until she realized this time Meg hadn't meant the appellation.

"Maybe we're meant to find it together," Meg said. Then she looked down the aisle.

Mary followed Meg's gaze. She turned and saw Ariel with a red daylily in her hand. The real Hope was following behind.

Nineteen

A pair of Scooby-Doo underpants, half a bowling ball, a Barbie doll with a nail through her hand, a home pregnancy test, a set of divorce papers, a Led Zeppelin album, a set of Dracula teeth, a half turtle shell with a leg still attached, a Styrofoam Tiki god, a headstone for a departed cat that read 'Your soul is safe now' . . ."

Mary was listening to local public radio station on her way back to the restaurant, to a representative from the Coastal Cleanup Committee who was rattling off some of the most unusual things they'd ever found washed up on Cape area beaches. That someone had actually kept a list of such things was as remarkable as the things themselves.

The list made Mary think about people, all the ones who had washed in and out of her life, the many who'd gone unnoticed, undocumented. Perhaps this was one of the biggest lessons of the summer thus far, that everyone had a story, a past, a perspective, a humanity that made him or her worth knowing. Even a nineteen-month-old child had something to teach.

By the time Mary dropped Lovey off at Audrey's house so that Audrey could take the old woman back to Hyannis, by the time she got Lovey to understand what was going on ("Is this where I'm living now?" Lovey had asked in Audrey's driveway), and then got Carleton home and settled down after what must have been one of the most exhausting days of his life, it was already after six o'clock. The raffle was to be held at seven.

Mary was glad she hadn't actually told anyone exactly where Carleton lived, and was relieved to hear he hadn't either. They had both agreed he should speak with someone at one of the museums in the coming week to figure out what to do with the paintings he had. Given their value, they certainly couldn't remain on the floor of Carleton's cottage. Mary assumed that he wouldn't be living there much longer. If he did leave, she'd miss having him as her neighbor, but she felt sure they'd remain friends. With his Parkinson's and all the Celia Brandeises out there, he needed someone to look out for his best interests. Still, what a find he'd turned out to be, even before she knew of his illustrious past—that old man was a Styrofoam Tiki god and a half.

In her hurry to make it back in time for the raffle, Mary realized that she'd never found out what had originally been intended to be the grand prize. Whatever it was, it had taken a back seat to Carleton's painting. Considering all the people who'd shown up to buy the tickets at a hundred dollars apiece, plus all the tips and food receipts, this day would end up meaning serious money for Meg and Ariel, probably close to the value of the painting itself, which Mary and Nate had thought they might withdraw from the raffle and sell privately until they realized how many tickets they'd already sold. It amazed Mary, the amount of money people on the Cape were willing and able to throw down for even just the chance to win one of Carleton's paintings. Not only that, but galleries as far away as Boston were scooping up ten tickets at a time.

As Mary approached the entrance, there was still a line of people waiting to get into the dining room. At the raffle table, Megan had been relieved by Shawn, the boy who'd admitted to the group that morning that he'd had a crush on Anicca. How differently this summer might have turned out. Meg could just as easily have found herself with a future grandson-in-law, a father for Ariel, instead of losing the girl who had been her world. Now that role fell to Ariel.

Meg's grace had surprised Mary today. She'd seen right through Mary's lies to her intentions, and that must have been what made her able to forgive. Loss had drawn the two women together, yet Mary felt that she'd found a friendship with Meg that would survive the painful events of the summer. She knew in some way she'd always be part of Ariel's life too. She couldn't be grateful for the circumstances that had brought them together, but she was grateful for the outcome.

Mary walked into the kitchen, where things were humming but under control. It was always a thrill for Mary to watch the kids when they were in their zones, performing their individual tasks with a confidence and rhythm that didn't afford them the time to think. By this time of the year, they had it down. And this was a better crew than most years.

Nate was working the fryers. She stood behind him until he turned to check the three green order tickets held in the metal groove. Then she asked, "Nate, what was the grand prize going to be, before we found out about the painting?"

He took one of the tickets and stabbed it on a skewer and looked up. "A cruise," he said. "It's still the second prize." He turned and dredged a handful of clams through the batter. He threw them in a basket and plunged them into the oil. As they sizzled, he checked a batch of fries in another basket, gave that one a shake, and dropped it back into the oil.

"A *sunset* cruise?" Mary asked. A few of the men who captained the touristy sunset cruises out of Rock Harbor were regulars at the bar. "Who donated—?"

Wayne came over waving a spatula. "You're killing me here," he said. He flicked the paddle down on the steel counter like he was swatting flies. "He's so far behind he's still dropping orders from fucking Monday."

Mary raised her hands. "Sorry. Never mind." She turned on her heel.

Maureen was sitting on the stool in front of the take-out window, scribbling on a large sheet of the white paper they used to wrap take-out sandwiches. "Maureen, do you know anything about the—?" Mary started to ask.

"Oh, Mary." Maureen jumped to her feet. "Could you do us a huge favor and tell everyone out there that we're low on specials?

Right now we have five left. I'm posting a countdown, so have them come in and check to make sure we can cover their orders. Okay?" Maureen tore of a long strip of tape from the dispenser by the register.

"Yeah, sure," Mary said.

Mary went out to the floor. The air had cooled but it was still dry and clear. It would be a good night for stars.

She made the rounds, telling each of the servers about the limited number of specials. While she was out there, a few customers came up to introduce themselves. Mary realized it really wasn't as bad being out there on the floor, playing owner, as she'd feared it would be. How silly to have hidden out in the kitchen all these years. People were generally nice and said things about the place that made her feel proud. One of the people who came up to her was a kid who'd known Anicca from the convenience store last summer. She'd brought her folks in and was asking about Ariel. Then there was Carmen DeLuca, one of the deli owners in town, a short woman with heavy arms and a helmet of thick black hair, who invited Mary to join her Bunko group, and then went off about the same thing everyone in town was irate over this summer, how they'd closed the Outer Beach to four-wheel-drive vehicles for the entire month of July because of two—count them, *two*—endangered plover chicks that were nesting in the dunes. And how that had single-handedly *killed* her sandwich business, and how she'd even offered to have her own two middle-schoolers out there following each of the *damn* chicks around 24-7 so they wouldn't get crushed under tires, but was that enough for the do-gooders at the Massachusetts Division of Fisheries and Wildlife? Of course not. *Two* birds. Carmen held up two fingers, and through the gap, Mary saw Nate approaching from the kitchen.

"Excuse me, Carmen," she said. "I think it's time for the raffle."

She met Nate at the ticket table. He had a sheet of paper under his arm.

"Okay, we're ready," he said. He wiped his hands on a towel looped around his belt. "All you have to do is pick two names out of the box. The first will be the winner of the fishing trip—?"

"I thought you said it was a cruise."

"Did I? Nope, it's a fishing trip." He took the paper in his hands.

"But who—"

"And then you announce who wins the painting. Now, figure the winners probably won't still be here. We told them they didn't have to be. But you should thank the donors," Nate said.

"Who donated—?" Mary started again.

"It's all right here," Nate said. He handed the paper to Mary. She started to look at it. "Hold on, this is important," he said. Mary looked up. "Once you announce the winners, give the two names to Maureen so she can read them over the loudspeaker, okay? And then we'll start trying to reach them, assuming they're not here."

"Okay, but—"

Maureen's voice, in sex-kitten mode, broke through the restaurant ambience: "Ladies and gentlemen, sorry to interrupt your dinner but we wanted to announce that it's time for the raffle drawing." Mary heard a few chairs being pushed back from tables and the sound of shuffling feet. People gathered around. "Clambake owner Mary Hopkins will now draw the two winning tickets. Mary?"

Nate moved to where the painting was hanging. Mary looked over at him. She was nervous. She didn't like to speaking to crowds. Even small ones. She looked down at Nate's notes. He'd written out what she should say. Mary read the first couple of lines, looked up at Nate, then at the faces. She could do this.

"Hi, everyone," she said. With no microphone, she had to raise her voice. "Thanks for coming out today. On behalf of Anicca Sutherland's family and everyone at the Clambake, I just want to let you know your generosity is greatly appreciated. So let's get down to it." Mary felt like there should be some kind of fanfare, a drumroll. She looked over at Nate, who smiled and nodded, urging her on.

"Okay. The first name I pick will be the winner of the second-prize fishing trip."

A flashbulb went off. Mary looked up to see a cameraman and one of the reporters from earlier in the day. Mary reached into the citronella-candle box that had been brought down from the attic to replace the foil-wrapped mayonnaise jar when no more tickets would fit into it. Now she dug down through the entries and clamped down on a ticket. She held on and pulled it out. "Okay. Here it is." This was exciting. "The winner of the fishing trip is . . . Frank Hewer." Mary looked up. "Frank Hewer?" And when there was no reply: "I guess he's not here. We'll call him in a few minutes with the good news. And many thanks—" Mary looked down at Nate's notes. She read the name of the person who'd donated the trip. Her throat went dry. No wonder no one wanted to tell her. "Many thanks to Dan Bassett for donating a full day's excursion with Frank and five of his friends aboard the *Proud Mary*." Could that really be the name of his boat? "Including lunch, beer, and bait. Congratulation, Frank, and thank you, Dan."

People in the group turned toward where Nate had been standing and clapped. More flashbulbs. Mary looked, and there was Dan, his eyes locked on hers. He nodded to the group and gave a little wave.

Mary's face caught fire. She felt like a summer carnival had let loose inside her, her head spinning like a merry-go-round, her stomach on the Tilt-A-Whirl. Her mouth felt like it had been stuffed with cotton candy, and a dizzying sound was ringing in her ears.

People were looking at her now, waiting for the next name to be picked. She looked up again, hoping Dan had gone, or had never been there in the first place, that perhaps it had just been her imagination playing tricks. But there he stood, tanned and handsome in dark jeans and a navy blue linen shirt, untucked, the sleeves rolled up to where his scar began.

"All right," Mary said. "And now for the grand-prize drawing." She took a deep breath. *Look at the people, not where he's standing.*

Mary looked down at Nate's notes, read some, then decided she didn't need them. Not for this. She knew what she wanted to say. She cleared her throat.

"When we started the day, we had no idea of the value of this next prize. It was a painting given to me by a nice old man I'd recently met, who just wanted to help out. I guess the rest is history. You'll probably be reading all about it in the paper tomorrow, how it turned out that this nice old man is really the one and only Carleton Dyer, a celebrated artist who'd vanished from the local scene over thirty years ago, giving up a promising career in oil painting in favor of a simpler life. A man whose work, I was told today, hangs in the Smithsonian, of all places."

Mary looked at the picture of Anicca and Ariel. "I can't being to explain the reasons behind the chain of events that brought us all here today," she went on. She took a breath. The air was crisp, and smelled of onion rings. "It began with the tragic death of a young mother who, together with her daughter and grandmother, has touched many hearts. As a result of this family's tragedy, at least one long-standing mystery has been solved." Mary paused to give Dan a sharp look. *Maybe more than one mystery,* she thought. "Cape Codders have been given back a living legend and a piece of their cultural history. So, for whatever it's worth, thank you, Carleton Dyer, for your body of work and for this generous gift, this lovely painting. I wish you many more productive years." Mary blew a kiss into the air. She imagined the old man must be snoozing by now. "Now let's find out who gets to hang this painting in their home."

Mary plunged her hand back into the box, rummaged around a little for dramatic effect, and pulled out another ticket. "The grand prize winner is . . . Jane Harding."

Some women near the entrance squealed.

Mary looked up. "Is Jane Harding here?"

"No, but we know her," one woman said. She had on a green gingham shirtdress and Barbara Bush pearls, and had to be in her mid-seventies.

"From the garden club," added another woman, younger and more heavyset, in teal cropped pants and a striped blouse.

"Yeah, and *he* knew her too," said a third woman, clearly the tomboy of the group. She was a boardinghouse owner from a neighboring town; Mary recognized her from one of the chamber of commerce meetings for the Outer Cape. The woman was wearing a yellow rain slicker even though there wasn't a cloud in the sky, and her silver hair was cropped in a hard line to her chin. Flash-forward to Maureen Donovan in forty years. "Old *dog*," the woman added.

"Cooper!" the first lady scolded, though her smile betrayed that she didn't disagree.

"You mean Carleton?" Mary asked. She noticed the reporter scribbling furiously on his pad.

"And *Jane,*" the lady in the green dress continued. The others giggled—except for the one in the raincoat. "It's true. They were an item once."

Jane and how many others? Mary smiled. Maybe Jane was the one who'd given him the necktie. Mary couldn't wait to tell him who'd won and get his version of the story. Then again, he didn't strike her as the kind who'd kiss and tell.

The woman with the teal pants reached into her wicker purse and pulled out a cell phone. She started dialing.

"If you reach her before we do, give her our congratulations," Mary said. "Thank you all again for coming out today. Enjoy the rest of your summer."

Mary took the two winning tickets and brought them to the take-out window, where she slid them under the screen for Maureen. "You should be proud," Mary said. "That goes for all of you," she added, speaking so that everyone in the kitchen would hear. "You did a great job today." She turned. "Even Nate," she said under her breath, "who I'm going to *kill*." Mary suspected that hitting up Dan for the prize had been his idea. Or maybe Wayne's.

Mary looked up. The crowd had dispersed and, as she'd feared,

Dan was standing no more than a few feet in front of her. The carnival rides started up again.

"Hey," he said. He buried he hands in his pockets.

"I didn't know it was you," Mary said.

"I know. I told them to keep it a secret," he said.

"More secrets, I'd have thought you learned—"

Maureen's voice came back over the loudspeaker: "Once again, we're pleased to announce the winners of tonight's raffle. They are Frank Hewer of Orleans, who wins the second-prize charter fishing trip, and Jane Harding of Nauset, winner of the Carleton Dyer oil painting valued at over forty thousand dollars."

The dining room erupted in applause.

"Always a bridesmaid," Dan said.

"It was nice of you just the same." Mary took a step toward the dining room.

Dan took her by the elbow. Sparks shot up Mary's arm. "We need to talk," he said. She looked down at his hand, how his fingers wrapped around her entire arm.

"We do? I think the events of the last decade or so pretty much speak for themselves."

"Like I said all those times I tried to call you and left messages," he said, "there's more to it."

As with every time she'd heard it, she felt that same pressure building behind her ears. What more could she possible need to know?

"Can't we just go someplace quiet?" He let her arm go.

"You want to talk? Fine. There's something I've got to take care of first," Mary said. She walked to the bar. Dan followed. She flagged down the bartender. "Chuck, pour me a Jameson's," Mary said. "A tall one." She'd never had whiskey at her bar in all the seventeen years she'd owned the place. But for some reason the name had sounded good rolling off her tongue tonight. She hoped the whiskey would taste as good on it. "What'll you have?" she asked Dan.

"The same," he told Chuck, his lips curled in a smile, in reaction to her impulsiveness, no doubt. He was the only one who'd ever found it amusing.

As they stood waiting for the drinks, Dan looked around. He seemed impressed. Chuck set the drinks on the bar.

Mary took a glass and secretly raised it to Dan's first foray into the dining room, and possibly his last. "Cheers," she said. She took a gulp. The strength of the booze brought tears to her eyes. "Follow me."

She wasn't sure where she was taking him. She could bring him upstairs to her office, but there was only one chair, the ceiling was slanted, and there was too much of her personal junk lying around. She could bring him down to the basement, though that was more his territory than hers. Either way, they had to go through the kitchen. Mary supposed it was too late to care what the rest of the staff thought. By now, despite her protests, and judging from her behavior tonight alone, she and Dan had to be old news. As they filed through, enormous drinks in hand, all work came to a halt.

"Knock it off," she said. They knew it meant stop staring and get back to work.

Wayne grinned. Mary caught him giving Dan a nod. Dan shrugged. At the last minute, Mary opted for the basement. Why not return to the original scene of the crime, even though she now knew Dan hadn't been the original criminal.

With each step down, the temperature seemed to drop about a half degree. Mary wished she had thought to bring her sweater. Hopefully, the whiskey would keep her warm. After a whole day in the sandals, Mary's feet were killing her. Leaning against the staircase were a couple of rusty folding chairs. Mary thought about setting them out but then figured this conversation probably wouldn't take long. She'd just let him have his say and be done with it. She couldn't think of anything he could say that would change how she felt about what he'd done. Or *not* done.

She set her drink down on the butcher's block table. Dan followed suit.

"So, let's recap," Mary said. Why dance around? "You knew Robbie had been messing around on me practically since the day we were married. You didn't tell me. Maybe I can understand that, in the beginning, at least, seeing as Robbie was your best friend. But then the accident happened, and you knew how I blamed myself for the things I'd said to him that night." With every sentence, Mary's heart rate picked up a few beats. "Through the nightmares and the crying spells, you held me and reassured me that it wasn't my fault. But, in the end, those were just words. They didn't change the things I'd said to Robbie. All that time, you had the power to take away my pain but you chose not to. All you had to do was tell me where Robbie'd been headed that night and I would have known my whole marriage had been a lie, that there probably wasn't anything I could have said to him that would have made a difference." Mary felt her fingernails digging into her palms. "And when I became curious about the past and asked a few simple questions, you just took off for good, leaving my calls and letters unanswered, leaving me to wonder what I'd done wrong and, even worse, to think that you'd simply moved on to greener pastures. Now, suddenly, twelve years later, here we are." She smacked her palm on the butcher block. The crack of it echoed in her ears. Mary realized she'd given the entire speech to her drink. She looked up.

Dan appeared the picture of calm, a billboard for inner peace, his hands folded in front of him. Like all he needed to do was bow his head and someone might sound a gong. His reaction only made Mary feel more frustrated, like she'd fired a cannon and missed the target by miles.

"You really still are beautiful," he said without smiling. "You haven't changed."

He'd always had that way of just undoing her. Mary shivered.

Dan came over and rubbed his hands up and down her bare arms, creating more friction, only the good kind.

"Dan," Mary said. She collected herself, took a step back so that the table was between them again. "What do you *want?*"

"I want a chance to tell you how I feel. How I've always felt."

Mary took another draw off her drink. She wished it tasted as good as it smelled. She wished she'd asked for a glass of wine instead. You couldn't just slug down Jameson's like you could wine. Maybe some people could, but she couldn't.

"I knew Robbie was cheating," Dan started. "I thought he was a fool for doing it and I told him so. Plenty of times. But it wasn't my place to come running to you. And there was another reason I didn't." Dan ran his fingernail along one of the knife grooves in the table. That Zen confidence of his seemed to be slipping away. "The reason was, I had feelings for you myself, even all the way back then. I thought Robbie was crazy to risk losing you. I figured sooner or later you'd find out on your own and leave him, or he'd run off with Katy and I'd be there to pick up the pieces. But the way things turned out, those pieces ended up being too damn heavy."

"What's that supposed to mean?" Mary asked.

"You thought *you* were carrying guilt? If I'd just told you what was going on or had the courage to challenge him and tell him how I felt about you, the whole thing might have played out different. Instead, I betrayed you both. Sure, in the end it seemed like I got what I wanted, but the price had just been too damn high." Dan looked at her. His eyes had changed, sunken deeper into his face.

Mary felt she should say something but she didn't know what. If she thought too much about those old days when they were all still kids, she'd well up herself.

He continued, "Underneath it all, there was this feeling that it was wrong, like I'd just stepped into a dead man's life." He rested his knuckles on the table. "And that damn earring." He shook his head.

Mary faked a smile. "Remember that first day? I found it right here." Mary pointed at the spot with her toe. "I just assumed it was you. I never dreamed—"

"Yeah." Dan took a gulp of his drink. "I suppose I should be flattered. I think I was, then."

What a pair, the two of them, Mary thought. Some of what he'd said made sense, but there were still big fat gaps in his logic. "I still don't get why you left," she said.

"That day I went to Alaska, when you asked me about the earring, when I realized you still had it, it all just hit me, that I'd kept this huge secret from you and the window for telling you the truth had long closed. And then you told me Robbie said *I'd* been the one who brought a girl down here. That hurt. In some ways he used both of us."

Mary nodded.

"It wasn't like I just decided that minute that I wasn't coming back," he said. "When I got out west, we launched and I just focused on what needed to get done. During the quiet times, I thought about how it might be easier on all of us if I just never came back. In truth, the longer I stayed away, the more I was afraid to come back." He looked at the fish crates behind her, then dropped his head and rapped on the table with his knuckle. "That doesn't mean I didn't miss you."

"But things were *good*. Why couldn't we just forget about Robbie?" Mary kicked the leg of the heavy table with her toe, and the ache in her sore, tired foot shot up her calf.

"Be honest. Did you ever forget about Robbie? You brought him up all the time."

She may have brought him up, but not because she wished they were still together. "I was angry at him for how he'd treated me," she said. "I was angry at him even for getting himself killed. It was just stuff I needed to work through." She remembered how patient Dan had been. "And you helped me with that, I'll admit."

Dan shook his head. "Every time we talked about him, it reminded me how he might still be alive if only—"

Mary bolted to the sink. "Jesus, it feels like we're in some kind of competition: Who's the most to blame for Robbie dying? You know what? I think that award goes to *Robbie*." She turned back around. "I'm sorry, but you talk about how the whole thing between us was wrong." Mary felt that whale in her throat again. It was breeching, hurling itself out of the darkness, then crashing back down. "It didn't feel one bit wrong when we were together. Not to me." *Don't cry,* she told herself. She coughed and cleared her throat. "You never acted like it was wrong either. I think what we had was something special. And I think you threw it all away." There, she'd said what she'd wanted to say to him for the last dozen years. And she'd done it without crying.

For a few moments, the only sounds: the drip, drip of the old sink; the creak of footsteps upstairs; some muffled Asian swears. The walk-in motor kicked on.

"You're right," Dan finally said. "It was other women who made me see it most."

Mary's spine stiffened a little. Other women. *What* other women? *How many* other women? Wasn't this what had gotten her into trouble in the first place? This time, she kept her mouth shut.

"I never had anything like it again," he continued. "Made me realize the *us* part hadn't been wrong. It was just all the other stuff swirling around."

"You *let* it swirl. It didn't have to swirl." Whatever that meant. It made sense to her.

Dan dropped his head. He didn't say anything right away. Then he started, "I'm a simple guy, Mary. Back in those days, when things got complicated, I ran. Ever wonder how I wound up out in Alaska in the first place? How many kids go that far to get away from their folks? For as long as I remember, all I've ever wanted was to find a place where I could just fish, be around nature and lead a simple kind of life. My parents wanted me to go to college for business. Can you see it?" Dan stepped back and opened his arms. He shook out his hair. Mary tried not to smile but didn't quite pull it off. "Yeah, thanks. Me either," he said. "I've always been happiest outdoors, on the water, working on the boat or walking in the woods. That's never changed."

"So, what has? You just told me when things get complicated you run. Well, guess what? My life's pretty complicated. Running this place sure as hell is complicated. *I'm* complicated."

Dan smiled. "I'm not so sure. I think in some ways we're a lot alike. We both like to work hard, play hard. We're good at what we do. We get a charge out of a nice meal and some stupid fireworks, or watching stars out on the beach."

"Falling chunks of rock," Mary corrected. She felt herself softening toward him. Maybe it was the drink, but everything in that cold, hard room was beginning to warm up. "You could get hit with the urge to run again."

"Remember I told you about this?" He pushed up his sleeve. In the shadows of the dimly lit room, the groove in his arm seemed deeper. "The best way I can explain it is, in those seconds while I was treading that frigid water, I could feel my body starting to shut down. I could feel things slipping away, not how they say your life passes in front of you or anything, but more like I was shedding the stuff that was *not me,* like the guilt or grudges I'd carried around all my life, my ways of thinking about things. It all felt meaningless and it kind of washed off, and I was left with just this deeper understanding of who I was, that I was somehow connected to everything else. I stopped feeling cold. I stopped panicking. In those last seconds before the life preserver splashed down next to me and all I had to do was rally enough strength to pull my arm through it, I felt less attached to the outcome, like I could be okay with whatever happened. After that, even after the ordeal with my arm being torn up, the surgery and how long it took to heal, I seemed to find the peace I'd always been looking for. I realized the stuff I'd been running from was just noise in my head. You can't run from your own head. I knew then I could be anywhere. I could go home."

Mary imagined an experience like that could change someone. But—"You were home a long time before you came looking for me," she said.

"I just didn't think I had much of a right to come back and expect you to still have anything left for me," he said. "When the girl died, it gave me a reason. But I'd been thinking about you anyway. I think I said as much that first phone call."

"You thought I was too proud." Mary smiled. "Proud Mary."

He wiped his hand over his whiskers, a little embarrassed.

"Did you really name your boat after me?"

"I tell people it's from the song. But you can think that. There's probably some truth to it."

Mary stepped around the table. She walked up to him and patted her hand on his shirt pocket.

"No cigarettes?" she said.

"Quit ten years ago." He smiled and pressed her hand to his chest. "And you might as well give it up. You never were very good at it."

"I suppose," Mary said. She looked into his eyes, then closed her own and rested her forehead on his shoulder. When she finally drew away, something in the room had shifted, a spaciousness had arisen from the dark corners and melted out into something infinite. And then she realized it wasn't the room at all, but an expansiveness that seemed to blossom from within her, an acuteness of her senses, unfolding like a late-summer rose. Everything took on a sacredness. The grimy old sink. The hooks on the ceiling. The battered butcher block table. Even the plastic crates stacked up against the wall. Suddenly there seemed enough room in her life for all of it, for everything and everyone who wanted in: Carleton, Meg, Ariel, the kids upstairs, the customers, Lovey, Lovey's disease, even Dan. And though her heart was beating fast, Mary felt cradled in a stillness she'd never experienced before: perhaps her peace at last.

Mary was overcome by an urge to breathe in the night air, to take this spaciousness outside to see just where and how far it might take her.

She sprinted to the bulkhead. "Let's get out of here," she said. She didn't wait for a response. She undid the lock and pushed open the double doors, which pealed their metal shriek into the night.

Stars and chunks of celestial rock rained in on them. She turned around. Dan's eyes were bright.

"Where do you want to go?" he asked.

"How about you show me my namesake? I haven't been on a boat in years."

"You live on Cape Cod and you haven't been on a boat in years," he said. He shook his head, then reached out his hand. "Let's go, Sunshine."

"Clambaked" Oysters

"This one's all about the bumps."

4 strips of bacon
half of a 9-ounce bag fresh baby spinach
½ teaspoon minced garlic
½ tablespoon olive oil
¼ cup Pernod
1 cup half and half
salt and pepper
2 to 3 tablespoons cornstarch
cold water
1 dozen fresh oysters, top shell removed
grated Parmesan cheese

Preheat oven to 400 degrees. Cook the bacon slices until crisp. Drain and set aside. Roughly chop the spinach. In a large saucepan, sauté the garlic in the olive oil. Add the spinach and Pernod. Cook until the spinach is wilted. Add the half and half and cook until the liquid is reduced by half. Add salt and pepper to taste. Place cornstarch in a small bowl and add water little by little, mixing until smooth. Gradually add to the spinach, stirring until blended and the mixture thickens. Place the opened oysters on a baking sheet. Spoon 1 tablespoon of the spinach onto each oyster. Top each with a generous amount of Parmesan and ⅓ strip of the cooked bacon. Bake for 6 to 8 minutes. Broil for a few minutes more until cheese turns golden.

Serves 2 to 4.

Summer Secret Salad

"A cool curve on a hot summer day."

1 package elbow macaroni (1 pound)
1 cup mayonnaise
½ cup sour cream
¼ teaspoon dry mustard
salt and pepper to taste
4 hard-boiled eggs, chopped
1 cup chopped celery
½ cup chopped onion
¼ cup chopped sweet pickle with 2 tablespoons juice
2 carrots, chopped
1 green bell pepper, chopped
2 tablespoons celery seeds

Cook pasta al dente according to instructions on the box. Prepare the dressing: in medium bowl, mix the mayonnaise, sour cream, and dry mustard. Season with salt and pepper to taste. In a large bowl combine the rest of the ingredients. Add the dressing and mix well.

Serves 6.

Orleans Swordfish

"Just the right amount of points."

2 tablespoons butter, softened
1 tablespoon anchovy paste
½ cup olive oil
4 fresh swordfish steaks, each about 1 ¼ inches thick
salt and pepper to taste
2 tomatoes, diced
4 lemon wedges

In a bowl, mix butter and anchovy paste. Set aside. Rub the olive oil over swordfish steaks. Lightly season them with salt and pepper. Grill approximately seven minutes on each side or more, according to their thickness. Spread the anchovy-butter mixture on the hot steaks as they come off the grill. Garnish with the tomato and lemon.

Serves 4.

Hopkins Haddock

"The pecans create waves that seem to go on forever."

4 fresh haddock fillets (about 8 ounces each)
salt and pepper to taste
1 cup flour
1 cup milk
½ cup pecans, finely minced
2 tablespoons olive oil
splash of white wine
8 ounces homemade or store-bought pesto
4 lemon slices

Preheat oven to 350 degrees. Lightly season the haddock fillets with salt and pepper. Dust with flour and dip in milk. Press skinless side of each fillet firmly into the pecans so they stick. Place the fillets skin-side down on a clean plate.

Heat the olive oil in a sauté pan over medium heat. Place the haddock fillets pecan-crusted side down in the hot pan. Lightly brown the pecans. Remove the fillets and place them on a baking sheet or oven-safe dish, crust side up. Add a few splashes of white wine to keep fish moist. Cook for 6 to 8 minutes until fish is cooked through.

Drizzle serving platter or individual plates with pesto and place fish on top. Garnish with the lemon slices. Serve with rice and fresh steamed vegetables or green salad.

Serves 4.

Proud Mary's Portuguese Mussels

"The one makes my left wrist twitch, but in a good way."

1 small onion, diced
1 pound diced linguica (Portuguese sausage)
1 tablespoon chopped garlic
3 pounds cleaned mussels
2 cups white wine
½ cup lemon juice
3 plum tomatoes, diced
1 package of pasta (1 pound any variety), cooked and drained
fresh chopped basil for garnish (optional)

In a large saucepan, sauté the onion and linguica until the onion is tender. Add the garlic, mussels, white wine, and lemon juice. Cover and cook on high heat for five minutes or until all the mussels are open. (Discard any that don't open.) Add the tomatoes. Serve over hot pasta with fresh chopped basil as garnish.

(Without the pasta, this dish is great as an appetizer. Serve with French bread or garlic toast.)

Serves 4 to 6.

Acknowledgments

Thanks to Molly Lyons at Joelle Delbourgo Associates, and to Danielle Friedman, Kelly Bowen and copy editor Janet Fletcher at Touchstone Simon & Schuster. And special gratitude to Trish Grader;

to Richard E. Cytowic, author of *The Man Who Tasted Shapes* (MIT Press, 1998) for writing a fascinating book on synesthesia; and to Elizabeth Reynard for her wonderful collection of lore *The Narrow Land: Folk Chronicles of Old Cape Cod* (Houghton Mifflin, 1934);

to Lisa and Scott Moss, purveyors of the Saltwater Grille in Orleans, MA, for their help in creating the recipes and for their enthusiasm;

to family and the many friends who contribute in ways both tangible and intangible, including Lorrie, Lisa, Jeff, John, Lynne B., Deb, Therese, Martha, Jen, Jessica, Barbara, and Alex;

to independent booksellers and libraries on the Cape for their support;

and, finally, to the servers, cooks, bartenders, kitchen staff, bus people, hosts, and hostesses who populate eateries all over the Cape and beyond—the ones I worked with during my six years as a waitress at restaurants in Orleans, and outside Boston, and the many who've served me and my family. As a friend said recently, no one should be able to eat in a restaurant until they've worked in one. Amen.

SUMMER SHIFT

Mary Hopkins, a successful Cape Cod restaurant owner, is reasonably satisfied with her stable life. But at the beginning of a new season, when Anicca, a young waitress, is killed in a car accident, Mary realizes she knows nothing about the people who work for her. Meanwhile, she struggles to cope with the fact that her beloved great-aunt Lovey has just been diagnosed with Alzheimer's disease. Finally, when an old flame shows up at her doorstep, Mary is forced to abandon her careful existence and confront her own dark past.

As Mary fights to regain her footing, she becomes inextricably involved in the lives of the surviving members of Anicca's family and ultimately finds that moving forward usually involves forgiving the past.

FOR DISCUSSION

1. What effect does the beginning of the novel, in which Mary and Robbie open the restaurant, have on the theme of failed expectations that pervades the story?

2. Many of the characters, such as Mary and Dan, express a deep sense of guilt in relation to Robbie's death. How does the author handle the irrationality of this guilt while still acknowledging its inevitability? Does the last scene of the novel provide evidence for an ultimate transgression of guilt?

3. Early in the novel, Mary introduces the "smooth stone with a vein of quartz running though it given her by Robbie on their honeymoon that she'd been waiting to skim on the waves for fourteen years" (page 26). Later, it becomes a symbol of "her acceptance that he was now part of something greater even than the sea itself" (page 235). Do you think that the stone has come to represent something other than this acceptance? If so, what?

4. When Mary visits the crash site, she notes that trees have the capacity to mend themselves and predicts that "years from now, there'd be just a scar, some imperfection in the surface that would hold the memory of what had happened" (page 42). How does this mirror Mary's healing process?

5. Bonasia gives the reader a contradictory image of time when she foreshadows that a shard of glass that has been thrown into the ocean will, "like everything else in time's cauldron . . . be sufficiently pulverized" (page 68). How are these contradicting ideas reconciled in the end? Which proves to be a more accurate symbol?

6. Mary removes a stuffed bear from the crash site to save it from imminent ruin. Why does she do this? Further, what does it signify that Ariel is ultimately given the bear during the charity event?

7. Mary's reaction to her aunt's Alzheimer's diagnosis is very different from Lovey's own calm reaction. Compare and contrast Mary's and Lovey's reactions. How do they play off each other?

8. How does Lovey's ability to live completely in the present affect Mary? How is she able to learn a valuable lesson from observing her aunt enjoy such things as "the scent of cinnamon. A yellow robe. Warm coffee on the lips" (page 179)?

9. Why do you think Mary chose to lie to Meg about her true identity? How do you feel about Meg's ability to completely forgive Mary for this falsehood?

10. Mary's new friend and neighbor Carleton Dyer asks her, "What is *ugly*? For there to be beauty, there has to be ugliness" (page 219). Do you agree with him? Cite examples from the novel to support your claim.

11. Discuss Dan's account of his near-death experience, in which he claims, "I was shedding the stuff that was *not me,* like the guilt or grudges I'd carried around all my life, my ways of thinking about things. It all felt meaningless and it kind of washed off, and I was left with just this deeper understanding of who I was, that I was somehow connected to everything else" (page 308). Where else in the novel do you see moments of this "deeper understanding"? And how is it achieved in those cases?

12. Toward the end of the novel, Mary asks herself (in regard to Alzheimer's), "Where was the grace in such a horrible disease? Where was the grace in any of it?" (page 259). Do you think that Mary is eventually able to answer this question? When? How so?

13. Discuss the scene in which Mary asks her employees to form a circle and share one thing about themselves. At the end of this scene, Bonasia writes, "it was as if they all at once remembered why they were there" (page 273). What have they remembered? What is the catalyst for this memory?

14. Revisit the closing lines of the novel: "And though her heart was beating fast, Mary felt cradled in a stillness she'd never experienced before; perhaps her peace at last" (page 309). Which previous scenes do these last images evoke? How do they resolve the prevailing themes of guilt and loss?

Where did the idea for this novel come from? Is there a particular scene or character that you wrote first?

The first novel I ever tried to write was a sprawling story about a woman who ran a clam bar. It ended up collecting dust on a shelf. After *Some Assembly Required* was published, I went back and reread the manuscript to see if there was anything salvageable. There's a cyclical rhythm that seasonal business owners get caught up in that has always struck me as monotonous and challenging. And so there was still something compelling to me about my original main character and her situation. Nothing remains of the original work except Mary Hopkins and her clam bar, and even Mary underwent significant changes. But I'm glad I took the time to find Mary's voice.

Summer Shift seems to echo your previous novel, Some Assembly Required, in that it spends a significant amount of time on the theme of moving beyond loss. How, if at all, do you think your perspective on this theme has evolved between the two books?

Loss is something I've always been thematically drawn to in my writing, and so, yes, both books do deal with the process of moving past it. While I was writing *Summer Shift,* I was reading a lot of Eastern philosophy and trying to incorporate some of this thinking into my own life. A lot of these ideas ended up in the book; for example, allowing oneself to be at ease with what is rather than constantly wishing things were different. Sometimes by merely shifting the way we see things, resisting our reaction to always judge, we can ease our own suffering. Carleton really embodies this wisdom for me, his being able to let go of the past and live his life in the present moment. Lovey's disease forces her to live this way as well. Mary, like myself, is a student.

You have listed "waitress" among your previous professions. How much of your restaurant experience is present in the novel? Which restaurant employee do you most identify with?

I waitressed at a number of different establishments when I was in high school and college, including a couple of seafood restaurants on the Cape. I definitely drew from that experience in writing *Summer Shift*, the controlled chaos, the internal caste system, and the alliances that develop between coworkers. I think one of the interesting things about being young and having a summer job was that we all knew this was just a brief stopover in our lives and that we'd all be moving on to something else, most of us sooner rather than later. And yet we were learning some pretty important life skills. While I don't see myself in any particular character, I can identify with each in some way, as an author must, I imagine.

One of your more striking images is that of the "shard of glass" being first pulverized by the ocean before ultimately becoming sea glass. How do you see the Cape Cod landscape as a reflection of Mary's progression throughout the novel?

As many Cape Codders do, Mary turns to nature in difficult times. I believe if we're open and in tune enough with our surroundings, we can often derive answers from our natural world, finding useful metaphors for our own lives. Standing at the edge of an ocean that's been around for hundreds of millions of years, one's problems are immediately weighed in a greater context. Nature has so much to teach, whether it be a lesson about perseverance from a fiddler crab; about the transient nature of all things from a shift in the tides; or how, through contemplating a shard of glass, we might learn that everything inevitably loses its sharp edges and yet there is beauty to be found even in that.

Wayne's synesthesia is a particularly interesting character trait. Was this character drawn from any personal experiences? What sort of research was involved in bringing his gift to the page?

I've always been interested in peculiar neurological afflictions, especially ones that create ironic situations. I may have Dr. Oliver Sacks to thank for that (*The Man Who Mistook His Wife for a Hat*). I had read about synesthesia years ago and had always planned to give it to one of my characters. The manifestation where people "taste shapes" is far more rare than the kind where people attribute colors to letters, number, or music. I recently saw the Kandinsky exhibit at the Guggenheim in New York (2009). He was purported to have the "seeing sound" variety and, for much of his career, his work was inspired by music. There's a book called *The Man Who Tasted Shapes* by Richard E. Cytowic, M.D., that I used as reference to understand Wayne's particular type of synesthesia and then proceeded to explore how, as with Kandinsky, such an affliction might be transformed into an artistic advantage.

How would you compare the writing process of *Summer Shift* to that of *Some Assembly Required*? Did either come more naturally? Why or why not?

Some Assembly Required was my graduate school thesis for my masters of fine arts degree. It took several years to write and saw lots of critical feedback from professors and fellow students along the way. There were interruptions in the writing, as I had to put it down to do other schoolwork from time to time. *Summer Shift* had a much easier birth. It took me about eighteen months to write. Not another person set eyes on the manuscript until I sent it off to my agent. Throughout the process I kept wondering if it was all too easy. After all the hand-holding with the first novel, I worried whether I'd be as successful on my own. But I've heard other authors talk about how some books just seem to flow from them. That was the case for me with *Summer Shift*.

Two characters in the novel suffer from serious diseases: Lovey is diagnosed with Alzheimer's; Carleton is living with Parkinson's. How would you compare their coping mechanisms? Do you see a greater degree of resignation in either character?

I had a great-aunt who suffered from Alzheimer's disease and I was very involved with her care. I saw a tremendous amount of frustration in her at the beginning that eventually gave way to her settling into the inevitability of her situation. I think much of this was a function of the disease running its course. They say that Alzheimer's is harder on the caregivers than it is on the patients. While I'm not sure if I agree with that, I did feel it was harder for us to let go at times. Parkinson's affects the body dramatically and the mind to a much lesser extent. And so I think someone would have to work harder to find a place of acceptance. Even Carleton, wise as he is, has moments of shame and frustration, particularly when faced with the prospect of having to interact with other people. I imagine that's how it is in real life. No mater how enlightened and at peace you may be with your situation, there are going to be those moments you resist what's happening to you. I believe coping with pain, loss, illness, and life, for that matter, is a practice, something you work on rather than something you achieve.

Discuss your research for the character of Carleton Dyer, a painter who bears a striking resemblance to Henry Hensche, a Provincetown painter. Did you learn anything else about the history of the arts on Cape Cod?

I have many friends who are visual artists on Cape Cod, and I've have had the good fortune to be drawn into their world, which includes gaining an appreciation for the history of the Provincetown art community. I saw Carleton as an amalgam of painters like Henry Hensche, Edwin Dickinson, Ross Moffett, and others. I imagine how exciting it must have been to be a part of such a cluster of talent all living and working in the same small town, bouncing ideas off one another, and achieving worldwide recognition. From Charles Hawthorne's arrival at the turn of the century through to the Abstract Expressionists of the 1940s and 1950s, Provincetown, for all its beauty, light, and freedom of spirit, has always managed to capture and inspire artists, a legacy that lives on today.

Do you have any new projects planned? Will you set another book in Cape Cod? Why or why not?

I recently had the opportunity to spend a week of pure solitude in one of the legendary Provincetown dune shacks. These are fabulously rustic little cottages with no electricity or running water, situated just yards from the ocean on the backshore of town, accessible only by four-wheel drive vehicles. My intention had been to use this time to unplug and develop thoughts around a premise I had for a third Cape novel. All I'll say is that my week was very productive and I'm excited to get going. I feel so lucky to be able to live and work in a place that has so much to offer in natural beauty, history, and an abundance of fascinating characters.

Enhance Your Book Group

1. Throw a dinner party with some of the authentic Wayne Chen recipes offered at the back of the book (no synesthesia required)!

2. The character of Carleton Dyer bears a striking resemblance to Henry Hensche, a Provincetown painter who also suffered from Parkinson's disease. To learn more about Hensche and Provincetown's art history, visit: www.thehenschefoundation .org/ (and make sure to support your own local community arts).

3. Visit the author's webpage at: www.lynnkielebonasia.com. Make sure to read the article about the inspiration for her previous novel, *Some Assembly Required*.